HEAT WAVE

Also by Maureen Jennings

Murdoch Mystery Series

Except the Dying (1997)

Under the Dragon's Tail (1998)

Poor Tom Is Cold (2001)

Let Loose the Dogs (2003)

Night's Child (2005)

Vices of My Blood (2006)

A Journeyman to Grief (2007)

Let Darkness Bury the Dead (2017)

Christine Morris Series

Does Your Mother Know? (2006)

The K Handshape (2008)

Detective Inspector Tom Tyler Series

Season of Darkness (2011)

Beware This Boy (2012)

No Known Grave (2014)

Dead Ground in Between (2016)

Novella

Shipwreck (2011)

Screenplays for Murdoch Mysteries TV Series

"Staircase to Heaven" (co-writer) (2011)

"Victoria Cross" (co-writer) (2012)

"Murdochaphobia" (co-writer) (2013)

"Shipwreck" (adapted from the novella) (2014)

"House of Industry" (2015)

"The Missing" (2016)

"Game of Kings" (2018)

"One Minute to Murder" (2019)

HEAT WAVE

A Paradise Café Mystery by

MAUREEN JENNINGS

Author of the Detective Murdoch Mysteries

Cormorant Books

Canada Council for the Arts | Conseil des Arts du Canada

ONTARIO CREATES | ONTARIO CRÉATIF

Patrimoine canadien

Canada

The publisher gratefully acknowledges the support of the Canada Council for the Arts and the Ontario Arts Council for its publishing program. We acknowledge the financial support of the Government of Canada through the Canada Book Fund (CBF) for our publishing activities, and the Government of Ontario through Ontario Creates, an agency of the Ontario Ministry of Culture, and the Ontario Book Publishing Tax Credit Program.

LIBRARY AND ARCHIVES CANADA CATALOGUING IN PUBLICATION

Jennings, Maureen, author
Heat wave : a Paradise Café mystery / by Maureen Jennings.

Issued in print and electronic formats.
ISBN 978-1-77086-542-6 (softcover).— ISBN 978-1-77086-543-3 (HTML)

I. Title.

PS8569.E562H43 2019 C813'.54 C2018-906264-9
C2018-906265-7

Cover art: Nick Craine
Interior text design: tannicegdesigns.ca
Printer: Friesens

Printed and bound in Canada.

CORMORANT BOOKS INC.
260 SPADINA AVENUE, SUITE 502, TORONTO, ON M5T 2E4
www.cormorantbooks.com

To Iden, for always.

Also, this one is in memory of Angie,

my cousin who set me on this path by

demanding stories when we were children.

Chapter One

USUALLY THE WALK from my house to the office takes me twenty-five minutes at the most, but this morning I was moving slowly, very slowly. The city — indeed, the country — was in the grip of a record-breaking heat wave, and already, at eight o'clock, the temperature was ninety degrees. The sky was a clear blue, except for a few flimsy clouds hanging over the lake in a weak, uncommitted way. It was so humid I could have wrung out the air and made a river.

The *Daily Star* had reported that fledgling seagulls nesting in a colony on top of the Toronto Bank building had been jumping off because the roof was too hot. As they were not yet able to fly, this was a disastrous move. I sympathized. Never mind the apples baking on the trees, I felt as if I could boil over myself. It didn't help that I was wearing what I tended to think of as my "uniform": a white cotton blouse with long sleeves and a prim collar, and a navy blue linen skirt. Mr. Gilmore, my boss, was a stickler for proper appearances — no bare arms, and hems had to hover closer to the ankles than the knees. At regular intervals, he would say, "Miss Frayne, you are the face of the company. When a prospective client enters the office, they want immediate reassurance that T. Gilmore and Associates, Private Investigators, are completely respectable." He never failed to give me a sly grin at this point. "Add to that reasonable rates and we have a winning combination."

In fact, I was the only other associate, and I still had my jobs as secretary and general dogsbody. I thought perhaps getting a swankier office with windows and decent chairs might improve the "face" considerably, but I hadn't yet shared this insight with Mr. Gilmore. He was right about his winning combination: in spite of the depression, business was steady. We weren't getting rich, but we were covering expenses. Perhaps clients drawn to the boast of "reasonable rates" didn't expect a fancy decor.

One good thing about dressing like a respectable debutante was that I wore a hat with a wide brim. It helped to shade my face from the killing sun. Despite this helpful accessory, by the time I reached the Arcade, sweat was trickling down the back of my neck and my stockings were plastered to my legs.

When it was built over fifty years ago, the Arcade Building had been Toronto's pride and joy. Like a lot of our early piles, it had a vaguely ecclesiastical look, with a huge arched entrance and elegant classical pilasters. In fact, it was then and is now devoted strictly to commercial operations. The red bricks are getting a touch shabby with age, but it is still impressive: four storeys high, with an inside atrium lit by overhead plate glass windows. In winter, the roof brought in yearned-for sunlight; fortunately now the owners had wisely installed an air-cooling system. Without it, the Arcade would have been a greenhouse fit only for tomatoes, and nobody would have been shopping. Smart shops, albeit small, were on the first and second floors, business offices on the third. There was a hydraulic elevator, but it was constantly out of service. Today was no exception. Stairs it was. In the humid heat, I climbed as if I were ancient. The offices of T. Gilmore and Associates were at the end of the hall, and I trudged past the three other tenants. Nobody seemed to have arrived as yet. All the doors had their "Closed" signs turned out.

I let myself into the office. To my surprise, Mr. Gilmore was already at his desk. He usually didn't get in until nine at the earliest. As soon as I opened the door, he stood up and came to meet me. He looked terrible.

"Mr. Gilmore, what's wrong?"

He was holding an envelope, and he handed it to me.

"Take a look."

It was addressed to him: "Mr. T. Gilmore. The Yonge Street Arcade. 3rd floor. Suite B. Toronto."

Bold black letters. Neat handwriting.

I took out the single piece of paper. Dead centre were the words:

FILTHY COMMIE JEW. YOU DESERVE TO DIE.

At the bottom were drawings of rats with vicious teeth. Each had a knife protruding from its side.

"Mr. Gilmore! What on earth is it about?"

"A good question, Miss Frayne."

"Why would anybody send you such a letter?"

"I was wondering the same thing. All I can think of is that I have been mistaken for somebody else. I live in a neighbourhood where there are people of the Hebrew persuasion."

"And it was here when you came in?"

"It was in the letter box. As you can see, the envelope isn't franked. It was a private delivery."

"Have you received any other letters like this?"

"Not at all. This one has the dubious distinction of being the first."

"Has anybody else in the neighbourhood been targeted?"

"Not that I am aware of." He reached out for the paper. His hand was shaking. He noticed and steadied himself. "It is not something they might want to reveal." He gave me his typical wry smile. "I know these people, Miss Frayne. If they can ignore such nastiness, it might go away. Mr. Hitler is capitalizing on this trait over in Germany."

I felt a pang of shame. I was well aware of what was going on in Europe. I knew laws were being enacted against the Jews — book burnings, discrimination — but like a lot of us in Canada, I sort of hoped it would go away. Or that they would deal with it over there. These days I was wrapped up in what was happening in my own country, where unemployed men were being jailed for no good reason except that they were protesting their desperate condition. Besides, since the Christie Pits riot three years ago, overt anti-Semitism in Toronto seemed to have abated. "Should we contact the police?"

He made a burring noise. "What will they say? 'Let us know if you receive any further such missives'?"

"But there is an implied threat."

"As you say, implied only. There has been no violence to my person or my property."

Technically, he was correct, but holding that piece of paper in my hand it didn't feel quite like that. It was an attack all right.

"But ..."

He was already replacing the letter inside the envelope. "I should not have shown you. I was taken off guard for a moment. There is nothing you can do. And, as I say, a case of mistaken identity."

"I can speak to the other tenants. Somebody might have noticed whoever delivered it."

"Not likely. It could have come any time after we closed last evening. The Arcade is open to the public. Dozens of people linger in here to escape the heat. Besides, even if somebody were to have seen our private postman, and even if we found such person, it doesn't mean he was the one who wrote the letter."

"You say it is a case of mistaken identity and that you are not personally being targeted. How do you know that?"

He blinked. "Because quite simply, Miss Frayne, I do not consider myself to be a filthy Jew, Communist or not."

Mr. Gilmore was middle-aged, round of chin and girth with grey hair that he combed across his balding head. He wore wire-rimmed glasses. Usually, his conservative blue suit was well pressed. This morning he looked no different, except that he was in his shirt sleeves and he had a couple of angry scratches along his jawline.

I indicated the marks. "What happened to your chin?"

"Oh, that." He touched the scratches gingerly. "I had an argument with a rose bush. I wanted to confine it, and it had other ideas. Roses can be like that."

He gazed down at the envelope in his hand. "I should probably burn this thing."

"No, don't do that. Give it to me, and I'll lock it in my desk. If, God forbid, any more show up, I will personally make sure I find the culprit if it's the last thing I do."

His eyes met mine. "Thank you, Miss Frayne. Your concern warms my heart." He handed over the letter. "Perhaps we can keep this between ourselves?"

"Of course."

I opened my desk drawer and consigned the envelope to the back.

Mr. Gilmore pursed his lips. "I think I ought to check in at home. Just in case the postman has also paid a visit there. I do not want my wife to be upset. She does not tolerate the heat well, and she is rather fragile these days." He got his hat and jacket from the stand. "I suggest we get on with business, Miss Frayne. Always the best antidote to distress, don't you think? I left a report on the Dictaphone for you. The Walsingham case. You can type it up. And perhaps we can get some action on any money we are owed. Mr. Epping is dragging his feet. Give him a bit of a prod."

"When do you think you will be back?"

"I shan't be gone long. As I said, just a little reassurance required."

He left.

Chapter Two

Mr. Gilmore and I had been colleagues now for some two years, but we shared almost nothing about our personal lives. He knew I lived with my grandfather because sometimes I'd had to take time off if Gramps was poorly. I knew Mr. Gilmore had a wife, no children. She suffered from what he called neurasthenia, and she had bouts that required his presence at home. That was about it. Neither of us was inclined to unleash personal disclosures on the other. He called me Miss Frayne, I addressed him as Mr. Gilmore, but there was an ease between us that I valued.

He was not telling the truth, of that was I sure, but I had no idea what he was trying to conceal.

I switched on the overhead fan and went into the tiny cupboard we referred to, with great optimism more than accuracy, as our kitchen. There was a shelf in there, a postage stamp-sized sink, and a hot plate. A cup of coffee seemed like a good idea.

I put the kettle on to boil and returned to my desk. In my short career as a private investigator I'd already brushed up against some of the less wholesome sides of the human condition, but I can't say I was inured, and this whole occurrence was disturbing.

I took out the letter. Mr. Gilmore hadn't seemed to want to examine it, but I certainly did. It was written on lined paper and had been torn from a top-opening notebook. Looked like typical school issue. The paper was ever so slightly yellowed, as if it had been around for quite a while. I reached for my magnifying glass to examine the letters. The writer had used a wide nib fountain pen that was obviously in danger of drying up. He or she had needed to overwrite the letters C and *d*. The drawings of the rats were crude, but rather more skilful than ordinary. There was an unpleasant-looking brown stain in the corner. Cautiously I sniffed at it. Smelled like tea. This certainly wasn't leading me on some magical straight path to the perpetrator, but at least there were enough individual distinguishing points. If we did have another visit from our mysterious postman, we would be able to compare any further letters with some confidence.

I returned the letter to the drawer.

The overhead fan seemed to be simply stirring the air around without making much dent in the heat. The stifling atmosphere wasn't helping with my concentration. I decided to remove my stockings. If anybody did come into the office, my legs would be hidden behind the desk.

I unfastened the suspenders and rolled off my stockings.

Pure bliss. I undid the buttons at my wrists and neck. Wonderful! The relief from the heat and humidity was immediate.

All right, back to work.

I pulled a file folder toward me from the TO DO tray. I had another tray labelled DONE WITH. At the moment they were about even. Time to send out follow-up remittance notices to delinquent clients who, now happy and contented in their lives, seemed to have forgotten the debt owed to the ones who had brought about their reinstated sense of well-being. Beautifully written thank-you cards were sweet, but they didn't pay the electricity bill, which had the irritating habit of showing up on a regular basis. In this case, a certain Mr. Neville Epping seemed reluctant to settle his account now that his divorce was finalized. The preliminaries had gone on for months. I'd been handed the case shortly after Mr. Gilmore had hired me. In his typical, slightly pedantic fashion, he had warned me that "domestic situations," as he referred to them, could often be unpleasant. "Like breathing in the foul air that exudes from a sewer," was how he'd put it. "Estranged couples can build up a lot of odoriferous bitterness." But these were our most lucrative accounts, and this past year I had already worked on four of them. My job was to stand witness to the fact that Mr. Husband had been seen going into a hotel with a woman-not-his-wife, thereby furnishing Mrs. Real Wife with grounds for divorce. I did not have to catch said couple *in flagrante delicto*, thank goodness, just report that they had entered the hotel and stayed there for some time. Hey, they may have been having a wild game of dominoes for all I knew.

I far preferred the cases where people were reunited. With beloved pets, cherished jewellery, even lost relatives. I didn't need a psychoanalyst to explain to me why I was so partial to this kind of case. Suffice it to say, my father, a young soldier, had died in South Africa, never having clapped eyes on me. My mother, equally young, had stuck it out as a mother for two years then also headed out, leaving me with my paternal grandparents. These early upheavals seemed to have left me with a need for order and stability and my predilection for finding lost things.

I picked up a sheet of paper and rolled it into the typewriter. I hadn't liked Mr. Epping, who struck me as a bully who wanted his own way no matter how many other people were damaged.

July 8, 1936

Dear Mr. Epping,

In my opinion you are a lout and a bully.
You have caused your wife untold suffering
for no good reason other than that she is
not a strong woman and has not been able
to conceive and deliver a live child.
Didn't you take an oath to be together "in

sickness and in health"? Lot of clout that had. She's better off getting a divorce, but I'm sure you won't give her a generous settlement. You and Henry the Eighth have a lot in common, including the fact that you have jowls.

I grinned to myself. I know: a touch childish, but it was satisfying. I rolled out the paper and put it into the file marked, CONFIDENTIAL. Mr. Gilmore would never look in there. But even if he did, I didn't think he'd mind.

I put a carbon between two sheets of fresh paper and rolled them into the typewriter. With a demure countenance, I typed the standard number three letter, finishing with, "Your immediate consideration to this matter will be appreciated."

I folded the top sheet, shoved it into an envelope, licked the stamp, and thumped it on.

I sniffed. There was a strong odour of cooking onions drifting on the air. Our immediate neighbour on this floor was making his breakfast. This happened on a regular basis, and I suspected Mr. Patchell was living in his office. This was strictly forbidden by the management of the Arcade, but I wasn't going to turn him in. If he could survive in that tiny space, washroom down a flight of stairs, bed on the couch, I sympathized. He repaired watches, but these days people were more likely to pawn their watches than to get them fixed. The expense of sustaining home and office must have been too much for him.

I typed up another couple of invoices, at the end of which I was fighting the inclination to put my head down and have a nap. Three sleepless nights in a row, tossing around in a stiflingly hot room, were definitely catching up with me. If Gramps had been in agreement, I would have trekked us down to the lake and slept on the beach. Being a proper Englishman, however, my grandfather had been appalled at the suggestion. I might have insisted, but I'd heard it wasn't really that much cooler down there unless you wanted to lie submerged in the water.

I took up the headphones to the Dictaphone. Mr. Gilmore preferred to dictate his reports rather than writing them. I switched on the machine. A tinny voice came out.

"Good day, Miss Frayne. This is my report on the Walsingham case to date. First. Charming as she was, Mrs. Walsingham was not entirely forthcoming. It was a simple matter to discover that she is in fact about to be married to a wealthy man from Edmonton. He himself is a widower with two grown children. He is a former general in the army and served with distinction in France. His reputation is that he has little tolerance for slackers or wayward youths. I don't think she will be too happy to learn that just as she feared, her son is a wastrel and a sorry piece of work. He frequents the gambling dens on Elizabeth Street, coerces the Chinese to sell him opium, pays for prostitutes. A rather advanced state of depravity for a seventeen-year-old. I believe he is unacquainted with the word 'No.' If he lives to see his majority, it will be a miracle. My advice to our client is to get him to enlist in the army as fast as possible. Hopefully they will straighten him out. She should certainly keep him out of sight of her new fiancé. Nothing good will come of their meeting. Phrase this anyway you want, Miss Frayne, but don't be mealy-mouthed about it. She must face the facts or more than one life will be ruined. You can add another thirty dollars to her bill as I did spend at least one sleepless night worrying about this wretched young man. You can list this charge as surveillance."

I had to smile at that last remark.

My feet were itching, and I rubbed them on the carpet. I lifted my face to the fan overhead. The breeze on my hot cheeks was pleasant.

I was debating whether or not to ring Mr. Gilmore to see if everything was all right at home when I heard somebody coming along the hall. The gait was rather fast, not too heavy, definite. The steps halted outside our door, and there was a knock. I slipped my bare feet into my shoes.

You'd be surprised how much information is conveyed in a knock. A sharp *rat-a-tat* usually indicated a man, most likely a husband out to find out what his errant wife was up to. A timid, barely audible *tap-tap* was invariably a female looking for help finding her missing pet. She was coming to us without confiding in her husband, who wouldn't approve and never did like the blasted dog anyway.

These knocks now were loud enough, confident without being belligerent. I stayed seated and called out, "Come in."

In stepped a tall, slim man, neatly dressed in a tan-coloured summer suit.

He removed his straw boater. "Good morning. I wonder if I might speak to Mr. Gilmore."

He didn't look like the kind of man who would send a hate-filled letter, but I was cautious.

"I'm afraid he's not in at the moment. May I be of assistance?"

I suppose the following moments were ones of mutual appraisal. I'm on the disconcerting side of thirty, and he looked a little older. His hair was light brown and smoothed back from a high forehead; his eyes were brown, intelligent. He was clean-shaven.

"Thank you, Mrs., er ..."

"Frayne. Charlotte Frayne. *Miss*."

Not all women over thirty are married, but people typically assume we are.

"I beg your pardon. *Miss* Frayne. I was particularly hoping to talk to Mr. Gilmore. We are acquainted."

Were they? I certainly hadn't seen this man in the office before. I'd have remembered.

The visitor continued as if I'd asked the question. "He's a regular customer at my café. I brew him the coffee he likes. Strong and black, no cream or sugar."

I already knew Mr. Gilmore's culinary preferences, so

I suppose that was a bit of a confirmation. Was that the intent?

"I can get a message to him if you wish. What name shall I say?"

"Taylor. Hilliard Taylor. I am one of the owners of the Paradise Café on Queen Street. He'll know who I am." He glanced around. "It must be difficult for you to not see daylight for hours on end. You can only deduce the weather if somebody comes in with a wet umbrella and a mackintosh, I suppose."

I gave him a polite smile. "That's a good deduction yourself, sir. But you'd be surprised. I do get out a lot."

He nodded, not excited by my itinerary. He was twisting his hat round and round. "Do you think Mr. Gilmore will be available tomorrow?"

"I expect he will."

"I'll come back then."

"I am his associate. Perhaps I can help."

"I, er, I don't think so, Miss Frayne. Thank you anyway."

He turned for the door. It wasn't unusual for prospective clients to dismiss me out of hand, especially when I was seated at the desk. Female private investigators weren't that common. I'd have let it go, but there was something about this man that made me soften. He looked physically strong enough, but there was an unexpected vulnerability to his face.

"Mr. Taylor. Why don't you tell me the nature of your business? I promise that if I think it is beyond my skills, I will say so."

I must admit I rather hoped it wouldn't turn out to be a domestic. He turned and studied me for a moment. I must have passed some kind of test, because his shoulders lowered and he smiled.

"Very well. Fair enough."

I waved at the single chair.

"Please have a seat."

I pulled over my notebook and picked up my pen while he walked over to the chair and sat down. He seemed to move more stiffly than he should for a man his apparent age.

"As I said, I am part owner of a café called the Paradise. We are located on Queen Street, near Simcoe. Do you know it?"

"I'm afraid not."

He looked disappointed. "We have only been in business since January, so I guess I can't expect world recognition." He chewed on his lip. "It's about the café that I'd like to consult."

Good. Not a domestic, unless it was to do with alimony. I smiled my encouraging smile.

It seemed to work, because he continued. "Perhaps I should give you a bit of background."

"Please do."

Most of the clients I had dealt with to that point needed what I'd call an indirect entry into their real problem. Hilliard Taylor was no exception.

"Initially, I'd say our first few months of business were good. We keep our prices low and cater to people who can't afford to spend much money away from home. The café is always full. Our costs have not changed. We should be making a small but steady profit." He hesitated, then, with a sigh, he went on. "However, some irregularities seem to have occurred that I do not understand. As of the past month we appear to be slipping into a hole."

He picked up on some expression that must have flitted across my face.

"You're probably wondering why I'm consulting a private investigating agency about such a matter and not an accountant."

"I can only assume you suspect some nefarious reason for these irregularities?"

He gave me a slightly lopsided grin that I found endearing.

"Precisely."

I tapped my pen. "And to your mind, what might be that reason?"

He started to fan himself with his boater. He looked as if he would do anything to avoid what he had to say. I helped him out.

"You suspect somebody is stealing?"

He nodded. I could see a nerve twitching in his jaw. He said, so quietly I almost couldn't hear him, "It looks that way."

I came out from behind my desk, forgetting I wasn't wearing my stockings.

"I made a pot of coffee earlier. Would you like a cup?"

"No, thanks. I'm fine. I'd just like to get to the bottom of this whole mess as soon as possible."

I retreated back to my notebook. I would have liked some coffee, but it would have to wait.

"Do you have anybody in mind?"

He flinched. "I've gone over and over everything, and I can only conclude that it is somebody who is familiar with the operation of the café."

"I see."

He got to his feet. "I need to stretch my legs."

Considering the size of the office, unless he walked up the walls he wasn't going to get much exercise. He began to make a tight circle around the chair.

There was something about the way he did it that made me think he had made many such tight perambulations before. Had he previously been in jail?

"Please continue, Mr. Taylor. How many people do you consider are familiar with the running of the café?"

"There are the four of us, the partners, and we have two staff, a mother and her daughter, who wait on the tables. We have a part-time baker."

"Have you talked to your partners about the problem?"

He glanced at me as if I were a doctor waving a large needle at him that he knew he had to accept.

"Not yet. I didn't want to worry them unnecessarily. I preferred to be absolutely sure about what was happening." He held up his hand as if to stop me speaking. "I know what you are thinking. But I must insist. I trust my partners absolutely."

I decided to enter the arena obliquely.

"How long have you all known each other?"

"Many years. Since 1917."

"Soldiers?"

"Yes. As a matter of fact, we were all prisoners of war together. At Doberitz."

Prisoners of war would not have had extensive areas in which to stretch their legs; this explained his walking in circles. And the touch of defensiveness in his tone. Not all of society accepted the fact that soldiers often had no choice but to surrender to the enemy and become prisoners of war. I'd heard it voiced more than once that this was an act of cowardice. Why hadn't they simply given up their lives instead of giving in?

I continued my own cerebral form of circling. "You all first met nineteen years ago. Did you stay in touch over the intervening years?"

"We did. Conal and Wilf both went back to the Prairies. Eric is from Toronto. I returned to Sudbury. And to answer your question, yes, we stayed in touch, wrote letters, visited when we could." He sat down abruptly, perching on the edge of the chair. "We met up again about two years ago. A veterans' reunion here in Toronto. We got to chatting, and one thing led to another. Turned out we were all at loose ends. Eric and Wilf weren't married anymore. Conal had never tied the knot, and as for me ... well, I was on my own too."

I was curious about that, but now wasn't the time to ask. He continued his narrative.

"By the end of that particular night, we decided to throw in our lot and go into business together. We were all sick to death of being dependent on some boss who didn't give a toss for our livelihood." He snapped his fingers. "You're hired. Snap. You're fired. Snap. Felt like we were back in that hellhole camp where our fate was in the hands of other people. We decided to start a café."

I was genuinely surprised. "These days, an enterprise like that would be considered very risky."

He nodded. "I know it sounds mad, but we did have some grounding in reality. Eric had experience as a chef. He'd been working in a restaurant out west for a few years. Wilf is an electrician. Conal is an artist, but also a fine carpenter."

"And you?"

"Me? I'm a good dishwasher. Handling the financial side of things devolved onto me."

His self-deprecating humour was sweet.

"Every restaurant has to have a good dishwasher."

"What we all agreed on was that we'd had it to the gills with the present state of affairs. At least, doing this, we'd only have to answer to ourselves."

"The four of you? No other partners?"

"No. Just us. We each scraped up enough money to cover a couple of months' rent and then we went out looking. I was the one who found this little place on Queen Street. It had gone bust. The landlord was glad to unload it for a reasonable sum and to have us move in right away. We slapped on some fresh paint, blocked up the rat holes, and Bob's your uncle, the Paradise Café was born."

He stared up at the ceiling.

"I like the name," I said.

"There was never a doubt that was we were going to call it." His voice dropped. "Out there, the Paradise Café was biding her time, waiting for us to find her. And finally, after all those years, we did just that. But you can't say we adopted her. She adopted us."

For whatever reason, as yet undisclosed when he spoke as he did, his voice was drenched with sadness.

The shrill ring of the telephone interrupted us.

"Excuse me." I picked up the receiver. "Gilmore and Associates."

It was Mr. Gilmore. I hardly recognized his voice, he sounded so strained.

"Miss Frayne, are you in the midst of anything at the moment?"

"I'm speaking with a client."

I was about to tell him who it was, but I didn't get the chance.

"Would you be so good as to terminate the interview

promptly? An urgent matter has arisen here. I need to speak to you at once. Please call me back right away. I am at home. You know the number." He hung up.

I swivelled back to face Hilliard.

"I'm afraid I have to deal with another urgent matter. Would you be able to return later, so that we may continue at another time? I do apologize."

He frowned at me, but I don't have a poker face. His expression softened.

"I can come back."

I hesitated. I had no idea what was happening to Mr. Gilmore.

"Tell you what," said Hilliard. "I assume you would need to see the Paradise with your own eyes and get the lay of the land? Why don't you do what you have to do and then come over to the café this afternoon?"

"All right. I will if I can."

He smiled. "Have you ever had waitressing experience?"

"As a matter of fact, yes. I worked part-time when I was in high school."

"Good. We would have to get extra help anyway because Mrs. Reilly has lumbago and we've only got one waitress on tonight. I could hire you temporarily. If you could handle it, it would be the best way to get some idea of the routine. You'd be undercover, as it were."

I had done undercover work before. Last time was as a lady's maid at a posh house on Jarvis Street. Disastrous. This sounded like a piece of cake in comparison.

"Okay."

"Excellent. The first dinner sitting is at five. Let's say I'll expect you about three-thirty, and if it looks as if you can't make it you can give me a ring."

He collected his hat from the floor.

"Miss Frayne, I need hardly tell you how important it is to me to clear this up as soon as possible. My partners and I have invested all our dreams in this project. I cannot bear the thought it might fail."

He looked so relieved I almost slid by the question of my fee. Almost.

"I will need to charge you my investigator's fee. I have an hourly rate, which is charged no matter what the outcome. Unless, that is, you consider I have been grossly incompetent."

Another smile. "Why do I doubt I would ever think that? And in addition, I shall pay you what I would normally pay a waitress. Fifteen cents an hour, less five each time the uniform is cleaned."

"Done."

"Miss Frayne, do I have your absolute assurance that nobody will know about this arrangement? Unless, that is …"

His voice trailed off, but I didn't need him to complete the sentence. Unless one of his closest companions turned out to be a traitor. For his sake, I hoped that wouldn't prove to be the case.

He saluted and left.

Chapter Three

I DIALLED MR. GILMORE'S home number, and he answered right away.

"Miss Frayne, bless you for responding so promptly."

"Of course."

"Somebody broke into my house while I was away. They attacked my wife."

"Good heavens! That's dreadful. What happened?"

"We don't know as yet. She hasn't recovered consciousness. She's been taken to the hospital. The police are here now. I am so shocked, Miss Frayne, I hardly know what I'm saying. They seem to be implying I am responsible."

"What! What do you mean, responsible?"

"For the supposed break-in and the attack on Ida."

"That's ridiculous."

"Apparently not. I wonder if you would come here."

"I'll be there right away."

"Thank you, I would appreciate that. I don't quite know where to turn."

We hung up, and I realized he'd forgotten to tell me his address. As we kept our relationship on a professional basis, I'd never been to his home. He didn't live too far from the Arcade, but that was all I knew. I was just about to ring him back when I remembered we kept special papers in the tiny safe in the office. We didn't have to use it very often, and I hadn't memorized the combination. I pulled open the drawer of my desk and rummaged at the back where I kept a cigar box thrust underneath a pile of old invoices. The number was in there: 17-5-34. I retrieved it and hurried over to the safe. It was an ugly black thing with no pretensions except for appearing impregnable. I squatted down in front of it and turned the dial.

It opened easily. I was experiencing rather irrational feelings of guilt. I knew that the safe contained reports on cases that he considered sensitive; Mr. Gilmore was the one who handled that material, not me. It wasn't that I wasn't allowed to see them; however, I always felt I was discouraged to do so.

There were only a handful of labelled folders. I pulled them out. One on the top said, APPLICATIONS I couldn't resist a quick look. It was a form I had filled out when I was applying for the position of assistant private investigator. Mr. Gilmore had attached a note: "Excellent candidate. No reservations. Job offered."

I was chuffed.

The folder underneath was labelled, PERSONAL PAPERS. FOR EMERGENCY PURPOSES ONLY. I thought this qualified as an emergency, and I opened it. Inside were three sheets of paper. One was a copy of Mr. Gilmore's licence as a private investigator, the second was his marriage certificate, and the third was a certificate of name change. It read, "On the 3rd April, Daniel Jacob Goldenberg changed his name by deed poll and is henceforth to be known as Thaddeus Gilmore."

The certificate was dated 1928, which was when Mr. Gilmore established his investigating business. I sat back. That was a bit of a shock. It had certainly never come up in any of our talks. But I had been right about Mr. Gilmore dissembling. Given his original name, I had to assume he was Jewish. His carefully phrased comment came back to me: "I do not consider myself to be a filthy Jew, Communist or not."

I wondered if the piece of hate mail that had arrived earlier was in any way connected with what had just happened at his house. Was the snake of anti-Semitism only scotched, not killed?

I took Might's City Directory off the shelf and consulted it quickly. Mr. T. Gilmore was listed as living at number sixteen Phoebe Street. I wrote down the names of the immediate neighbours in case I needed to talk to them.

I resumed respectability with stockings, straw hat, and cotton gloves and hurried out of the office. Briefly I considered getting on one of the streetcars clanking down Yonge Street, but I couldn't face being in such close proximity with other overheated humanity. Phoebe Street wasn't that far away, and I decided walking would be just as fast. The oppressiveness of the heat and humidity was worse than ever. I turned west on Queen Street. Just as I went past Osgoode Hall Law School, an open-topped Packard Roadster turned out of the driveway. The car was the colour of a robin's egg; there was a uniformed chauffeur driving, and two young women in gauzy summer frocks were in the back seat. I felt a stab of envy. Not particularly because they were in a car that would have cost more than I might earn in ten years, nor because the women were young, pretty, and rich. I envied them the breeze in their faces.

I continued on. Just ahead of me was a straggly lineup, mostly men, all silent. I realized they were lined up in front of a café. The name? The Paradise. It was squeezed between a shop selling second-hand goods on one side and a shabby boarded-up storefront, with the words "FOR RENT" scrawled across the plywood, on the other. The Paradise stood out like a lighthouse in a dreary sea. The trim was a bright, cheery yellow, and the name above the window was picked out in orange lights. It didn't look like the kind of place that would draw the law school crowd, but it did convey warmth and friendliness. Clearly the customers waiting outside thought the same.

Phoebe Street was only ten minutes' walk from the café by way of Soho Street. Unlike its rather rakish name, Soho was sedate, empty of traffic. Phoebe intersected to the left. I paused to get my bearings. It was a short street, lush with trees, lined on each side by Victorian-era row houses. Black wrought iron railings enclosed tiny front gardens filled with shrubs and flower beds. Ensuring some individuality, each door had its own stained-glass skylight and different coloured trim around the windows. These houses conveyed a sense of permanence, order, and calm — an illusion shattered by Mr. Gilmore's recent call and news.

From the corner, I could see a small knot of spectators were gathered on the sidewalk in the shade of a linden tree, all focused on something nearby. This had to be Mr. Gilmore's house. Rather like the owner, it appeared to be neat and unassuming.

A uniformed constable was standing in front of the gate. I paused, just long enough to wipe off my face and neck with my handkerchief, and approached the house.

Perhaps the officer, an older man, normally had a red face, but I assumed he was scarlet right now because he was boiling hot in his serge uniform and helmet. I sympathized with the suffering caused by the high collar and long sleeves. He held out his arm in order to block me.

"Sorry, madam. You can't go in there."

"I'm a friend and an associate of Mr. Gilmore's. He sent for me."

The constable had an expression on his face that suggested he wouldn't have believed Queen Mary herself if she'd claimed the present king was her son.

"You'll have to wait until the detective gives permission."

"All right. Where is he? I'll speak to him."

I didn't have to wait long. The front door opened, and a man emerged. He was dressed in a light blue summer suit, and he looked a lot cooler than the constable. He had the demeanour of a man of authority. He walked down the path toward us.

"Excuse me, sir," said the constable. "This lady here says she's an associate of Mr. Gilmore's. She wants to see him."

The constable managed to convey deep suspicion as to my motives, not to mention my honesty. The detective regarded me dispassionately, and I was sure he was going to deny me access to my poor boss. Then I realized I knew him. I stepped forward, hand outstretched in a rather manly way.

"Detective Murdoch. We've met."

He obviously didn't have a clue as to who I was, but he smiled politely.

We shook hands. It was a little awkward, as I had to stretch over the railing to reach his hand.

"It must be two years ago now," I babbled on. "You gave a talk to the students at the school where I was teaching. St. Mary's. I'm Charlotte Frayne. It was my job to thank you."

He made a good recovery, and his smile seemed genuine. "Of course. Glad to meet you again, Miss Frayne."

I was slightly chagrined I had offered such a sticky palm. His was dry. Physically, he looked the same as I remembered. Dark hair, dark eyes, well-defined bone structure. He was still what my friend Polly would call "a dish."

"Your topic was 'What Next?' as I recall. There wasn't a lot to cheer about back then. The future looked bleak. You gave the students hope."

I was laying it on a bit thick, but, in fact, I had liked him. Never mind his good looks, his talk had been thoughtful and pertinent. My students had appreciated him.

He grimaced. "I'm glad to hear it. As you say, not a lot to cheer about. I wish it were significantly different nowadays, but I'm not sure it is."

The beefy constable was eavesdropping and doing a very bad job of pretending not to.

"I gather you're not a teacher anymore," said Murdoch. "The constable said you were an associate of Mr. Gilmore."

"That's right. I left teaching not too long after you and I met."

I wasn't about to go into the circumstances. I had been fired. The official reason was cutting down on staff, but we all knew it was because I had challenged one of the school trustees. I'd underestimated the amount of influence he had. Or more accurately, the amount of fear he was able to generate. Nobody could afford to lose their jobs.

"May I speak with Mr. Gilmore?" I asked Murdoch.

He glanced around. We were still on either side of the gate at this point.

"Let's move over into the shade for a minute, shall we." A few feet away, at the corner of the house, were a striped garden umbrella and a couple of canvas chairs.

Murdoch swung open the gate, and I stepped through and followed him. In the front garden, the flowers were in dire need of resuscitation, and the tiny lawn was already turning dry and brown. For the past week, the city council had ordered all citizens to refrain from any watering until the weather broke. Mr. Gilmore was evidently obedient. I wasn't sure about the rest of the houses on the row.

There was some relief from the day's sun under the umbrella. It was also out of earshot of Beefy. We sat down.

"Can you tell me what has happened?" I asked.

He shook his head. "I can't go into a lot of details at this point, as I'm sure you can understand. All we know is that Mrs. Gilmore was attacked. A Mrs. Kaufmann, who lives at the end house, found her lying unconscious in the hall."

"When was this?"

"Just after nine o'clock. She ran across the road to Alexander's repair shop. The owner has a telephone. He rang the station."

"Did the neighbour see the attacker?"

"She says not."

"You said she found Mrs. Gilmore about nine. Do we know when the attack itself actually took place?"

"Not at the moment. I did speak with Mr. Gilmore, and he was adamant his wife was sleeping peacefully when he left at seven-thirty this morning. He said he went directly to his office."

"I can vouch for that. He was there when I arrived at eight o'clock."

I wanted to say that there was no way Mr. Gilmore could have just clobbered his wife. True, he was upset, but I attributed that to the nasty letter he had received. I bit my tongue. Better to wait and hear what the police had to say.

"Assuming he is telling the truth," Murdoch continued, "his wife was attacked between half past seven and ten past nine. A window of more than one hour and a half."

Murdoch removed a rather handsome watch from his inner pocket and flipped it open.

"Mr. Gilmore returned here about a quarter to ten. Did he remain at the office from when you saw him at eight?"

What the heck was I going to say? Murdoch was doing what he should do to investigate this crime, but I was reluctant to reveal that Mr. Gilmore had high-tailed it out directly after he read the letter. This was about twenty-five past eight.

I stalled for time. "Is that what he said?"

"Not precisely. He was rather vague about it. But he was emphatic about not returning to the house since he left this morning."

Mr. Gilmore had said he was going to check on his wife. If he had gone straight home, he should have been at his house a lot earlier. What was he doing? There seemed to be more than an entire hour unaccounted for.

"Where is he now?"

"Inside."

"He's afraid that you're considering him a suspect."

"All possibilities are open at the moment."

I saw that Murdoch was watching me. For the second time this morning a man was sizing me up. Nothing lascivious in either case. Apparently, I passed Murdoch's inspection as well as I had Hilliard Taylor's.

"I should tell you, Miss Frayne, I do not seriously suspect Mr. Gilmore. Unless he is a consummate actor, I believed his distress when he found out what had happened. The blow to his wife was on the back of her head, and there was quite a lot of bloodshed. There is no blood on Mr. Gilmore's clothes. He does have a couple of nasty scratches on his face, however."

"He explained that to me. He said he was doing some gardening and was scratched by a rose bush."

Murdoch nodded. "That's what he told me as well. I did take a look at the back garden. There are a couple of rose bushes, but they don't appear to have been tended to recently."

"I suppose he gave up the fight after he was scratched."

"Possibly. As I said, he is not a prime suspect."

"Of course. Wouldn't Mrs. Gilmore be able to enlighten us as to what happened?"

"I hope so. She has not recovered consciousness as yet. Her condition is grave, but let us hope for a full recovery."

I saw the curtain move in the front window, and I glimpsed my boss peering out.

"Is it all right if I go and speak to Mr. Gilmore?"

"Certainly. I will come with you. I'm sure he's eager to go to the hospital. I'll have him driven there."

We headed to the door.

"You haven't said what time Mr. Gilmore did leave the office," said Murdoch casually.

Once again I was put into the position of having to choose.

"I wasn't paying a lot of attention." Sort of true. I fervently hoped it wasn't significant.

I glanced at Murdoch and had the feeling I didn't fool him one little bit. I was saved further venery by Mr. Gilmore, who opened the front door and came out. Gone was the mild, immaculately dressed man I was used to. His mouth was tight, his face flushed and sweaty. He was in his shirt sleeves.

"Miss Frayne. Thank you for coming. Perhaps you can assure the detective that I was with you in our office, not here attacking the woman I love and cherish."

That sure put me on the spot, as I knew that strictly speaking I could not give him the alibi he wanted.

"I'm sure Mrs. Gilmore will be able to say what happened."

He looked at me, aghast. "Let's pray she recovers."

Murdoch intervened. "Mr. Gilmore, I have no desire to add to your distress. As soon as one of our detectives arrives, I shall have you taken to the hospital."

Mr. Gilmore looked as if he might shove past Murdoch and take off down the street, but right then a car turned onto Phoebe Street.

"Ah, that's the police car now," said Murdoch. "If you will wait here, sir, I'll give him instructions."

This was the first opportunity Mr. Gilmore had had to speak privately to me. He leaned in closer. The scratches were livid, and there was a drop of spittle on the corner of his mouth; his breath was foul. He lowered his voice. "Miss Frayne. I ask you not to mention the letter I received this morning. It has nothing to do with what has happened here."

"Can you be sure of that, sir? It might help the police to know about it."

"If that proves to be the case, I shall tell them. But for now I don't want to muddy the waters."

I didn't have a chance to pursue this further because Murdoch returned. He was followed by a heavy-set man who was sporting a decidedly unfriendly expression.

"Detective Arcady will drive you, sir," Murdoch said.

Mr. Gilmore addressed me. "I shall ring as soon as I learn anything more."

He hurried down the path to the car, with the unrelenting detective right behind him. Not under arrest, but, in spite of what Murdoch had said, at least one of the detectives was holding him under suspicion.

Murdoch turned. "Come inside. It's a bit cooler."

We went into the house. It was a traditional design with a narrow hall leading to the back, the stairs directly to the right. Opposite, through open French doors, I glimpsed a pleasantly furnished living room. Not too cluttered, not too sparse. There was a rug on the hall floor, and interwoven with the pattern was a dark, ominous stain. A silver candelabra was lying near the door.

Murdoch pointed. "The attack seems to have happened

here. There's no doubt that was the weapon. We'll get it tested for fingerprints. Mrs. Gilmore was a little further into the hall, near the kitchen. She was lying face down, and she had been attacked from behind."

"Was she dressed?"

My question elicited a shrewd glance. "She was in her nightclothes, but she was wearing a dressing gown. I assume her assailant entered by way of the front door; whether he forced his way in is not clear. She might have been running away, or …" He hesitated.

"She knew the man, let him in, and might not have realized she was in danger. She might have been simply heading back toward the kitchen."

"Precisely."

He didn't have to fill in the blanks. If Mrs. Gilmore had not been alarmed by her visitor, her husband was still under suspicion. But why would he attack her? There was absolutely nothing to indicate that he was a violent man or that there was any animosity between the two of them. Quite the opposite. Unfortunately, his own words came back to me. *Things are not always what they seem, Miss Frayne. Never jump to conclusions until you have conducted a thorough investigation.* He'd smiled at me. *And even then, you might not be right. People can be astonishingly duplicitous.*

Chapter Four

MURDOCH HAD LEFT the front door ajar, which allowed the sound of another car arriving to reach us. Murdoch could see it was a police car.

"I have to talk to them," said Murdoch. "Good to see you again, Miss Frayne. Don't worry, we'll get to the bottom of this. Now, if you'll excuse me, I'll have to let you out."

He led the way out the door and back down the path. Two uniformed constables were waiting, getting an update from Beefy. I noticed Murdoch's right arm wasn't totally mobile. When he'd given his talk at my school I remembered he'd told me that it was the result of an old war wound. He was probably the same age as Hilliard Taylor. Maybe they knew each other. Band of brothers and so on.

I stepped away from the gate as the constables went through. Beefy wasn't looking any friendlier, but I could see no valid reason why I shouldn't have a chat with the neighbours. The onlookers were dispersing. One woman walked past and opened the gate to what was presumably her own house at the end of the row. I didn't want to lose her, so I trotted after her, calling out, "Excuse me, Mrs. Kaufmann?"

I was taking a guess that she was the woman who had found Mrs. Gilmore, and I proved to be right. She turned and stared at me, a deep suspicion in her eyes.

I flashed my cheeriest smile. "My name is Charlotte Frayne. I'm an associate of Mr. Gilmore's. I wonder if I might have a word with you."

At first, given how she moved, I'd thought she was elderly but, closer, I could see that wasn't the case at all. She might not be much older than I. But her face was thin and without colour. The shapeless, drab cotton dress she wore aged her considerably. She was wearing a calico sunbonnet and a grey striped apron over her dress that would have been suitable in the workhouse.

"This must have been a terrible shock for you." She didn't answer, and I began to wonder if she was deaf or an immigrant who couldn't speak English.

She turned and began again to walk away down the path. I took a chance and followed, at which point a man came out of the house and stood at the top of the steps. He appeared to be older than Mrs. Kaufmann, whom I presumed to be his wife. He was wearing dirt-stained overalls; his hair and beard were unkempt, his expression pugnacious.

"What you want, missus?"

I tried to include both of them. "I'm an associate of Mr. Gilmore's, and for everybody's sake, I'd like to get to the bottom of this dreadful incident as soon as possible. Would you mind if I come and talk to you?"

The woman looked up at her husband. He answered for her.

"What do you want know?"

I was starting to feel a bit ridiculous hovering on the path while he talked down to me. Cautiously I advanced and addressed his wife.

"I understand you were the one who found Mrs. Gilmore?"

She half turned. At least there was some response.

"Why did you go to the house?"

She was given no chance to answer.

"Why shouldn't she?" her husband said harshly.

I gave in. I wasn't going to get anywhere without addressing Mr. Kaufmann. I tried the soothing voice routine.

"It's a good thing she did. She probably saved Mrs. Gilmore's life. I'm just wondering if she'd heard anything. A cry? A shout?"

Mr. Kaufmann said something to his wife in what sounded like German. Obviously, he gave his permission for her to answer. Her voice was lightly accented.

"I want make lemonade. Ida owed me a lemon from last week, so I went collect it. The door was part open. I thought this strange. I thought she might have faint. She not well sometime. I went in and there she was. On floor."

"Was she conscious?"

"No." The woman paused. Her lips began to quiver. "I thought she dead."

"Thank goodness you were able to get help immediately."

"I went to get Mr. Alexander. I know he has telephone. Police arrive soon." Mrs. Kaufmann wiped her mouth with the end of her apron. "Who did this?"

"I don't know. Have there been any other such occurrences in this neighbourhood? Any break-ins?"

"No. We are quiet here." She actually swayed a little, but before I could offer help she turned away. Kaufmann did nothing.

"Excuse. I must go lie down."

She shuffled up the steps. There was a small wooden crucifix hanging on the doorpost, and she touched it reverentially as she went past. Kaufmann stepped aside, and she squeezed past him. The way she shrank away made me think she was afraid, but that might have been the situation. When she was inside, her husband sat down on the top step. He was not a tall man by any means, but he had what I can only call presence. He had the broad shoulders of a labourer; his cotton shirt was rolled up to the elbows, revealing muscular forearms decorated with intricate tattoos; as far as I could see from my hasty scrutiny, they were military style. His thighs were thick.

I shifted. I would have been happy to sit down, but there was nowhere, and he wasn't making any space available to me.

He was studying the scene at the Gilmore house. Another constable was at the door. Beefy had gone.

"My wife is a good woman."

I had no reason to think otherwise, and I nodded.

He put his own finger to his temple. "Mrs. Gilmore's not always right in the head."

Now he did look at me. His eyes had the yellowish tinge of a habitual drinker, but they were still keen. "She shouts and screams sometimes."

"Why is that?"

He shrugged. "Her brain's not working properly. She goes to the past. She sees things that aren't there. So she screams."

"Is this a frequent occurrence?"

"No. Not frequent. Every so often."

"Your wife said she didn't hear anything this morning. Did you?"

"If my wife says it was quiet, then it was quiet. Why should I call her a liar?"

Why indeed?

"It's not a matter of calling her a liar, Mr. Kaufmann. Perhaps you might have been somewhere else where, if there was a scream, you would have heard it. Or you didn't take it seriously, given Mrs. Gilmore's history of shouting."

This was getting too convoluted.

He frowned at me, stupid woman that I was. "I was still sleeping. It's been hard to get a good night's sleep with this heat. There was no sound from Mrs. Gilmore. First I know of any trouble is when wife comes to get me. Tells me what is happening."

"Do you recall what time that was?"

"No. I don't have a watch."

He scratched hard at his wrist as if punishing it for this lapse.

I persisted. "We don't know at exactly what time she was attacked. It could have been shortly after Mr. Gilmore left the house, which was about half past seven."

"Then I was asleep."

"Which means you would not have seen a stranger going to the Gilmore house. Is that correct?"

"Even if I was awake, which I was not, I do not sit on my steps and watch the world go by. I am a working man." He waved his hand in the direction of the row houses. "I take care of them."

"You sound just like my grandfather. Loves to work. Can't nail him down."

I'd been hoping to find Kaufmann's soft spot. A little flattery can go a long way. He gave me a brief nod.

Time to leave while I was ahead. "One more thing, Mr. Kaufmann. This seems like such a friendly neighbourhood. People know each other, help each other out if necessary. Not like where I live. I'm lucky if any of my neighbours even knows my name."

I'm afraid this was a flagrant lie. I knew all of my neighbours, and they knew me. I was fishing. "Would you say that you and your wife were friends with the Gilmores?"

He frowned. "Why are you asking? You're not the police."

"That's quite true; it's just that I've worked with Mr. Gilmore for some time now, and he strikes me as a very decent man. He's afraid that the police might think he was the one who attacked his own wife. I find that a ridiculous idea, but you know him in a different way from me. You said Mrs. Gilmore has shown signs of being a troubled woman. Did you ever see or hear them arguing?"

"No. To my mind, Gilmore shouldn't have put up with it. He should've shown her who was boss."

Right!

"And as a friend, did you ever offer your opinion?"

Oops, I'd gone too far. I'd lost my tiny foothold of approval. The expression on his face would have done justice to a disturbed wasps' nest, if they had expressions.

Without another word he got to his feet and went back into the house.

I called after him, "Thank you for talking to me, Mr. Kaufmann."

The screen door banged open. He leaned out.

"Leave! Now."

I did. I must admit my heart was accelerating.

Chapter Five

I THOUGHT THERE WAS still time to ask more questions. The police would be doing that officially all too soon. I hoped I could glean some information before it was either embellished or buried.

Across the road, at the corner, was an auto repair shop. Presumably where the telephone was housed. I could hear clanging coming from that direction. I walked over.

A husky man in stained overalls was banging out dents from the fender of a car that looked as if it had lost a fierce argument for road rights.

"Hello there."

I tried to time my greeting in between bangs. I had to repeat it, and the second time the man turned around. I beamed a full wattage, admiring smile. I have no hesitation in using feminine wiles if they will get me somewhere.

"That must be hot work. I hope the owners appreciate it."

He shrugged. "Doubt it. Most like they'll buy another new one."

"Too bad to just toss it on the trash heap, considering it's such a beauty. It's an Auburn Speedster, isn't it?"

That really got his attention. He used his bandana to wipe the sweat off his face.

"How'd you know that?"

"Why shouldn't I? Not all of us women are empty-headed."

"No, of course not. I didn't mean to give offence …"

His voice trailed off.

"No offence taken. It's just that I've made it a bit of a hobby to study cars."

That at least was true, but I wasn't about to go into the reason for this unfeminine interest. Knowing the makes of cars was an essential part of the business of surveillance.

"Me, if I ever get enough money, I'd buy a LaSalle. Used, naturally."

He guffawed. "Ha. Fat chance. They never come up for sale."

"Oh, well. A girl can dream, can't she?" I held out my hand. "Hi, I'm Charlotte."

He wiped his palm down his shirt and shook hands with me. "Vince. Vince Alexander." He jerked his head. "Me and my dad own this place. That's our name, Alexander Auto Repairs."

"Good thing people like you exist. There seem to be more accidents every day. You'd think there'd be fewer cars on the roads these days, given the price of gasoline." I screwed up my mouth. "Never seems to bother rich people, does it? Tough times, I mean. They just go on buying whatever they fancy."

"You're right about that."

I flapped my hand in the general direction of the street. "Not much traffic on this street, obviously. What you'd call a quiet neighbourhood."

He mopped his face again. "True. It is that. Say, you're not a reporter, are you?"

"Me? No. Why would I be? Did something happen here?"

"It sure did. One of the neighbours was attacked this morning. Word is she might not survive."

"My goodness! Fancy that. Who did it?"

"Nobody knows. I was talking to one of the constables, and he says they've taken the husband into custody." He pushed a strand of greasy hair out of his eyes. "Me, I'd never have suspected that. Gilmore is a quiet sort of fellow. But you never know what goes on behind closed doors, do you?"

"Indeed not. On the other hand, maybe they've got it wrong, the coppers. They're not infallible. Maybe it wasn't him. Could've been a tramp looking for something to steal."

He nodded. "You could be right. God knows there're enough of those around these days. She might've surprised him. I have to make sure I lock up real secure at night. I've had some tools nipped about a week ago."

"Did you yourself see anybody hanging around?"

"Nope."

"And you'd notice, I'm sure. You've got a good view of the street."

"I don't spend my time watching. I've got work to do."

He stared at me for a moment. He was getting suspicious, I could tell.

"I'll let you get back to it, then. Don't forget, if a used LaSalle comes up, let me know. Any condition."

"How would I get hold of you?"

I fished in my purse and took out one of my business cards. He looked at it.

"What? You a private cop?"

"I work for the company."

He waved away a colony of flies that were exploring his face and arms. He looked at the card again.

"Wait a minute. This says Gilmore. Is it the same man?"

"Yes, it is."

"You should have said so right off the bat."

"Sorry. Sometimes people get the wrong impression … 'off the bat.' Mr. Gilmore hasn't been charged, by the way. The police took him to the hospital to be with his wife. Needless to say, he's very upset about what has happened, and he's asked me to see if I could find out anything."

Vince was silent for a moment, chewing on his lip. Then he gave me a sly little grin. "Are you really interested in a used LaSalle?"

I grinned back. "Who wouldn't be? They're the best."

"Well. Now that you ask, I did hear something early this morning. It was so bloody hot, my old lady was tossing and turning like she was on a ship. I got up and went out to the back garden to have a smoke."

He paused, either remembering the discomfort of the night or what it was he had heard and was about to reveal to me. I nodded encouragingly.

"I'd just lit up when somebody let out one hell of a scream. A woman. Now, sometimes Mrs. Gilmore shouts in her sleep. She has nightmares, according to what I understand. But this didn't sound like the usual. It was only the once. Quiet after that."

"Do you think it was Mrs. Gilmore?"

His gaze shifted. "Wouldn't swear to it, but it was coming from that direction. Seemed like their house."

"What time would you say?"

"I must've got up at half past six, and I'd almost finished my smoke so it could have been close to seven. Might have been later, might have been earlier."

"Did you tell the police?"

"No. It slipped my mind until just now."

I suspected my desire to purchase a used La Salle had jogged his memory.

"D'you think it's important?" he asked.

"It could be. Thanks for telling me."

He touched his forehead. "Sure. If I remember anything else, I'll let you know. We're on the phone, I could ring you."

"That would be great. Much appreciated. I'd like to get to the bottom of this. As you said, Mr. Gilmore is a mighty decent man."

He nodded. "Never given me any trouble, anyways."

"I haven't met his wife. She suffers from bad health as I understand."

"So I hear, but doesn't slow her down none." He frowned. "Sometimes I think she's organizing a wives' union on the street."

"Really? Never heard of such a thing."

"She comes over to visit my wife regularly, and after, you can bet your boots, Lillian is going to have something to complain about."

"What sort of thing?"

"You know, why don't I help out more around the house? Why don't I take her to the pictures once in a while? Even a dance, God forbid. She seems to forget I'm working to put food on the table. I'm fagged out at the end of the day. I don't want to go anywhere."

"I see your point. And you say Mrs. Gilmore seemed to be instigating these discontents in your wife?"

"Definitely."

He wiped his face down. He was still a young man and good-looking in a rough way.

"Not a reason to attack a defenceless woman, though, is it?"

"Hey, you're not implying anything, are you?"

"Not at all. But if Mrs Gilmore was interfering in your marriage, maybe she was doing it with other couples. Maybe with somebody not as tolerant as you."

"Well, you can take your pick on this street. Like I said, you'd think she was organizing a union." He thrust his fist in the air in a mock salute. "'Women of the world unite. Down with tyrants.'"

I rather liked the sound of that, but this was not the moment to take sides.

"I assume Mr. Gilmore doesn't object to his wife's politics?"

"Doesn't seem to. To tell the truth, I think he might agree."

He said this with a note of incredulity. Then he turned back to the auto. "I've got a lot to do. 'Less you have any more questions, I'll get on with it."

He slapped at his arm, picked off a dead fly, and dropped it to the ground.

"Bloody flies. They's out in full force."

He picked up his hammer and gave the damaged car a hard blow on the snout as if it were responsible.

It was time for me to get going. "Thanks a lot. I'll keep you informed of any developments."

He grunted a reply, and I continued on my way.

This information put a different slant on Mr. Kaufmann's statement that Mrs. Gilmore was a madwoman. But then, I suppose from his point of view, inciting wives to stand up for themselves was a kind of madness.

Chapter Six

VINCE HAD BEEN aggravatingly vague about when he was outside having his smoke. Was he telling the truth? Had I overdone it with the car thing? Had he construed that as possible payment? For any information, made up or not?

Somehow, I believed him. But if the shout had come from Mrs. Gilmore, where was her husband? At seven he had said he was still at home. Was it a nightmare? Had anybody else heard it?

There seemed to be no more action at number sixteen. The police hadn't seriously embarked on an investigation yet. I imagined they were waiting to see what happened to Ida Gilmore. I could continue my own questioning.

I decided to concentrate on visiting the rest of the houses on the row.

After talking to Vince Alexander, I had a different slant on the situation of the street. Was this attack personally motivated? Had Ida Gilmore offended some person, yet unknown, to the point that he — or even she — had gone to the house with a view to confront her?

I took out the list of names I'd made from Might's

before I left. I went to number eighteen first, which was the house immediately attached to the west of the Gilmores'. According to my list, it was the residence of Mario Ano.

Although identical in design to the others on the row, this house looked a bit more polished. That included the large brass door knocker in the shape of a lion's head, which gleamed in the sun. The windows had definitely been washed recently, and the lace curtains were snow white.

I took the ring in the lion's mouth and rapped. The door was opened at once. A smallish round woman, with dark hair and a dark complexion, stood on the threshold. She'd answered so quickly I wondered if she'd been waiting. For a visitor? For life to start?

"Good morning. Mrs. Ano?"

"Si."

"My name is Charlotte Frayne. I am an investigator, and I wondered if I might come in and ask you some questions. It's in connection with the attack on Mrs. Gilmore, which I assume you know about."

She stared at me for a moment. "I no speak good English. What you want to know?"

I fanned myself. "It's such a hot day, do you mind if I come inside and talk?"

There was a long pause as if she were translating my words. I was about to repeat myself when she nodded and stepped back.

"Come."

She led the way to the parlour and gestured to a brocade-covered chair. I could tell the room was not used frequently.

I took out my notebook. I'd become very good at taking discreet notes. I could almost write without looking at the page. Almost.

"May I ask your full name?"

"Angelina Ano. My husband is Mario."

She perched across from me on the matching sofa. The parlour smelled strongly of furniture polish. There was a white crotched doily protecting the surface of three side tables, and similar antimacassars on the backs of two chairs and the matching sofa. Above the mantelpiece was a rather muddy painting of Jesus holding out his arms to some puffy children crouched at his feet. The shelf was crowded with knick-knacks.

"Is your husband at home, Mrs. Ano?"

"No. He work since six o'clock this morning. He not home until seven. He is teamster."

I gathered from a silver-framed photograph on the side table that they had two young children. They obviously didn't visit this room, which managed magically to be jammed with stuff and yet very tidy.

I didn't stay long, just long enough to elicit that Mrs. Hodge from number twenty had been the one to tell her about Mrs. Gilmore.

Mrs. Ano kept repeating, "Terriblee. Terriblee. Mrs. Gilmore good woman. So sorry."

I asked her if her husband objected to Mrs. Gilmore's

views on women, especially wives, but either she didn't understand or pretended not to.

Not much else was forthcoming. She walked me to the door. I imagined her watching as I walked down the path. Her flower beds were flourishing.

Number fourteen was the house right next to the Gilmores' east side. It had a deserted air: all the flowers had succumbed to the heat, no curtains at the windows.

I knocked anyway.

Mrs. Ano had remained at her door, and she called over to me, "You won't get no answer. They moved out. Evicted. Couldn't pay rent."

"Sorry to hear that. When did they leave?"

"About three weeks ago. Here five years like us, but don't matter. No rent pay, no house."

"Right. Thanks."

I moved on to number twenty. Mrs. Ano went back inside.

EARLY ON IN our association, Mr. Gilmore had shared a little technique about interviews. "Go inside the home whenever you can. You can learn a lot about a person from his environment. It is always the silent witness."

The following notes more or less comply with that injunction.

MRS. EDITH HODGE lives at number twenty. She is in her late twenties, has reddish hair, which is unbrushed.

Skinny frame. Flowered house dress. Medium height.

She didn't invite me in, so I had to content myself with paying attention to the outside of the house.

Door and trim freshly painted. Brown. Well-maintained.

She declared herself to be English, here for four years. Married to James Hodge, Canadian born. Printer. He works in Markham and has to leave for work at five in the morning. Winter and summer. Returns by eight. Six days a week.

She speaks with a strong accent, Yorkshire, I believe. She was carrying a toddler in her arms, and they both looked hot and miserable. I followed the same procedure as with Mrs. Ano, showing my licence, etc. Yes, she'd seen the police car arrive. She was sitting on the steps to get some air. She'd enquired and was told what had happened. She went to tell Mrs. Ano.

"Awful thing. Wicked." But, no, she had no idea who would have attacked Mrs. Gilmore. "Probably some poor sod of a tramp" was how she put it. Lot of desperate men around. No, she had not in fact seen any such poor sod in the area. She herself had been preoccupied with tending to her Jimmy, who was teething. The heat was getting to him. She had to keep bathing him. I asked her if she had heard a woman's cry sometime about seven or so, but she hadn't. I didn't have a chance to ask her about Mrs. Gilmore's politics or if indeed she had said anything to her. The baby started wailing, and she took him inside.

Number twenty-two. Mrs. Belinda Parker. Elderly. Widow. Tiny frame. White hair still in night braid. Maroon silk dressing gown, gold piping. Left over from husband? Slippers.

The house trim could definitely do with a coat of paint. Flower pots rather than plants in front bed. Lawn wilting.

Here the problem turned out to be the difficulty in getting away. Mrs. Parker answered my ring right away and invited me to come inside. I followed her into the living room, which was suffocating. It seemed to be more used than the Ano parlour, less stuffed, the furniture worn.

There was a photograph in pride of place over the mantelpiece. A regal-looking man in formal clothes. I guessed he was the deceased Mr. Parker.

A large white cat had been sitting on the fireside rug, but it seemed to take a shine to me and jumped onto my lap. This made me even hotter, but Mrs. Parker didn't move to shoo it away. As it started to purr vigorously, I didn't have the heart to shove it off. I had the impression Mrs. Parker hadn't talked to anybody in weeks and wanted to make up for lost time. She insisted on getting a glass of water for me. She had a rather loud voice, which is typical of somebody who is hard of hearing. She actually had an old-fashioned ear trumpet, which she aimed at me so I could speak into it. She put on her wire-framed glasses. Said she could hear better with them on! She was a sweet old soul and didn't want to dish out the dirt, just to express concern for her neighbours' hardships. Poor Mrs. Ano. Husband out of work like everybody else. (Mrs. Ano had said he was a teamster who left for work every morning and returned every night. Is he employed or isn't he?) Poor Mrs. Hodge with that sickly baby. She should take him to a doctor, but she probably couldn't afford to. I asked her about Mrs. Gilmore stirring up the women, and she laughed. "She certainly did. And good for her, I say. About time women started to stand up for themselves. Wished I'd done that earlier in my life." She didn't explain, and I didn't press her. I might have been there for another hour. She hadn't heard anything untoward this morning, but that was hardly surprising. These days she wouldn't hear Gideon's trumpet if he played it just outside her house. As gently as I could, I moved the cat, whose name was Blanche, to the floor. I promised to inform Mrs. Parker of any developments.

I went to the next house. It looked well taken care of; the flowers had been watered. Lots of yellow daisies in these beds. Anxious white butterflies fluttered around. The owner was listed as Horace Pouluke. Mrs. Pouluke answered the door. She had wide Slavic cheekbones and, given her name, I'd expected her English might be rudimentary, but it wasn't. She was most articulate. She had heard what had happened but didn't say who had told her. Two very solemn-looking children, girls who might be twins, were clinging to her legs.

I said who I was and showed my card, at which point she burst into tears. It took her a while to compose herself, and both children began to whimper. What she eventually said was more or less the following.

Mrs. Gilmore is a saint. When Horace ran off and left her with two young children, Mrs. Gilmore was wonderful. She referred Mrs. Pouluke to a woman she knew who was in need of a house cleaner. The wages are good, and she's allowed to take the children with her while she worked. Jarvis Street wasn't too far, and Mrs. Gilmore often bought her streetcar tickets. Once again she was overwhelmed by crying. When she calmed down, I asked her if she had ever been witness to a quarrel of any kind between Mrs. Gilmore and anybody else. Never. Oh, she knew that Mrs. Gilmore might ruffle feathers of some people. Mrs. Kubay and her daughter at number twelve, for instance. She knew they could be nasty. Very nasty. They made that clear when Horace left. As if it were her fault and her shame. Arthur Kaufmann hated Mrs. Gilmore, but he's like that with everybody. Sour as turned milk. He's a returned soldier, and he'll let you know every chance he gets how hard done by he is. If she were his wife, she'd leave him. They don't have children, so there's nothing to keep her, really.

Vince Alexander, from the repair shop, didn't like Mrs. Gilmore. She knew that, but he's a good man. He might get all surly, but that's not to say he'd hit a defenceless woman half his size.

I threw in that people kept mentioning Mrs. Gilmore might have been attacked by a vagrant, a potential thief. Did Mrs. Pouluke see many such men, I asked. Regularly. At least once a week there's somebody at the door, asking if they can work for food. The soft-hearted woman wept again when she told me this. "I give them what I can. They're always so grateful."

I said goodbye, making the same promise I'd made to Mrs. Parker. I could hear the clang of Vince's hammer against the auto fender.

I went back to the other side of the Gilmore house, to number twelve. Same iron railings keeping guard on an extremely neat garden bed and straight path. The steps had been whitened. The curtains in the windows were white also. I already knew that a Mrs. Kubay, a widow, and her daughter, Cassandra, lived here. It was she who answered the door. Her elderly mother was hovering behind her. Miss Kubay must be close to seventy, and, not surprisingly, her mother is ninety. She made this a matter of pride and lost no time in telling me her age. They insisted I come in out of the heat, and it was in fact a relief to step into the dark living room, which had a large ceiling fan. Like Mrs. Parker's, the furniture was solid and Victorian with lots of burgundy plush. Several gilt-framed portraits covered the walls, and on first glance they all seemed to be of dignified, stiff-looking men in dignified poses. Mrs. Kubay noticed my glance and said they were all portraits of her late husband and his board members. She didn't expound on what board and seemed to assume I would know, which alas I didn't. Miss Kubay disappeared into the kitchen and returned with a tray with glasses and a pitcher of cold and very tart lemonade, also welcome. After that it was downhill all the way. A more unpleasant, mean-spirited pair of women would have been hard to find. Mrs. Kubay almost spat when I brought up Mrs. Gilmore's name. "A disgrace" was how she put it. She knew all about Mrs. Gilmore's philosophies and activities and thoroughly disapproved. What she said was, "God made Eve to be Adam's helpmate, and as far we are concerned that's how it should always be, amen." I looked at her daughter's bony hands and for a moment found myself wondering if they were capable of whopping somebody over the head with a heavy candelabra. I would have said no, but she didn't have any problem carrying the laden tray. She was certainly no frail old lady. Like Mrs. Parker they wanted to talk; but, unlike the other elderly woman, they did indeed want to dish the dirt. They are against, in no particular order, the "Eye-ties up the street. Would you believe they introduced chickens into their backyard? Well, we put a stop to that immediately. Can you imagine, chickens?" The Hodges, who are propagating like rabbits. The Alexanders, who are not to be trusted as far as you could throw them. The grocer on the corner, who constantly sells them poor quality fruit, and so on. The only one who got the stamp of approval was Mr. James Baker and his wife, Elizabeth, who lived at number ten. They were English and distantly related to minor aristocracy. They spent a lot of their time in England looking after their affairs. It was obvious that the Kubays were not above taking on some reflected glory.

I managed to elicit their opinion of Mr. Gilmore, as opposed to his wife. "A fool," the younger woman declared emphatically. I brought the conversation back to what had happened. "Unimaginable. And on such a good Christian street," was how Miss Kubay phrased it. "Not quite," said old Kubay. "The Anos are Papist, as to be expected. And the grocer on the corner is a Hebrew. He's the only one." She didn't say that this was one too many, but that's what she conveyed. So much for Mr. Gilmore's declaration that the letter he'd received must have been a mistake, intended for somebody else. This stretch of the neighbourhood had definitely not turned out to be predominantly Jewish. The two women were emphatic about not hearing a sound this morning, although they were early risers. They liked to listen to the wireless in the morning. Religious music, usually.

I extricated myself from them and the dark, stifling house and continued on my way.

There was no answer at number ten; presumably the Bakers were in England supervising the ploughing and breeding of their serfs.

The grocer at number eight is Jacob Selfman, a tiny man who has a club foot. He was not usually at home, he told me, as his grocery shop is on Huron Street, although it is mostly managed by an assistant. Today, however, he'd felt unusually tired and was taking a bit of time to rest. He expressed great regret at what had happened but could offer no theories. Perhaps a vagrant? Mr. and Mrs. Gilmore were good people. Would offend nobody. Perhaps because he is a bachelor, he hadn't been subject to Mrs. Gilmore's views and was surprised when I repeated them.

I asked him as discreetly as I could if he had received any hate mail that could be considered anti-Semitic, but he said no. "We get along here. All I get is bills. And the occasional letter from one of my cousins who is in Germany." He shook his head. "The situation there is unimaginable." I would like to have heard more, but he didn't seem to want to talk about it, and he excused himself.

That was it. It was time for me to get back to the office.

Chapter Seven

I THOUGHT I MIGHT as well have a look in at the Paradise, as it was on my route back to the Arcade.

The temperature had climbed even higher, and I felt as if I was trying to suck oxygen from air reluctant to yield it up. It took me twelve minutes to reach the Paradise. Hilliard had said Mr. Gilmore was a regular customer, and that made sense as the café was directly on the way to the office.

The lineup of men had vanished, presumably into the café. I pushed open the door and entered. A bell tinkled merrily, and a few of the customers looked up to see who had come in. The space was long and narrow with a single long table down the centre and individual small tables along both walls. It was full and noisy with chatter, a mix of men and women, though mostly men. There was a delicious smell of cooking food. Two large overhead fans whirred. Hilliard Taylor was behind the serving counter, accepting money from a rather down-and-out-looking customer.

A pretty young woman in a staid black maid's dress and white apron walked toward me.

"Good day, madam. Here for lunch?"

"Actually, I'd like to speak to the owner, please."

She gave me a fast head-to-toe scan then nodded toward Hilliard. "That's him over there."

He saw me, but made no acknowledgement except for a slight raise of his eyebrows. He wasn't expecting me this early. I edged over to him and waited while he finished counting out change for his customer. A table was squeezed into the corner, where two men were playing chess. A large, ornately framed mirror hung behind the counter, and I watched the reflections of those behind me. There was no doubt the Paradise catered to a poorer class of people. For the most part, they were scrawny and shabby. Several of the men were hunched over their soup bowls. They were eating quickly, as if they hadn't seen a meal for a while and weren't sure if they would see any more soon.

The café itself was anything but shabby. There were white cloths on the tables, the dishes looked of good quality. The walls were painted yellow, a paler colour than the outside trim but also sunny and bright.

"Can I help you?" Hilliard asked. He evidently wanted to keep up the pretence that we hadn't met before.

"I understand you can use an extra hand here. I'd like to offer my services."

I noticed one of the chess players look up at us.

"Have you got waitressing experience?" Hilliard asked. He was trying to suppress a grin.

"I do."

"Excellent. When can you start?"

"Any time."

"How about tonight?"

"Sure. I can do that."

"Done. Come back at half past three. I'll show you the ropes. We have three dinner sittings. First is at five. The others are at six and seven."

Another customer was waiting to pay. The chess man appeared to be still paying attention to me. I was rather enjoying my new role.

"I'll need to know what wages you're offering."

"The usual. Fifteen cents an hour to start. You'll get a raise after three months if your work is satisfactory. Five cents a fortnight deducted for the uniform. You can expect to put in forty-eight to fifty hours a week when we're busy."

"And gratuities? Do I share them?"

He chuckled. "This is not a clientele that hands out gratuities. If anybody does, you get to keep it."

I was glad this exchange was all for show. Who the heck could live on those kinds of wages?

"Sounds good to me. I'll be here."

"And your name is?"

"Frayne, Charlotte Frayne."

I began to retreat toward the door, but before I could get past the chess players, the one who'd evinced such interest caught me by the arm. He stood up.

"Excuse me, miss. I'm one of the owners. My partner

should have introduced us if you're going to be working here."

He was smiling at me, but his eyes were angry. Hilliard came from behind the counter at once.

"So sorry. Miss Frayne, may I introduce my partner, Mr. Wilf Morrow."

The other chess player sneaked in his chance to move a piece.

Hilliard indicated a poster pinned to the wall. It was announcing an upcoming chess competition.

"Among other things, Wilf is also a chess whizz," said Hilliard. "Probably the best in the city."

"Ha. Flattery will get you everywhere." Hilliard's comment seemed to mollify Wilf. His voice was raspy, as if he had laryngitis.

Another customer had come to the counter, and Hilliard excused himself to tend to him. Before I could leave, Wilf sat down, leaned back in his chair, and surveyed me from head to toe. Less obtrusively, I did my own scrutiny.

The most obvious thing about him was his thick thatch of fair, curly hair. It sprang out of his head in an electric sort of way. He had a short, bristly moustache that didn't suit him. His best feature was his blue eyes. They would have been nicer if he weren't angry with me. For what reason, I didn't know.

"I must say, you don't look as if you are out of work, Miss Fane. Exactly why are you in need of a job?"

"The name's actually Frayne. Charlotte Frayne. Like a

lot of people these days, I was suddenly turfed out on my ear. They could get the same help for less money."

"What did you do?"

"I worked in an office."

"Doing what?"

"Fetch and carry position."

Out of the corner of my eye, I could see Hilliard was listening intently. It might scuttle our proposed arrangement if I didn't pass muster with his partner. So far I wasn't sure I was going to make it.

Wilf frowned at me. "We're not an office. What have you got to offer us?"

"I'm experienced, for one thing." I allowed myself a cheeky grin. "And, like I said, I'm very good at fetching and carrying."

"We could get ten women in a minute for the job. And at less wage. What else do you do?"

I glanced down at the chessboard.

"Beautiful set you've got there."

It was indeed exquisite. The chess pieces were polished wood, and each seemed to be individually carved. Wilf's opponent was an older man with a sun-darkened, weather-beaten face and shrewd but sad eyes. He wasn't paying attention to me but was focussed only on the chessboard before him.

I was surprised when he said, without looking at me, "Wilf makes them himself. He might sell you a set if you ask him nice."

Wilf guffawed. "She won't know how to play, Pete. I've yet to meet a woman who could tell a knight from a bishop unless he was in the bedroom."

I was stunned by Wilf's statement. How about that for provocation?

Pete glanced up at me in embarrassment. I leaned over Wilf's shoulder.

"Speaking of bishops, if you move your rook to bishop three you can put Pete in check. He won't get out of it."

Wilf gaped at the board. His shock was immensely satisfying.

As I headed for the door, I tapped Pete on the shoulder. "Sorry. It's not that I wanted you to lose, but the move was too obvious not to mention."

"Anytime," said Pete, flashing me a grin.

I looked at Wilf, who was still studying the board. "I'll see you later, Mr. Morrow." Then I turned and, with a wave at Hilliard, I left.

In ten minutes, I reached the office. I felt like a wet dishrag. Mindful of the warnings in all the newspapers about heatstroke, I went straight to the sink and splashed water on my face and wrists. Stockings off again, buttons undone, I began to feel more human. I soaked a tea towel in water, draped it around my neck, and went to my desk. I had just sat down when the telephone rang. I answered it on the first ring. It was Mr. Gilmore.

"Ida has regained consciousness," he said abruptly. His voice was tight and strangled.

"Thank goodness."

I had no chance to continue.

"She is still not really lucid. The detective tried to question her, but with no success."

I was at a loss for words.

"Do you realize what this means, Miss Frayne?"

I wasn't able to answer fast enough.

"She cannot exonerate me."

"I'm sure nobody suspects you, Mr. Gilmore. That would be too ridiculous."

"Would it?" He paused. "I was sitting at her bedside. She opened her eyes, saw me, and started to scream. A detective was also in the room."

"Oh, no!"

"I'm afraid so. She wouldn't stop. The nurse rushed in to calm her down, but couldn't. Finally the doctor gave her a sedative, but she appeared not to recognize me. I was not her beloved husband, I was somebody to be feared."

"What does the doctor say?"

"He says she is having a delayed reaction to the trauma. I told him she has had bouts like this before. I'm not sure that anyone believed me."

"But Mrs. Gilmore will recover?"

"The doctor could not give me that reassurance. In his words, 'All we can do is hope.'" He paused. "What if she doesn't, Miss Frayne? Not only will I lose my dear Ida, I will be under suspicion of having attacked her."

I could hear him struggling for his equanimity.

"Try not to dwell on that, Mr. Gilmore. We are an investigating firm, after all. We will find out exactly what happened."

"I hope so."

I was tempted to ask him about the hour for which I was unable to account, but decided this wasn't the time. However, I had underestimated him. He went straight to it.

"I'm sure the police detective asked you if you could provide an alibi for me."

"He did."

"You are probably wondering what I was up to that it took me so long to get home."

"Yes, I was so wondering."

"The weather, I'd say. I walked down to the lake and sat by the beach to cool off. I took much longer than I anticipated."

"Did you explain this to the detective?"

"Of course. He didn't believe me."

I could not answer Mr. Gilmore in the manner he was expecting, as I wasn't sure I did either. He had seemed in a big hurry to check on his wife. Having worked for a year now as an investigator, I knew only too well there could be a dozen reasons he'd changed his mind about going straight home. Unfortunately, in similar circumstances, they were rarely above board.

I heard someone in the background calling his name.

"I must go, Miss Frayne. I will leave a message with our answering service about the situation here."

He hung up.

I wiped my face with the wet towel. I felt terrible about all of this. I wasn't closing my eyes to the facts. Mr. Gilmore's demeanour was not merely odd. It was very unlike the man I had come to know professionally. Could the unaccounted time be as simple as he'd said? A walk to the lake?

Given Wilf Morrow's remark about my appearance, I thought it might be a good idea to change my clothes into something evincing a salary a little less fortunate. Besides, Gramps would be happy to have me at home. He never complained, but I knew he got lonely when I was away for long stretches of the day. A significant incentive for me to work with Mr. Gilmore had been that my hours were flexible. Even if I was out on a case, he didn't mind if I took time to look in on my grandfather.

I reached for my damp stockings, wondering if I could be so bold as to walk home with bare legs?

I'd missed the sound of footsteps in the hall. The first thing I knew was the rattle of the mail slot. An envelope dropped into the letter box. The handwriting was all too familiar. Even from my desk, I recognized it.

Same bold handwriting, but this was addressed, "Miss C. Frayne. The Yonge Street Arcade. 3rd floor. Suite B. Toronto."

Not bothering to put my shoes on, I ran to the door, opened it, and went into the hall. There was no one in sight. Fast as I could, I raced to the stairwell at the far end. It, too, was empty. The postman must have already reached the bottom. In bare feet, I galloped down the stairs to the exit door, which opened into the arcade itself. There were a few people strolling about. All very normal, calm-looking people. There were literally a dozen places the postman could have gone, including outside to Yonge Street. A few of the passersby gave me curious glances. I can only imagine what I looked like, without stockings or shoes. I turned and climbed back upstairs.

I waited until I was inside the office before I opened the envelope and took out the one sheet of paper. The message was direct.

HOPE SHE DIES. ONE LESS BREEDER OF JEWS.
THE SAME THING COULD HAPPEN TO YOU UNLESS YOU BREAK OFF ALL CONNECTIONS WITH THE FILTH.

I took the first letter out of the drawer and placed both envelopes and letters side by side. They had obviously been written by the same hand. The letter addressed to me did not have any tea stain and looked a little cleaner, but it too had been torn from a top-opening school note-book with lined pages, slightly faded. I examined the new epistle through my magnifying glass. There were no over-writes on this one, but the writing had been done with a fountain pen, medium width nib. The envelope didn't reveal much more. Except for the name, the address was exactly the same on both. Did the writer know my first name and omitted it? Or did they not know what the *C* stood for? Rather important information.

The most obvious and most sobering fact about the second letter was that the writer knew what had happened to Mrs. Gilmore. How? The possibilities at this stage were limited. A neighbour? A police officer? The attacker himself?

I placed the original letter in an envelope and sealed it. I did the same with the second letter and locked both of them in my desk drawer. Mr. Gilmore had been keen to destroy his letter, but I was not so inclined. After my initial feeling of shock and fear, I was angry. I was not going to let this go. The feeling of security in the office that I had taken for granted these past two years had been shattered.

It was getting to be too late to consider going home, changing, and then back to the café in time to arrive at half past three. I'd have to return as is, wearing clothing that identified me as gainfully employed. I reached for the telephone to call Gramps and warn him it might be a while before I came home.

Not long after I had started to work with Mr. Gilmore, I'd had a telephone installed in my house. The machine was totally new to Gramps, and he never used it himself to call anyone. He viewed it with the suspicion of an old soldier who was confronting a strange-looking parcel that might blow up at any moment.

After four or five rings, he answered.

"Yes?"

As usual, he shouted into the phone, not because he was hard of hearing but because he thought that was the only way to make himself heard over the distance.

"Gramps. How many times do I have to tell you? You must answer by giving the number. Main 7425."

"Why do I have to do that? You know who you're calling, don't you?"

"I could be a stranger."

"Who? Nobody calls here except you. The others are wrong numbers or people trying to sell me something. Just got one about an hour ago."

"Wrong number?"

"Yep. A man. He wanted to sell me an insurance policy. I told him I didn't need it. I was properly insured, thank you very much. I said my beneficiary would be left well off."

"What? You told him all that?"

"I was having him on. Irritating bloke. He's called before. Thinks I can't tell."

"When did he call before?"

"Ages ago. But I've still got my marbles. I knew it was the same bloke."

"What did he sound like?"

"How should he sound? Like a man trying to sell me insurance."

Gramps was exasperated. I knew he wasn't going to be able to tell me the fine points of the strange caller. Educated?

Old? Young? In his mind there were only two kinds of people: the English and the others.

"Why are you ringing, Lottie? I'm in the middle of listening to my program. According to the farm news we're going to have a terrible harvest. The fruit is rotting on the trees. The ground is so parched, nothing is growing."

"I'd hoped to get home early, Gramps, but I have a new assignment that I have to go to. I wanted to make sure you'll be all right."

"Of course I'll be all right. Don't rush around. It's too hot. What's your assignment? Not another irate husband, I hope?"

"No, not this time. It's to do with theft."

"Ha. It's a miracle every house in the city isn't being robbed, given the state of unemployment."

I headed him off before he could go galloping into one of his rants about the government.

"There's some cold chicken in the icebox, Gramps. And there's some salad left you can have with it."

"Don't worry about me. Mrs. Johnson said she'd come by and fix something."

Mrs. Bertha Johnson was a widow who had moved into our neighbourhood two months ago. She had expressed a lot of sympathy for my grandfather's lonely state and made a point of coming over when I was working late to keep him company and make dinner. She seemed to be coming over a lot. Frankly, I didn't know quite what to make of her.

"Go back to your program, Gramps. I'll try not to be late."

"Don't worry. I'll manage. By the way, I made up another Mary had a little lamb joke."

My grandfather loved making up jokes. Some of them execrable, some funny.

"I told Mrs. Johnson, and she almost split her sides laughing."

"Did she? That must have been painful."

"What?"

"Never mind, Gramps. Go ahead. Tell me the joke."

"All right. Here we go. Mary had a little lamb who thought it was a pig, and everywhere that Mary went, that lamb became a ham."

I groaned. "That's awful."

"Bertha thought it was hilarious."

"Different funny bones, I guess."

"She's a good woman, Lottie," he said huffily. "We enjoy a laugh together."

His response didn't make me any happier.

"I don't think I'll be too late home, Gramps. Have a good evening."

"I'll leave you the leftover chicken."

We hung up.

I gathered up my things, forced myself to put on my stockings, and headed out.

I checked the hall before going to the stairs. It was deserted. My neighbours all had their doors closed. Business wasn't jumping. I thought about asking Mr. Patchell, the onions man, if he'd seen anybody come to my door, but I thought it was a waste of time.

THE PARADISE WAS closed between three o'clock and five o'clock (after lunch and before dinner), and I had to ring their bell to gain entrance. Hilliard Taylor came hurrying to open the door.

"Miss Frayne. Come in."

"Am I still hired?"

"Yes, of course. You impressed Wilf. That's for sure. The other two are happy to go along with my recommendation." He stepped back. "Conal is upstairs working on one of his paintings. Wilf has gone out. Eric is in the kitchen preparing the dinner plate. Come this way and I'll introduce you."

I trotted after him, and, as we went past the counter, he grabbed an apron that was hanging on a hook.

"Would you mind putting this on? It will put them in the right frame of mind."

Wilf had taken exception to the way I was dressed, so it was a safe assumption that Hilliard was trying to make sure my image was different for the other two partners. I slipped on the apron.

"Would you roll up your sleeves?" he said.

I did. I also undid the buttons at my collar. Now I was ready to tackle anything.

THE KITCHEN WAS hot, but there was another big overhead fan going, which made things bearable. Eric was standing over the sink, peeling potatoes. The naked ones were halved and dropped into a massive pot on the stove. He turned and gave me a pleasant smile when he saw me.

"Hello, Miss Frayne. Welcome. Hill told me you'd be filling in for a while."

Hilliard slapped him on the shoulder. "This is Eric Fenwell, chief cook, partner, all-round good fellow."

Like Hilliard, Eric was a tall man. No stereotype of the jolly, red-cheeked cook. He was thin and lean, with a long, narrow face; he didn't have much hair left, and the stragglers were grey.

"Whatever you're making smells good," I said, ever agreeable.

"Simple vegetable soup. I'm just adding to it for the dinner sitting." He kept on with his task, but addressed me over his shoulder. "Did Hill fill you in about our camp days? Every Wednesday we have one."

Hilliard answered, "Not yet."

"What's a camp day?" I asked.

Eric picked up another potato and peeled it rapidly. The peeling he dropped into a bowl that seemed to have various tag ends of vegetables in it.

"You tell her, Hill. You're our chronicler."

Hilliard shrugged. "We call it that to commemorate our time in a POW camp during the war."

"That must have been tough."

"Tough is a mild word for it, Miss Frayne," said Eric. "We were being steadily starved to death. A bowl of so-called soup was dished out once a day. Really it was the leftover water from the boiled potatoes that the guards had had for their dinner." He grinned at me. "Don't worry, that's not what we serve on our camp day." He gave the soup a brisk stir. "This is potato soup as it should have been."

Unasked, Hilliard picked up a potato from the basket and started to peel it. He took up the tale.

"We were young men, healthy and hearty until we were captured. It didn't take long before we were skeletal." Playfully, he poked Eric in the ribs. "Hey, pal, you still could do with a bit of meat on your bones."

"I try, but it won't stick."

"You'd better stop digging those ditches then."

They laughed at the shared joke I could guess at.

"We had to work," Hilliard said. "Hard physical work. At the end of the day we'd be marched back to the camp, to our bowl of hot water, a slice of black bread every other day."

"Ugh. Don't remind me of the bread. I think it was made of sawdust." Eric scowled and dropped a sliced potato with some force into the pot. It splashed up hot water.

"We ate it anyway. Amazing what you'll eat when you're starving."

I frankly didn't know what to say. All I could do was look sympathetic.

"You were in the same camp, I take it?" Hilliard had already given me this information, but I thought it might be a good idea to maintain the fiction that I was a complete stranger. And I must admit I was gripped by a strong desire to let them both know somebody was interested in what had happened to them.

Eric started to busy himself scrubbing down the cutting board. Hilliard peered into the pot. "That's probably enough, Eric. Let's add more carrots."

Without waiting for Eric to agree, Hilliard picked up a handful of cut carrots from a bowl on the counter.

"Hey, who's the cook here?" protested Eric.

Hilliard returned the carrots to the bowl. "Okay. You are. Sorry."

"Go and sit down. Finish the story."

Hilliard pulled out a chair for me at the table. He sat down across from me.

"There were four of us, all Canadians, and we formed a bond, a pack you might more accurately call it. Me, Eric here, Wilf Morrow, whom you've met, and Conal Pierce. Actually, Conal's Irish, but he had immigrated to Canada just before war broke out, and he joined up. To fight for the Empire."

Suddenly, Eric put both hands on the counter and leaned forward. He began to cough, a hard, dry coughing that shook his frame.

"What's up?" Hilliard asked. "Are you all right?"

"I think I need a break. I should go out for some air."

Immediately, Hilliard jumped up and went over to him. He put his arm around Eric's shoulders.

"It's too hot to go outside. Why don't you have a lie-down upstairs? I've got the fans going, and it's not bad up there. I'll call you in an hour."

"All right. Pop the shepherd's pie in the oven. Low heat. The gravy's ready. Just needs heating up."

"Got it."

For a moment, Eric didn't move, then he straightened up. He nodded over at me. "Sorry, Miss Frayne. I'm not contagious, honest. The heat's getting to me. See you later."

He was heading for the door when he stopped and grabbed a tattered book that was on the shelf above the sink.

"Recipes," he said to me. " I've got to find something that doesn't need much oven."

He left.

Hilliard went back to the counter and picked an onion out of a wire basket. He began to slice it into chunks.

"I just don't know if it's better never to bring up the past or if by sharing it we can let it go."

"It's hard to tell sometimes. Does Eric always react like that when you talk about the camp?"

"Not always, but it does happen."

He let go of a deep sigh. I could see why finding out what was happening to the café was so fraught for him. He reached into the basket and took out another onion.

"As Eric said, we were slowly starving. We would lie on

the bunks in those fetid barracks and, to keep ourselves sane, we'd share stories about food. Meals we'd eaten back home, the taste of things we loved to eat. I think that's where the idea of a café was first conceived. We vowed that when we started the café, we'd include those special meals, but we'd also have a camp day when we'd reproduce the food that we were served. We wanted to educate the public as to what it was like." He fell silent. I waited.

"Of course, we couldn't really do that. Who on earth would voluntarily choose to pay for a bowl of soup that was mostly water with the occasional piece of rotten meat thrown in? Instead, we make a version of that food. The potato soup is delicious. The black bread is a favourite. It's been a while now, so mostly the customers aren't curious as to why we call it camp day. They just like the soup and the bread."

"What are some of the special favourite meals?"

"The ones we'd remember when we were lying on that flea-ridden mattress trying to do whatever we could to survive, you mean?"

"Yep."

He wiped tears away with the back of his hand. "Damn onions."

I gave him a moment to get his pesky watering eyes under control. Before he had the chance to answer, the kitchen door swung open and Wilf Morrow entered, followed by a man I hadn't yet met. They were both heavily under the influence.

When he saw me, Wilf beamed.

"If it isn't miss chess whiz. I should tell you, madam, that I did make the move you suggested, and my opponent capitulated. I had two dollars riding on that game, so I thank you."

He gave me an ostentatious bow, sweeping his hat off.

"You'd have seen it yourself in a minute," I answered modestly.

Hilliard added the last onion to the pot on the stove and lit the gas.

"Introduce Conal," he said to Wilf. The tender moment had vanished.

"Yes, sir. I was about to." Wilf indicated the man behind him. "Miss Frayne. This is Conal Pierce. He is the fourth member of this illustrious quartet. Don't let the fact that he is Irish and therefore, ipso facto, an ignorant, probably drunken, peasant deter you from making his acquaintance."

Conal didn't seemed bothered by the insult, and I got the feeling this was what passed for regular banter between them. He gave me a shy nod. He was definitely the shortest of the four of them and, although they must all have been close in age, he looked a lot younger. He had dark hair, blue eyes, and prominent ears.

"Glad to meet you, Miss Frayne, I understand you will be helping out for the next little while."

He had retained an Irish lilt to his voice.

"Conal has finally finished his next masterpiece," said Wilf. "Mr. Pierce, unveil if you please."

"Certainly." He pronounced it, *Shertainlee*.

He was carrying a wrapped parcel under his arm, which he placed on the table.

Wilf said to me, "There is no doubt Conal here is a genius as lofty as any that hang in the Louvre. Unfortunately, the world at large has not yet recognized this fact." He gave the other man a rather hard slap on the back. "Do not despair, Conal. Your time will come. Let's have a look at what you've done."

Again, the Irishman seemed unperturbed by the banter. Hilliard was busy dealing with the soup. There were a couple of pans on the stove that had dough in them. He put them in the oven.

"Where's Eric," asked Wilf. "Why are you playing mom?"

"He was tired out. I sent him upstairs to have a rest."

"Good idea. I think I might do the same."

"Oh, no, you won't. You've got to set up the boards for tonight's contest."

"Our new helper knows chess. She can do it."

I didn't have a chance to respond. Hilliard snapped at his partner.

"No. It's your job. Conal, are you going to show us your masterpiece or not?"

"Sure. I was just waiting for you two to stop bickering." He gave a mock pout. "I will not throw my pearls before swine."

Wilf drew himself up in mock belligerence. "Who are you calling a swine, peasant?"

Hilliard directed a smile at me. "Don't mind us, Miss Frayne. We go on like this all day."

"I hope you don't expect me to join in," I said in my sweetest voice.

All three of them stared at me. Hilliard recovered.

"Of course not. Now, Conal. Unwrap your damn painting and let's get on with the job of bloody running a successful café, shall we."

Stumbling a little, Conal did as he was told.

I can't say if the canvas that emerged could have been called a masterpiece, but it was without doubt one of the most striking and troubling works I've seen.

At the centre of the painting was the figure of a man who appeared to be tied to a post. His head had fallen forward, onto his chest, and his body was slumped. In the background were rows of huts. All the colours were sombre except that one of the windows in the nearest hut was lit. The light was blood red.

"What do you think, Miss Frayne?" Conal asked.

I wasn't sure how to respond. Probably there were paintings out there that were better executed, more technically skilful, but this one had captured some raw feeling that seemed to leap from the canvas and grab the viewer by the throat.

Hilliard and Wilf were both regarding the canvas. I was trying to muster up some answer, but Hilliard spoke first. His voice was low.

"We've got to let it go, for God's sake. You, me, Wilf, Eric. We must let it go."

"Can't you paint some nice daisies or petunias, even cute puppies?" Wilf said, but the joke went flat.

Conal began to rewrap the painting. "My apologies, gentlemen. I didn't want to upset the apple cart."

Hilliard grabbed his hand. "Stop it."

I'm not sure how the situation would have resolved itself, but, at that moment, a man walked into the kitchen. I recognized him; he was the defeated chess player, Pete.

"Where's Eric? There's a pal of his wants to come in and talk to him."

"We're busy right now. Who is it?" Hilliard asked.

"It's the detective fella. Name of Murdoch."

I caught the warning glance that flashed between Hilliard and Wilf.

Pete surveyed the group. "What's up with you lot? You look like you dropped a dollar and picked up a dime."

Hilliard took charge. "Wilf, go and rouse Eric. Conal, put your painting somewhere safe for the time being. We'll talk about it later."

He reached over and ruffled the other man's hair. "Don't fret, there's a good chap. You've done a super painting. It's just that …" His voice trailed off.

Conal had a stricken expression on his face. "I know, I know. We should have done with all of that."

I was contemplating jumping in the deep end and

asking them what the hell it was they should have done with, but Pete spoke first.

"I'll go and set up the chess set."

He scuttled out of the kitchen, passing Eric at the door. His face was crumpled from sleep. Wilf was right behind him.

"I understand Jack Murdoch is asking to talk to me. What shall I do?" Eric's question was aimed at Hilliard.

"Don't leave the poor chap frying on the sidewalk. Bring him in. He'd probably like some cold lemonade."

I was feeling like a fifteenth wheel, if there's such a thing. Hilliard addressed me.

"Miss Frayne. You must be wondering what sort of group you've got yourself mixed up with. Don't worry. Most of the time we're all as sane as the next man — which isn't saying much these days."

I was uneasy with the fact that Detective Murdoch was on the premises. I didn't want my undercover persona to be flushed out before I'd even started. None of the other three partners needed to know I was a private investigator, and Murdoch might mention it.

"While they're dealing with the law, why don't you show me around the kitchen? You might need me to chop vegetables or scrub the floor or some such."

Eric looked at me. "This is my domain. You'll be out front with the customers."

"Maybe playing chess," said Wilf with what sounded like false heartiness to me.

Eric turned to Hilliard. "Hill. You didn't give me an answer. What shall I say to Jack?"

"I suggest you find out what he wants first before worrying about what to say to him."

"If it's to do with the café, you and Wilf should be present."

"And Conal," said Hilliard.

The man in question had finished wrapping his painting and was sitting by the table. He didn't seem to be part of the conversation at all. Hilliard walked over to him.

"Con, I promise we'll have a proper look at the painting after closing. It looks stunning to me."

"And to me," said Wilf. "Great job."

"What are we talking about?" Eric asked.

"Con's finished another painting," answered Hilliard.

"Oh. That's good. Now I suggest we go and have a chat with Murdoch. All of us. Even you, Conal."

They began to file out of the kitchen. Hilliard came close to me.

"Perhaps you could come too, Miss Frayne. You never know what you might pick up on."

Frankly I didn't know what to do. He was the client, after all. I didn't have a chance to tell him I'd just met Murdoch. Wilf still seemed ambivalent about my employment, even though I was concentrating on sending out innocuous, sweet vibrations. Neither Eric nor Conal seemed to care. But Hilliard was right. I might pick up valuable information.

Chapter Eight

I FOLLOWED THE MEN into the café, hanging back and trying to be inconspicuous. Murdoch was standing in front of the poster about the upcoming chess tournament. He turned when we came in, and he and Eric Fenwell immediately exchanged friendly greetings.

"What's up, Jack?" Eric asked.

"Just wanted to check out something with you. It's to do with a case I'm working on."

"Would it be all right if all of us participate?"

"Sure."

Hilliard indicated one of the corner tables.

"Let's sit down over here."

They began to settle themselves at the table. I slipped behind the counter. Against the wall was a large blackboard, neatly printed.

Wednesday Is Camp Day

Dinner Plate

Bowl of hearty potato soup

One slice of "war" bread (extra slice with dripping OR parsnip marmalade, 5 cents)

Shepherd's pie and gravy
Two green veg
Choice of salad: apple and beet OR dandelion
Choice of dessert: one of trench pudding
OR Eccles cake OR chocolate biscuit
Cup of coffee OR tea
35 cents per plate

There was a drawing at the bottom of a row of stick men dancing merrily.

Hilliard called out to me, "Miss Frayne. Would you mind bringing over that jug of lemonade and some glasses?" He addressed Murdoch. "Miss Frayne is new here. She's learning the ropes."

Murdoch blinked.

How he managed to pick up on less than a second's hesitation, I do not know, but Wilf jumped on this like a terrier on a tasty rat.

"Do you two know each other?"

I saved Murdoch the difficulty of lying. "I have the kind of face that people always think they've met before."

Jack was smooth. "I think you're right about that, Miss Frayne. Did you say the name was Frayne?"

Wilf still looked suspicious, but he didn't pursue the matter.

I brought over the lemonade and the glasses as requested and placed them on the table. All five men began to light up cigarettes. Eric offered his cigarette case to Murdoch.

"Here. These are Sweet Caps. Your favourite, I believe."

Murdoch beamed. "Indeed they are. Fiona keeps on at me to stop smoking. She says it has to be bad for you to swallow all that burning smoke."

The others, except for Conal, laughed at the absurdity of this idea. I did not laugh, as I was on Fiona's side.

Conal had shrunk into himself and was hardly participating in all the brotherly banter.

"Listen, Jack," said Wilf. "I noticed you taking a gander at the notice about the chess tournament. Why don't you join us? Only two dollars for the pot. Winner takes all. We've got some good players signed up already. It'll be a round robin tournament, starting at ten o'clock on Saturday."

I couldn't help myself. Contrary to all rules about private investigators staying out of sight, I blurted out, "Are women allowed to play? If so, count me in."

For a moment, they all gaped at me, as surprised as if the dog had suddenly started to speak. Then Hilliard shrugged.

"I see no reason why not. If you think you can put up a good game, that is. No playing on feminine weakness to dupe us."

"Wouldn't dream of it."

"I thought she was going to be our new help," said Wilf with a frown.

"This counts as help. An attractive woman playing with the men could be a big draw."

Wilf looked at me. Once again, his eyes were not friendly.

"Where did you learn to play chess, Miss Frayne?"

"My grandfather taught me. He's a tough taskmaster, believe me."

Murdoch smiled. "My father was the one who taught me. Also a tough master."

Eric gulped down some of the lemonade. "How's he doing, your dad? My father's always talking about him. The cases they worked on. He says he wants to go out east and visit him. Maybe in September."

"I'm sure he'd like that. He gets bored easily out in the pasture."

Hilliard started to stub out his cigarette. "Good. Now that we've all exchanged our thrilling and extraordinary histories, shall we get on with the purpose of this visit? No offence, Jack. It's just that opening time is coming up fast, and I don't think we're ready."

It was Murdoch's turn to extinguish his cigarette. I retreated back to the counter, but I could hear what they were saying. Hilliard had made sure of that. The corner table was convenient.

"I'm following up on one of my cases," said Murdoch. "Routine confirmation of whereabouts. The person I'm enquiring about claims to have stopped in here for a coffee sometime after eight-thirty this morning. He says he's a regular customer and that you'd know him and be able to confirm this. His name is Thaddeus Gilmore."

If ever you can describe men as freezing in shock, this would apply to all of them, even Conal.

It was obvious to me that Wilf, Eric, and Conal were expecting Hilliard to answer. If it was obvious to me, I assumed it would be obvious to Murdoch.

Hilliard said, "I was out most of the morning. There were people coming and going from about eight, when we opened the doors. I didn't notice Mr. Gilmore, but then he is just one of our many customers."

"Did anybody else see him?" Murdoch asked.

"One day tends to melt into another," said Wilf. "Is he in some kind of trouble?"

Murdoch didn't answer right away.

"Conal, what about you?"

"No good asking him," said Hilliard. "He doesn't get out of bed until noon. Right, Van Gogh?"

Conal smiled. "Depends on the night before."

Murdoch shifted rather impatiently in his chair. "So this morning? Were you in the café?"

"Not me. I think I got up about eleven."

"Busy night, I assume?"

"It was that."

Murdoch turned back to Hilliard.

'"Last time I was here, there was a young woman waiting on tables. Fair hair, petite. Can I have a word with her?"

Hilliard shook his head. "No need. Pearl works lunch and dinner."

Murdoch leaned back in his chair. His jaw tightened. "Let me get this right. One of your regular customers, Gilmore, says he was here for at least forty minutes this morning, but nobody can verify that. Not too observant, are you chaps?"

"Come on, Jack," said Eric. "We're busy. I'm in the back doing prep for lunch, Wilf has a lot to do to get ready for the chess tournament, Hill has to place orders for our supplies. You heard what Conal had to say."

Murdoch shrugged. "From what you've just told me, I'm surprised any of your customers get served. Who waits on them? The Holy Ghost?"

It was Hilliard's turn to lean back. "Look, we want to co-operate, but you're asking questions we can't answer. Why are the police interested in Thad Gilmore?"

"I'm looking into a nasty incident that occurred this morning. Mrs. Gilmore was attacked in her home."

Hilliard sat straight up. "Good Lord. That's terrible. I am sorry."

The others looked shocked as well. Their reactions seemed genuine.

"We have to investigate all possibilities, of course, and I'm following up on a statement her husband made. He says he was not at home when the attack may have occurred, but I'm having a hard time pinning down any kind of corroboration of his whereabouts."

He didn't give any indication he could have been talking about me, but I felt guilty. I hadn't exactly been co-operative.

"Does that make it any easier to recall this morning's clientele?" Murdoch continued.

There was little doubt the three men looked to Hilliard for guidance.

"I can only repeat what I've already said. I am as sure as I sit here, however, that Thad Gilmore would not be guilty of attacking anybody. Especially his wife. He's a thoroughly good man."

"Quite an endorsement, considering you say you hardly know him. So cursory is your acquaintance, in fact, you don't know if he came into the Paradise this morning or not."

Hilliard flushed. "Let's say I've got good instincts."

Murdoch looked around at the other three men. "Anything you'd like to add?"

Each of them shook his head.

I felt as stunned as they were.

Apparently in all the shock of receiving a hate letter and his urgency to get home to his wife, Mr. Gilmore had forgotten to mention that on his way to a stroll by the lake, he had stopped in at the Paradise for a cup of coffee. And if that were true, I was with Murdoch on his surprise at the strange vagueness of the four men. The Paradise wasn't that large a space. How could Mr. Gilmore have gone unnoticed? Why did they want it to be so ambiguous? Not a denial nor an affirmation.

"Just that I hope you find the culprit," said Eric.

Murdoch pushed back his chair. "I'll wish you all a good day then. Thanks for the lemonade. Wilf, I think I would like to enter that chess tournament." He looked over at me, where I was pretending to be invisible. "Perhaps I could draw a match against you, Miss Frayne. I'm sure you would give me a run for my money."

Before I could pursue the point, the side door opened and Pearl came in.

Murdoch spoke to her first.

"Just the person I was hoping to talk to."

Pearl didn't seem too happy to hear that.

"What about?"

She glanced over at Hilliard, but he was staring at his own hands.

"It's all right, Pearl. This is Detective Murdoch. You can answer him. Jack, this is our invaluable helper, Miss Pearl Reilly."

"Did you help out with serving this morning?" Murdoch asked.

"What's the problem?"

Before Jack could answer she went on.

"Are you talking about the complaint about the coffee? Old Mr. Cohen says as it was weak. He wanted a refill. I didn't give it to him. That's not a crime, is it?"

Hilliard jumped in. "That's not what the detective wants to ask you. But we will take that under advisement. Eric, was the coffee weak?"

"Course not. Same as usual. That old man always complains about something. He just wants to get something for free."

Conal piped up. "Maybe that's because he's got no money and he's starving."

"We don't run a charity here, Con," said Eric. "We can't feed the entire damn city for nothing."

This seemed to be a topic that ran along well-defined lines, but as a diversionary topic it didn't work. Murdoch fidgeted impatiently.

"Never mind that now. Miss Reilly. I'm enquiring about a Mr. Thaddeus Gilmore. Was he here this morning?"

Pearl shifted. "Who's he when he's home?"

She might be a good waitress, but she was a lousy actress.

"He's a slightly chubby chap, glasses, soft spoken. Always nicely dressed. Did you see him?"

The girl checked with Hilliard, who quietly gave her a nod.

"He might have been. I can't say for sure."

"If he was here, what time might he have arrived?" Jack asked.

She shrugged. "Just after me, I suppose."

"What time was that?"

"Probably after eight-thirty? I wasn't checking the clock."

"How long did he stay?"

"I couldn't say. I was serving other customers."

"An estimate?"

"No idea."

"And you would have served him coffee?"

"If he was here, that's what I would have done."

"And if he was here, how long roughly would it take to serve him his coffee? How long do your customers usually stay?"

"It varies, doesn't it. Am I right, Mr. Taylor?"

I took back what I said about Pearl not being a good actress. She was doing a fantastic job of evading Murdoch's persistent questions.

Hilliard nodded with too much enthusiasm. "Quite right, Pearl. Some people whip in and out, some linger."

"Why does he want to know?" Pearl asked Hilliard.

"Shall I tell her?" Hilliard asked Murdoch.

"By all means."

The other three men were not saying much, but I could tell how intently they were taking this all in.

What the hell was going on?

Hilliard spoke to Pearl. "There has been an incident involving Mrs. Gilmore, and the detective was enquiring about Mr. Gilmore."

"Why?"

Hilliard flapped his hand. "Over to you, Jack."

"I'm afraid Mrs. Gilmore was attacked. At the moment we don't know who did it, so we are following all lines of enquiry. Mr. Gilmore says he was here at the café this morning. We are just verifying that was indeed the case."

Pearl looked at Jack directly. "Did the others say they saw him here?"

"Nobody can recollect."

"Then me neither. Like I said, it got busy."

That closed the ranks. It was obvious as the nose on my face that the little group were hiding something, but I didn't know what it was, and neither, it seemed, did Murdoch.

He got to his feet. "Thank you for your time, gentlemen, ladies. I will keep you apprised of the situation."

He was clearly annoyed at being stymied, and I didn't blame him.

"I'll let myself out."

"I owe you and Fiona a dinner," Eric called out.

Murdoch appeared not to have heard and he left.

Nobody spoke for a few moments, then Conal muttered, "Thad shouldn't have said anything."

"Given the potentially graver charge of assaulting his wife, I'm not surprised," answered Wilf. "I think we should have acknowledged he was here, Hill. We just made Murdoch suspicious."

Hilliard frowned. "I didn't know why he was asking, did I?"

"Shall we tell him?"

"If he comes back to the question and if it's vital for Thad, yes, we can say we saw him."

Wilf suddenly noticed I was within earshot, although I thought I was doing a good job of being totally caught up with the notice board.

"Miss Frayne, this must all seem most mysterious to you."

I offered him a bemused look.

"Sorry, Mr. Morrow, I wasn't paying attention. What is mysterious?"

"Never mind."

Eric got up. "Come on we're late. Come and help me,

you two. Hilliard, you were going to show Miss Frayne the ropes, I believe."

There was an expression on Pearl's face that I couldn't quite fathom. She had lowered her eyes and was staring at the floor. Suddenly she looked up and her eyes met mine.

"Poor Mr. Gilmore. You never know what life's going to throw at you."

I suddenly liked her a lot better.

Chapter Nine

PEARL OFFERED TO show me the routine, but Hilliard took over. She looked a bit resentful once again, and I was afraid she'd insist on shadowing us or think that I might have been hired to replace her. She agreed to help out in the kitchen, and she followed after the men. I was relieved. There were things I needed to ask Hilliard in private.

He showed me where the serving utensils were kept behind the counter and introduced me to the cash register, which he affectionately referred to as "Bessie." It was a splendid old machine with ornate trim.

"At the close of the day, I count the cash and fill out a deposit slip from the bank noting the amount of each denomination of coin. You know. Ten dimes, five nickels, and so forth. That, together with the day's receipts from the cash register record, I put into a lockbox and stash in the safe —"

I interrupted him. "Where is the safe?"

"In the back room, behind the kitchen."

"And the combination?"

"It's in an old tea tin on the plate shelf."

I made a face.

"Behind the plates." He grinned. "I know, I know. But we haven't been expecting theft."

I didn't need to spell it out for him. Almost anybody could have found out where the combination was kept.

"The following morning, I take out the lockbox and make up a float for the day, leaving the rest of the money in the box. Once a week I myself take that money to the bank. That's usually on Sunday, when we're closed. The bank has an after-hours deposit box."

"Do you check the receipts and money every day to see if they balance?"

He looked a little shamefaced. "I find that sort of thing too tedious. I've always left it up to the bank to do their own tally. It is their job, after all. As I said, nobody complained until a few days ago. When the manager rang me up was the first time I knew something might not be right."

"His reason for calling you in wasn't because you weren't balancing, was it?"

"No. Everything was fine on that score. He said our cash intake had dropped to an alarming level."

As if on cue, Pearl popped her head through the door.

"Everything all right? Need any help?"

"No, we're fine, thanks. I was just about to show Miss Frayne where we keep the money pouches."

"Why don't I do that? It is my job, after all."

There was no way around it. Pearl wanted to be involved. Hilliard conceded.

She came behind the counter, reached below the register, and took out two leather pouches.

"Here you go. You might have to loosen the strings a bit."

The pouch was fastened by two strips of leather. I tied it on, and it fitted perfectly.

"That's the one my mother uses," said Pearl. "So, when you arrive, you get your pouch and Mr. Taylor gives you the float for the sitting. You know what a float is, don't you?"

I wanted to be sarcastic and say, "Why yes, isn't that the same as a raft?" But I held my tongue. My brief liking of Pearl was rapidly dissipating. I nodded.

She continued. "You put that money into each compartment, nickels, dimes, quarters, pennies. If you're handed any paper money, put it in the back of the pouch. You won't get much of that, though." She raised her eyebrows. "All right so far?"

"Yes, got it. Coins in their own place, paper at the back. Ingenious."

Hilliard had been listening in, and I saw him trying to hide his grin.

"Might take a while, but you'll catch on," said Pearl. "Lunch costs thirty cents a plate; dinner is thirty-five. If they want an extra slice of bread, that's five cents. Okay so far?"

"Uh-huh." I nodded.

"At the end of the sitting, everybody is shoved out and you take your pouch to Mr. Taylor, who counts it, takes away the float, and puts the money in the register."

I turned to Hilliard. "And you are the only one who handles the cash register?"

"That's right."

"Do you have a printed record of the transactions?"

"Not lately. Poor old Bessie isn't very reliable. The spool jams all the time, so I just count up everything as I'm given."

"Do you have any way to confirm how many customers are actually served?"

"We have a maximum capacity of thirty people. We're always close to that mark, and because there is no coming and going as such, it's easy to count them for each sitting."

Pearl was looking a little puzzled at this line of questioning, so I didn't pursue it.

It seemed highly unlikely for the waitresses to fudge the amount of money they were collecting. The theft must indeed be happening from the safe itself.

Pearl happily showed me where the trays were and demonstrated how to carry them properly.

"They get heavy," she said with enthusiasm.

I picked one up, just to show off, carrying it at shoulder level, executing a neat behind shove on the swinging door so I could go through. All my old skills were coming back rapidly. I just hoped my feet would hold up.

Ending the charade, Hilliard said I could take a break until the café opened at five. When she heard this, Pearl pouted.

"How come she gets time off and I don't?"

"Because you're booked to help Eric in the kitchen, remember?"

"Righty-oh. Just asking. He's fine. Don't forget we've got that group tonight as well."

Hilliard frowned at her. "What she means, Miss Frayne, is that we have regular meeting groups that make use of our back room. They pay a small sum for rental, and we serve them food and beverages."

"Who is it tonight?'

He hesitated for a moment, then retreated into mystifying vagueness. "It's some sort of men's debating society."

"What do they debate?"

"I haven't the foggiest idea. The state of the world, probably. They can get pretty heated at times. But you won't have to serve them. Pearl takes orders, and one of them picks up the food directly from the kitchen."

Pearl was listening to all of this. "Bunch of cheapskates. The tip they leave wouldn't pay for a mouse."

The source of the rather poetic reference was obscure, but I got what she meant.

Crash course over, I decided to go back to the office. I wanted to see if Mr. Gilmore had called. Given the circumstances, I was prepared to challenge him on his strangely spotty account of his movements this morning.

I agreed to be back by five.

Chapter Ten

THE HEAT ON the street was like a blow. The fans in the café really did make a difference, and outside in the sun the temperature shot up. I thought going along Richmond Street might be a little cooler than Queen, and I began to walk north on McCaul.

I hadn't gone far when I heard a man yelling.

"Get up, you lazy beast! Get up!"

There was a big dray in front of me, the teamster standing on the boards. He was lashing his whip across the bony back of his horse, which appeared to have fallen to its knees.

"Giddy-up," the man shouted again and whipped the horse hard.

I must admit I didn't stop to think. Not always a good idea, but frankly I couldn't bear it. I jumped on the running board of the dray. Before the man could raise his whip again, I grabbed his arm and yelled in his face.

"Stop it! You're going to kill that horse."

I had the advantage of surprise; he had the advantage of both size and inclination. For the moment, surprise won out.

"If you beat that horse one more time, you'll be on a charge. He's overheated."

"Wha—"

"If you want to save him, we've got to cool him down. NOW."

I snatched the whip out of his hand so he couldn't do any more damage and jumped off the running board. The poor horse was still on its knees, its sides heaving. Fortunately for all concerned, a few feet away there was a horse trough.

"Give me those sacks," I commanded the teamster. He looked as if he was about to protest, but I didn't give him the chance. "You heard me. If you want to save this creature, do as you're told. Throw them down."

He had been sitting on a pile of sacks as cushions. He tossed them to me.

"Now get down, unhitch your horse, and walk him over to that shade. If you so much as raise your voice, I'm going to make you very sorry."

I waited to make sure he dismounted from the dray, then I picked up a couple of the sacks and ran to the trough. There wasn't much water left. When I tried the spigot, no water came out. The city was preserving all water sources. All I could do was soak the sacks in the little water that remained in the trough. In the meantime, the teamster was doing what I had told him, and he was leading the horse slowly over to the shade of a big tree. The creature's gait was heartbreakingly unsteady. I grabbed up the wet sacks, hurried over, and draped one over the horse's head, squeezing water out of the other sack so it dribbled down his nose. He didn't flinch or protest.

"Have you got a bucket?" I yelled at the teamster.

The man went back to the dray and reached under the seat. "I've got this."

"Get whatever water you can from that trough. HURRY UP."

He obeyed, and I concentrated on bathing the horse's neck and nose gently with a wet sack. His desperate panting started to slow down. The teamster returned with the bucket. It was only a quarter full, but I carefully dribbled the water over the horse's withers. His body was so hot the water almost evaporated on contact. I shoved the bucket at the teamster.

"Get some more."

"There's none left in the trough."

"This is what you're going to do, then. Just around the corner on Queen Street there's a café called the Paradise. You're going to get there as fast as you can … don't argue."

The man spluttered. "I can't run; I'll get heatstroke."

"I don't care. You were only too ready to kill this poor creature. Bring lots and lots of water. Got that? Tell them that Miss Frayne sent you. Ask for Hilliard."

"Yes … but —"

"If you utter one more 'but,' you will live to regret it. Repeat. What's my name?"

"Miss Frayne."

"Who are you asking for?"

"Somebody called Billiard."

"Wrong. Hilliard. Repeat."

"Hilliard."

"Correct. Now go." I picked up one of the damp sacks. "Put this over your head."

He skittered off while I continued to fan the horse. The exchange had sure raised my own temperature, and I was sweating copiously. I wiped my own face and draped a wet sack around my neck. It wouldn't help the horse if I passed out. I stroked his nose. He was a faded ginger colour, and he had a white blaze.

"Don't worry, old fellow. You're going to be all right."

He did indeed look like an old fellow with protruding bony ribs. The dray appeared to be loaded with bricks. A heavy load indeed. There was lettering along the side. ROGERS HAULAGE. As far as I was concerned, they were going to get a visit from the Humane Society.

Fortunately, I didn't have to wait too long before the teamster returned. He was carrying two buckets. Close behind was Hilliard, also with a bucket.

Once near enough, Hilliard said, "Do you mind if I take over? I was with a cavalry unit during the war. I'm familiar with horses."

I was only too happy to relinquish my responsibility. My knowledge of horses had mostly been gleaned from reading *Black Beauty*.

Hilliard put his bucket on the ground in front of the

horse. It showed no reaction.

"He might not want to drink anything just yet. Let's concentrate on cooling him as best we can. We need to make sure his heart is cooled, and his head. Keep pouring the water on him."

Hilliard spoke to the hapless teamster, who had dropped to a heap by the tree. I'd have been happy to throw water over him, but it was too precious.

"What are you doing even working your horse on a day like this?"

He didn't raise his voice, but there was an authority to him that was unmistakable. I had briefly intimidated the teamster, but Hilliard did that and more.

The man muttered something inaudible.

"Where's your stable?" Hilliard asked.

"Over on King Street."

Hilliard moved a little closer. "Here's what you're going to do. When your horse has sufficiently recovered, you will walk, I repeat, walk him to the stable. You will not work him for at least two days, and certainly not until this heat breaks. Got that?"

Full of resentment, the teamster glared at him. "How am I going to make a living without the horse? I've got deliveries to make. I don't deliver, I don't get paid."

Hilliard bent over him. "You won't have a horse if this one dies, will you? It's in your own interest to treat him properly. If he collapses on the street, you will have to pay to have his carcass taken to the glue factory."

"No!"

"Yes!"

"What about my load? Can't just leave it on the street. Somebody could pinch it."

"When you've made your horse comfortable, you can notify the police station. The beat constable will keep a lookout to make sure nobody steals anything."

I had the feeling a mutually friendly relationship with the police was not one the man was familiar with. He noticed me watching him, and he scowled. If looks could kill, I would be dead and buried. He was blaming me for interfering. At that moment, I had to admit I was glad Hilliard was present.

The horse lowered its head and began to drink from the bucket of water. Hilliard stroked its nose and wiped its nostrils with the wet sack.

"There, that feels better, doesn't it, old chap?"

The poor nag was indeed looking better. It was breathing more normally, and it even raised its head.

Hilliard handed the reins to the teamster. "Here. Now go slowly. Keep in the shade as much as you can."

The man started off when Hilliard called to him. "Come by the café tomorrow and I'll give you a coffee on the house."

The teamster looked over his shoulder. "Can't stand coffee."

They went off down the street.

Hilliard turned to me. "Poor bloody creature. I doubt

very much its life is going to be much easier no matter what we've done today."

"I should report him to the Humane Society."

"I can understand how you feel. Problem is the man's right. He's probably hanging on to this job for dear life."

"You're certainly being kinder toward him than I feel. I'd like to see him charged."

Hilliard shrugged. "Desperation can turn the best of men into cruel creatures."

There was the same tone in his voice as when he'd talked to me in the office. I might have continued, but, before I could say anything, a wave of dizziness swept over me and I staggered against the dray. Hilliard was beside me at once.

"Hey, you need to sit down." He half carried me to the tree, and I sank to the ground. "Hold on." He grabbed one of the buckets. There was some water left in the bottom, and unceremoniously he poured it over my head.

"Sorry, Miss Frayne."

I was in no shape to worry about what this was doing to my appearance; I just wished there were two more buckets of water he could throw on me. Hilliard began to fan me with one of the sacks. Heavenly.

"Perhaps we should reconsider your coming to work tonight," he said.

I was feeling much better, although my mouth felt so dry I would have drunk out of the horse trough itself if there had been any water left.

"I'll be okay in a minute. It's all the excitement. Got me hot."

He knelt beside me. There seemed to be genuine concern in his eyes. His face, too, was damp with sweat.

"Why don't you come back to the café? At least you can have a cool drink and a lie-down if you want. There's time."

I was ready to get up. "Thanks for the offer. I'll be all right."

"Were you going to go home?"

"No, I was going back to the office."

"The café is closer. I suggest we go there."

"I can't. I have to check for messages."

"All right. If you insist. At least let me accompany you."

I stood up, but the dizziness wasn't too far off. I had no desire to collapse on the sidewalk.

"Thank you. Perhaps I will take you up on that offer."

He took me by the elbow. "Steady as she goes."

"What about the empty buckets?"

"I'll collect them on the way back."

We set off. I wanted desperately to be in charge of my own legs, but they weren't co-operating. We had reached the end of the block before I could quite trust myself to continue under my own steam.

Hilliard tried again to persuade me to take a rest, but I was keen to honour the assignment. I promised to return by dinner and said I would cancel if I was still feeling groggy. He left me at the Arcade, where I made my way upstairs to the office. Once inside, I locked the door and stripped down to my brevvies. What a relief that was. I doused myself with water from the sink, then I switched on the fan, dragged over a chair and footstool so they were directly underneath it, and stretched out as well as I could. There had been no message from Mr. Gilmore, so I could only assume there was no significant change in his wife's condition. I rang his home number, but there was no answer.

Was I any further ahead in knowing what had happened? I had to say no, but I was hoping that Ida Gilmore would be able to provide some answers.

I had a short nap, woke unrefreshed, and wiped myself down as best I could. For some reason, I could feel the touch of Hilliard's hand on my elbow. It seemed like such a long time ago that he'd walked into the office, rather than just this morning. What was it he'd said? "I was on my own, too."

Did that mean what I was beginning to hope it meant?

It was time to head for the café.

Chapter Eleven

When I got to the Paradise, the lineup was already outside the door. The customers, men and women, were quiet, as if lining up in an orderly fashion were part of their hearts and souls.

What did you do today? I stood in line.

I was glad that the café appeared to have a loyal clientele, but I knew already that part of the reason was because Hilliard and his partners were subsidizing the unemployed.

Hilliard had told me to enter by the side door, so I went around and knocked. Wilf opened the door, which led into a small hall. He had a glass in his hand.

"Ah! Our mysterious Miss Frayne. Come in."

He stood back to let me through. His breath smelled of beer. I'd thought he was already plastered at lunchtime. I guessed he was continuing to maintain that state.

"Why mysterious?"

"Come now, Miss Frayne. You show up on our doorstep looking for work, which alas does not pay well. Wish it did. However, you are not bothered by the insultingly low wage even though you look like a woman who has had some success in life."

I was taken aback by this, and I certainly didn't want to spew out a whole raft of lies that I couldn't support. We were inside now, too close together for comfort — at least on my part it was uncomfortable. I had the feeling Wilf was rather enjoying himself. I wished Hilliard would appear.

Wilf hung over me, swaying a little. Bad sign.

"Not only that, you seem to have a good deal of expertise in playing chess. Most unusual for a woman. I'd say this is all very odd, Miss Frayne."

I mustered up a wide and perfectly innocent smile. "Not these days, Mr. Morrow. Many people are resorting to work they might not normally do."

"No, truly, tell me the truth. I'm betting you were once a schoolteacher."

Well, at least I could admit to that.

"Bang on. But as you know, there have been cutbacks on every front."

"Sometimes I wonder, Miss Frayne, exactly what we were fighting for all those years ago. I don't see an appreciable change in the way the working class is treated. We wanted to build a better, more equal world. Would you say that happened?"

"What happened?" Hilliard came into the hall from the kitchen on these last words.

Wilf lifted his glass. "Miss Frayne and I are having a deep philosophical talk. I told her she is mysterious, and she doesn't agree. She seems to think she is no different from every other intelligent, good-looking woman in need of work who just happens to end up on the doorstep of the Paradise. No ulterior motive in sight. What's your opinion, Hill?"

Before Wilf could take another swig, Hilliard took hold of the glass and removed it from his grip.

"In my opinion, you need to back off from the sauce, get sobered up, fast, and get out there to greet our customers. You've promised to play a couple of games of chess. The state you are in at the moment, a child of three would beat you."

His voice had the same authority I'd heard when he confronted the teamster. Wilf flushed and gave a mock salute.

"Yes, sir. Whatever you say, sir."

"I suggest you go upstairs and stick your head under the cold water tap."

"Yes, sir."

Without another word, Wilf headed for the stairs. Hilliard watched him go. There was an apron hanging by the door, and I reached for it.

Hilliard grinned at me. "You seem to hold your own very well, Miss Frayne. Angry teamsters? Inebriated café owners? No problem."

I didn't know how to reply to that. "So the plan is for me to work until closing, keeping my eyes open for any indication of nefarious goings-on. By anybody."

"Exactly. I might not have the opportunity to get your report tonight. I'll be doing the closing up. See if you can hang around for that, please. But unless we say otherwise, I'll come to your office in the morning, as I did today."

"All right. By the way, please call me Charlotte. I am technically your employee. Miss Frayne sounds too respectful."

"Ouch. There's an implication in that remark I don't really like."

"Not at all. I'm sure you treat your waitresses very well."

He laughed. "You haven't seen me in action yet. You don't know that."

"When we get cozy, I'll ask Miss Reilly what she feels."

"I call her Pearl, but I always refer to her mother as Mrs. Reilly. Does that sound respectful enough for you?"

"Absolutely. And I shall respectfully call you Mr. Taylor."

He considered that. "Let's say that as long as our pretend official relationship is in place, you can address me as such, but you have to promise to call me Hill at such time as that ends."

I felt a little flutter in my throat. Yes, I realized I had not known him for even a day yet, but my little love-starved heart had a very different sense of time.

"Okay."

"Are you ready?"

"Ready."

"Let's go."

He led the way into the kitchen.

Eric was back at the stove, spooning out the soup into bowls on a tray. Pearl was standing by. He smiled. She didn't.

"Hello, Miss Frayne. We're about ready. Pearl will take out the first batch."

"Are you quite sure you know what to do?" she asked me with unmistakable hostility. And I thought we'd bonded.

"If I don't, I'll be sure to ask." Bees could have gotten stuck in the honey of my tone.

"Give her a bit of help, Pearl," said Hill. "She'll catch on fast, I know it."

He reached for the leather pouch and gave it to me. "Here you go. Your badge of office. Come to the register and I will give you your float." He winked at me. "I'll go and let in the hungry hoards."

Pearl picked up her tray. "I've cut the bread. It's in that basket. You can follow behind me and give each person a slice. Some of them will ask for seconds, but don't give it to them. If they want more, they have to pay more. A second slice is five cents. With dripping or parsnip marmalade."

"Got it."

"The first course is easy. Soup and bread. Then there's choice of salad, apple and beet or dandelion. A lot of people turn up their noses at dandelions, but they're very good. We only use the new leaves. Quite delicate, like lettuce, only cheaper."

"I'll have to give it a try."

"Mr. Fenwell's good about experimenting. The second course is shepherd's pie with green peas and gravy. That always goes over well. We allow them a choice of three desserts. Today it's Eccles cake, which is popular, a chocolate biscuit, also popular, and trench pudding."

"What's that?"

I was tempted to make a joke about rat juice, but didn't think Pearl was in the mood.

"It's basically cooked rice and milk with some dates and coconut butter. I don't mind it, but I've told them to name it something else. I mean, it brings up bad associations, wouldn't you say? After what happened and all."

"You've got a point there, Pearl. But I suppose it fits in with the camp day theme."

"I guess so. Anyway, back to what I was saying. Some of the customers take the earth to make up their minds. You have to hustle them along or they'd be here 'til the cows come home."

"It's probably the highlight of the day for some of the men."

She grimaced. "Do you think so? Well, they should count their lucky stars they can even get a sweet for the price they pay. All right. Let's go. They're in."

Hilliard had indeed let in the customers, and they were filing in obediently. Most went directly to what I assumed were their familiar places. Except for the cheery decor and the fact that they had to pay, we could have been in a soup kitchen.

When faced with the customers, Pearl underwent a transformation. She was obviously popular. She knew most of them by name, and there was a lively banter and joshing back and forth. Two or three of them asked for the meal to be put on their tab, but most had their thirty-five cents ready on the table. Pearl scooped up the money and dropped it into her pouch. She only had to make change a couple of times. The men were curious but polite about me.

"New, are you?"

"Don't let them run you ragged, miss."

"When are we getting the steak and kidney pie again?"

Pearl answered that with a sharp, "When you're lucky."

And so the evening went. The customers all ate quickly. While they were waiting for the pie, many of them sat with their faces upturned to the fans, looking like sunflowers following the sun, but in reverse. Wilf came out and immediately started up a chess game with an old, wizened chap with no teeth. I'd sort of liked Pete, but he was nowhere to be seen. I hoped the new chap would clobber Wilf. He didn't, nor did the next three players. Wilf might have been heading for total inebriation earlier, but it didn't seem to have any impact on his ability to play chess. I was too busy serving to be able to scrutinize the games, but Wilf seemed to move his pieces quickly and aggressively. I was itching to give him a match. As I'd said, Gramps had been a tough teacher.

Shortly after the first course had finished, one of the men took a harmonica from his pocket and started to play. The song had been very popular last year. Plaintive and melancholy. "When I Grow Too Old to Dream." He wasn't that accomplished, and he wasn't old, but he played from his soul. The café grew quiet. He finished the piece, and another man shouted out, "Give us something a bit livelier, Charlie. We're all going to slit our throats at this rate."

"Yeah," called out another man. "How about 'Strutters Ball'?"

The harmonica player didn't seem fazed by the comments, and he immediately launched into the lively number. Some of those who had finished their soup joined in, keeping up a beat on their bowls with spoons. Even Pearl did a little hop and skip as she gathered the money.

She was right about the dessert course. We each brought out a revolving lazy Susan. Dishes of trench pudding on the lower rack, Eccles cakes and biscuits on the upper. It was a serious decision to make, and many lingered over it. I'd have liked to say, "Have all three" to a few of the skinny, ragged men.

Pearl would have none of that nonsense. "Make up your mind. We haven't got all day," was her refrain. They all seemed to know the routine. They ate quickly, but then lingered on to chat and share a smoke. I was too busy to sample the food myself; from what I could tell it was most palatable. Cheap it might be, but quality was not compromised.

At ten minutes to the hour, Hilliard rang a bell and called out, "Next sitting please, everyone." They began to stand up, gather hats, and head for the door. The next group were already lining up, some of them pressing their noses against the windows.

Hilliard closed the door behind the first lot and began to clear the tables, changing the tablecloths if it seemed necessary. Wilf, apparently now quite sober, started to sweep the floor with vigour. Pearl hustled me into the kitchen. Conal was washing the dirty dishes that were piled in the sink.

"Start drying," said Pearl. Frankly, I would have been just as glad to sit down and ease my suffering feet for a few minutes, but I refused to show any weakness. Pearl helped herself to one of the biscuits on the tray. It looked delicious.

Conal gave me a sweet smile. "Do as many as you can."

Halfway through, we heard the next group surge into the café.

"I'll let them get seated and take the orders," said Pearl as she wiped a biscuit crumb from the corner of her mouth.

Eric started to lay out the bowls ready for the next round of soup.

"That certainly smells good," I said. I hadn't meant to sound wistful, but it must have come across that way because he immediately ladled out some into a bowl.

"You've got time. Have some. Take a piece of bread and soak it."

It tasted as good as it smelled. I forked a piece of bread, soggy with the soup, and stuffed it into my mouth. I managed to down a few spoonfuls before Pearl returned.

"We're all ready out here."

She loaded up the tray, I took the breadbasket as before,

and we went out to the café. It was crowded. Two or three women this time, and a couple of young children, but mostly men. Like the first group, they were roughly dressed with weather-scoured faces. Hungry.

We began to hand out the soup and bread.

Near the end of the sitting, something rather peculiar happened.

There were three doors that opened into the café proper. One was from the street, one swung into the kitchen, and the other was just to the left of the counter. I was collecting the empty soup bowls and waiting for Pearl to come out of the kitchen with a tray of pie slices. I suppose I blended into the scenery in my white apron. One of the new customers approached the closed door. I'd noticed him come in and scan the crowd. He was ordinary enough, wearing a workman's cloth cap and rumpled suit. Nothing to distinguish him, except that I picked up on a certain jumpiness. He didn't sit down to order any food, but slowly made his way to the back of the café. He didn't greet any of the customers, nor they him. Once at the rear door, he knocked twice and the door was opened promptly. I couldn't see who was there, but I was close enough to hear a male voice, and it sounded like Conal Pierce.

"What do you want?" he said.

"Our glowing dream," was the answer.

"Come in and welcome."

The newcomer did so, and the door closed. A very brief interaction, but obviously the two men were exchanging some kind of code. The answer sounded vaguely familiar, but I couldn't immediately identify it. Hill was at the far end of the counter, busy adding up somebody's tab, and he didn't appear to have noticed what had transpired. Or if he did, it didn't bother him.

Pearl emerged from the kitchen. "Take out the bowls and pick up the plates," she said in her bossy voice.

I obeyed. By the time I returned, I was plunged into the serving melee. If the code-uttering man came out, I didn't see him. Two other people, however, did go through that door. One was a tall, stately woman who was better dressed than any I'd seen so far. The man was likewise smart. They seemed to be a couple. She knocked on the door. He answered the question posed.

"A glowing dream."

They went inside.

At ten to eight, Hill called out, "Closing up, folks. Finish your meal. See you tomorrow."

Like the first two groups, they left fairly promptly. At five past eight the café was empty. Hill locked the door and reversed the sign. "Open" facing us meant the restaurant was "Closed" to the public. The word was never so wonderful. He and Wilf both dived into the same routine of cleaning up. I gathered the dirty dishes onto a tray and carried them into the kitchen, where Pearl waved at me to bring them over to the sink.

"You done good," she said, but as she was concentrating on scrubbing a recalcitrant bowl I wasn't entirely sure she was addressing me.

Conal was nowhere to be seen. Eric was sitting at the table, smoking.

"So how did you get on, Miss Frayne?"

"Fine. Other than being crippled for the rest of my life."

Pearl made the snorting noise she had perfected.

"Now you know what it's like."

I wasn't aware I had been in a state of denial about the hard work waitresses did, but I nodded agreeably.

"There's bread left," said Eric. "Help yourself."

I actually craved a chocolate biscuit, but I took a slice of bread from the basket as offered.

"Put some dripping on it."

I did so. "Scrumptious."

Pearl banged some plates onto the draining board.

"Shall I dry them?" I asked her, ever helpful.

"No need. They can dry like that."

She reached into the sink and pulled the plug then started to take off her apron. "I'm done for tonight."

Eric was rapidly disappearing into a cloud of tobacco smoke. "Thanks, Pearl. Great job as usual. See you at lunch tomorrow."

For the first time she looked at me directly. "Will you be on?"

"I believe so. I'm filling in while your mother is away."

"I see."

It was hard to tell if she liked that news or not.

"Did you get all your prep done?" she asked Eric.

"Yep. All done. We're having stewed oxtail tomorrow. It's marinating. Cut down on cooking time. I didn't want to overheat the kitchen."

"According to the papers, this weather is here until Friday. We're all going to fry in our beds," said Pearl. She reached for her straw hat and jammed it on her head. "Good night, then. See you tomorrow."

She headed for the swing door and almost collided with Wilf, who was coming in.

"Whoa. Oops. Sorry, Pearl. My fault. Allow me."

He held the door open, and as she went through he gave her a friendly pat on her behind. She pursed her lips but didn't seem to mind. Wilf saw me.

"Still here, Miss Frayne? I'd have thought you'd have fled by now."

"She's having something to eat," said Eric.

"That sounds like a good idea. Any soup left?"

"I believe so, help yourself."

Wilf went to the pot on the stove, ladled out some of the soup into a bowl, and came over to the table.

"How did your games go?" Eric asked him.

"Fine. No difficulties. I won all three. My opponents played like schoolboys." He glanced over at me. "Or should I say schoolgirls?"

"You might not have won against schoolgirls," I said with a smile.

Eric chuckled, but Wilf didn't. He didn't reply at all but began to spoon up his soup with the same intensity I'd seen with some of the rough customers. He must have realized I was observing him because he paused.

"Good soup, Eric."

"I second that," I said. "It's delicious."

"You also get a dessert," said Eric to me. "Did you try one of the Eccles cakes? I made them myself."

"No, I didn't get a chance."

He swung around and reached for a plate, plucked off one of the cakes, and gave it to me. I took a bite.

Like any creative artist with his work, Eric watched for my reaction.

"Do you think it could be a bit flakier?"

"Nope. It's perfect."

Hilliard came in as I said that. "No good telling him that, Charlotte. He believes in Plato. There's only one Really Real Eccles Cake, and he'll never be able to make it."

He was carrying the cash tray from the till, and he came over to the table and put it down.

"Seems like we had a good day," said Wilf.

"Excellent."

Hill began to count out the coins, noting the amount of each denomination on a slip of paper. He worked swiftly while I focused on munching into my Eccles cake. Wilf seemed lost in thought, or the soup. Eric stubbed out his cigarette and was seized with a coughing fit that was painful to hear. Only when the cough subsided was he was able to speak.

"I'm going to go home. Good night, Miss Frayne. Congratulations on surviving your first night at the Paradise

Café. See you later, Hill, Wilf. If Conal comes down, tell him he can finish off the soup. Make sure he washes out his bowl. You too, Wilf."

Wilf threw up his hands. "More than my life is worth not to."

"Night."

I called after him, "Sleep well. Take care of that cough."

Both Hilliard and Wilf looked at me in surprise. What? Weren't the help allowed to relate to the bosses? Obviously not.

Hilliard had finished his task, and he went to the safe. It was a large, ornately decorated affair that looked as if it should contain the crown jewels or at the least multiple bars of gold bullion. He dragged over a small stool, which he sat on as he dialled the combination. There was a series of soft clicks, and he turned the handle. The safe opened. He removed four linen bags and brought them back to the table. I could see each was marked. One cent. Five. Ten. Twenty-five. He scooped the corresponding coins out of the till tray and put them into the bags. There were two one-dollar bills.

"What's the total?" Wilf asked. He had helped himself to a couple of biscuits and literally stuffed them into his mouth. He had more flesh on his bones than the other two men, but he wasn't by any means chubby. Amazing.

"Including ten breakfast teas and coffees, less two tabs for seventy cents, we took in fifty-nine dollars."

"Deduct Miss Frayne's wages and we can say we had a good day."

"Indeed, we did. We'll pay Charlotte on Saturday."

Wilf picked a piece of pastry out of his teeth. "Let's hope your feet hold out, Miss Frayne."

Hill gathered up the bags of money, went back to the open safe, and stashed them inside. The bills he clipped to a pile. The daily tally went into a box. He closed the door and turned the handle.

Any lingering doubts were dispelled. Any lost money would have to have been taken from the safe.

I tried to suppress a yawn. Unsuccessfully.

"Keeping you up, are we, Miss Frayne?" said Wilf. "Off you go then. We all need our beauty sleep these days."

Hilliard stood up. "Thank you again for stepping in at such short notice. We'll see you tomorrow."

I headed for the door, but just as Pearl had almost collided with incoming traffic, so did I. Conal was bursting in.

"Sorry, miss." He hardly waited for me to depart before I heard him say to the two men, "Listen, you fellas. I've got to tell you something."

I would have liked to linger in the outer room, but it would have been too obvious. I took my time hanging up my apron. There was only silence on the other side of the door. I let myself out.

Dusk was creeping in reluctantly, as if it didn't want to disturb the dying sun. The air was somewhat cooler but still sticky. I headed for home.

Chapter Twelve

DUCHESS STREET WAS typical of Toronto, a mixture of industry and residential. To get to our house, I had to walk past a delivery warehouse where idle vans lined up on the asphalt. I don't know how they survived in this economy. They never seemed busy. At least the driver couldn't take out his frustration on the engine with a whip.

I moved on past the row of residences. The McCraes and the Greens were entertaining or burying their misery or whatever the unemployed did to distract themselves. They were sitting out on their respective porches. Both families were large, the sons returned from jobs that no longer existed. Lights from cigarettes and pipes glowed like fireflies in the gathering dusk. Bursts of laughter punctuated the air. It made me feel oddly lonely. I wasn't married, and with nobody in the offing I can't say I was happy about that. I'd have liked to have a fella to snuggle up to, as my grandma would have said. I missed her a lot. She'd died suddenly four years earlier of an aneurysm in the brain. We'd been sitting around the kitchen table when she put her hand to her head. "Ooh. Ouch," were her last words — if you can even call them words. At that she collapsed forward. That's it. The end. She was dead. "At least she didn't suffer," said Gramps. I knew that was true, but it had been a terrible shock to both of us.

When I was effectively orphaned at the age of two, Gran and Gramps didn't hesitate for a second. They took me in, showered me with love, and brought me up to be as independent as a girl can be in this society of ours. With Gran's passing, Gramps and I turned to each other.

My best friend, Polly, declared that my reliance on my grandfather was what was contributing to my lack of romance. "It's safer than trusting an available man. You're afraid of being abandoned." Polly took a university course in Freudian psychology, and now she puts it to use, analyzing situations whenever possible.

At the moment, she was up in Muskoka working at a summer camp for disadvantaged children. She didn't like it, really. "How can you adopt fifty children? They all need adopting, but they're going back to whatever situation they call home at the end of the summer, where they will sink into their miserable lives. What we do for two months is a drop in the bucket." I'd tried to convince her that drops in buckets can add up to rivers and seas, but she tended to have a pessimistic turn to her nature. Since she had been gone, we had exchanged letters and a couple of phone calls, but I missed chewing things over with her.

My reverie was broken by a shout from Mr. McCrae.

"Good evening, Miss Frayne. Hot enough for you?"

"Indeed it is." I waved back at him. What else was I supposed to say? *No, I'm quite chilly as a matter of fact?*

As I approached my house, the usual delicious smell of baking bread wafted toward me. The next house but one was the location of the Ideal Bakery, and the air was always permeated with the smell of their goods. Even in these stringent times, people wanted bread and biscuits.

I was reminded of the Paradise Café. I had to admit that even though the evening had been physically tasking, I had enjoyed myself. I hoped the case Hilliard had brought me would require investigating for a while longer. So far, I certainly wasn't ready to point the finger.

I expected to see Gramps sitting outside, but the porch was empty. There were lights on in the house. I walked up the steps and let myself in.

Gramps called from the kitchen. "That you, Lottie?"

"Who do you think it is?"

I was irritable with the heat and exertion of the evening, but there was an odd tone to his voice. I walked through the dark hall, back to the kitchen where the lights were bright. To my surprise, Gramps wasn't alone. Nothing odd about that, except for the fact that his companion was our neighbour, Mrs. Johnson. I could swear that a moment earlier she'd been sitting on his lap.

As I entered the room, she was smoothing down her dress, and Gramps was most definitely smoothing down his hair.

"Hello, Lottie," he mumbled. "I wasn't expecting you until later."

"It is later," I said, not too nicely. "It's after nine."

I looked at Mrs. Johnson.

"I'd better be going," she said. "I was just keeping your grandfather company. He gets lonely when you have to work all the time."

Her voice was polite, but she managed to convey a reproach that made me bristle. Gramps and I had had many talks about my going to work. He swore he was all right with it. He wasn't home alone all the time, and if he was lonely, he went to his veterans' club.

To tell the truth, my suspicions (and Polly's) about our buxom widowed neighbour were confirmed. She had set her cap at Gramps, and from the way he was looking so sheepish I'd guess she'd introduced the powerful bait of her sex appeal to get what she wanted. What that might be I wasn't quite sure.

"Good night, Mrs. Johnson. Thanks for keeping my old sad sack of a grandfather from dreadful misery."

"Lottie!" exclaimed Gramps. "Bertha and I had a very pleasant evening."

"I'll bet you did, Gramps. But it is late, and I am tired. So if you don't mind, Mrs. Johnson, I'll hit the wooden trail. Shall I see you out, or do you know the way?"

"I can see myself out, thank you, Charlotte. Good night, Arnie. Shall I drop by tomorrow?"

"I certainly hope so," said Gramps. "Thanks again for keeping me company."

I can't say she exactly flounced out of the room, but she

gave a pretty good imitation of a flounce.

Gramps and I waited until we heard the sound of the front door closing. Then he turned to me. He was mad.

"Charlotte, I don't know how you can be so rude. She is a very nice woman, and she's lonely."

"Gramps! She was sitting on your lap. You were canoodling."

He glared at me for a moment, then he actually smiled. "And why not. We're both single."

"You're seventy-five, for God's sake."

"So what? That has nothing to do with it. Doesn't mean there's no life in the old dog. Bertha makes me feel young again."

"Really? And just how does she do that?"

Gramps got to his feet. "I'm not going to talk to you when you're in this mood. I'm going to bed. I'll see you in the morning."

He stomped out of the room. I felt wretched, of course, but I just didn't have the energy to settle the issue tonight. I didn't think it was something that would be easy to settle anyway. He was quite right. Why shouldn't he have a romantic life, no matter what his age?

Trouble was I didn't trust Bertha Johnson as far as I could throw her. She'd only moved into the house next door three months before, and it seemed to me that as soon as she'd sussed out the situation, she'd made a beeline for Gramps. At first, I was only too happy that he had somebody to keep him company when I was out, but her attentions began to escalate. A little junket here when he was under the weather, a fresh piece of cake there, a nice pork chop she'd got at the butcher's. You get the picture. So what's wrong with that, you might ask? As Gramps said, they were both single. But I wasn't a PI for nothing. Mrs. Johnson seemed inconsistent in her recounting of her own history. First she said she was from Vancouver, then she was from Victoria. Okay, they're both on the west coast, but surely you'd know the difference if you lived there. One you needed a ferry to get to. She was also vague about her first marriage. At one time she referred to her supposedly dead husband as Tom, another time as Tim. He seemed to have died from pneumonia first, then resurrected himself sufficiently to die later in a boating accident. When I casually queried Gramps about these peculiarities, he shrugged them off. "We all get forgetful as we get older." And how old was she, anyway? She claimed to be sixty, but I'd guess she was younger. Most women shave off a few years if they have to rather than adding to them. However, if you're hoping to snare a seventy-five-year-old widower, saying you were closer to that age might give you more credibility and him more security.

Gramps shut his bedroom door emphatically. I hated to upset him, but I also wanted to protect him from possible heartbreak and exploitation. We'd have to talk about it.

I went into the hall, where we had the telephone. I considered ringing Mr. Gilmore at home, but he hadn't called me so I assumed there was no change in his wife's condition.

I made my way upstairs, stripped off my clothes, and plopped on the bed. I had an electric fan that didn't make much difference. There seemed to be nothing to do except wait it out until the heat wave broke. I vowed I'd never complain again in January or February about frigid winter temperatures.

Chapter Thirteen

WHEN THE MORNING light slid around the window blind, I was already awake. I'd been dreaming I was standing outside the office. I could hear the telephone inside was ringing, but I couldn't find my key to the door. It wasn't in my purse, where it should have been, where I always keep it. Where had I left it? I felt desperate. As I came to consciousness, I realized that a telephone was indeed ringing — it was our house phone. I sat up quickly. My bedside clock showed ten past seven. Who the heck would be calling at that hour? I grabbed my dressing gown and ran downstairs.

"Hello. Main 7425."

"Miss Frayne. Mr. Gilmore here."

My heart was thumping.

"Yes, sir." In my state of alarm, I fell back to my former way of addressing him.

"I do apologize for calling you at this hour; however, I could not wait."

I thought he was going to tell me that his wife had died. Thank goodness he didn't.

"Ida is still in critical condition. It is clear that the police are gearing up to charge me with her assault. Detective Arcady was present when she screamed the way she did, and I fear that confirmed any suspicions that I am responsible." He paused. "I tell you, Miss Frayne, if she dies, I will be accused of murder."

"Surely not, Mr. Gilmore."

"I am the only likely suspect." He paused to take in a long, slow breath. "I did not attack my wife. I wish to find out who did. It is not something I can do easily. I have not left her side since yesterday. I do not want to. More importantly, I doubt it's something the police would agree to. I must ask you, Miss Frayne, to tackle this case. You will be doing this by yourself. Please do what you can to find out who attacked my wife."

"Of course I will, Mr. Gilmore. I have already spoken to most of the people on your street. Vince Alexander says he heard a shout. Might have been about seven o'clock, but he couldn't be definite about that."

There was silence at the other end of the line.

"Mr. Gilmore? I presume you didn't hear anything?"

"No. I would have said. When I left, Ida was asleep. I was awake about six-thirty."

"Mr. Alexander was vague about the time. It might have been later."

"It must have been. If he heard a shout, I'm sure I would have also. Our windows were open."

"He says it was a woman's voice, but it might have been the Hodge baby. He's been restless in this heat. Same with the Pouluke twins. Could have been one of them, maybe."

I was giving him an out.

"That baby does cry a lot, it's true, but surely Vince could tell the difference. The twins are rather quiet on the whole. Nobody else heard anything?"

"Not the people I spoke to. Mrs. Ano, Mrs. Parker, the Kubays, mother and daughter. Mrs. Hodge and Mrs. Pouluke. The Kaufmanns. They each said they heard nothing at any time that morning." I paused for a minute. I wanted to be tactful, but I had to be direct as well if I was going to be truly helpful. "Vince Alexander did say that Mrs. Gilmore might have offended some of your neighbours."

I heard Mr. Gilmore sigh. "She's a woman of decided opinions, my Ida. Not necessarily orthodox opinions. Let me guess, Vince Alexander didn't understand it, Arthur Kaufmann was nasty, Mrs. and Miss Kubay probably served you tea and cakes and slipped in some poison about everybody else."

"Lemonade, no cakes. Lots of poison. Most of those I spoke to seem to admire your wife."

"Quite so. One thing I have considered, Miss Frayne, is the timing of the attack. The police cannot pinpoint the time with any accuracy. Obviously, I was absent. Was that chance or deliberate? There was no forced entry. If the culprit was a tramp, Ida would have dealt with him kindly. She always did. She may have been turning away to go to the kitchen. We have a jar there with some small coins, which she hands out to people who come to the door in need."

This information was followed by another long silence. I waited.

"On the other hand, we keep the telephone in the kitchen. She may have been running to it."

There was another possibility, of course. Ida was not aware of being in danger and was simply heading back to the kitchen to finish her breakfast. And the man she did not consider dangerous was her husband. But why? Everything so far indicated a crime of impulse. I simply could not believe Mr. Gilmore was the culprit.

"Thank you, Miss Frayne. At the moment I have begged the use of the hospital telephone. It might be difficult for you to reach me here. I will call you later this afternoon."

He was obviously about to hang up.

"Mr. Gilmore, before you go, I do have a question."

"Yes?"

"I was at the Paradise Café yesterday —"

He interrupted me. "What were you doing there?"

"I haven't had a chance to tell you yet. Hilliard Taylor, one of the owners, came to the office shortly before you rang about your wife —"

He interrupted me again, a discourtesy uncommon to him. "What did he want?"

"He is worried that somebody is stealing from them. He wanted our firm to investigate. It looks as if the culprit might be one of the partners."

There was a long pause on the other end of the line. "I rather doubt that. They've gone through a lot together. Did he tell you? They were all prisoners of war."

"Yes, he told me. I agreed to take on the case, and I am now undercover, working for them as one of the waitresses at the café. That's why I was there, in the Paradise, when Detective Murdoch came in."

I did not continue, leaving Mr. Gilmore an opportunity to speak.

"Yes?"

"Detective Murdoch wanted to verify your statement, which he said you amended later, that you were at the café in the morning … you first said you went straight home."

"I was confused from the shock."

I had to persist. "I do understand that, Mr. Gilmore, except the odd thing is nobody could remember whether you had been at the café or not."

"Is that what they said?"

"Yes. I was present when they answered Murdoch's questions."

"Hmm. Well, it was busy. They must not have noticed me."

"Am I to understand, then, that you left the office to go home, but you went to have a coffee before proceeding to your house?"

"That is correct."

"And from the café, you went down to the lake to get some cool breeze?"

"Miss Frayne. I feel as if I am being interrogated all over again."

His voice was sharp with anger.

I'd been about to bring up the question of his being Jewish. Good thing I hadn't. This was the first time he'd ever spoken to me like that.

"I'm sorry to sound that way, Mr. Gilmore, but I need firm ground to stand on."

"Of course. Of course. It is I who should apologize. My nerves are somewhat frayed. But yes, I did exactly as you have related."

"Nothing else? No shopping? You know you like to shop sometimes."

I tried to make my tone jocular; from his response, I don't think I succeeded. Although I would have sworn that Mr. Gilmore was a completely uxorious and faithful man, his evolving story was all beginning to sound not only vague but untrue, and to my ears he was sounding guilty. Perhaps my view was coloured by my encounter with Gramps and Mrs. Johnson. I was quite conversant with how powerful *cherchez la femme* can be. The divorce cases we dealt with were all based on it. Did this apply to Mr. Gilmore?

"Miss Frayne. I ask you both as your employer and, as I hope, your friend to give your attention to finding out who has perpetrated this murderous attack. You must drop the café case. It will simply sap your energies and take up too much of your attention, which would be better employed. Nothing will be gained by your further investigations on behalf of Mr. Taylor. I'm sure there is a simple explanation for the missing money."

At that moment, I heard somebody calling his name in the background.

"I must go. It's one of the nurses. I'll ring back later."

He hung up.

I stood by the telephone. Frankly, I was all churned up. I had no desire to drop the café case. I was already committed to it. Almost two years ago, Mr. Gilmore had hired me to work at the agency. I'd begun as general dogsbody and secretary, but with his encouragement I'd soon qualified for my investigator's licence. From the beginning, we got along famously, and in short time he made me an associate. Surely now he didn't have the right to tell me what cases I could or could not pursue? Besides which, no matter how much he insisted he was telling the truth, I heard prevarication.

On impulse I picked up the telephone and dialled the general operator. I didn't want to go behind his back.

"Operator, will you put me through to the General Hospital."

"Certainly, madam. Please hold."

After only two rings the phone was answered. I used my nicest voice.

"Good morning. A Mr. Gilmore just rang me from your telephone. Would it be possible to speak to him? We didn't finish our conversation, as he was called away."

Not giving the receptionist a chance to act I rushed on.

"I'm a friend of the family. It was utterly shocking what happened to Mrs. Gilmore. I do hope she is all right."

It was still early in the morning, and perhaps the woman on the other end of the line was hungry for a bit of chat. Perhaps it was what Mr. Gilmore said. I had a way with people. Or perhaps it was prurient curiosity.

Whatever the reason, she said breathlessly, "I'm afraid her condition isn't much changed. She's still listed as grave."

I pushed a little.

"He sounded so tired just now. It would have been a long night for him having to sit in a chair by the bed and all that."

"Absolutely. Such a devoted husband. I hope if and when I get married, and if I ever get ill, my husband will be as doting." I heard her sigh. "But that's hoping for a lot, isn't it?"

I murmured something unintelligible.

"Do you want me to have him fetched to the telephone?" the nurse asked.

"No, don't bother. I'll speak to him later. Thank you so much. Try to stay cool."

"I'm not sure that's possible. If this heat wave doesn't break soon, we'll all be six feet under."

We hung up. At least I'd nailed down one indisputable fact. It would be nice if I could winkle out a few others.

There was no sign of movement from Gramps's room, so I went into the kitchen, made myself a cup of tea, and buttered a slice of bread. I didn't like to leave without seeing him and making amends. I scribbled him a note on a scrap of paper.

Gramps. Sorry, but I have a big case I have to deal with. I will ring you, so answer the phone. We'll have a proper talk when I get home.

I wanted to say, *Don't have anything to do with that Mrs. Johnson,* but I restrained myself.

I went back upstairs, got dressed, skipping the ubiquitous girdle and selecting a cooler (but still demure) blouse, and tiptoed softly out.

Chapter Fourteen

EARLY ON, MR. GILMORE had taught me the importance of keeping very careful and precise records of all active investigations. A second round of interviews seemed like a good idea. I also thought I'd like to take a look at the early morning coffee crowd that frequented the Paradise Café.

The blinds were still down and the "Closed" sign on the door hadn't been flipped. Four young men were lined up outside, all having a smoke. They were better dressed than the lunch and dinner crowds I'd seen, so I guessed they worked in the businesses along Queen Street and wanted a coffee to start their day. This certainly appeared to be a part of Mr. Gilmore's routine. I walked on, slowing down, pretending to look in the shop windows just past the café. I stared admiringly at the work of Miss Helen Farber, whose sign declared her to be a "Skilled Tailoress." There was a single mannequin in the window; its smooth face expressed delight at the smart navy and white polka dot dress with matching hat it was wearing. I could see that another young man had strolled up to the café queue and greeted the others. Obviously, they were regulars. At that moment, somebody inside the café turned over the

"Closed" card and opened the door. I glimpsed Wilf. As I didn't want him to see me, I stepped into the doorway of Miss Farber's shop. I waited several minutes, but the only other customers were two young women who emerged from the greengrocer's shop next to Miss Farber's. They were laughing together over some private joke. The vegetables, perhaps. They didn't pay any attention to me as they passed before entering the café.

Only seven people at this hour, two of them female, and yet all of the partners declaring they couldn't swear whether Mr. Gilmore had been there yesterday at this time or not. How could they have missed him? Why the dissimulation? I had no idea. Perhaps this morning's crowd was unusually light? I waited a little longer. Two of the young men emerged from the Paradise. They walked in the other direction from where I stood. One, the better dressed of the two, continued on and rang the bell at the Canadian Bank of Commerce on the corner. Tut, tut. A little on the late side. The other young fellow, using a key, let himself into the United Cigar Store. I took out my notebook and wrote down a brief description of each man and where they appeared to work. You never knew when such information might be useful.

I retraced my steps and headed for the office.

Climbing the stairs to the second floor, I smelled something awful. The stench got worse and worse as I walked down the hall. I unlocked the office door and entered. Phew. Vile, pungent, dead matter. The source was immediately visible. A dead rat, already at the liquefying stage, had been pushed through the mail slot and was lying in the box. There was a single piece of paper with it, which I extracted as gingerly as I could.

I WARNED YOU. YOU WILL END UP LIKE THIS UNLESS YOU GET OUT.

Black, bold handwriting, as with the other two letters.

At this point I was holding my handkerchief up to my nostrils. I put the piece of paper aside and tried to get a better look at the rat. There was dried blood on its nose, which was squashed in. It had been caught in a trap. But not recently, from the look of the deterioration. Had my tormentor come across it by chance, or had he saved the dead creature for just this purpose?

Still trying to defend myself against the stench, I walked over to my desk. I had a plain wooden pencil holder, which I was willing to sacrifice to the cause. I emptied out the pencils across my ink blotter and returned to the rat. Picking it by the tail with my handkerchief, I lifted it out of the mailbox and placed it in the pencil holder. It dripped necrotic fluid. I slid the lid on the holder closed and, almost gagging, went to the sink to wash my hands.

I could have washed and washed for the next hour. Never mind carbolic soap, I felt as if all the perfumes of Arabia would not sweeten my rat-stained hands.

When I had done my best, I returned to the desk and looked more closely at the piece of paper. It was unpleasantly stained, and not with tea. It was certainly similar to the others. Torn from a notebook, slightly yellowing. The writer had used a straight pen, moved quickly and decisively. It might or might not yield identifiable fingerprints.

I checked the clock. It was almost half past eight. I wasn't going to sit here with my stinky companion while I waited for the world to get started. I picked up the telephone and rang police headquarters.

"I'd like to speak to Detective Murdoch."

I was connected right away.

I explained what had happened.

"That's disgusting. Is it the first time this has happened?"

"First time with a body, second time with a nasty letter."

I told him about the epistle I'd received yesterday. He asked me to read it to him, which I did.

HOPE SHE DIES. ONE LESS BREEDER OF JEWS.
THE SAME THING COULD HAPPEN TO YOU UNLESS YOU BREAK OFF
ALL CONNECTIONS WITH THE FILTH.

"I assume the letter is referring to Mrs. Gilmore. Are the Gilmores Jewish?" Murdoch asked.

I hesitated. I wasn't sure what to say. "I don't really know."

I still didn't feel I could break my promise to Mr. Gilmore by revealing the letter he had received. And his response.

"Any ideas what it's all about?" Murdoch asked.

"None."

"Given what has happened, we have to take these letters very seriously," said Murdoch. "I'd like to see them. And the rat. I can run some tests. It's probably what you say, it was killed in a trap, but it might be helpful to know how it died."

"I can bring them over now if you like."

"Grand. Sooner the better."

"I'll be there shortly. You'll know I'm coming."

"I'm on the second floor. Don't be put off by the receptionist."

We hung up.

I dug out several sheets of newspaper from the waste-basket, wrapped up the pencil coffin, and put the two letters into two separate clean envelopes. With notebook, wrapped pencil box, and envelopes in hand, I set out.

Chapter Fifteen

THE POLICE HEADQUARTERS were housed in the Stewart Building on College Street. It was a sumptuous Romanesque pile of red sandstone with pointy towers, the roofs once burnished copper, now oxidized into a soft green. Elaborately carved friezes rimmed the walls. The entrance was by way of a two-sided flight of stairs that swept up to two arched entrances. Aside from the architectural symmetry, I thought the dual arches made a pithy statement about the primeval dichotomies we humans like to set up. *Saved* on the left, *sinners* on the right; *the rich* on the left, *the poor* on the right; *men* on the left, *women* on the right. Not surprisingly, the building hadn't started out as a home for police with cells for low-life criminals in the basement. It had been built originally for the elite Toronto Athletic Club, peopled by men of wealth and privilege. Swimming, golf, billiards, all offered. At some point the golden balls had tarnished and the club had run into financial difficulties. A technical school moved in for a while; the swimming pool was drained and functioned as a classroom. The police department took it over a few years ago, and the empty pool became a good place to store lost and confiscated bicycles. To my mind it was like various hermit crabs stuffing themselves into a discarded shell. An exquisite shell.

I hadn't wanted to risk travelling on the public transportation with the rat. No matter how tightly wrapped it was, the vile smell still escaped. So I walked over. It took me about half an hour, and in this heat I was dripping wet by the time I got there. The heat intensified the smell from the dead rodent.

I slowly climbed the steps, right side. The side for the poor, the sinners, and women. At least both arches led to the same door, which was heavy and metal-studded. I pushed it open and stepped into the outer foyer. It seemed dim after the bright sunlight outside, an impression reinforced by the rich, dark-hued wood panelling.

The decor changed drastically when I passed through another set of doors.

The large interior foyer had been partitioned into two areas. The walls had been painted what I could only call "depression beige" and ran floor to ceiling; there were no windows, one door on each side. I assumed one went through the respective doors into the office areas beyond. They had a graceless, makeshift look to them, unlike the beauty of the external design of the building and the aristocratic pretentions of the panelled inner foyer.

A narrow staircase was directly ahead, and to the right was an open counter above which a small sign ordered visitors to check in.

I walked over. A young man in police uniform was sitting at a desk typing. For a moment I had to admire his skill as his fingers flew over the clacking keys. He was listening to a Dictaphone.

"Excuse me," I said and rapped on the counter.

He stopped what he was doing and removed his earphones, albeit conveying a certain reluctance.

"Can I help you, madam?"

"I'm here to see Detective Murdoch."

"Is he expecting you?"

"Yes."

At that moment, the young man sniffed. It's possible he might have been coming down with a cold. However, he gave me what I could only think of as a strange look. I had the feeling the rat was making its presence known.

"Just a minute."

He turned to a board just behind him and pushed a switch.

"Detective Murdoch, there's a lady here who says you're expecting her. Name of?"

He looked over at me, eyebrows raised.

It was a perfectly correct procedure, but there was something about the disdain that this constable was conveying that got my back up. I felt like saying, "Lady Godiva" or "Mary Pickford."

Before I could confuse matters, one of the side doors opened and Jack Murdoch emerged. He greeted me with a smile.

"Miss Frayne. Good morning. Come this way." He nodded at the constable. "Thank you, Evans."

The fellow returned to his desk and typewriter. The door had hardly closed behind us when I heard the keys clacking away.

"He types fast, that chap," I said to Murdoch.

"He sure does. He won the Canada–U.S. typing championship last year."

That explained it. He must be intent on practicing for a repeat performance.

Jack led the way down the hall past one or two offices. It was pleasantly, delightfully cool.

"You've got an air-cooling unit."

"We certainly do. Put in last year. It has made all the difference. I can't imagine how we would have coped without it this summer." His lips twitched. "It can get pretty heated in here, especially when we bring in the usual crop of D and Ds."

I began to wonder if I could feign a ladylike fainting fit that would take some time to get over, thereby delaying my returning to the furnace outside.

Jack ushered me into his office. He put two sheets of fresh writing paper on the desk.

"All right then. Let's see your epistles."

I took out the letters and laid each one down carefully. The deceased rat I kept back. Jack removed a large magnifying glass from the drawer.

"They seem to be written by the same hand. Same style,

pen, and ink. Do you agree?"

"Totally."

"I'll send these to the lab and see if we can lift any fingerprints."

He sandwiched the letters between the clean papers and moved them to one side. He laid two more sheets on the desk.

"Now let's have a look at poor Yorick."

I placed the pencil box on the desk, unfolded the newspaper, and slid off the lid.

"I put it in here, but it came untrammelled."

Jack jumped back. "Whew. I'd know that particular stink anywhere."

Holding his breath, he used the glass to examine the rat.

"It's hard to know what killed it exactly or how long it's been dead. In this heat it would deteriorate very quickly. I doubt it was hard to find a dead rat in certain areas of this city. Or, for that matter, a live rat that was deliberately killed."

He straightened up. I thought he had an odd expression on his face.

"It became quite a sport, killing rats. We'd take bets on how many we could dispatch in one go. One of the men adopted a little lost terrier. Great dog. We named it Flash. It could kill two dozen rats in fifteen minutes. It wasn't difficult. They were so fat with gorging themselves, they couldn't run fast."

For a second, I didn't know what the heck he was

talking about, then I realized he was referring to his experience in the trenches.

I wasn't sure how to respond, so I just made a sympathetic murmuring noise. It had been almost eighteen years since the war had ended, and I constantly encountered evidence of its continuing aftermath. And now all the signs seemed to indicate we might be heading for another war. It was unbearable to think about.

Jack rewrapped the box.

"I'll put a rush on these. I hope we can have some results immediately."

I took the bull by the horns. "There is no reason that I can see why you and I should not co-operate on this case. I'll pass along any pertinent information I get."

He chuckled. "You said that so circumspectly. I take it you will be the one to decide what is pertinent or not?"

"You'll have to trust me."

"And you, me. I might not be able to reciprocate in kind, but I will do my best."

"Okay."

"I plan to drop in at the hospital later on today. I'd like to talk to Mrs. Gilmore, if she's able. Have you been in contact with Mr. Gilmore?"

"He rang this morning. He told me Mrs. Gilmore had still not regained consciousness."

"Does he know about these letters and the rat?"

"No. He called before I got to the office. I think I'll hold off telling him. He's got enough worries on his mind."

"You're probably right." He looked up at me. "You will, of course, notify me if you receive anything else."

"I will indeed."

Jack pushed back his chair. "I'll see you out."

He seemed to have recovered from his sojourn in the past; however, he made me think of the Paradise Café men and the painful memories they still seemed to bump into.

As I exited the cool building, the heat fell upon me like a blanket.

I headed back to the office.

Feeling like an old nag, I was plodding up the stairs to the third floor of the Arcade when I encountered Hilliard Taylor on his way down.

"There you are," he said. To my ears the ordinary phrase carried unnecessary impatience. "I said I'd come over this morning. Did you forget?"

"Of course not." I saw no reason to reveal I had only remembered the instant I saw him on the stairs.

"We probably should talk on the way over to the café. We might not have time otherwise."

We'd halted on the stairs during this conversation, and suddenly he leaned in closer and peered into my face.

"You look bagged. Are you up for coming?"

All of my muscles wanted to say, *No, I'm not*. But he was a client, after all.

"What do you take me for? I certainly am."

He squinted at me. "I'll have to take your word for it rather than the evidence. We'll walk slowly."

So we did, more or less. I am not naturally a stroller, and neither, it seemed, was Hilliard. We proceeded down Yonge Street at a fairly brisk pace.

"I should tell you that the intake money was fiddled with again."

"Darn. How much?"

"Strange thing is, some money has been returned, not taken. First thing this morning I checked. Last night, I made a duplicate of the deposit slip and put it in my desk. When I compared it with the one in the safe, I could see they didn't match. Somebody had changed that one. Five dollars in one-dollar bills have been put back."

"Have you come to any conclusions?"

"None except the obvious. First, it must have happened in the middle of the night when I, at least, was fast asleep. Second, the person fiddling knows the combination to the safe."

"Don't you think it's time to speak to your partners?"

He frowned at me. "Not yet. I couldn't tell who changed the slip. Officially there are just the four of us who know the combination, but you don't have to be Moriarty to notice where we keep it. Anybody coming and going in the café could have seen me get it out of the tea tin."

"From what you've told me, that could only be Mrs. Reilly and Pearl or your baker. Perhaps you could speak to him. If he's coming in the early hours of the morning, he might have run into somebody."

"I don't want to start rumours."

"Did you bring the slips with you?"

"I did. I was intending to show them to you."

"Sorry."

At that point we were trotting around an older couple who were shuffling slowly along. They both looked so hot and uncomfortable, I felt a surge of pity. Where did you go if your own home was like a furnace? As we passed by, the woman suddenly stumbled. The man caught hold of her just in time. Hilliard stepped forward.

"Can I help?"

Neither of them answered, but the man said something to the woman in a language I didn't understand. She shook her head.

"We'll be all right," the man said to Hilliard. He had an accent, Ukrainian perhaps.

"I think you should be out of this heat," said Hilliard. "It's going to get even worse by this afternoon."

The man looked at him through weary, red-rimmed eyes.

"Thank you, sir," he said. "We thought we'd make our way down to the lake."

"It's a bit of a walk."

His wife's head was drooping, and she was so listless I wasn't sure she could stay on her feet.

He didn't need to say they didn't have the money for the streetcar fare. I could see it.

"You know what?" said Hilliard. "I own the Paradise Café on Queen Street. Why don't you come over there? You can have some lunch on me. Great soup, and I can promise you it's cooler." Some time ago the old couple had lost whatever pride they'd once had. The man translated what Hilliard had said to his wife. She lifted her head. She faced Hilliard and said something in her own language. It was clear she was saying thank you.

"We thank you, sir," the man said. "God bless you. We do accept."

"Good," responded Hilliard briskly. "We'll go on ahead then. Keep walking along Queen Street. You can't miss it. The Paradise."

Hill and I continued on in silence, leaving them to follow.

"That was kind of you, Mr. Taylor."

He shook his head. "Nobody should have to suffer like that. Surely at their age they have a right to some peace of mind. We should be cherishing them, not treating them like mouldy potatoes to be tossed out at the earliest opportunity."

It was a rather odd expression, but I understood his feelings. Thank God I had been able to take care of Gran and Gramps.

We were approaching the café when Hill paused. "I suppose having the money returned is preferable to having it stolen, except that I can't leave it like this. I need to know what's going on."

"I can understand that."

"Are you all right to continue our arrangement for the time being? Mrs. Reilly is due back next week. We could take stock then."

"Of course. I enjoyed myself."

This was true. I could survive a few more days of heavy lifting, never mind the ice maiden who wanted me out of the way.

There was a lineup already, and most of them recognized Hill and called out a greeting. "We're getting fried out here! Hurry up."

"Give me five minutes," said Hill. He and I went to the side door, where I'd entered yesterday.

He sniffed. "Cabbage soup today. Not my favourite, I must admit. Brings back too many bad memories." He didn't elaborate, and we went through to the kitchen where Eric was at his familiar post over the stove, stirring the soup in a large pot. Pearl was waiting beside him. She greeted me with an astonishingly powerful scowl.

"There you are. I was starting to think you'd jumped ship. We've got two minutes, and the tables aren't even set yet."

"I'll get to it." I put my hat on the hook, slipped on the apron, and took down the money pouch.

"Where're the others?" Hill asked Eric.

"Conal's writing up the menu. Wilf said he'd be back shortly. He's nailing up some posters about the chess tournament." He nodded over at me. "Good morning, Miss Frayne."

I took the tray of cutlery from the counter and went into the dining room. Hilliard was behind me.

"Don't let Pearl bother you," he said. "She's protective of her environment."

"Is that what it is?"

Conal was working on the blackboard. Soup of the day was indeed cabbage, and he'd drawn a cabbage with human features beside the line. It was beaming — presumably at the thought of providing sustenance to hungry people. He gave me a shy smile but didn't stop what he was doing. He was as close to the board as he could get. Even with his glasses, he appeared to be very short-sighted.

"Hey, Hill," he called out. "What's the dessert choice today? I forgot what Eric said."

"Ginger pudding, Bakewell tart, or dates and custard."

Conal wrote it on the board, adding some cheery-faced fruits. I hurried to put the cutlery on the tables. Again with the down-to-basics approach, the spoons, knives, and forks were all in separate jars ready for the customers to help themselves.

It was true what Hilliard had said earlier. With the two whirling fans and the shades down, the temperature in the café was quite pleasant. The sticky flytraps flapped in the breeze from the fans, and I, too, could have done without the cabbage smell — but it was definitely preferable to trudging the hot pavement looking for some relief.

Pearl poked her head through the door.

"Are you ready?"

"Ready as we'll ever be," Hilliard answered.

He went to unlock the door.

EACH SITTING WAS packed, and because the customers were reluctant to leave and go out into the heat, things dragged. The couple Hilliard and I had encountered did accept his kind invitation; they came in time for the first sitting. I was pleased to see the gusto with which they ate. I thought they were lonely as well as hungry. They both chose Bakewell tarts for their desserts and ate them very slowly and with great satisfaction.

Three men, all nicely dressed, arrived about noon just as the sitting was changing. They went directly to the back door that required such a strange code to enter. This time I made sure I could see who was on the other side; it was indeed Conal Pierce. Nobody re-emerged, so either there was a second exit or they were having a long meeting.

After two hours, I was more than ready to sit down. I did so when the last customer was ushered out. As he'd done before, Hilliard took the money that Pearl and I had collected and deposited it in the till.

"The Bakewell tarts were popular," he said. "All of them went. I'd better warn Eric and see if he has time to whip up something else for the dinner sittings."

"I'll be off then," I said. "See you later on."

"Or thereabouts," added Pearl, just low enough that I could hear but not the other two men.

I checked my impulse to dump a jug of cold water over her pointy little head and left.

I wanted to go straight home and have a nap, but first

I needed to go to the office and see if there were any messages. Or private posts.

I'D HARDLY SAT down at my desk, kicked off my shoes, and peeled off my stockings when the telephone rang. It was Mr. Gilmore.

"Miss Frayne. I have to tell you. Ida died this morning."

Chapter Sixteen

It was a message I'd been half expecting, but still I was stunned.

"Mr. Gilmore, I'm so sorry."

"Except for the one time, she did not recover consciousness." He halted. "I think the police are going to charge me with homicide."

"Mr. Gilmore. You must tell them about the letter you received. It might be related to the attack."

"Possibly you are right, Miss Frayne. Would you be able to bring it here?"

"Of course. I'll come right away."

I heard a male voice in the background.

"Oh my God, I believe they're here. Miss Frayne, will you contact my solicitor? His name is Geoffrey Grier. He'll be in the files."

I heard the voice again, then the line went dead.

I immediately rang the hospital. The receptionist wasn't the same woman I'd talked to before. This one was frosty and formal. I asked if I could speak to Mr. Gilmore. She said she had no way to contact him, as he wasn't a patient.

I said that his wife had just died, something she refused to confirm. It was against hospital policy.

I wanted to yell over the phone, "Where is your humanity?" But I knew that was unfair and I was being irrational. I hung up and went to the filing cabinet to see if indeed we had Mr. Grier's number.

We did. Mr. Gilmore had recommended him to a divorcing couple who were engaging in a world war about who got what. I hadn't met him personally, but he had seemed very competent.

He himself answered my ring right away. I explained why I was calling, my words tumbling out. He listened, not saying much one way or another. I filled him in about the first letter, the charming notes I myself had received, and the dead rat.

"And the police have these?"

"The ones that I received. Not the one sent to Mr. Gilmore. The detective is having some tests run on them for fingerprints. Surely this has something to do with the crime? It can't be a coincidence."

"That's up to the police to decide. It's not my job. I simply need to know on what grounds they're holding Gilmore."

"He said they're going to charge him with the murder of his wife."

"I realize that, but that's the charge, not the grounds." He made a sort of clicking noise with his teeth.

I thought he could have used a little training in customer relations. A better jail side manner, as it were.

"More than likely they've taken him to headquarters until he has a bail hearing."

"I was just about to go there myself and hand over the first letter to the detective in charge."

"What is his name?"

"Murdoch. Detective Jack Murdoch."

"Thank you, Miss Frayne. I shall make a call."

His voice remained cool, uninvolved.

Before he could hang up, I yelled into the phone, "Wait! You will keep me informed, I hope."

"If you wish."

"I wish."

We hung up. I sat for a moment, face turned up to the fan, trying to cool off. Mr. Gilmore and I maintained a formal relationship, but I was very fond of him. I respected him a lot. He worked hard and conscientiously, charged a fair fee, and was universally decent and kind to the troubled people who came to us for help. I was inclined to be more judgmental. Now he was in need, and I wanted to make sure I did the very best I could to help him.

I took the letter that he had received out of my desk drawer and put it carefully into an envelope. I was about to set off for police headquarters when the telephone rang again. This time it was my grandfather.

He had never gotten accustomed to using the phone, and he deemed it necessary, seeing that I was so far away, to shout into the receiver.

"Hello. Hello. Charlotte. Is that you?"

"Gramps, it's okay. I can hear you perfectly well if you speak in a normal voice."

"Oh. Right. Good." He was still too loud. "I just wanted to let you know that Bertha and I are going on a little excursion. I didn't want you to worry if you did happen to get home early and I wasn't here."

"Where are you going?"

"Not far. The city is running special streetcars to take people out to Sunnyside. Half fare. We can have dinner in the Pavilion and take the last car back."

He sounded like boy with a mix of guilt and excitement in his voice.

I tried to be grown up.

"That sounds like it could be fun, Gramps. Should be cooler, anyway."

"Hope so. I've had enough of this weather. They're forecasting it'll continue through the weekend. Are you all right at your end? You seemed quite frazzled yesterday."

"I'm fine, Gramps."

"Good." He paused, and this time his voice dropped to normal levels. "Listen, Lottie, I know you're not too fond of Bertha. But you'll like her when you get to know her better. She really wants you both to be friends."

"Does she?"

He was definitely talking as if his intentions, at least, were serious.

"Give her a chance, Lottie. For my sake."

There was no other possible reply. "Of course, Gramps.

I want you to be happy."

His voice boomed again. "I am. I haven't felt this good since I met your grandma."

"I'll probably see you in the morning, then. Enjoy your excursion."

I probably don't have to spell out what I was feeling.

Mary had a little lamb
Its heart was filled with grief.
And every time that Mary left,
That lamb, it gnashed its teeth.

Chapter Seventeen

CONSTABLE EVANS, THE receptionist, was as disinterested as he had been the first time we got acquainted. He could barely break off what I presumed was a vital typing practice for the world cup. I asked for Detective Murdoch, and he rang through to him. Jack came promptly and greeted me in a friendly manner that was reassuring.

I could hardly wait until we were in his office. I sat down, trying to exert some control over my tumultuous thoughts so they didn't pour out unedited.

"I presume you already know that Mrs. Gilmore has died?"

"Yes. I received the call not too long ago."

"Mr. Gilmore says that he's to be charged with homicide."

"Yes. Detective Arcady is leading the case. He was at the hospital. He has been convinced from the beginning that Mr. Gilmore was responsible."

"And you?"

"I am still not convinced."

"Will I be able to talk to Mr. Gilmore?"

"I don't see why not. He was brought over here immediately. He is in the cells."

"There is something I must show you. Mr. Gilmore also received an anonymous letter. It came yesterday morning. I didn't mention it before because he asked me not to."

"Why was that?"

"It's anti-Semitic, and Mr. Gilmore is not admitting to being Jewish. I don't think he wanted to shine a light on that."

Jack sighed. "I hate to think that sort of discrimination is happening in this city, but I'm afraid it is. We can't rule it out as a possible motive in the attack on Mrs. Gilmore."

"I realize that now. I'm sorry I didn't show you the letter sooner, but I was respecting Mr. Gilmore's wishes."

"I understand." His expression was kind. He didn't reproach me for holding back on evidence — which he had a right to do.

"Have you brought the letter with you?"

I took the envelope out of my handbag and gave it to him. He slid out the original letter carefully.

"At first glance it does look like it's from the same perpetrator as the ones you received. We'll do a finger-print check to see."

"Any result from the tests?"

"Nothing at all, I'm afraid. The paper doesn't hold prints well, so there was nothing we could use. The stain was tea. The rat showed no signs of poison; it died from a broken neck. Caught in a trap. Could have been anywhere. By the way, it was female and was carrying babies."

I can't say I was particularly fond of rats, but somehow that seemed like a pity.

"We have examined the candelabra and managed to lift a couple of thumbprints. They will no doubt belong to Mr. Gilmore, but as it was a household item that proves nothing. Now that there is a homicide charge, we will have to return to the house and do a more thorough examination." He tapped the envelope that had contained the anonymous letter. "We cannot discount this or the letters to you." He looked at me. "You seem like a sensible person, Miss Frayne. I don't need to worry about your safety, do I?"

"I think I can take care of myself."

For a moment I felt a twinge of fear. I hoped that was true.

Jack got to his feet. "Let me take you downstairs."

He led the way out to the main foyer. Evans was typing like a madman; otherwise, the area was quiet.

"This way," said Jack.

The way to the cells seemed like a throwback to an earlier time. Not when attention was paid to the comfort of wealthy young men, but the time when criminals were universally despised no matter what they'd done.

The stairs were uncarpeted and the electric light dimmed.

Jack opened a door at the bottom; it led into a small hallway. It was completely bare except for a desk at the far end in front of another door. This was metal and had bars halfway up. At the desk was seated a young, fresh-faced constable who jumped to his feet, military fashion, as soon as we came in.

"At ease, Constable Curnoe," said Jack, also military style. "This lady is here to have a word with Thaddeus Gilmore. I believe he's just been brought in?"

"Yes, sir. He's in the second cell on the right."

"Good. Let us through then, if you will."

The constable took a large key that was attached to a long chain on his belt and unlocked the door.

Jack went through first and, as if a switch had been pressed, we were immediately assailed by the sound of a very drunken and most tuneless rendition of an old army song. Soldier version.

"It's a long way to tickle Mary, It's a long way to go."

The singer was in the first cell. He was dishevelled, unshaven, and dirty. He was gripping the bars of the cell, but it looked like more for support than a yearning for freedom. When he saw us, he stopped in mid-throttle and said, "Hello, folks. Spare a dime for an old soldier fallen on hard times?"

The drunk was by no means an attractive figure, but he wasn't really that old. Certainly young enough to have served in the war. There were many such men on the streets, scrounging food or money, dodging the police when they could. He didn't seem to realize he was in jail and probably put there for illegal soliciting.

"Tell you what," said Jack. "If you promise to be quiet for a while, I'll ask the constable to bring you a cup of tea. You must be parched from all that singing."

The man touched his finger to his greasy cap.

"Much appreciated, sir. I am indeed."

With that, he stepped away from the bars and collapsed onto his cot. He lay back and was almost instantaneously asleep, though not before releasing a series of putrid-smelling farts that threatened to blister the whitewash on the walls. Neither Jack nor I could stop our involuntary response. We fanned ourselves vigorously.

The holding jail accommodated six prisoners. I could see somebody lying on the cot in the far cell; he might as well have been dead for all the interest he showed in us.

Jack moved to Mr. Gilmore's cell. He was sitting on the single cot, his head bent to his chest. For a moment, I thought he might even be asleep, but he looked up at once.

"Miss Frayne. Thank you for coming. And you, detective, for giving permission."

"I'm going to allow you a little privacy," Jack said. "I'll be on the other side of the door. Constable Curnoe, if you please."

The constable had followed us in and locked the connecting door behind him. He immediately stepped forward and let Jack through.

Mr. Gilmore waited until that was concluded, then got up stiffly and moved closer to the bars. Only a couple of feet, I might add. The cell was not much bigger than a closet.

He nodded over his shoulder in the direction of the drunk.

"Thank the Lord you shut him up. He has been going non-stop for the past hour. I might not object, except he seems to know only one song, which he repeats over and over."

Mr. Gilmore looked terrible. Red-rimmed eyes, grey stubble on his chin, uncombed hair. His suit was rumpled. Where was the immaculate boss I knew?

"I am dreadfully sorry about your wife, Mr. Gilmore."

"And I, Miss Frayne. And I. But at the moment, I tell you frankly my mind seems to be focussed on finding the culprit. Not only to save my own skin, but because the very least Ida deserves is that her killer be brought to justice."

He was speaking quietly, his intensity unmistakable. Out of the corner of my eye, I could see that Jack Murdoch was himself speaking softly to the constable on the other side of the barred door. Even though he was engaged, I had the feeling he was completely aware of what was transpiring between Mr. Gilmore and me.

"Did you get hold of Grier?"

"I did. He said he's coming here right away."

"Good." He leaned in closer. "Obviously I am in no position to investigate the crime for which I am charged. I have to rely on you completely."

"I have to ask you, sir. On what grounds have the police laid this charge?"

"They haven't yet told me. They just say they have sufficient evidence to do so." His eyes filled with tears. "Ida had a very difficult early life. She didn't grow up here. She was born in Poland. Very turbulent times for many people. She witnessed things no child should ever have to witness. She sometimes relived those early years. I wish I could have made things easier for her. I couldn't."

"Was she under a doctor's care?"

He blinked at me. "A doctor? Oh, no. She would have none of that. We just waited it out. The bouts would come and go."

I hesitated, trying to find the best way to broach the subject I needed to broach.

"So far the police haven't been able to pin down the exact time of the attack. You left the house at seven-thirty; Mrs. Kaufmann found Ida shortly after nine. That gives us a window of opportunity of about an hour and a half."

He looked at me. I thought it was a wary look.

I took a breath, although I must admit I didn't inhale too deeply given the singer's copious output of foul air.

"Mr. Gilmore. You said that after you left the office, which was about eight-thirty, you went to the Paradise Café and had a coffee."

"That's right."

"They don't seem to remember whether you were there or not."

To my surprise, he actually chuckled. "What did they say?"

"They were very vague. Maybe yes, maybe no."

"Miss Frayne, I would like you to take them a message from me." He leaned forward so he could see Jack Murdoch. His voice dropped even lower. "Tell Conal, I said, 'We have a glowing dream.'"

"Really! What is that supposed to mean?"

"That doesn't matter. Conal will know that it comes from me. Please tell him that I do need his confirmation of my presence at the café." He held up his hand. "I know what you are going to say, Miss Frayne. If I am in need of an alibi for that crucial period of time, why don't I have Conal go to the police?"

"And why don't you?"

"If things get desperate enough I will, but if it's not necessary I prefer to keep it to ourselves. This is for your reassurance only. I have been touched by your loyalty, but it is better if you have something a little more definite to hold on to."

He gave me a woebegone smile. I had to jump in.

"Mr. Gilmore, when I was looking for your address I came across the deed poll whereby you changed your name.

"Did you indeed?"

"From Goldenberg to Gilmore. We have been dancing around the question of whether or not you are Jewish. I assume you are."

He ran his hand through his hair so that it stood up from his head. "My parents were Jews who came to this county to escape a pogrom in Russia. They thought it prudent for us to live a secular life, although I believe it caused them much grief to do so. As a young man I worked as a clerk in a solicitor's office. Good training in the observance of the less gentle ways of the world. When I decided to become a private investigator, I realized that the clientele I could most likely draw on would be, shall we say, reassured if I did not have an obviously Hebrew name. So I changed it to something nice and English. Thaddeus Gilmore is reassuring, wouldn't you say?"

I had to smile at him. "I suppose so. But, Mr. Gilmore, we cannot rule out that the attack on your wife might have been racially motivated. Who else in the neighbourhood would have known you are Jewish?"

He gave a little shrug. "Anybody. Perhaps from Ida herself. When she was in one of her states, she would lose discretion."

I thought he wanted to say more, but at that moment we heard a telephone ringing from the other side of the barred door. Constable Curnoe answered. He said something to Jack, who nodded at him.

Curnoe stood up and unlocked the door with his medieval key. Jack came in.

"Your solicitor has arrived, Mr. Gilmore. I will take you to the consulting room."

Mr. Gilmore reached out to me.

"Miss Frayne, I am forever in your debt."

I placed my hand in his, and his lips brushed my fingers with a delicate, old-world courtesy that wrenched my heart.

Constable Curnoe let him out.

As the door clanged shut, the singer next door sat bolt upright.

"What about that cuppa?" he bellowed. "I'm dying of thirst in here."

Chapter Eighteen

WHEN I GOT to the café, the second sitting was already underway and Pearl was bringing out the bowls of soup. I didn't feel like apologizing; I simply went straight to the kitchen to get my cash pouch and apron. Eric was slathering dripping from the jar onto slices of bread.

"Thank goodness you made it. Tonight everybody wants dripping. Take these baskets out, will you? We're having an oxtail stew with peas for the second course. You'll serve it on plates. When you've done the bread, come back and help me cut up some more celery for the salad."

The last thing I wanted to be doing at the moment was waiting on tables, but there was no way out. I picked up four of the baskets and went back to the dining room. Hilliard was at the cash register. He raised his eyebrows questioningly. I mouthed, "I'll tell you later."

As had been the case yesterday, there was a fairly loud chatter. Mostly men were at the tables, but there was a family at one end. Two ragged boys and a woman, presumably the mother. I put a basket in front of them. The boys looked at the woman, and she nodded permission.

Immediately they each took a slice of bread and began to wipe out their empty soup bowls.

"Say thank you," said the woman.

"Thank you, miss," they said in unison.

The bread vanished so quickly it would have been a credit to any conjuror. The mother was eating more slowly, but I could see it was an effort for her to do so.

I moved on.

During the next hour, four people passed through the café to the rear door. Three men, one woman. She was young and fashionably dressed. Very pretty. Even so, nobody paid her much attention. Neither did she court it. They each went through the same ritual. All very discreet and quiet.

At ten to the hour, Hilliard called out to the customers that it was time to leave. They slowly made their way out, and the lightning-fast cleanup jumped into action. Hilliard managed to whisper to me as he was changing one of the tables, "Are you all right, Miss Frayne?"

I would have liked to pour out my distress, but this was not the time or place. The last group were ushered in and sat down at the tables. I don't know how they'd spent the day, but every one of them looked hot and tired. The smell of sweat permeated the room immediately. Pearl came out with the soup. I got the bread. During the next hour I noticed only one more visitor enter and head straight to the back room. Nobody seemed to have left.

Once this sitting was ushered out, Hilliard locked the door behind them and turned over the "Closed" sign. He plopped down on one of the kitchen chairs and put his head on the table.

"I don't know about all of you, but I am completely and utterly bushed."

Pearl sat across from him, kicking off her shoes as she did so.

"The last shift is getting worse. The pong was awful."

"They probably haven't got anywhere to wash themselves."

Eric came over to the table and joined us. "The stew seemed to go over well, wouldn't you say? I wasn't sure at first."

"I don't think this lot cares what you serve them as long as it's cheap and hearty," said Pearl. There was an edge of contempt in her voice. I noted Eric's reaction.

"I care. Just because they don't have much money doesn't mean I can't give them good food."

She shrugged. "Suit yourself. I'm just saying." She stood up. "I'm off then. I'm going to the pictures tonight." She put her shoes back on.

"What's playing?" I asked, ever friendly.

"Clark Gable in something or other. They're staying open until one o'clock on account of the heat. Nice and cool in there. Of course they get more business, so everybody benefits."

She got her hat from the peg by the door. "See ya tomorrow." She looked over at me. "Will you be in, Miss Frayne?"

"I sure will."

"Suit yourself," she said enigmatically.

There was a silence for a moment after she left, then Eric said, "Shall I kill her now or later?"

Hilliard laughed. "Later. We need her help for a while longer."

"What's wrong with the girl? She's too young to be so cynical." He addressed me. "You seem to have dealt with her very well, Miss Frayne. I don't know how you've done it."

Before I could polish my halo, Conal came in. He looked as sweaty and unwashed as the customers who'd just departed.

"I'm famished, Eric. Any grub left?"

"Shoot, Conal. You should have had some earlier. There's no soup or salad left. All I can give you is some bread and dripping, maybe half a bowl of stew."

"Sounds like manna to me."

He went over to the stove and served himself what was truly half a bowl of stew. Eric watched him in an exasperated way.

"For god's sake. You're making me feel guilty. At least have some of the dates and custard."

"No Bakewell tarts?"

"No. All gone. I keep telling you, if you're not going to be here for the sitting, tell me and I'll put something aside."

"Sorry, Eric. I forgot."

"You'd forget your head if it was loose," Eric responded. "Look at you, you're skin and bones."

"Sorry," muttered Conal. Like the two boys I'd served earlier, he was busy wiping his bowl clean with a piece of bread.

"Reggie's coming in tonight, isn't he?" interceded Hilliard. "Let's have him bake extra loaves. We can always freeze them in the icebox. Here, Con." He reached behind him and took a dish of custard and dates from the lazy Susan and put it in front of the other man. "Do you want some tea?"

"No, thanks. Just a glass of lemonade."

"I'll get it," Hill said, and he went to the icebox. "Would you like one, Miss Frayne?"

"Sounds good."

Conal seemed to notice me for the first time. "Miss Frayne. How are you doing in this madhouse?"

"Very well. Everybody has been most supportive."

"Ha. She's been a real Christian about our little Pearl," said Eric.

Hilliard put the two glasses on the table.

I decided to jump into the lion's den.

"Somebody told me about a good movie. It's called *A Glowing Dream* or something like that."

That certainly got their attention.

"A movie?" said Conal. "What one? I've never heard of a picture called that. Who told you about it?"

"Thaddeus Gilmore did. He said if I repeated those words to you, Mr. Pierce, you'd understand I was of like mind. That's how he put it, anyway. I guess he meant we have the same taste. In movies."

Conal gaped at me. "How do you know him?"

Now what? Hilliard was staring at me. He didn't have to say anything. I could tell the last thing he wanted me to do was reveal our connection.

"When did he say those words to you?" Conal asked.

My bacon was saved by Wilf, who chose that moment to come into the kitchen.

"Listen everybody." He gestured excitedly. "I just ran into Reggie Fox. He's heard that Thaddeus Gilmore's wife has died. Today. The police have charged Gilmore with murder."

"Bloody hell. Poor sod," said Hilliard.

There was a silence. Conal looked over at Hilliard, then at me. He didn't look scattered or vague.

"What's the truth, Miss Frayne? How do you know Thaddeus?"

"I've done some work for him in the past. He told me that his wife had been attacked and that the police suspected him. He said you would be able to provide him with the alibi he desperately needs. Now that she has died, it is even more imperative. He said he was here yesterday morning when the attack happened. He said you, Mr. Pierce, would confirm that. He said he would not tell the police unless he absolutely had to."

Conal didn't answer right away. He looked again at Hilliard. Wilf and Eric were staring at Conal.

I felt a sudden wave of anger sweep over me. I liked

these men well enough, but my loyalty was totally with Mr. Gilmore.

"Why are we tiptoeing around this? A man's life is possibly at stake. I know you have a little secret, pardon me, private room back there. I know you have to have a password to get in. I don't give a damn if you're in there playing hot games of tiddlywinks. I just want you to come with me to the police and confirm that Thaddeus Gilmore was in that bloody room all morning until he went home, so he could not, emphatically not, have killed his wife."

I realized I was shouting.

Conal stood up. "Of course. We can go right now."

"I'll come with you," said Hilliard.

"What are you going to say you were doing?" Wilf asked.

Conal shrugged. "We were doing what we always do, we were having a political discussion. Thaddeus is a member of the club."

I hadn't cooled down yet. "I've never yet heard of a club that is for political discussion that requires a secret password to get into. What else is it?"

Wilf scowled at me. "You don't need to know. Conal will confirm Mr. Gilmore's alibi. As you say, they could have been playing tiddlywinks. It doesn't matter."

"It might matter to the police. What you were doing might have something do with the fact that his wife was murdered. I mean, we are interested in finding the killer, aren't we?"

Conal sat down abruptly. "Surely there is no connection."

Eric spoke up this time. "She's right. They will want to investigate thoroughly. Jack Murdoch is no fool. He's a conscientious officer. Gilmore being a member of the party might have something to do with the attack on his wife."

Another silence. I could hardly contain my exasperation. "What party are you talking about?"

Hilliard took over. "The Communist Party. Conal is a member of the party, as is Thaddeus Gilmore. They meet here on a regular basis."

"Why all the secrecy? That's not illegal anymore."

Conal answered. "Supposedly not, but believe me, we can be harassed at any moment. We are not popular with the government. A strike that is totally justified but that gets out of hand because of police brutality and *wham*, we're all in jail."

He spoke with the fervour of a disciple. I thought about the letter that Mr. Gilmore had received. *Filthy Commie Jew*.

It was true what Conal had said. There were many people in this city, including the chief constable himself, who hated and mistrusted the Communists, whom they saw as determined to bring down the established order. The Communists saw themselves as trying to bring equality to the working classes and relieve the suffering of the unemployed.

"I can't see any reason to hide the truth from the police," I said. "These are high stakes."

"All right. Let's go now, then. No need for poor Gilmore to be in jail a moment longer than he has to."

"I'll stay here," said Wilf. "Eric and I can start on food prep for tomorrow."

I'm not sure what part of me took over next, the investigator or the curious child; regardless, I surprised even myself by saying, "Before we go, can I have a look at this mysterious room? I do know the password, after all."

Conal regarded me with some suspicion. "There aren't any guns or explosives stashed away, if that's what you're thinking."

"Of course not. But let's put it this way. The police are sure to want to have a look, especially if they feel the room is in any way connected with the attack. Better to be prepared."

"Good idea, Miss Frayne," said Hilliard. "Show her, Conal, and then let's get going."

THE ROOM WAS small, windowless, and tidy. Chairs were lined up around the perimeter. Perhaps a dozen or so. A school desk was on the far side. It looked like a proper church meeting room. But there were no crosses on the wall, just a photograph of a field of corn, the significance of which escaped me. This was hanging above the desk. I went over to have a closer look at it. Conal followed behind. While I was studying the enigmatic picture, he picked up a wooden box that was on the desk and slipped it into a drawer. He did this so quickly that I might not have seen him, except that the photograph was in a glass frame. Not only did I see Conal's reflection, I had already taken note of the box. There was a label on one side, but he moved it too quickly for me to see it. Obviously it was significant.

I'm not an investigator for nothing.

I pointed at the cornfield. "Nice photograph. Did you take it?"

He regarded me in a blank sort of way, almost as if he didn't understand the question. There was definitely something a bit off about Conal, but there was also something that drew out softer feelings from me. He certainly had the perpetual air of a beaten or defeated dog. Or horse, for that matter.

"What? Oh, no. That's Eric's. He's got a thing about grain and bread. Loves making it, serving it. I believe he snapped that when he was visiting Alberta."

"I'm surprised he lets you put it in here and not the dining room."

Conal looked over at the photograph. "Bread is the staff of life, isn't it?" He gave me a painful smile. "We thought about it often enough when we were in the camp. Fresh crusty bread, dripping with golden butter and homemade strawberry jam. Red as blood itself. That was Eric's favourite memory. His mother used to serve it for their afternoon tea. She's dead now. She passed away before he came back. I believe that's why he prefers the picture to be in here."

The door opened, and Hilliard came in.

"Ready to go, Miss Frayne? You've seen the room. Nothing scary about it, right? Just a place to talk."

"That's what it looks like for sure."

Conal had already begun to drift toward the door.

"All right, Con?"

"All right, Hill. Miss Frayne asked about the photograph, and I was telling her about Eric and his bread."

Hilliard glanced over at the picture. "Maybe he'll hang it in the café one of these days. It's a damn good photo." He reached over and put his arm around Conal's shoulders. "You look tired, my man. Let's get this over with, and then you should get yourself to an early bed."

"Sounds good."

Chapter Nineteen

It was after nine by the time we arrived at the police station. Jack Murdoch had already left, but Detective Arcady was still there. The receptionist, not a typing champion in training this time, was polite. He sent for Detective Arcady, who came out in a desultory fashion.

"Come this way."

The three of us followed him into the same hallway I had followed Jack Murdoch through the day before. Arcady's office was adjacent. The two spaces were no doubt identical, so there was no rational reason to feel that Murdoch's office was pleasant as well as businesslike but that Arcady's was not at all. Neither pleasant nor businesslike. His desk was piled with newspapers, and the two available chairs likewise. He took a pile from one chair, shoved it onto the floor, and gestured to me, the lone female, to have a seat. He gave no indication that he recognized me from the day before. Hilliard cleared a place on the other chair for Conal, and he himself stood by the door.

As I sat down, I noticed that there was a photograph on a single shelf behind Arcady. The frame was jet. Next to it was a black vase in which stood two red paper poppies.

The stems were bent, and the flowers looked dusty. I glimpsed a young woman in a war nurse's uniform in the picture. Who was she? A sister? A sweetheart? I had no chance to find out, but the indication of loss might explain why the detective seemed so sour and grey.

"What can I do for you?"

Hilliard spoke. "We understand you are detaining Thaddeus Gilmore on the charge of murdering his wife. We both wish to testify that he was present at our café yesterday morning from eight-forty until nine-thirty."

I threw in my two cents. "He was with me at the office from eight o'clock until twenty-five past. I understand that Mrs. Gilmore was found shortly after nine."

Arcady's lips twitched. "My, my. You're full of understanding, aren't you, dearie. In other words, you wish to provide him with an alibi. If in fact that is the time period in question."

"That's right. Detective Murdoch spoke to us yesterday, and it was that particular time that he was concerned about."

"Was he indeed?"

Arcady didn't look too pleased, and I wondered if there was rivalry between the two detectives. I couldn't imagine it would come from Jack.

He nodded in my direction. "And you, madam, what do you understand? Were you present in the café when Gilmore was presumably enjoying a morning cup of coffee? Which the gentleman here seems to have suddenly remembered."

Even with the red poppies drooping over Arcady's shoulder, I found it hard to feel anything but annoyance. I dearly wished we were talking to Jack Murdoch.

"I work for Mr. Gilmore. When I arrived at the office at eight o'clock, he was there. As I said, he left at about twenty-five past the hour."

I glanced over at Conal, but he didn't seem startled at my admission. I suppose I'd convinced them I was essentially moonlighting as a waitress.

Arcady opened a drawer in his desk and fished around, finally taking out some sheets of paper.

"I'll have to get a sworn statement from each of you. You can write it out, then I'll get the commissioner to come and administer the oath. I presume you are all Christian and prepared to swear on the Bible. Mr. Pierce, what will bind your conscience, or dare I ask? The Communist Manifesto, perhaps?"

So they knew. The police knew. Arcady's tone was harassing. No wonder Conal and the others had been so evasive when Jack had come to talk to them.

Conal straightened up. "I will affirm on any book you so desire. What I have to say is true."

Arcady handed us each a sheet of paper. "Write out that you were with Thaddeus Gilmore from such and such a time to such and such a time. Constantly. If you had to leave his sight, toilet break, stroll around the block. Doesn't matter. Even if it was for only a minute, say so. Make a note. Sign it at the bottom."

He leaned over and pressed a switch on the intercom on his desk.

The receptionist answered promptly.

"Carter. What time is Judge St. James due in?"

"Nine-thirty tomorrow, sir."

"Thanks."

Arcady disconnected. "You'll have to come back tomorrow to be sworn."

Hilliard spoke. "Does that mean Mr. Gilmore won't be released until then?"

"Good heavens, man. Of course he won't be released until he's appeared before the judge. Surely you didn't think you could just walk in here, say we the police have made a mistake, expect an apology, and, Bob's your uncle, out walks your pal, a free man."

Hilliard refused to rise to the bait. His voice was quiet.

"I suppose we might have expected some sort of justice like that. You have made our error abundantly clear. We will come back tomorrow. Conal, let's go."

Conal finished writing his deposition and signed the paper. He had to lean close in to write, and his hand was shaky. Hilliard was beside him, and he squeezed his arm.

"Well done."

He sounded like a benevolent teacher encouraging a struggling pupil, or a father helping his son.

Arcady collected our sheets and put them in a folder. He frowned at Conal.

"By the way, that's quite a long time for Gilmore to be

sitting in the café. What were you doing?"

"Doing? Nothing much. Just talking."

"Was anybody else present? Anybody who can verify your statement?"

"A few people." Conal's tone was wary.

Arcady pushed another sheet of paper toward him.

"Jot down their names."

Hilliard intervened. "Conal is speaking for himself. What more do you need?"

"More the merrier," said Arcady. "We'll need to question them."

Conal shrank. "I don't know their names. They're customers."

"And after all this time, you don't say, 'Hi, Bill, hello, John, good morning, Mary'?"

"No."

"Pity. I'd think it was good public relations to know your customers by name." Arcady pursed his thin lips. I could see he was enjoying himself.

Hilliard tugged on Conal's arm. "Let's go."

I stood up as well. "Can we see Mr. Gilmore?"

"Not at this hour, you can't."

I deliberately shifted my gaze to the photograph on the shelf. So full of pathos. Arcady could see what I was looking at, and I was certain he got the message I wanted to convey. If so, he didn't soften at all. If anything, his face became even stonier.

"No matter what you three say, I'm not convinced we

have the wrong man. This investigation is far from over." He waved his hand. "Check out with the constable at reception before you go."

He made no attempt to usher us out.

Chapter Twenty

THE BIG DOOR closed behind us.

"Why are there always men who want to be yahoos, no matter what side of the law they stand on?" Hilliard muttered.

"I have no answer to that," I said, and he smiled.

"Pity. So, Conal, off you go. Straight to bed. We'll sort all this out."

"I will. Good night, Miss Frayne."

If I could, I would have scooped him up in my arms and soothed him. What was it about the man? He was probably older than I was, but he appeared so much like a young child. What the heck had happened to him in his life? I couldn't help but think of the disturbing painting he'd showed us.

Hilliard took me by the elbow. "I'll see you home."

I was happy about that. The warm night air wrapped around us; without the punishing sun, it was fairly pleasant walking. More people were out and about, spirits lifted by a short reprieve from the heat. It was almost like a normal summer night.

"I get the feeling Conal is mentally fragile," I said to Hilliard as we walked. "Is that true?"

"I suppose so."

Hilliard didn't seem to want to expand on this statement, but he was the one hiring me to delve into shady doings at his own café. Some more background information might prove to be helpful.

I persisted. "Left over from the war?"

"Yes."

"What happened?"

We'd walked on a little further before he answered.

"A lot of things. First off, he was gassed just as he was being taken prisoner. If his eyes had been treated properly, he might have been all right, but the Krauts weren't in the mood to mollycoddle the enemy. Nobody looked after him. Left him almost blind. He had shown signs of being a talented artist, but that was before he was so rash as to sign up. No chance after that."

"I don't know if I agree with you. The painting I saw was very impressive."

Hilliard actually stopped in his tracks. "When do you think he did that?"

"I don't know. A couple of days ago?"

"No. He painted it first eighteen years ago. Right after we were released. He's been touching it up ever since."

"And he hasn't done a new painting since then?"

"He paints them, all right, but he can't get his colours

right, or his figures, so as soon as they are finished, he destroys them. Then he goes back to fiddling with his original painting."

Hilliard hadn't moved while we were speaking, but abruptly he started up again. He jumped forward so quickly that for a minute I thought he was going to walk on ahead by himself. I trotted after him.

"It seemed so specific. The man slumped on the post. Does that painting depict something that actually happened?"

"Yes."

We turned onto Yonge Street. There were more people, and it appeared that many of the shops were staying open to take advantage of the prospective customers. I was getting the hang of this strange rhythm with Hilliard. I wouldn't push him. I'd just keep talking and walking. However, this silence was going on for a long time. I was just about to prompt him when he said, "Tell you what. Why don't we sit on one of the benches over there and I'll tell you the whole story."

The bench was set slightly back from the street, not private at all really, but, with the typical anonymity of a big city, we were able to talk as quietly as if we were in the middle of a prairie. Passersby didn't give us a second glance. That said, I was glad of the covering darkness. I didn't want anybody to see that, as Hilliard went on talking, I wept. So did he.

"The four of us weren't in the same regiment, but we were captured at the same time, and we met up when we found ourselves jammed into some kind of railway car that was normally used for cattle. There was dried excrement on the floor, hardly any air or light."

He stopped, and in a gesture that was rapidly becoming familiar he began to pat at his jacket pocket.

"Do you mind if I smoke, Miss Frayne?"

"Not at all. And please do call me Charlotte."

I hoped that by bringing in some informality, he would find it easier to relax. Right now, he appeared tense in a way I hadn't seen before. He fussed with his pipe and tobacco, then continued.

"There were too many of us to sit down properly. We were wedged together in an upright position. Somebody figured out we could help each other if every second man knelt on one knee and made a bridge with his other. This his neighbour could then sit on for a few minutes. An old manoeuvre we learned from amateur boxing."

He didn't say he was the organizer with this clever tactic, but I guessed he was.

"We turned and turned about. The stronger ones held up the less strong. I don't know how long we travelled in that manner, but ..."

He didn't finish his sentence. He didn't need to. I couldn't help it — I reached over and squeezed his hand. He looked surprised, as if he wasn't used to being the one comforted.

"It must have been hell," I said.

"Hell? Is there a worse place than hell? If so, I'd say it is being in that stinking cattle car for all eternity. A man actually died in the car I was in. He simply collapsed. Nothing we could do until the train stopped. Those closest had to hold up the corpse for God knows how long. Somebody started to sing a hymn. A few joined in, but mostly we'd lost the energy even for that."

Hilliard actually shuddered, rather like a dog shaking off water.

"I happened to be jammed beside Wilf Morrow, and it turned out we knew each other from training camp. I hadn't met Eric or Conal before, but they were both shoved against us."

He drew on his pipe and flashed me a wry smile. "I suppose being like that for an interminable length of time creates a certain intimacy. Eric, who was quite religious at that time, later described it as a rope that God had thrown down. 'You, you, you, and you. Gotcha.' We were all in the same circle, like we had been caught by a lariat. We talked to each other because we had to. We hit it off. Not sure why, we're very different in personality and background. But when we were finally let out of the cattle car we kept together. Nobody wanted to let the others out of their sight. We managed to get assigned to the same hut in Doberitz."

His pipe was fading, and I waited for him to go through all the rituals: poking at the bowl, relighting the tobacco. When he was done, I said, "How long were you in the camp?"

"We were captured at Passchendaele in late seventeen,

and we were in Doberitz until the Armistice in November of eighteen. As the war progressed, we got less and less to eat. The Kraut guards weren't exactly living in the lap of luxury, and they saw no reason to treat us better than their own lower ranks."

He puffed at his pipe.

I focussed on the few people walking past us. A well-dressed woman with a small white dog; two young lovers gripping hands tightly in case the wind of reality swept one of them away.

Hilliard continued. His voice seemed to have dropped lower.

"Hunger, severe hunger, makes you desperate. After a while, when you are in fact starving to death, you lose interest in food, your joints hurt. You have a bellyache all the time as your own stomach acid starts eating at you. In the last few months of the imprisonment, we didn't do much work. The Krauts knew they were losing the war. That made some of them even more savage than usual, but others became more neutral. Who knew if they'd need us as friends before too long? We spent long hours lying on our bunks talking about food. What we'd loved. What we'd eat, if we could. We'd end every sentence with the words 'If I could have that right now, I'd think I was in Paradise.' It became our mantra."

"And that eventually led to the café?"

"It certainly did."

"What was your favourite food?"

"I grew up on a farm just outside of Sudbury. My mother was an excellent cook, and we had plenty of fresh vegetables and fruits to eat. But when it comes down to it, what I thought about all the time when I was a prisoner of war was the fresh whipped cream."

He contemplated the bowl of his pipe as if it could provide solace.

I waited. I liked the occasional dollop of cream when I could get it, but it wouldn't be at the top of my list of favourite foods.

Hilliard took the plunge and jumped back into his memories. They were certainly happier than the others, and he began to smile as he related them to me.

"We raised dairy cattle, over a dozen Guernseys. There were three of us kids. I'm the oldest. I've got two younger sisters. We all had our daily chores to do. I'd muck out the stalls, and my sisters, when they were old enough to pull on a teat — which requires strong hands, by the way — would help my mother with the milking. If we'd done a good job, and only if, my mother would give us each a dish of fresh cream. Thick and yellowish. Add a little sugar, just a pinch, and you have … paradise."

I made "yum, yum" noises, although it was certainly not an experience that I'd ever had in my urban upbringing.

"In the summer, we'd put fresh cream on top of the strawberries we'd just picked. They were still sun-warm, red, and luscious. When you bit into them you got a mouthful of sweetness. God alone made that treat."

He stopped to draw some more on the pipe. I wondered if God liked tobacco as well.

"We got cream throughout the winter, of course, and my mother would boil up some potatoes, all grown in her garden at the back of the house, mash them up with a bit of salt to taste, then put some cream on each serving. I'm practically salivating as I think about it."

Me, too.

"We'd add cream to a lot of things."

"Even pork chops?"

He snorted with laughter. "Especially pork chops. You've never tasted real pork chops until you've had them fried up in homemade lard then slipped onto the plate among the peas, served with a topping of fresh cream."

An indecisive breeze had come up. A young man on a butcher's bike with bedding in the front basket rode past us, presumably on his way to the lake. I didn't really want to interrupt Hilliard's bucolic reveries, but I was dead tired and I wanted to get home. I thought it was time to bring him back to his tale of life in the prisoner of war camp.

"Sorry, I think I diverted you," I said. "You were telling me about your experience with your current partners when you were incarcerated. You were all virtually starving."

"We had no idea what was happening in the world. The camp was closed off. You have no idea how desperate men can scrounge bits of information. Some of the men spoke German quite well, and they overheard the guards talking to each other. The general sense was that the Axis powers were losing. But we had been prisoners of war for almost a year. By October we were all giving up hope. The food parcels from the Red Cross were getting more and more scarce. Later we discovered one in three were being pilfered."

He halted. I felt we were coming to the nub of his story.

"Then one day, at the beginning of November, there was a huge ruckus. The Krauts came bursting into the hut. Somebody had stolen food, two oranges no less, from the commandant's store. *Verboten*. We had plenty of food. What were we? Petty criminals? The culprit must be found immediately. If he did not confess or if he was not handed over within twenty-four hours, the entire camp would be punished. Bread and water only for four days. If he was not identified by then, the punishment would be repeated."

Hilliard said all this with a convincing German accent. A man walking past glanced over at us curiously.

"When we'd arrived at the camp, we had elected spokesmen according to protocol. I was the one from our hut. I tried to protest, but that was a joke. I got slammed in the face for my pains. It was a case of turn in the culprit or nothing. Oh no, they would not execute him even if he deserved it. He would be treated fairly. Punished only according to the martial law."

I could see Hilliard was fighting for control. Even after all this time, it was obvious the affair still grieved him.

"Fairly! What a farce that was. Fairness, if it had ever existed in that hellhole, had disappeared a long time ago.

The guards stomped off yelling, 'Twenty-four hours! That's it.' … There were fifty men jammed into our hut. We knew who had stolen the oranges. It was Billy Mosely, a young fellow originally from England. He'd immigrated to Toronto from London's East End just before the war broke out. He'd signed up right away, survived, but like us was taken prisoner at Passchendaele. He was incredibly light-fingered. Said it came from growing up in the slums. He was always sneaking in hunks of bread, a carrot, a potato. He always shared his prize, and usually the guards didn't notice what had been taken. The bread was frequently mouldy anyway."

Hilliard pursed his lips as if the taste still lingered in his mouth.

"Billy was the one who devised the system of cutting up our daily loaf. One small loaf to be divided among three men. He showed us how to do it fairly. There's that word again. But this time it's true. One man measured out the loaf into three portions while the other two turned their backs. Then without looking they would call out which slice they wanted. The one on the right. In the middle. The one on the left. Kept things scrupulously fair.

"But stealing oranges. That was suicidal. We all knew how carefully fruit like that was counted. It was for the commandant only. He was a *schwein* named Neimeyer. Even his men hated him. Not enough to rebel, alas, but we could see how disliked he was. He was often drunk, and that was when his sadism was at its most extreme."

Hilliard stared out into space. "One afternoon, he ordered the entire camp to assemble in the yard. He was sitting on a platform in front of us. At a table. He snapped his fingers, and a troupe of orderlies came up. Each was carrying a tray on which were various dishes of food we could see. And smell. Then Neimeyer slowly ate his meal. He waved his fork in the air with each bite. 'Watch this, you men,' said he. 'Learn some manners.'"

At this point, Hilliard leaned forward and rested his head in his hands. "We weren't getting beaten or locked up, which happened all the time. All that was happening was that a group of starving men were being forced to watch a man eat his dinner. Probably doesn't sound that bad."

I grabbed his shoulder. "Yes, it does. It sounds utterly dreadful."

I don't know if I was of much comfort. How can you remove such anguish from a man's experience? It's impossible.

Hilliard shuddered. "Sorry. I got distracted for a minute. Where was I?"

"The German guards had asked for the blood of Billy Mosely. You all knew he was the one who had stolen the oranges."

"Yes, yes. That evening after roll call, he'd come into the hut, all excited. He'd been on cleaning detail at the commandant's house, and for one magic moment, the guard had been distracted. Billy snatched two oranges from the pantry and slipped them into his shirt."

Hilliard chuckled. "He'd put them under his armpits and managed to keep them in place all the time they were being walked back to the huts. It's a miracle it wasn't noticed, but the guard was either sympathetic or stupid. We never knew. Billy got away with it."

Hilliard wiped his mouth in a gesture I thought was subconscious.

"You can imagine the challenge of dividing two oranges among fifty men," he went on. "Probably none of whom had tasted fresh fruit for months and months. But Billy did it. First we whittled down the number to twenty by throwing dice. I won a slice. I remember to this day how I tried to savour that tiny piece of orange, making myself eat so slowly. Some men chewed the peel itself. When the Krauts left, we all gathered around, trying to decide what to do. Billy volunteered to give himself up, but we wouldn't hear of it. Matter of pride. He'd become like our mascot. He was a little chap with bandy legs, long arms. Sort of monkey-like. He had several teeth missing, which he said his old man had knocked out of his mouth because he'd been cheeky. He never moaned, was constantly on the lookout to scrounge something, which he always shared. We loved him. Nobody was going to turn him in."

Hilliard took a handkerchief from his pocket and rubbed it over his face.

"I gather somebody did turn him in?"

He nodded. "Next night they came for him. We'd just got into our bunks when in burst the Krauts. Shouting, throwing their weight around like they always did. They said they knew who the thief was. One of them went straight to Billy's bunk and dragged him off. He gave him a hard blow on the head, which almost knocked him out. Two of the others got him to his feet and then, semi-conscious as he was, they dragged him out. We couldn't do anything to stop them. We just watched helplessly. It was a wet, cold night, and they took him out to the parade ground and tied him to a post. The commandant was there. 'You can stay here until morning and think about your sins.' For some reason, he had good English. A lot of the Krauts did, actually. Sins. That's the word he used, 'sins,' as if stealing two oranges for starving men was a sin. But the guards left him out there in the pelting rain and cold. Wilf, Eric, me, and Conal had our bunks by the window, and we could hear him crying for help. After a while, his voice got fainter and fainter. Conal wanted to go out and get him, but we held him back. It would only bring punishment on him. And on us, too. We told him to wait until morning. Then we'd get Billy. I said I'd go and talk to the commandant myself."

Hilliard's eyes were full of tears. I knew what he was going to say.

"We had to wait until after morning roll call before we were allowed to cut him down. The four of us went, but when we got there he was dead. Exposure. The blow to the head. Starvation. The commandant made himself scarce. It's one thing to treat your prisoners badly; it's another to have one die as a result of your orders. We buried the little fellow as honourably as we could. And we waited out the war. Ironically, the Armistice was signed ten days later. If only we could have held on. Billy was so enterprising he would probably be a millionaire by now."

"I presume he is the figure in the painting that Conal touches up over and over?"

"They were particularly close friends. He was teaching Billy how to draw. He took his death very hard. Frankly, I don't think he's ever got over it."

"Did you find out who had betrayed him?"

Hilliard shrugged. "Could have been anybody in the camp. Everybody knew it was likely Billy who'd taken the oranges. But they didn't want to be punished for his crime. As I said, hunger tends to throw us back to a more primitive self. They wouldn't have expected he would die. So, no. We don't know what man betrayed Billy Mosely." He sighed. "In a way, we all did. Neimeyer couldn't have done much against two hundred men if we had banded together. But we were weak, afraid. Hungry. We just wanted to survive. And we didn't know how close we were to the end of it all. Some men found God, some lost Him. Conal found Communism."

His story over, he stashed away his pipe and tobacco pouch. He reached out his hand to me. "Come. It's getting late. Neither of us will be fit for work tomorrow."

We didn't speak for the rest of the way, but our silence was not isolating. I think he knew how much I sympathized.

He didn't bring up the issue of the missing money at the café. Neither did I.

Hilliard said goodbye as he left me at my house, and I went inside.

Chapter Twenty-One

NONE OF THE lights were on, and I assumed Gramps had called it an early night. But then I saw a note propped on the kitchen table.

Hi, Lottie,

I will probably be late getting in so don't wait up for me. Bertha and me plan to stay as long as possible at Sunnyside and take the last streetcar home. Hope you had a good day. Bertha made you a sandwich, which is in the icebox. I told her you often don't get to have any dinner. It's a cheese and chutney, your favourite.

See you in the morning.
Gramps

Why did I have the feeling I was being courted? And why did it make me angry? It seemed as if Gramps was quite smitten by this woman. If their relationship continued, I had better get myself sorted out.

I was in fact somewhat hungry. I went to the icebox and took out the sandwich that Mrs. Johnson had so kindly and thoughtfully made for me. It was all right. Strange, though, how cheese and chutney on bread can taste like sour grapes.

Hilliard's words kept repeating and repeating in my head. I'd been only a child during the war, but Gran and Gramps talked about what was happening all the time. The sorrow and desperation of those years had permeated my life.

I undressed and got into bed. My room was hot in spite of the fan, and I rolled back and forth restlessly. I expected to hear Gramps come in at any time, but he didn't. When I last checked, it was two o'clock. I fell asleep, and nasty dreams got hold of me. In one dream I was at the Paradise, ready to work, but the door was locked. I knocked, and poisonous Pearl answered. "No, we don't need you today," she said and tried to close the door. I pushed against her.

"Yes, I am working today. You do need me. Let me in. Get Hilliard."

"He's busy. He says you're not needed." I tried desperately to shove against the door, but the girl was fiendishly strong. She finally slammed it in my face.

I woke up suddenly. "Gramps, is that you?" I called out. It was seven o'clock.

"Yes, it's me, pet. Sorry to wake you up."

I heard him coming up the stairs, and with a little polite tap on my door he came into my room.

I sat up. "Where were you?"

"It got so late coming back from Sunnyside I didn't want to disturb you, so Bertha offered for me to stay at her house."

"You wouldn't have disturbed me. It was more disturbing not knowing where the hell you were."

"I'm sorry, Lottie."

I knew he was sorry. For upsetting me, not for staying out all night.

"Shall I make you a cup of coffee?"

"No! Stop trying to mollify me. What were you doing staying the night like that?"

In spite of my tone, Gramps actually chuckled. "What do you think I was doing?"

"Gramps! Are you telling me you had carnal relations with that woman?"

"And why not? The nether regions are functioning properly."

"The nether regions!"

He reacted to that, and I could see he was getting angry.

"Lottie. I know this is difficult for you, but Bertha is a mighty attractive woman. She's single. I'm single. There's no reason we shouldn't pursue intimacy if we want to."

I knew I was being absolutely childish, but I was finding it hard to rein in everything I was feeling.

"Gramps. I don't want you to get hurt. You hardly know the woman."

"Lottie, I am not the silly old fool you are making me out to be. Let's say I'm getting to know her. And so far, I like what I see."

"And that is obviously getting to be quite a lot."

He knew what I meant.

He stepped back. "I'll go and make you that coffee."

BREAKFAST WAS STRAINED. Gramps munched on a piece of bread and jam, sipping his tea. It was clear he was thinking happy thoughts. He didn't even ask me about my case, which he always did. Eventually, he glanced over at me.

"Bertha made up a great Mary had a little lamb joke. Do you want to hear it?"

"Save it for later, Gramps. I've got to get going."

I got up to leave, and I gave him my usual kiss on the cheek. His skin smelled faintly of violets. I wonder how that came about!

THE HEAVY, HUMID air got hold of me at once, but I walked as fast as I could to the office. I went inside, turned on the fan, and set the kettle to boil for my coffee. No stinking rodents today, no letters. So far, so good.

I phoned police headquarters.

"Detective Murdoch, please. Tell him it's Charlotte Frayne calling."

Jack answered promptly.

"I have to come to headquarters at nine-thirty to swear an affidavit about Mr. Gilmore's whereabouts. Conal Pierce is also coming in. I wanted to make sure you had seen Detective Arcady's report."

"I just finished reading it."

"So, it looks as if Mr. Gilmore is in the clear?"

"It does appear so."

"When will he be released?"

"That depends on when we can get the Crown judge to have a look at the depositions. Might be later today."

"Good. He has to arrange for his wife's funeral."

From the kitchen, I could hear the kettle was whistling to advise me the water was boiling.

"Jack, I wonder if I might ask you a favour?"

"Ask away."

"Could you do a background check on somebody for me? She says she's from Vancouver. I have doubts that she is who and what she says she is."

"One of your cases?"

"Hmm. Hmm."

"I can make a telephone call. See if she has any outstanding charges out there."

"I would appreciate that."

"What's the name?"

"She calls herself Bertha Johnson. A widow. About sixty or so. Fair skinned, red hair, although that could be more from a bottle than nature. Between five foot three and five foot five. Approximately one hundred and fifty pounds."

"I'll get on to it."

"Thanks. I'll see you shortly."

We hung up. I went to appease the kettle and make a cup of coffee.

I had just sat down at the desk when I heard the rattle of the mail slot. An envelope dropped into the box.

My heart thudded, but I got up at once.

It was not a nasty anonymous letter. The opposite. It was a thank-you note from Mrs. Epping. And a cheque. Fully remitted. She'd added underneath her signature: "A free woman, Hallelujah." That was a nice start to the day, I must admit.

Chapter Twenty-Two

I MET CONAL AS he was approaching the police station, and we walked in together. Same arch. He looked even more fragile than yesterday. I thought about what Hilliard had told me about their experiences as POWs. I gave him as warm a smile as I could, and he responded briefly.

Jack Murdoch came out to greet us, and we followed him to his office. The commissioner of oaths was early and was waiting for us. He was a tall, elegant man with cropped grey hair and a trim beard. He got to his feet as I entered. The statements that Conal and I had made yesterday were on the table. We had just to read them through and sign on oath that they were true. Judge St. James handed us a Bible, and we swore on it. Conal didn't seem to object to doing that. He, too, asked Jack when Mr. Gilmore would be released, and Jack gave him the same answer. The judge left.

Jack addressed me. "Might I have a word before you go?"

"I'll be off then," interjected Conal. "I'll see you at the café, Miss Frayne."

Jack escorted him out. While I waited, I took the chance to look more closely around his office. A window rather high up looked onto the outside car park. A large desk took up most of the room, with two identical metal files on either side. There was a portrait of the late King George V on the wall. His expression was serious, as he was probably contemplating the shenanigans of his eldest son. He was right to worry. His heir, currently King Edward VIII, had a reputation for shenanigans, all of them involving married women. Across from King George was the obligatory portrait of Chief Constable Dennis Draper. He also looked severe, although no doubt for a different reason. His expression reflected what Jack and I had talked about previously. Pesky union men threatening strikes and general disruption of society. Communists, Hebrews, all anarchists. Draper's moustache bristled, and if a portrait could have spoken it would have been shouting, "Stamp 'em out. Every last one of them."

There was a low bookcase behind Jack's desk. Three photographs took pride of place along with a small wooden frame in which hung a silver medal that looked like a prize of some kind. I stood up and went closer. In one of the photographs, a young woman was sitting with a ventriloquist's dummy on her knee. The same woman was in the next photo, but this time as a pretty bride on the arm of a young Jack Murdoch. He looked happy and handsome. Predictably, the third photograph was a family portrait. More recent, obviously, as there were now two young children, a boy and a girl. The ventriloquist was still attractive, as was Jack.

I was heading back to my chair when Jack came in.

I indicated the photographs. "Your family?"

"Yes. That picture's two years old. Will is fourteen now and Amy is twelve."

"Was your wife a ventriloquist?"

He chuckled. "She was indeed. A very good one." He went over and picked up the photo. "She named the dummy Miss Happ. The act was Fiona's way of expressing her anger about the war. She was very opposed to it, but the majority of people in this city were for it. When she performed her piece one night at Shea's, she caused a riot." He replaced the photograph on the shelf. "I was a complete wreck returning from the Front. My poor father hardly knew what to do with me. Fiona was instrumental in helping me to snap out of it."

For a moment, his face had the same expression I'd seen on Hilliard's when he was telling me what had happened in the POW camp.

He turned around. "She is still a fiery one, is my wife." His voice was fond.

I pointed. "Isn't that the Military Medal? That is certainly something to be proud of."

"Is it? Sometimes I wonder."

Tender territory, this.

He didn't seem to want to elaborate, so I didn't pursue it.

He sat down at his desk, opened a drawer, and took out a folder.

"I was able to get that information you asked for."

"That was fast."

"A pal of mine was on duty in Vancouver, and he checked their files." He pushed the sheet of paper over to me. "Bertha Johnson has various aliases. Brenda Jackson, Beulah Jones, Bonnie Jensen. Five years ago, she was charged with issuing forged cheques. Got six months for that. Four years later, a charge of using false information with the intent to defraud. She was Beulah Jones then. She was about to marry some man, listed as Arthur Andrews, but at the last minute it was discovered she was already married under the name Brenda Jackson."

"Would that be considered a legal marriage?"

"The name on her birth certificate is Brenda Frominger. The husband's name is given as Terrence Jackson. They married in 1925. She is still married to him. That hasn't stopped her from claiming to be the widow of one Gerald Jensen. She applied to receive his life insurance in 1935. As they were not legally married, she didn't get it. That was last year. Since then she has dropped out of sight."

Not too far out of sight.

"It would appear that Bertha Johnson, or more correctly Brenda Jackson, has made a career of entrapping older men with the intent of getting her hands on their money. In two cases, through a life insurance policy."

I certainly didn't like the sound of that.

"Did the hubbies die from natural causes?"

"Looks like it. They were all elderly. Seems as if she got them to the altar, had them change their insurance policies in her favour, and when they kicked the bucket, she stepped forward as the supposed widow."

"But she's still doing it? You'd think she had enough money by now."

"In each case the claim was denied. She's probably living on the vapours of previous conflagrations."

"And the original husband? Terrence Jackson?"

"He's still around. According to my chum, he might be the one instigating the schemes."

"In other words, he's pimping."

"I'd say so."

I had the urge to rush home and pour all this out to Gramps; however, I knew that might backfire. He was quite besotted. Who was he going to believe? His luscious new love or unproven police reports?

"Thanks, Jack, much appreciated." I took the piece of paper and put it in my purse. "Any further developments on the Gilmore case?"

"We're stalled. Thaddeus appears to have a tight alibi, so we're still looking for the killer."

The only thing that would change that would be if Conal had lied under oath. Reasons as yet undisclosed.

Mr. Gilmore had told me he went to the lake for a while. That didn't jibe with what Conal had sworn was his departure time. Who was telling the truth?

Chapter Twenty-Three

I HAD TO GET back to the café if I was going to be in time for the lunch sittings, and I knew I wouldn't be moving too quickly. Surely it couldn't be hotter today? I walked past a newspaper stand, and the handwritten sign said indeed that: "Another Scorcher. 92 F." The vendor had a good idea. That or he was altruistic. He'd made room on his newsstand for jugs of iced tea. Five cents a glass. I stopped.

"I'll take a glass."

He poured out one for me.

"You look cool as the proverbial cucumber, miss, if I may so."

A compliment is a compliment, even if the good fellow did look as if he might be the same age as Gramps. The glass he handed me had a rather suspicious looking smudge at the rim, but at that point I didn't care. He was keeping the jugs in a bucket of ice, and the drink was frosty. If I'd had time to gulp down a second one, I would have. I returned the glass to the vendor, who gave me a little bow, gave my glass a quick wipe with his apron, and returned it to its place on the stand.

I certainly didn't feel as cool as a cucumber, and I went

on my way none the wiser as to his compliment. Maybe it was the hat.

As with yesterday, there was already a queue outside the Paradise. A couple of women today, both looking decidedly down at heel. Neither was young, and I wondered where they lived. Was the café a treat or a necessity?

I went around to the side door and let myself in. There was a strong smell of curry in the air.

Pearl was already loading up her tray with bowls ready for Eric to spoon in the soup of the day.

"There you are," she said in her inimitable fashion. "I was beginning to wonder if you'd show up at all."

I didn't bother to answer. "I'll get the bread ready."

Eric called over his shoulder, "Good morning, Miss Frayne. Another scorcher to cope with. We're doing mulligatawny soup today, tomato or cold veg salad. No dripping left, but there is a nice parsley butter. The blancmange didn't set too well, so see if you can push the roly-poly pudding or the biscuits."

"Will do."

Hilliard and Conal were both seated at the table, having some of the soup. Hilliard beamed at me. "Good morning."

Conal glanced up and smiled a greeting.

I thought about Hilliard's story, and I felt even more sympathy for him.

"Excuse me, Mr. Pierce, but I think I may have dropped my handkerchief in the side room when you showed it to me. Do you mind if I just take a quick look?"

"What?" Conal looked up at me. "Er. The room's locked."

Hilliard jumped up. "You finish your soup, Conal. I've got to get out there anyway. I'll show her."

Conal pushed back his soup bowl. "No. I'll do it."

"Won't take a minute. Why don't you help Eric with the fish cakes?"

Pearl scowled at me. "Don't take long."

Hilliard beckoned to me, and I followed him out to the dining room. He said quietly, "Five dollars missing from the deposit as of this morning."

He reached under the counter and lifted a key.

"This is the one. Now, Miss Frayne, you don't strike me as the kind of woman who loses handkerchiefs except when you need to. Why do you want to see the room again?"

"I just need to confirm something."

He opened the door as he spoke, and we went inside. I went straight to the desk. The wooden box that Conal had made pains to move out of sight was back on the top of the desk.

A handwritten sign was pasted on one side: "Strike Money." I pointed at it.

"Any idea what that refers to?"

Hill went to the box, slid off the lid, and tipped the box upside down. Three one-dollar bills and several coins fell out. He poked at the coins.

"Five dollars. Exactly."

He leaned his hands on the desk and bowed his head. He muttered something I didn't hear.

"As with the combination to the safe, I assume everybody knows where the key to this room is kept?"

He looked at me, his eyes dark with anger.

"That is true, but essentially this is Conal's domain. Even if he's not the thief, he has to know who is." He banged on the desk with his fist. "Or does he just believe money magically appears in his damn collection box? 'My goodness gracious, where did that come from?'"

"Is it strike money?"

"Oh, I'm sure that what it's intended for. It's Conal's obsession. Always has been. Justice for the masses." He banged again. "Damn. Damn."

"What do you want to do?"

He straightened up. "Find out the truth. As soon as we close after lunch, I'm going to get everybody together. Time to face facts."

"I'm sorry. I feel bad about the way it's looking."

"*You* do? I'm just getting used the idea that one or more of the men I trusted most in the world has stabbed me in back."

He scooped up the money and returned it to the box.

"Come on. I've got to open the café." He hustled me out. "I want you to be at the meeting."

"Okay."

He went into the dining room. I was heading back to the kitchen when Conal came out.

"Did you find what you were looking for?" he asked me.

"No, I didn't. Must have dropped it at home. Thanks."

He had a key in his hand, and he began to unlock the door, bending in close so he could see, as was his wont.

"There's a meeting tonight. I'd better make sure everything is tidy."

I left him to it. I could hear the bustle of the incoming customers.

I'd encountered betrayal and deceit before, but this situation was making me feel particularly bad. I'd been hired to find out what was happening to the money, but I almost wished I hadn't. I couldn't get the expression on Hilliard's face out of my mind. I remembered what Mr. Gilmore had said to me early on. "Objectivity, however hard won, is our stock in trade as investigators. Don't get emotionally involved with the clients."

Unfortunately, it seemed a little too late to follow his advice.

Chapter Twenty-Four

THE TWO HOURS of lunchtime were non-stop, and once again I was glad when Hilliard flipped the "Closed" sign over after the final customer left.

"We're meeting in the kitchen." He looked angry.

Wilf and Eric were already there. Eric was sitting down for once. Pearl was just leaving.

"See you later. You too?" This question was aimed at me.

"That's right," I answered her in a cheery voice.

No response to that one way or the other.

She left.

Hilliard poured himself a glass of water and joined the other two.

"Where's Conal?"

"He said he'd be here," answered Wilf. "What's up? What's the urgency?"

"You'll find out," Hilliard answered.

At that moment, the side door opened and Conal came in.

"Sorry, chaps, just got caught up in something."

Behind the thick glasses, his eyes looked wild to me. The pupils dilated. I knew it wasn't the refraction from the lenses. Was he taking drugs? Unlike the sad sack exterior previously, he seemed giddy and effervescent. He sat down and grabbed one of the biscuits from the trolley, stuffing it into his mouth with gusto.

"Yum. All righty. I'm ready. Hill you said you wanted a meeting. Urgent."

Wilf nodded in my direction. "Surely you're not going to let her stay?"

I must say I didn't appreciate the anonymous "her", but before I was going to remind him of my given name, Hilliard answered.

"Yes, I have asked Miss Frayne to be present." He looked around the table. "You should all know that she is a private investigator. She is an associate of Thaddeus Gilmore's. I have hired her to investigate some irregularities."

They gaped at him.

Wilf was the first to speak. "What the hell are you talking about, Hill?"

"A few days ago, I had a call from our bank manager, Mr. Strawbridge. He said that he'd noticed that over the past few weeks, our intake of cash has dipped. He was concerned we might be in financial difficulties. The bank owns the mortgage, and they could foreclose if we miss our payments."

"That doesn't make sense," spluttered Eric. "We've been busier than ever. We can't be in financial difficulties."

I was making myself as unobtrusive as possible so I could observe the reactions of the three men. Not surprisingly, Conal didn't seem surprised. He had shrunk into his own shoulders like a dog who anticipated being beaten. His giddiness was gone.

Hilliard clenched his hands together. "As you know, I make up the daily accounts and put the money with bank slips in the safe. It seems that somebody has been altering the slips and lifting some of the cash."

"Who? Who the hell would do that?" Wilf went red with anger.

"Somebody who knows the combination to the safe," said Eric with a measured calm that was hard won. "How much money are we talking about?"

"Twenty-seven dollars over three weeks," said Hilliard. "It won't sink us, but it's not money we can afford to lose."

"Why didn't you discuss it with us first?" Wilf was glaring over at me as if I were the cause of the problem.

"I wanted to make sure this was the only answer. That's why I hired Miss Frayne to investigate."

"And what conclusion did our little waitress come to?"

Hilliard intervened and saved me from bopping Wilf on the nose.

"I believe Conal can answer that."

The Irishman was fiddling with a spoon on the table, and he didn't speak. He didn't really need to. Guilt was written all over him.

Eric spoke up. "Conal, what's this all about? Have you been filching money from the safe?"

Conal still didn't meet anybody's eye. "I wasn't filching."

"Don't play with us. You were either taking the money or you weren't," snapped Wilf.

Conal fidgeted some more. "I borrowed some cash. I will return it by the end of next week."

Wilf leaned across the table and grabbed Conal by the arm. "Will you please tell us what you are up to? If you need more money, why didn't you ask?"

"It's not for me."

"What then?"

"I'm not at liberty to tell you."

Wilf looked as if he was about to shake an answer out of him.

Hilliard said, "Five dollars was taken last night. In Conal's private room there is a box. It contains that exact amount in bills and coins. The note on the box says, 'Strike money.'"

Almost simultaneously, Eric and Wilf exclaimed, "Strike money!"

"What strike are we talking about?" Eric asked.

"This has to be another little endeavour of your Commie Party pals!" Wilf was yelling. Conal shrank even further, but when he answered he had the strength and dignity of the dedicated.

"Don't belittle me, Wilf. This is no petty endeavour. The party has been trying to organize a strike of the Spadina Avenue garment workers. The conditions they are forced to work in are appalling."

"That's not our responsibility," snapped Wilf.

"I think it is the responsibility of every decent human

being. Negotiations are in progress with the various owners, but if they fail the workers will go out on strike."

"It won't work," said Wilf. "It hasn't before, and it won't now. They can bring in a dozen scabs in a day. A strike will be crushed immediately."

"We have faith that the unions will support us. But the workers, most of whom are women, by the way, with children to support, will need money to live on. Hence the collection box. Everybody chips in when they come to a meeting. We have to challenge this exploitation."

Wilf wasn't having any of this. He got to his feet.

"I don't have to do any such thing. We're trying to run a café here with the thinnest of margins. Why do we do that, Conal? Answer me. Why?"

"Wilf, leave him be," said Hilliard.

"Stop protecting him, Hill. It's about time he grew up." He leaned in toward the trembling Conal. "Are you going to answer me? Why are we running a café?"

Conal didn't speak.

"Cat got your tongue? Well, I'll tell you. Because we've each known what it's like to be starving. We all agreed we would do what we could to help those in a similar state."

Eric now joined in the fray. "Wilf. You've had too much to drink. Calm down."

"I won't calm down. Let him answer." He turned back to Conal. "What you are doing is sabotage. You've betrayed us just as surely as you did back then when we were behind barbed wire."

All the blood drained from Conal's face.

"I don't know what you mean."

"Come off it. You damn well do know. We've tiptoed around it for years. I think it's about time we told the truth."

Eric stood up and got between Wilf and Conal. "Forget it. It's dead and buried."

Hilliard also got to his feet.

"Wilf. Cut it out. There is nothing to be gained by raking up the past."

"Let's see, shall we? Weren't we told that if a wound got infected, we had to lance it? Clean it out? Well, this particular wound has been festering for years. Let's clean it up."

I was still pinned to my chair. I wish I could say I did something helpful, but I didn't know what to do. There was so much rage. It wasn't that I was frightened for myself. I wasn't. I knew any intervention on my part would be worse than useless.

Wilf was straining against the other two men. If they had released him, I don't know what he would have done to Conal.

"Answer me, goddamn it. Were you the one who turned in Billy?"

Conal was silent.

"Answer me!"

Conal simply looked up at him, his eyes obscured behind his glasses. Hilliard finally spoke.

"Conal. Can you say something?"

The other man almost whispered. "I thought I would save the rest of us."

"So you admit it," yelled Wilf. "You were the one who fingered him to the Krauts."

"We would all have been punished. I couldn't stand it anymore."

"But he was your friend. Our friend." Wilf wasn't shouting now, and this made his anguish even worse.

Conal put his head down on the table and began to cry. He was sobbing so hard, I could hardly make out his words.

"Billy was indestructible. I didn't know he would die. How could I know?"

Hilliard came around to him and put his arm around Conal's shoulders.

"How indeed."

Eric touched Conal's arm.

"Don't fret, Connie. Terrible things happen in war. Hill's right. We'll sort it out."

Wilf turned his back to them and was staring at the far wall. His shoulders were shaking, and I saw he, too, was crying.

I made a sign at Hilliard to indicate I was going to the dining room. He nodded, and I left them. Eric and Hilliard had their heads close to Conal's. Wilf hadn't moved.

I sat down at one of the tables and waited. Conal's sobs finally tapered off. There was a murmur of voices. I couldn't tell if Wilf had joined in.

I couldn't help but replay in my brain what had just happened.

There was a little niggling doubt in my mind.

"I'm not at liberty to say." Those were Conal's words when he was asked why he'd taken the money. He had not specifically admitted the money was for the strike fund, but it seemed to me he was relieved to jump off into the politics of social justice. Was that indeed why he was taking money from the cash box? But if not for strikers, what was it for?

It wasn't long before the kitchen door swung open and Hilliard came in. He looked ghastly. He joined me at the table.

"Thank you, Miss Frayne. You have been exemplary. We can consider the investigation is completed."

"I'm sorry. What do you think you'll do?"

"Nothing. He's promised he won't do it again. And I don't think he will. Maybe Wilf's analogy is right. Infections have to be cleared out if there is to be healing."

"Is Conal going to be all right?"

"Eventually. Wilf is sorry about blowing up, for one thing. He knows what it was like in that place. He doesn't have any right to be judgmental."

"Were you surprised by what Conal said?"

He shrugged. "Not exactly. Billy could have been turned in by anybody. Being tied to a post all night as a punishment was frequent. Nobody knew Billy wouldn't survive it. He did seem indestructible."

He looked as if he was carrying the weight of the world on his back. I was about to offer him some comfort, but I didn't get a chance. There was a sharp rapping at the front door. Hill went to open it, and there on the threshold was Jack Murdoch. Hilliard had no choice but to answer.

It seemed obvious to me from the look on Jack Murdoch's face that he was the bearer of bad news.

Chapter Twenty-Five

JACK TOUCHED HIS hat when he saw me.

"Good afternoon. I was hoping I'd find Miss Frayne here. I wonder if I might have a word?"

"Of course."

He stepped into the dining room. Hilliard regarded us both for a moment.

"I should get back to the kitchen. Give me a call if you need me. Jack, there's some fresh lemonade on the counter. Help yourself."

He scuttled off. I could tell he wasn't feeling up to more dire exchanges.

Jack grabbed a drink, then came over to where I was sitting.

"Mind if I sit down?"

"Of course not."

He pulled up a chair across from me.

"There has been another attack on Phoebe Street. Arthur Kaufmann has been seriously wounded, and his wife is in the hospital. He was stabbed, and she was hit."

"Good Lord. When did this happen?"

"Sometime earlier today. Neither of them is talking at the

moment. Fortunately, his injuries are not life threatening, and she is expected to recover."

There could be only one reason why Jack had sought me out.

"It can't have anything to do with Mr. Gilmore. He's still in jail."

"He was released two hours ago."

"Oh, I see."

"The judge thought there was sufficient credibility in his alibi to release him. At the time of this attack he was not in custody. However, he has been re-apprehended."

"On what grounds?"

"We received a call from one of the neighbours. She said she'd heard shouting coming from the Kaufmann house. We went right away given what had happened previously." Jack was running his finger around the rim of his glass, and it made a sort of whining noise. He stopped. "Sorry. We found Mr. Kaufmann on the floor, bleeding from a stab wound to the back. His wife appeared to have received a severe blow to the side of the head."

"Has she been able to say what occurred?"

"Not so far. When she was found she was not actually unconscious, but she appears to have gone into a state of shock and cannot speak."

"Do we know what the weapon was?"

"Only with Kaufmann. He appears to have been stabbed with a kitchen knife."

"Why do you think this has something to do with Mr. Gilmore?"

"When we went to the Kaufmann house, Mr. Gilmore was there. He was wearing a shirt that had substantial bloodstains on the front and the sleeves."

"His explanation?"

"He said he too heard shouts coming from the Kaufmann house. He went to investigate and found the situation as I have described. He says he was trying to tend to Mr. Kaufmann and got the blood on him in that way. When he had done what he could, he then went back to his house, where there is a telephone, in order to call the police. That done, he returned to the Kaufmann house until the police arrived."

"Don't you believe him?"

Jack shrugged. "Let's say the circumstances have to be clarified. We have a witness who says she saw him going to the Kaufmann house prior to the sound of shouting, which she says she heard several minutes later."

"Prior? That's a big discrepancy."

"It is. She also saw him leaving shortly afterward. At that point she noticed he had blood on his clothes."

He swished the lemonade around in his glass.

"We are continuing to question people on the street, of course, but I tell you frankly, Miss Frayne, things are not looking good for Mr. Gilmore. He has asked to see you."

I stood up. "I'll come right away."

Jack picked up his hat.

I dithered, not sure what to do about the lads in the kitchen. Hilliard solved my problem by coming through the swing door.

"Trouble?"

"And then some." I saw no reason not to fill him in. "There has been another attack on Phoebe Street. Mr. Gilmore is once again a suspect. I'm going to see him."

"Who was attacked?"

Jack answered. "A Mr. and Mrs. Kaufmann."

Hilliard looked startled.

"Do you know them?" asked Jack.

"Not exactly, but I think a Mrs. Kaufmann has come here a few times. She's a little woman, dark hair. Nervous?"

That fit her description. Especially the nervous part.

"Did she come here with Mr. Gilmore?" Jack asked.

It was obvious to me that Hilliard was backtracking rapidly.

"Possibly. Or they may just have arrived at the same time. Neighbours and all that."

Hill had the same guarded manner that he'd shown before when Jack was questioning him about Mr. Gilmore. I could only assume that Mrs. Kaufmann had been a visitor to the secret room, as I thought of it. No reason why a woman shouldn't like a good old argy-bargy about politics as much as a man did. I stopped myself. That's how Mrs. Gilmore had been described. A woman of strong opinions. Mrs. Kaufmann hadn't looked as if she could exchange harsh words with a goose, but perhaps that was misleading.

"Did Mr. Kaufmann ever come in?" Jack continued.

Hilliard hesitated. Jack helped him out.

"Muscular fellow with a beard. Wears his hair long and straggly."

"Lots of our customers fit that description. Can't afford a haircut."

Jack couldn't hold back a sigh.

"So would you say Kaufmann was a customer or not?"

"Not a regular, but I do recall a man answering to that description dropped in last week sometime. Unpleasant type. Claimed the soup was tasteless. Made a fuss."

"Was he by himself?"

Hilliard answered that one promptly. "Yes, he was. I had the impression his wife had to go to work. He complained about not getting home-cooked meals. Said that was the only reason he was eating in this flea pit. That's a direct quote."

Hilliard looked at me keenly.

"Charlotte. You've been a great help for us. Please come back this evening if you can. I'd like to know what has transpired."

"All right."

"I've got a police car," said Jack to me. "It's too hot to walk. I'll drive us over."

Suddenly, from the kitchen, came the sound of a man wailing. The sound was so full of anguish it made my blood freeze.

"What the heck is that?" Jack asked.

"Conal's gone into one of his states," said Hilliard. "They happen periodically. He thinks he's back in the trenches."

Jack nodded. "I'm familiar with it."

It was a rather ambiguous statement, but he didn't seem as if he were about to elaborate.

Hilliard began to head for the kitchen. "The doctor's given him some sedatives. I'll go and get them."

The cries ended abruptly.

Chapter Twenty-Six

THE POLICE CAR was scruffy and stank of stale cigarette smoke and tension. Jack himself was driving.

"You said before that you didn't consider Mr. Gilmore a prime suspect in the attack on his wife. You seem to have changed your mind about him."

Jack pursed his lips. "Not exactly. We need more evidence before we can reach a definite conclusion."

"I presume he denies attacking the Kaufmanns."

"Emphatically."

"May I ask who is the witness who claims to have seen him going to the Kaufmann house?"

"A Miss Kubay. Her mother also corroborates her statement. They were both sitting at their window getting some air."

"I myself don't think I would trust those two particular women as far as I could throw them. Pardon the expression."

"Why do you say that? I know they're both older, but they seemed able to see all right. I checked that out right away."

"It's their inner vision I'm worried about."

Unfortunately, we were just then turning into the car park that was attached to police headquarters. There was no opportunity to continue the talk.

CONSTABLE EVANS WAS apparently still in the grip of competition fever, but he stopped typing long enough to greet us.

"Mr. Grier is here, sir. He's with the prisoner."

As Jack and I walked to the stairs, the solicitor was just coming up from the holding cells. He frowned at Jack.

"I've taken my client's deposition. I'll be back tomorrow for the arraignment."

I might as well not have existed for all the notice I got from him. Why did I get the impression only males were within his sightlines?

Jack and I proceeded downstairs.

This time the only occupant of the cells was Mr. Gilmore. No musically inclined drunk, thank goodness.

"I'll have to be present while you talk," said Jack.

He opened the cell door, and I went inside.

Mr. Gilmore was sitting on the bunk. He looked even worse than he had before. He sprang to his feet and, as was his wont, shook hands formally by way of greeting.

"Have you heard how Mrs. Kaufmann is doing?" he asked Jack.

"Not since she was admitted to hospital. But I believe she will be all right. Physically, at least."

"Has she given an account of what happened?"

"Not as yet. She is apparently still in a state of severe shock."

"And Arthur Kaufmann?"

"He's lucky. He bled a lot, but basically the wound isn't that deep. He should recover completely."

"Has he made a statement?"

"He says he was taken completely by surprise. No idea who the attacker was. He must have lost consciousness after he was stabbed and only came to when you found him. Perhaps more details will come to him as he recovers."

Mr. Gilmore was silent for a moment, then he spoke to Jack.

"You have no objection if I inform Miss Frayne what happened?"

"Not at all."

It was starting to feel a little crowded in the cell, and the only place to sit was on the bunk or the toilet bucket.

Mr. Gilmore sensed my dilemma.

"Forgive me, Miss Frayne. My manners have deserted me. Please have a seat."

He moved aside so I could perch on the hard bunk. It didn't make much difference to the spatial inadequacy, but I accepted gratefully. I hadn't got my waitressing legs yet.

Mr. Gilmore waited until I was settled. Somewhere along the way, he'd lost his spectacles. There was a little mark across his nose where they'd pressed, and without them his face seemed soft and naked. He clasped his hands together, another familiar gesture, and addressed me.

"Detective Arcady brought me back to the station here, as you see. I told him what I will now repeat to you. I was in my own house beginning to take care of affairs that involve my wife's death. I heard a woman scream. It sounded as if it was coming from a few houses down. I went outside and determined it must be Mrs. Kaufmann. I went to see what was happening. I found Arthur Kaufmann lying face down in the kitchen, bleeding copiously. Mrs. Kaufmann was also in the kitchen. She was leaning against the cupboard. She had a gash on her head, which was bleeding profusely, as scalp wounds do. She indicated I should take care of her husband. I seized a cloth from the sink and handed it to her for her own wound. I then checked the condition of Arthur Kaufmann. I knew he needed professional help. At this point Mrs. Kaufmann appeared to have gone into a state of shock. She was conscious, but no longer seemingly aware of her surroundings. I managed to help her into the living room, where she could at least lie on the couch. Although I was not happy to leave her, I had to telephone the police from my house. Which I did as fast as I could. I then returned to the Kaufmann house, where I ascertained that Arthur Kaufmann was conscious. I instructed him not to move, and I got another towel and pressed it against the wound on his back. I remained like that until the police arrived. They were wonderfully prompt. Detective Arcady and two constables entered. The ambulance attendants got Kaufmann onto one stretcher and Mrs. Kaufmann onto another. I was bloodied from my encounter with both injured people. The detective questioned me, and I told him what I have just now told you. He said I would have to come to the station and make a statement. Which I have done."

He spoke as if he were delivering a report to the court on one of our cases.

He had said he'd made a statement already to Arcady, and I wanted to believe that was why his account sounded oddly rehearsed. A little too precise.

"Detective Murdoch said they have a statement from a witness that you were seen going to the house before there was any sound of shouting or disturbance."

"Do you know the name of the witness?"

"Miss Kubay. Corroborated by her mother."

"In that case I would say she is deliberately lying. Both of them are lying."

"Why would she do that?"

"Miss Kubay and her mother have been my enemies for a long time, Miss Frayne."

"Why is that?"

"My wife, Ida, held views about women that they did not agree with. I assume they tarred me with the same brush."

His hands were clenched, and they tightened even more. He was trying to fend off tears.

"Forgive me, Miss Frayne. I have not yet assimilated the reality that Ida is dead."

"I'll do everything I can to find out who has done this, Mr. Gilmore."

He glanced over at Detective Murdoch. "Thank you. I

have faith that the good detective here will clear my name."

I sure hoped so.

There wasn't anything more to be done, so I said goodbye, shook hands again, and left. He returned to his seat on the bunk.

My heart went out to him. I realized how fond I'd become of Thaddeus Gilmore.

The lonely constable on guard stood up respectfully as we walked past.

"See if Mr. Gilmore wants some tea, will you, Curnoe? And he might need something to eat."

The constable saluted. "Yes, sir."

I waited until we were upstairs in the lobby.

"What's the next step?"

"It's too much of a coincidence that two people have been violently attacked who lived mere houses from each other. I truly hope that this time we can get a statement from the second victim. Unlike Mrs. Gilmore, Mrs. Kaufmann was attacked from the front. Surely, she will be able to give us a description of her attacker. If she chooses to, that is."

"Mr. Gilmore says she went into a state of shock almost immediately."

"Unfortunately, that is not difficult to feign."

"Why would she pretend?"

"I don't know. I'm merely saying that her state may or may not be genuine."

"Do you believe the Kubays?"

He gave a little shrug. "I can't discount anything at the moment. If it is true that Mr. Gilmore went to the Kaufmann house before the shouting, that is, before the attack, it does suggest he was implicated. What else could it mean?"

"But why? What is the motivation behind both attacks?"

We didn't have the chance to explore this any further. A woman in police uniform was just entering the building. She saw Jack and came straight over to him.

"May I have a word, detective?"

She was an attractive woman in spite of the uniform, which was unbecoming as well as being hot as hell: heavy leather belt at the waist, dark stockings, sensible shoes, a stiff hat.

Jack addressed me. "Will you wait a minute?"

I drifted over to the reception to admire Constable Evans's dexterity. One quick glance assured him I didn't need anything urgently, and without breaking stride, or, should I say, stroke, he continued typing.

Jack's conversation with the female officer was brief. She headed off to the women's quarters. If it had been me, I would have been unleashing my waist from that monstrous belt immediately, but she had more discipline. She disappeared without disarray through the connecting door.

Jack came over to me.

"Constable Nicholls was reporting from the hospital. Mrs. Kaufmann has not recovered. She's virtually catatonic."

"How is the injury?"

"Nasty, but not serious. Her state is purely mental." He

regarded me with the intense scrutiny I was becoming accustomed to from him.

"Charlotte. I wonder if you would do something for me?"

"Name it."

"I directed one of the women police officers to be at Mrs. Kaufmann's bedside. I was hoping she could get a statement, but apparently the mere sight of a uniform sets her off shaking and retreating even more. I'm wondering if you could go to see her. She might respond to you. You've met her already. You'll be a familiar face."

I had been hoping I could get to Mrs. Kaufmann; this was a golden opportunity. I was also quite chuffed that he seemed to have faith in my abilities and reliability.

"Of course. I can go right now."

"Splendid. Let me get an authorization form."

He hurried over to the reception and rather sharply ordered Evans to stop typing for a minute and get him some letterhead paper.

He wasn't long, and he handed me the envelope. "The constable on duty at the hospital is now Miss Frobisher. Show her this. Do what you can. I'm going over to Phoebe Street first, but then I'll be back here. If you don't mind, I'd appreciate a report tonight. One way or another."

Chapter Twenty-Seven

THERE WAS NOTHING sumptuous or Romanesque about the Toronto General Hospital. It was grey coloured, built from start to finish to function as a hospital, and was serious and no-nonsense. A place that would not encourage lingering.

I made my way to the ward where Mrs. Kaufmann had been taken. She didn't have the luxury of a private room, but she was in the bed nearest to the door. There was a screen around her bed, and a policewoman was seated outside it.

I explained who I was and showed her the letter of authorization that Jack had given me. She didn't do a perfunctory check but examined it carefully. There was indeed nothing perfunctory about Constable Frobisher. She had a perpetual tight-lipped expression. Maybe that's what happens when your major job is to make sure young women don't fall into wicked ways. I considered my line of work at least had more variety, if not as much respectability.

"Has Mrs. Kaufmann said anything to you?" I asked.

"Nothing at all. The last time I went to see if she was

able to give a statement she started shrieking. The nurse had to come and sedate her."

"When was that?"

"About an hour ago. She's probably gone to the world now."

"I'll check."

I stepped around the screen.

Even though she had suffered a dreadful experience, Mrs. Kaufmann actually looked younger than when I'd seen her last. Prettier. She had a bandage over her left temple, and the side of her head had been partly shaved. The rest of her hair was loose and flowing out on the pillow. It was a rich dark brown, no trace of grey. She appeared to be breathing peacefully. There was a little colour in her cheeks.

I came closer and placed my hand gently on her bare arm.

"Mrs. Kaufmann. It's Charlotte Frayne here. We met on Wednesday."

She shifted a little, but didn't open her eyes. I could see a yellowing bruise on her jaw that I hadn't noticed before.

"Mrs. Kaufmann. Do you think you could talk to me?"

Her eyelids fluttered, but remained closed. She licked her lips.

I leaned over to the bedside table, where there was a glass of water. I dipped my finger into the water and ran it along her upper lip. I did that twice.

Suddenly, she opened her eyes and looked straight into mine.

For one brief moment an expression of joy crossed her face.

"Ida."

"No, it's not Ida, Mrs. Kaufmann. I'm Charlotte Frayne. I've come on behalf of Mr. Gilmore."

The delight faded.

"Where's Ida?" she murmured.

Before I could even stumble into some kind of answer, she jerked her head away. Her shoulders began to shake. A wail broke out, eerily similar to the sound Conal Pierce had made earlier at the café. Full of grief and anguish.

Constable Frobisher shoved aside the screen. "What on earth's going on?"

I didn't have a chance to explain.

"Fetch a nurse," she ordered.

I didn't have to go far. A nurse was already scurrying down toward us. She had a hypodermic in her hand and, without ceremony, she stepped up to the bed, pulled aside the sheet, and plunged the needle into Mrs. Kaufmann's thigh.

"No more visitors for today," she said briskly.

I was in agreement with that. I had no desire to participate in further torture for the poor woman in the bed.

I moved outside of the screen with Constable Frobisher.

"What happened?" she asked.

"She mistook me for somebody else."

The constable's expression had changed. Much more sympathy.

"A cry like that makes your blood run cold, doesn't it?"

It did indeed.

Chapter Twenty-Eight

I EXITED THE HOSPITAL just as an ambulance was drawing up to the front doors. The attendants jumped out and lifted a stretcher from the back of the van. The elderly man lying on it was sickly pale. There was a cloth across his forehead, and I guessed he was another victim of the heat. I felt a stab of worry about Gramps. Not that I thought he'd succumb to the weather. He handled the high temperatures better than I did. It was just that we hadn't really communicated since breakfast.

It would have to wait.

I decided to go and see how Jack was making out.

A few feet from the entrance, I passed a bench where a woman and a child were sitting. She had her arm around the girl. They were not particularly well dressed, and the slump of their bodies conveyed despair. I could see that the little girl was weeping. The woman was crying also, although she was trying to hide it. Was somebody they knew in the hospital? Father, for instance? I certainly didn't want to be intrusive, but coming from Mrs. Kaufmann and her sorrow seemed to have drawn me into the circle of suffering humanity. I stopped.

"Excuse me. Is there any way I can be of help?"

They both looked up at me in astonishment.

"Are you saying we should move on?" the woman asked.

"Heavens no. Not at all. It's just that … well, you are clearly both upset, and I wondered if you were lost."

"Lost? I was born here. I'm not lost." Her eyes were shrewd and intelligent. "Not in that sense. But my husband is in the hospital. We've been told he has consumption. 'If he can go to a sanatorium and rest, he might live.' That's what the doctor said. He was well-meaning, but he might as well have said that if we flew to the moon, John would get better."

Gently she pushed the little girl into sitting in a more upright position. "Come, Sam. We must get home." She took the child by the hand. "Thank you for your concern. We'll manage somehow."

I suspected an offer of money would be offensive. "My name is Charlotte Frayne. I work in the Yonge Street Arcade. If you do think of any way I can be of help, please contact me."

The woman took the card I was holding out to her. "Thank you, my name is Colloby. This is my daughter, Samantha."

I was glad to see she put the card in her purse. The two of them moved off down the street, the child clinging tightly to her mother's hand.

Rationally, I knew that the disease the woman's husband was suffering from couldn't be cured by money alone, but money could buy him some decent care and her a reprieve from worry. I thought of Mrs. Walsingham and her wretched pampered son. Talk about money going to waste. Perhaps I could plant a little thought in her ear.

EVEN MORE BLUE than I had been before, I headed off. Maybe plunging into the investigation of brutal crime was what I needed. Better still, the solving of brutal crime.

As I was turning onto Phoebe Street, Jack Murdoch was just leaving Vince Alexander's shop. Unfortunately, he was with Detective Arcady.

He saw me and waved. I joined them.

Arcady was the same cold fish as before.

"Any luck with Mrs. Kaufmann?" Jack asked.

"I'm afraid not. She's still too shocked. And it does seem genuine. I'm not sure when she'll be able to talk. I can go back tomorrow if you want me to."

"I would like that. I'm sure you're the best person to do it."

"Anything more this end?"

Arcady answered for him. "Nothing we've not already heard. Detective Murdoch and I are in agreement that we have to extend the investigation to the entire surrounding streets. But that is more for verification than anything else. As far as I am concerned, we already have the guilty party in custody."

"I still have trouble seeing any motivation."

Arcady leaned in to me. His ice chip eyes seemed an inch

away. Did he ever smile? I thought again of the photograph in his office and tried, not too successfully, to find some compassion.

"My theory is that Kaufmann and Mrs. Gilmore were having a liaison. Gilmore discovered this, confronted his wife, and, in a fit of rage, hit her with the candle holder. When he was finally released from jail, he was still seething. He went to confront Kaufmann. Again in a fit of rage at his perfidy, he stabbed him."

"And Mrs. Kaufmann?"

"She was an innocent bystander. She tried to protect her husband and got beaten for her pains."

Arcady wasn't so obtuse he couldn't see the incredulity on my face. "This might be difficult for you to accept, Miss Frayne, but logic will tell you I am right. There is absolutely no evidence of a stranger coming to either house. No vagrant has been seen in the area, there was no forced entry into the Gilmore house nor the Kaufmanns'. Everything points to the victims being familiar with their attacker."

There was a slight smirk wanting to break out of the corner of his mouth. He thought his position was unassailable. On a rational level it had some plausibility. However, he had not worked with Thaddeus Gilmore the way I had for two years. I would bet my own life he was not capable of killing anybody or hitting defenceless women. In addition, he had an alibi for the first attack. If, that is, his wife had been killed after eight. Alas, not yet confirmed.

"I can see your point about the familiarity, but there are other people living on this street."

His pesky smirk hovered into view again. "None of them, I may point out, were covered with blood. Nobody else's face was scratched. They are mostly female."

"Women can be strong if their blood is up. And Mr. Gilmore has explained both the scratches and the blood."

"Indeed, he has."

"I believe that Mrs. Kaufmann will eventually be able to tell us what happened."

This time Jack intervened. "Not necessarily, I'm afraid. I was dealing with many returning soldiers right after the war, and you would be surprised how many of them had no recall of the events that had led up to their being wounded. They remember going over the top and that's all. A complete blank as to the manner of the injury or the circumstances." He pulled out the fancy watch. "We should get back to headquarters."

"What's the next step with Mr. Gilmore?"

"He has already gone before the court judge. The judge refused bail."

Jack offered me a ride in the car, but I turned it down. I didn't fancy a cozy ride with Detective Arcady. Besides, I wasn't finished yet.

They left, and when the car turned the corner out of sight, I headed back to the Kaufmann house. There was a young constable stationed at the door. I waved Jack's letter under his nose. He wanted to examine it more carefully, but I whisked it away just in time and put it in the pocket of my skirt, where he could hardly yank it out.

"I promise I won't disturb anything," I said sweetly.

"I'm sure you won't, ma'am. But I'll have to keep this door open. I'd rather you didn't switch on the lights. Fingerprints and all that. I'll do that for you."

He was a nice young fellow, but it was obvious he had no intention of bending any rules and having any fallout land on his lap. I thought he had a good career ahead of him. What better combination can there be for advancement, especially in an institution like the police force? Good manners and a touch of rigidity.

I went inside.

The house was hot, and there was a nasty smell in the air that I knew was spilled blood. The layout of the house was exactly the same as the Gilmores', and I guessed all the houses on this street followed the same floor plan. The hall was uncarpeted with a linoleum covering. No rugs. No pictures on the walls, just a small brass crucifix near the entrance to the dining room. A flight of stairs, also uncarpeted, led to the second floor. The double doors to the dining room on the left were open, and I could see how sparsely it was furnished. There was a strange feeling to the house, as if the inhabitants were in the process of leaving or had just arrived and hadn't settled. As far as I knew, neither of these things was the case. More likely the Kaufmanns had gradually sold off the furniture they possessed in order to survive.

I walked down to the kitchen, noting how the linoleum made a slithery, squeaky sort of noise. The small kitchen was as spartan as the rest of the house. The police had left a rope across the door, and I didn't move it, but I peered in. Two wooden chairs, one with a broken back, were at a circular table that had been set for a meal. Mismatched plates, teacups, knives, and forks. The stove was beside the sink. There was one open-shelved cupboard for dishes, which was following Old Mother Hubbard's lead. The bloodstains on the floor were clearly visible. A larger congealed pool near the sink must have come from Arthur Kaufmann. Mr. Gilmore had said he found Mrs. Kaufmann leaning against the cupboard. There was a reddish smudge there that I assumed was also blood. Not as copious. Supposedly Mr. Kaufmann had been stabbed with a kitchen knife. The police had obviously taken it away. Where had it been? It had to be visible. No assailant would have time to poke around in a drawer or two in search of a weapon. A half of a loaf of bread was sitting on the counter. I assumed Mrs. K. had been making lunch when the assailant had attacked her. From the front. Mr. K. must have already been in the kitchen, standing near the sink. He hadn't had time to turn to face his attacker. Mrs. K. was closest to the door; she must have been the first one to be assaulted.

What exactly had happened?

An assailant had entered the house, presumably in a manner that did not alarm either Kaufmann or his wife. This attacker had walked down the squeaky hall. He, if it was a he, had then encountered Mrs. K. She received a blow to the head, which knocked her to the ground. The attacker then seized the bread knife she had been using and promptly stabbed Mr. K. in the back.

Why hadn't Arthur turned around? Had it all happened so fast that he didn't have time? That would have to be fast indeed. But if he had been the one attacked first, what was Mrs. K. doing? She could have fled into the hall, but she hadn't. Had fear pinned her to the cupboard?

But then what? Mr. Gilmore had heard shouts. From whom? Man or woman? He came to see what was happening. He walked into the house. Found the couple as he described. Mr. K. unconscious but alive, Mrs. K conscious but in a state of shock and unable to speak. After trying to staunch the flow of blood from her injury, he ran to his own house to ring for the police. He returned to the Kaufmanns' to give further assistance. At this point, Arthur was conscious but had not said what had happened to them. The police and the ambulance arrived quickly, and the injured couple were transferred to the hospital. Mrs. K. was still *non compos mentis*. The detective in charge was Arcady. He asked Mr. Gilmore to accompany him to the station. Once there, he said Mr. Gilmore was under arrest. They suspected him of attacking the Kaufmanns. Motive as yet undisclosed. Maybe the couple knew something about the death of his wife Mr. Gilmore didn't want them to reveal. But neither had been killed. They could still tell their tales.

Where did the attacker, possibly bloodstained, go? The time lapse seemed quite short. Had he been seen? I kept thinking in terms of a man, but I suppose it could have been a woman. As I had said so blithely to Detective Arcady, women can get their blood up just as much as men can. Once again, we were back to motive.

The constable was keeping an eye on me. I called out to him, "I'm just going to take a look upstairs."

The stairs were also squeaky, the walls bare of ornamentation. I couldn't help wondering how long they had lived in this state.

There were two rooms on the second floor and a bathroom.

The door was open to the first bedroom, and I stepped in. I was almost knocked back by the reek of stale tobacco and sweat, with an overlay of spilled liquor and possibly vomit.

The heat had cooked everything to a higher intensity than normal.

There was a double bed; a coverlet that looked handmade was dragging on the floor. There were no rugs, just a few sheets of newspaper scattered about.

I walked over to the window. The lace curtains had been pulled back and the sash was up as far as it would go to let in the bit of air. I was looking down into a narrow back garden. A straight, no-nonsense path divided it evenly, and it seemed as if the entire space had been given over to the growing of vegetables except at the rear, where there was a veritable riot of leggy sunflowers. Plump tomatoes were weighing down vines, no blush yet. Immaculate runner beans straggled up canes. Beets with glossy dark green leaves, veined with deep purple, took up one entire corner. Nothing looked thirsty. Despite the injunction against watering, somebody was taking good care of them.

I checked the bathroom next. It was very clean, also uncluttered. A sink, a tub, and a toilet. Two towels on a rack, both pristine. A man's shaving utensils were on a shelf by the sink. No creams or perfumes visible. Arthur Kaufmann might have been a bachelor for all the signs of a female presence.

From there, I went to the second bedroom. Although it too was sparsely furnished, it was considerably more cozy than the other. There was a single cot also covered by a pretty, colourful quilt. Beside the bed was a yellow and brown hooked rug. Several prints were tacked on the walls; all of them, as far as I could tell, were pictures of flowers. This was obviously where Katia Kaufmann slept. Her choice or his? Did he even allow her a choice?

I walked over to the wardrobe, which was too dominant for this small room. Hanging inside was a green polka dotted summer frock, a black wool skirt, and a pink blouse. It was hard to feel that a woman's life could be summed up by the contents of her wardrobe, but it seemed that way.

I went back to the landing. I was about to close the door

behind me when I noticed there was a bolt on the inside. It looked as if it was newly installed.

"See everything you needed?" the constable asked me. He looked relieved that I had returned to his jurisdiction.

"I get the impression this couple were on their uppers. No luxuries to be seen."

"Them and half the city. I don't know how this economy is going to turn around. Not unless there's another war. And it's looking more and more like that's going to happen."

He looked too young to have had direct fighting experience of the past conflagration, but his parents would have gone through it.

"Let's hope you're wrong about that, constable."

Chapter Twenty-Nine

I'D TOLD JACK Murdoch I'd report in no matter what, but while I was on Phoebe Street I thought I might as well continue a little longer with my directive. *Find out whatever you can. They might be more willing to talk to you.*

The street was slipping into dusk, the sun reluctantly giving up its hold on the day. I could see the Kubays had turned on a light. I opened the gate and walked down to the door. I didn't have a chance to ring the bell when the door opened abruptly and Miss Kubay was standing on the threshold. She was holding up her hand palm out as if she was stopping traffic.

"I saw you coming," she said, her voice a whisper. "Mother is resting. What do you want?"

"So sorry to disturb you," I said in my most conciliatory tone. "I realize it's getting late, but I'm just doing a follow-up on the incident that happened earlier."

"I've already spoken to the police."

"I know you have. But going over things with a different person can sometimes bring up things that were overlooked first time around."

"What sort of things?"

I resisted the temptation to be snide. We wouldn't know until they came up.

I glanced around. "Miss Kubay, is there anywhere we can speak more comfortably? I promise I will keep my voice down."

I had underestimated her. Either that or something had changed. Wednesday, she had been eager to chat. By her own lights, she had been friendly, co-operative. The urge to gossip about her neighbours had been paramount. Now there was an anger in her eyes I didn't totally understand. She was not going to be sweet-talked into opening up.

"I told you, Mother is resting. I gave my statement. Nothing has been overlooked, as you put it."

"I understand you said you saw Mr. Gilmore going over to the Kaufmann house and shortly after that you heard shouts. Then you say you saw him again, this time running to his own house. Have I put it correctly?"

"Yes. I said I saw him because I did."

"And you are positive it was Mr. Gilmore?"

"Of course."

She looked as if she were about to go back inside, but I literally got my foot in the door.

"Mr. Gilmore says he did not go to the Kaufmann house until he too heard shouting. He went to see what was happening."

"He's lying."

"Why would he do that?"

"How should I know? Ask him. All I know is I saw what I saw. He went to their house well before anybody started shouting."

I wasn't going to be able to keep her much longer.

"Miss Kubay. I do not doubt you saw somebody." Actually, I did seriously doubt, but never mind that for now. "Is it possible that you saw a man you thought was Mr. Gilmore? Might it have been a vagrant, for instance?" Poor vagrants. They were getting all the opprobrium.

"No."

But I'd seen a shadow of doubt flit across her face. Who had she seen, if anybody?

"Just one more question, if you don't mind."

"Actually, I do mind. My mother needs attention."

I made one last desperate attempt.

"She does look grand for her age."

A fat lot of good my self-abasement did. If anything, she became even more frosty. She could have made a living keeping houses cool.

"Does she indeed? I'm sure she will be gratified to know your opinion."

I had to step back or lose my foot.

She closed the door. "Firmly" would be an understatement.

I decided to leave.

I was going past Mrs. Parker's house, docked tail decidedly between my legs, when somebody called out to me.

"Miss Frayne."

It was Mrs. Parker. She was sitting in front of her open window in the gloom, hardly visible.

Much as I had liked her, I wasn't in the mood for an endless chat, so I was about to wave and keep walking, but she called again.

"Miss Frayne. Might we have a word?"

There was no help for it. I opened the gate and walked down the path. She leaned out of the window.

"You must be hot. Why don't you come inside for a moment? I have the fan going in the parlour. It's quite pleasant. I made some raspberry wine earlier. Perhaps we could share some?"

I couldn't turn her down.

"Thank you, that sounds lovely. I'm afraid I can't stay long, though."

She beamed at me. "I'll let you in."

She disappeared, and a moment later I heard her unbolt the front door.

"Come in, come in," she said, as delighted as if I were a long-lost relative. So much for not staying long.

She had been telling the truth about the parlour. A large fan in one corner was doing a good job.

"I only put it on in emergencies," said Mrs. Parker as I poked my head in its direction. "The electricity is so expensive. But I would consider this heat wave an emergency, wouldn't you?"

"Indeed, I would."

"I'll be right back," said my hostess. "If you want to slip

off your shoes and cool your feet, I don't mind."

She trotted off.

Never mind my shoes, I would have liked to lift my skirt and cool off my thighs.

Mrs. Parker soon returned with her tray, which she placed on the table in front of me. She poured the drink from a pitcher into delicate, slender wineglasses.

"An old family recipe. My late husband was very fond of it, so I make it regularly."

I took a sip. It was rather too sweet for my taste and had quite a delayed wallop. I exclaimed exuberantly.

Formalities over, she sat back.

"I won't keep you, Miss Frayne. But I thought there was something you might like to know. I am so dreadfully sorry about what has happened to the Kaufmanns." She paused.

"I'm sure it must be disturbing to everybody what has happened on the street."

She nodded. "That nice police officer spoke to me earlier. The dark-haired one, not the older man. Frankly, I find him most unpleasant. Quite unsympathetic."

I knew she was referring to Arcady.

"They asked me if I had heard anything coming from the Kaufmann house. Shouts or cries? I said no, I had not. They are a few doors down, after all. The first I knew of the attack was when a police ambulance drew up in front of the house."

"Were you sitting in the window?"

She dropped her head, embarrassed to be seen as a nosy old lady.

"I come and go. Walk back to the kitchen, even sit in the back garden sometimes, then take a little look at the street." She sighed. "I do get a little, shall we say, aimless now that Matthew has gone."

"That is quite understandable."

"Is it? I always reproach myself that I should be doing something. But I don't quite know what that should be."

I didn't know what to say. I sipped at the wine. It was starting to create quite a buzz in my head.

"But really, Miss Frayne, there was something I wanted to share with you. I might have told the nice detective, but I didn't want to tell the other man. He would probably make more of it than it is."

I said as gently as I could, "There have been two very serious attacks in the past two days, Mrs. Parker, so anything you consider relevant to the investigation I would be only too happy to hear."

"Will you pass it on only to that nice detective?"

"I can certainly do that."

"Good. The reason I am being so enigmatic, Miss Frayne, is because I do like Katia Kaufmann. I think her husband is a brute, and I'm quite sure he mistreated her."

I wasn't surprised to hear that.

"I did hear her cry out on occasion. Often when I was in the backyard, I heard him upbraiding her terribly."

Again, I waited. She was not to be rushed.

"What I wanted to tell you was that I did come briefly to the window earlier. I saw a man come out of Mr. Gilmore's house, walk down the street, and go into the Kaufmann house."

Oh dear. I might not believe Miss Kubay, but I didn't doubt Mrs. Parker.

"Did you see who it was?"

"Oh, yes. I recognized him. He has visited Katia Kaufmann before." She dropped her voice, but the whisper was not salacious, more like concerned. For a woman of her generation, this was not information you trumpeted from the mountaintops. "I do believe this man is her lover."

Chapter Thirty

I HAD TO ASK. "Can we be clear about this, Mrs. Parker? You don't mean Thaddeus Gilmore?"

"Good gracious me, no. I hope you didn't think that."

"Not really, but I needed to make sure. You said this man came out of Mr. Gilmore's house."

"He did. I believe they were friends. When I saw him before, he went there first, then he would visit Katia Kaufmann."

Out of deference to her feeling of propriety, I found myself lowering my voice as well. "On what do you base your opinion that this man and Mrs. Kaufmann were lovers?"

Heaven knows what she would say. She'd hardly be hiding in the wardrobe.

"As I mentioned, I like to sit in my backyard. On three separate occasions I saw Mrs. Kaufmann and this gentleman together. How shall I put it? They were expressing great affection toward each other."

"Can you describe him for me?"

"Average height and weight. Nothing too distinctive

about him, really. Brown hair. Modestly dressed. He wore glasses."

"Where was Mr. Kaufmann during these affectionate exchanges?"

"He leaves the house on regular occasions. Wednesdays and Fridays. Nine o'clock in the morning. That is when Mrs. Kaufmann had her visitor."

"Do you know what Mr. Kaufmann does when he leaves the house?"

"I do not. We do not have the kind of relationship where we exchange pleasantries about our daily routines. He is usually gone for two or three hours."

"Does Mrs. Kaufmann go out?"

"She didn't used to, but in the past while she has been going out at least once a week. Thursday afternoons. She gets a little dressed up on those days."

Does she indeed? Meeting the alleged lover? I must say I was impressed with Mrs. Parker. She was giving me these details in a dispassionate way as if she were reporting on the sunflowers or the dahlias. Yes, they were quite bright this morning.

I walked her through her statement again. She had a quiet certitude that was convincing. Shortly after this man had entered the Kaufmann house, she had heard shouts, a cry she was sure was from Mrs. Kaufmann. She hadn't known what to do when she saw Mr. Gilmore come out of his house and hurry to the Kaufmanns'. Not too long after that, perhaps less than ten minutes, she saw him return to his own house. She did see signs of blood on his shirt. He went back again to the Kaufmanns', and shortly thereafter a police car and an ambulance arrived. Mr. Kaufmann was carried out on a stretcher and was followed a few minutes later by his wife, also on a stretcher. Mrs. Parker had come out of her own house at that point to see what was happening, but the abrupt police officer had sent her back inside. She saw no sign of the first man, the lover. Nobody as yet had come to ask for a statement from her.

"Could the visitor have left from the rear door?" I asked her.

"He certainly could. There is a laneway that runs behind all our houses. He could have gone out by the back gate and gone along the laneway to the street."

She sat and looked at me over the top of her old-fashioned pince-nez. "I have no desire to get anybody into trouble. I do like Mrs. Kaufmann, and I consider the Gilmores to be splendid neighbours. What has happened, Miss Frayne? I am afraid to leave my house."

I reassured her as best as I could. But my words seemed hollow, even to me. Two savage attacks in three days. What was a vulnerable old lady going to do except be afraid?

"Keep your door locked and don't open it for anybody you don't know. Do you have enough food to be going on with?"

She did.

"I'll be back as soon as I know anything more."

I put the glass on the side table. I hadn't finished it, but if I was going to have any brain left I thought I'd better stop now. Promising to be back the next day, I left.

THE YOUNG CONSTABLE in front of the Kaufmann house greeted me happily.

"I think I dropped my handkerchief in one of the bedrooms. Okay if I pop up and get it?"

That pesky handkerchief was coming in handy.

"Sure."

I went inside the stifling house and hurried upstairs. I went to Mrs. Kaufmann's room first. I'd just given a cursory scan before, now I had more idea of what I was looking for.

When I was growing up, Gran had not always approved of my reading material. She was old-fashioned enough to consider certain novels unsuitable for developing minds. I got into the habit of slipping my current library books underneath the bed and reading them at night. I don't think she would actually have removed any of them, but the threat was there. If she had known I had accidently come across *England, My England* by D.H. Lawrence, she would have had a conniption. She would have been right. It was far too old for me. Scarred me for life.

I went straight to the bed and crouched down so I could see underneath. Katia Kaufmann obviously had the same need to conceal as I had had. There were no books hidden away, but there was a metal box. Not a speck of dust on it.

I should explain that although I was licensed as a private

investigator, I had no more legal rights than an ordinary citizen. I could not take anything or interfere with any property. By even looking at Katia's things, I was stepping close to the edge. I had to take that risk.

I pulled it out. It was locked, but the key was not hard to find. Katia had hidden it under her pillow.

I opened the box without any difficulty.

Inside, glued to a piece of stiff cardboard, was a pen-and-ink drawing of a young woman. She was looking over her shoulder as she smiled demurely at the artist. Her shoulders were bare, but whether the rest of her was clothed or not you couldn't tell. She had thick curly hair, loose and wild. It was a charming portrait, intimate and loving.

There was enough resemblance to know this was Katia Kaufmann when she was younger. The artist had written his signature on the bottom of the drawing: "Conal Pierce. '17." There was a small photograph. Conal in army uniform, looking young and hopeful.

I put both pictures aside on the bed. I had no idea what to make of it all. Obviously, Katia Kaufmann had a prior relationship with Conal Pierce. Mrs. Parker thought they were lovers, and looking at the sweet portrait that was not hard to believe. I assumed they had reconnected with each other, perhaps when he had come to Toronto to start the café.

I turned back to the box. At the bottom was a leather pouch. I opened that and spilled out the contents. Mostly coins, some notes. They added up to twenty-seven dollars.

My instincts had been right. Conal hadn't come totally clean. The money wasn't going to fund strikers. It had ended up in a box underneath Katia Kaufmann's bed.

I returned everything, locked the box, and replaced the key underneath the pillow.

I WENT TO the second bedroom. I wasn't exactly sure what I was looking for, but I had a feeling Arthur Kaufmann had his secrets just as his wife had.

A battered wardrobe was in one corner. No door, just a chintz curtain hanging from a rod. I walked over to it and pulled the curtain aside. There were only two pieces of clothing hanging up: a man's shirt, dark blue, and a pair of navy trousers. There was a white metal pin on the shirt with a distinctive red insignia.

My, my. It seemed Kaufmann was a member of one of the Toronto Swastika Clubs. They had sprouted up like ugly mushrooms about three years ago.

Chapter Thirty-One

I LEFT THE STINKING room and started to head downstairs. I was in the hallway when Kaufmann appeared. He appeared to be wearing a hospital issue shirt, and his left arm was bound close to his body. He looked pale. And very angry.

"What are you doing here?"

I stayed calm. "I could ask you the same question."

He actually bared his teeth. "I live here. This is my house."

I managed a smile. "Of course. I just meant that I'm surprised you have been released from hospital so soon. How are you feeling?"

I didn't give a toss as to how he was feeling, but it seemed a good diversionary move. He looked as if any minute he was going to grab me physically and throw me out.

He was not diverted.

"I will be better now I'm home."

"Indeed. And how is your wife?"

"Never mind. I repeat question. What are you doing here?"

"I'm helping the police with the investigation into the attack."

"You're trespassing. Get out."

I would have been only too happy to leave, but he was completely blocking the hall, and I didn't know how I was going to get past him without one of us pushing the other out of the way. I thought he'd win that contest. Over Kaufmann's shoulder I could see the constable, who was watching us. He looked worried. I called to him.

"Constable. Would you mind reassuring Mr. Kaufmann that I am working in conjunction with the police?"

He probably wasn't completely sure about that, but it was obvious what state Kaufmann was in.

He said confidently, "I can vouch for this lady, sir."

Bless him.

Reluctantly, and making his reluctance obvious, Kaufmann stepped aside so that I could get by. The hallway was narrow, and I had to squeeze against the wall. He smelled vile: stale sweat, fear, some carbolic he'd been daubed with for his injury, and whisky. He'd stopped somewhere along the way to throw back quite a bit of whisky.

He favoured me with yet another snarl. "If I see you within two feet of this house again, I'm going to lodge a formal complaint. I'll make sure you lose your licence. Assuming you even have a licence."

"Oh, I do. As I said, I am officially helping the police with their enquiries."

I couldn't let him have the last word, could I?

I got outside.

Kaufmann moved to the door.

"Are you planning to stay?" he asked the constable.

"I will until I'm relieved, sir. We want to make sure you are safe."

Kaufmann almost spat at him. "Safe? Of course, I'm sodding safe. I was taken by surprise before. It won't happen again." He came even closer. I was beside the constable, slightly behind him, and I could feel him tense. I did too. We might have been looking at a bear on the rampage. However, Kaufmann contented himself with slamming the door shut.

I think the constable and I both released the breaths we'd been holding.

"I'm sorry if I pulled you into something," I said.

He grinned a little. "Nasty piece of work, isn't he? You'd think he'd be glad to know the Toronto Police Force is looking out for him."

He had a boyish face dusted with freckles. He'd been afraid of Kaufmann, but he hadn't backed down. I felt like giving him a hug and telling him he had a good career ahead of him. Probably I was the one who needed a hug.

"I am going over to headquarters to report to Detective Murdoch. I'll tell him what happened. I'll make sure to tell him how well you handled the situation."

"Thank you, ma'am."

I set off along Phoebe Street. No lights in the Kubay house, nor Mrs. Parker's house. Didn't mean they weren't watching. Funny how some people can watch kindly and others maliciously.

Chapter Thirty-Two

THERE WERE ONLY a few lights showing on the upper floors of the police headquarters. Most of the workers appeared to have regular human hours and had gone home. There was yet another young constable at the reception. He greeted me in a friendly fashion when I entered. I had the impression he was bored and lonely.

"Is Detective Murdoch still here?" I asked.

"Certainly is, ma'am. Who shall I say is asking for him?"

Were all the new crop of constables as polite, I wondered?

He rang Jack on the intercom. As before, he came out promptly from the office section.

"Miss Frayne. Excellent. Come on down. Would you like some coffee?"

I'd actually consumed enough liquid refreshment for the evening, but I nodded enthusiastically. Coffee might be a good antidote to the potent wine Mrs. Parker had served. For a moment I had a twinge of paranoia. Did Murdoch offer it because I seemed a bit tipsy?

He turned to the young constable. "Constable Pagel, could you possibly conjure up some coffee for us?"

The young man jumped up with alacrity and headed to the door on the other side of the foyer.

"And if you can add a couple of sandwiches it would be appreciated."

I was in fact getting hungry, so my enthusiasm was not feigned this time.

I followed Jack down the hall.

"I'm surprised you're still here at this hour."

"Fiona and the children are up in Muskoka for the month, so I'm a bachelor except on weekends. Working gives me something to do."

He gave me a rueful grin. "I have to admit, selfish man that I am, I don't like it. I'd much rather be splashing around in the lake or sitting on a dock with a breeze on my face. Not to mention being waited on hand and foot by a devoted wife."

"That's typical married life, is it?"

Maybe I'd been sharper than I intended, but he glanced at me for a moment, then laughed.

"Hardly. There's nothing typical about my wife. You'd like her. Perhaps at some point, we could have you over for dinner."

I was absurdly pleased. Both by the invitation and by being linked to a woman about whom there was "nothing typical."

We'd just sat down when the telephone shrilled from the desk.

Jack answered.

"I see. Did he say anything? Nothing at all? And his wife? Okay. Come back to the station and turn in your report. Good work."

He hung up and gave the inside of his cheek a bit of a chew, a habit I was getting familiar with.

"That was Constable O'Grady. He was on guard at the hospital. He says that Kaufmann has checked himself out. Apparently it was against the doctor's advice, but Kaufmann insisted."

"I know. I was about to tell you, I ran into him, almost literally, over at his house."

I filled him in about our encounter in the hall.

"Sounds like a good thing Constable Davis was on hand."

"It was."

I sang the praises of young Davis.

"I suppose I don't have a reason to justify keeping a man there, but everything is so unresolved. Two assaults in three days."

"What about Katia Kaufmann?"

"She hasn't been discharged from hospital as yet. She's still in some kind of shock. Not talking."

"Did Kaufmann have anything to say for himself?"

"Nothing. He says he doesn't remember anything from the time he went into his kitchen to the time he woke up in the hospital."

"Pity."

"As I said earlier, I saw lots of that when I was at the

Front. Complete memory blank." He gave a rueful grin. "Sometimes I wish that had happened to me, but no such luck." I would like to have heard more, but he didn't elaborate. "Constable O'Grady also reported two enquiries into the state of Mrs. Kaufmann. The caller was a man who claimed he was a relative."

"No name, I presume?"

"None reported."

"Do you think she at least will be able to tell us anything about what happened?"

"We'll have to wait and see. It would certainly be helpful if one or the other could."

He leaned back in his chair. I thought he looked tired.

There was a tap on the door, and Constable Pagel entered with a tray loaded with two cups of coffee and two plates, each with a rather squished-looking egg sandwich.

I took a sip of the coffee. It was so weak as to be almost unrecognizable. It was also lukewarm. I turned to the sandwich, which tasted as bad as it looked. The bread almost fell apart in my hand. Out of shock, my slightly fuzzy head started to clear.

Jack took a big gulp of the coffee then tucked into the sandwich with apparent enjoyment. I assumed he was accustomed to police fare.

"All right, so what have you got to tell me?"

"Lots."

I started with what I'd found in Arthur Kaufmann's room. He listened attentively.

"So he's been a blue shirt has he? A Swastika Club member. Why am I not really surprised?"

"I haven't heard much about the clubs lately. Are they even still in operation?"

"Unfortunately, they are. The Balmy Beach Swastika Club became the Beaches Protection Association."

"Protection being a euphemism for exclusion?"

"You've got it."

"I have to admit, I'm a bit hazy about what the Swastika Clubs were. It all ended up in the riot at Christie Pits, but that's about all I know."

To tell the truth, that summer, I'd been caught up in my own affairs. The loss of Gran, for instance. Falling for an unsuitable man, for another.

Jack drank some more of the pretend coffee. "Back then they were mostly young toughs, unemployed and looking for trouble. And when you're a young aggrieved male and looking for trouble, you're going to find it."

"What did they have to be so aggrieved about? Other than the economy, that is?"

"That was secondary. They seemed to leap into action when they felt their turf was being contaminated by foreigners."

"Ah, yes. The eternal 'other.'"

"Thirty-three was a hot summer. Almost as bad as now. There were a lot of people going down to the lake to swim and cool off. The locals, some of them anyway, objected to the crowds who came and took over with their foreign ways what they thought of as 'their' beach. There were lots of complaints."

"Oh, Lord, I'm remembering now. They felt that the so-called invaders smelled of garlic, for one thing."

"That's right. And they didn't observe decorum and changed into swimming costumes in their cars, for another."

"Sounds very decorous to me."

"Obviously not to the proper residents. So out came the Swastikas. All inspired by Chancellor Hitler, no doubt. Badges, sweaters, banners. Stones arranged on the sand." He sighed. "It was very ugly. Anti-fascist groups picked up the gauntlet. The Communists, mostly. Some young Jews. Immigrant Italians. They became allies."

"And that erupted into the riot."

"It did."

He stood up abruptly, giving me a slightly shamefaced smile. "Excuse me, Charlotte. I'll be right back. Call of nature." He went off. Maybe he didn't like to spit out the egg sandwich in front of me.

For good manners, a principle drummed into me by Gran, I forced myself to swallow down the last of the coffee. Not even she could have persuaded me to finish the egg sandwich.

I fell into my own reverie.

Word of the Christie Pits riot had flashed through the city like a fire.

Gramps and I were having dinner when one of our

neighbours, Mr. McCrae, knocked on the door. He was very agitated.

"Some east-end rabble brought a blanket to the baseball game. They'd drawn a swastika on it, bold as brass. Sure enough don't they unfurl it during the game. When they saw that, the young Jewish lads went crazy and they flew up the hill to get the damn thing. Eye-ties were playing on the other team, but they've joined in with the Jews. Now they're all having a go at each other. In the streets and everywhere. It's still going on. The police can't stop it."

I'd had a hard time persuading my chivalrous grandfather not to rush over and intervene. He hated what he called "bully boys."

"I didn't lose my only son fighting bravely as a soldier to put up with ruffians beating up on people they don't like."

I'd sort of got used to him saying, "my only son." He meant my father, but that seemed to have fallen away from Phillip Frayne's identity. I suppose I couldn't blame Gramps. Phillip had never seen me. He'd impregnated my mother when he was home on leave. She was seventeen, "with the grass of Ireland still between her teeth," as my grandma described her one day. Not a lot of fondness there. Phillip was fighting in South Africa at the time. He was ignominiously kicked in the stomach by a pack mule and died from peritonitis shortly thereafter. He was four days past his twentieth birthday. Growing up without a father didn't mean much to me. Gramps had done just fine as far as I was concerned.

That evening, Gramps and I had argued at each other for quite a long time. I rarely raised my voice to him, but on that occasion I did.

"You think those men with blood lust will respect an old codger like you? If you go over there, I'm coming too."

"First of all, I'm not an old codger; second, speaking of lust, do you think they'd have any more respect for a woman?"

And on it went. Finally, he agreed that he'd wait and see what the reports were. We'd received various until late into the night. The fighting had gone on for hours. The few police officers on the scene were overwhelmed and could do little to stop it.

THE DOOR OPENED and Jack returned. "Sorry about that. Where were we?"

"You got me thinking about the riot. I've always wondered why Chief Draper didn't have more officers on the scene. There had been intimations of trouble brewing at the game just a week before. Hadn't the swastika sign appeared then?"

Jack clenched his teeth. "For God's sake don't quote me, but I'll tell you why there weren't more police there. Draper is an asshole, forgive the language."

I had to laugh. "Forgiven."

"He was more concerned with trying to suppress an orderly meeting of decent men who were desperate for employment. He thought they were all communists, which is still his big bogeyman." Jack shook his hands in the air. "Argh! Bogeyman! Help. Fee fie fo fum. I smell communists. Of course, he knew there might be trouble at the baseball game. He chose to ignore it. Imagine what the Jews felt when those louts unleashed their swastika banner and started to shout, 'Hail Hitler.'"

It was my turn to clench up. "I've often been surprised Draper is still our chief constable. At the very least, he's a rigid, unthinking fool. At worst, a bigot."

"That's putting it nicely."

I had the feeling Jack Murdoch had a lot more he could have said about the state of the police department.

"Thank God, Mayor Stewart ordered them to stop flaunting their signs or risk prosecution."

"I hate to say this," continued Jack, "but I think there is another war on the horizon. The War to End All Wars is the one I fought in, and it clearly didn't work."

We were both silent for a moment. Bringing up that ravaged time had a way of doing that to people as they fell into their memories.

"Do you think there is any connection between the attack on Kaufmann and his association with the Swastikas?"

I knew I could be pointing in the direction of Mr. Gilmore, but it was a question that had to be asked.

"I don't know, but I'm going to pursue it." He looked over at the clock. "It's getting late. I'd better rouse the justice of the peace and get a search warrant before he leaves. I'd like to take a closer look at what you found. If Kaufmann won't voluntarily let me in, I can at least do a legal search. Was there anything else you wanted to tell me?"

"There was. Mrs. Kaufmann appears to have had a prior relationship with Conal Pierce. They are probably lovers."

"Really!"

"Check the box underneath her bed."

"I will. Thank you, Charlotte. Keep all this to yourself for now."

"Of course."

He stood up to usher me out. At the door he hesitated.

"Sorry about the coffee and the sandwich. Not very good, were they?"

Chapter Thirty-Three

As far as people on the sidewalks were concerned, the city was dead. Nobody who didn't have to leave his home was out. A strip of light, purple as a bruise, was lingering on the edges of the night that had taken over, soft and suffocating.

When I got to the Paradise, even that remnant of day had vanished. Dim street lights were on. The city kept the wattage low for the economy's sake.

I went to the front door and rapped. I heard somebody say something, but the door was recalcitrant, so I knocked again.

"It's Charlotte Frayne," I called, and quickly the door opened. Hilliard peered down at me. Not too welcoming.

"Hello, Charlotte. Sorry. This isn't a good time to talk."

"I have some information. About the thefts."

Even then I think he would have put me off, but the door was open and Wilf Morrow was seated only a few feet away. He saw me.

"Well, if it isn't our industrious waitress coming in early to get ready for tomorrow or something." Yet again, he sounded plastered. "Bring her in, Hill. Let her join the party."

I knew that Jack Murdoch would be calling on them very soon. I thought it would be easier on them if I prepared the ground.

Hilliard stepped back to let me through.

All four partners were around the table. I must have come in the middle of a very intense talk, because the tension was thick in the air.

Hill pulled out a chair. "Have a seat."

Eric looked at me politely. "We were having a rather important chat, Miss Frayne. Would you mind coming back later?"

I would have been only too happy to do that, but I didn't get the chance to respond.

Hilliard dragged up another chair and sat down beside me. "No reason she can't stay."

"Perhaps she wants to give up snooping and become a waitress," said Wilf.

"We are rehashing what came out after lunch," said Eric. "Wilf is angry that Hill didn't tell us earlier that money was missing. I suppose I'm rather annoyed about that as well."

"I've told you at least three times," said Hilliard, who was also steaming. "I didn't want to bring it up until I was sure about what was going on."

Wilf sneered at him. "Until you made sure it wasn't the mice, you mean?"

Eric reached over and put his hand on Wilf's arm. "Cool down, pal. So he didn't tell us. He has now, and we should deal with it."

Wilf had a glass in front of him that looked like beer. He took a big swig. Hilliard glared at him.

"Don't you think you should slow down with that? We're not going to come to any sane conclusions if you drink yourself into oblivion."

"Oblivion? That might be nice."

Throughout all this, Conal hadn't uttered a word. He was at the corner of the table, sipping on something that could also have been beer, but he didn't seem drunk in the same way Wilf was. He just seemed far, far away. I wished I hadn't come. I supposed I would have to tell them what I'd found in Katia's room, and frankly, I dreaded it.

Conal saved me. Speaking into the air, not looking at anybody, he said, "I've said I'm sorry a dozen times. I will replace the money if it takes all year."

"I still don't know why you didn't just say you needed money," said Eric. "We could have floated a loan."

"Speak for yourself, Eric," spluttered Wilf. "I don't know if I would have been willing to cough up for some godforsaken Commie cause."

Conal lowered his head. "In answer to your question, Eric, I didn't tell you because I knew you would ask me why I wanted the money, and I wasn't at liberty to say."

That really ticked off Wilf. "You weren't at liberty? What the hell does that mean? Did the prime minister want money to buy himself a boat? Or was it the archbishop who wasn't raking in enough money on the collection plate but didn't want the world to know?"

"Get off his back, Wilf," said Hilliard. "Let him tell us himself."

Almost for the first time, Conal seemed to become aware that I was sitting there.

"I apologize, Miss Frayne. I didn't mean to drag you into the middle of a family row."

"Didn't you say she was a good intermediary?" This from Wilf. I would cheerfully have tipped a bucket of beer over his head.

"Even if it's sailing on a stormy sea. I suggest you listen to Mr. Pierce."

Wrong thing to say. I might as well have put a lit match to the very oil I was attempting to pour on the troubled waters.

Wilf Morrow literally jumped out of his chair. "Stormy sea? What are you, a poet? Stormy sea, my arse. We're dealing with betrayal here."

I don't know if he intended to come over to me and give me a wallop, but he didn't have a chance because Hilliard grabbed hold of him hard by the arms and pushed him away so that he actually fell to the floor.

"Wilf! Hill!" Eric cried out. "Stop it. Let's all calm down. She's right. We are getting to it. We can deal with this ourselves."

I must admit I was getting a bit fed up with this lot, especially as I knew about the purloined money sitting in a pretty box underneath Mrs. Kaufmann's bed. I suppose it aroused my stubborn streak.

"Mr. Taylor. I am still in your employ. Do you want me

to leave now and come back tomorrow? I do have pertinent information."

This time it was Conal who looked at me in alarm. I thought he had been about to tell the whole truth, but maybe he hadn't. Wilf wasn't moving from the floor, and Hilliard put out a hand to help him up. Boys after all.

"Certainly, I don't want you to leave. You're quite right. Conal, go on with what you were saying."

"I don't know what the big secret is," said Eric. "You've been collecting money for the strike. Isn't that what you said?" He reached into his pocket for his wallet. "Hell, I'll give you some more."

Conal waved his hands in the air. "No, no. It wasn't for the strike. I let you think that."

That seemed about to inflame Wilf all over again. Hill put a restraining hand on his arm.

"Go on, Conal. Why did you take the money?"

"I was helping out a friend."

"A friend? Who?" demanded Wilf.

Conal hesitated and was eyeing his friend nervously.

"I'd rather not say. It's not relevant. It's just a friend."

Hilliard took a deep breath. He turned to me.

"Is this information that you have, Miss Frayne?"

"Yes."

Back to Conal. "Do you want to tell us yourself, or do you want Miss Frayne to give us her report?"

Conal's eyes met mine. He desperately wanted to keep this a secret, but it was clear I knew.

Wilf was the one to prod him. Anger barely held in.

"Well? Spit it out."

"I loaned the money to Mrs. Kaufmann."

"What? The woman who just joined the party?"

"Yes."

"Why her?" asked Eric.

Conal shrugged, still holding back. Hilliard nodded at me.

"Miss Frayne?"

I was reluctant too, having seen the tenderness in that drawing, but we had to move on.

"I believe Mr. Pierce and Mrs. Kaufmann had a prior acquaintance."

Hilliard slapped his hand on the table. "Of course. You talked about her when we were in Doberitz. I remember now. Her name was Katia Kurth then. She was your sweetheart."

Conal lowered his head and looked bashful. He must have grown up on a diet of King Arthur stories.

"Yes. The woman I fell in love with when we were both twenty. She was working in France near the base."

"I notice she didn't wait for you," said the ever tactful Wilf.

"She was told I'd died. When I was released, I tried to contact her. But it was too late. I learned she had married. I didn't know where she was living." He slumped in his chair. "It was sheer chance that we met again. You can imagine how I felt when she walked into the café."

All three of the men stared at him, perhaps trying to

understand such a passion. I thought even Hilliard was struggling. According to what he'd told me earlier, true love hadn't quite hit the others yet.

"When she came into the café, I thought my life had been given back to me," said Conal. Now he was released from his secret, he seemed to want to talk. Words poured out. "We knew we still loved each other. But she revealed that she was trapped in an unhappy marriage with a man who mistreated her. She didn't say that right away. I know what you're thinking, Wilf. I can see it written all over your face."

"She's taking you for a ride."

"No, she's not," Conal burst out passionately. "She wouldn't tell me at first. Then I noticed the bruises. She said she tripped, she banged her head. But gradually, when she trusted that I wouldn't despise her, she admitted the truth."

"And the money? Our money? That is supposed to be healing ointment, is it?"

"Wilf! Stop it. Let's hear him out." Hilliard had raised his voice. Wilf subsided.

Conal continued. "Over the last two months, I have been giving her money so that she can leave him. She has nothing of her own. She insists it is a loan from me, and she will pay it back whe she's on her feet." He raised his head and looked at his comrades. "I'm sorry I didn't tell you, but Katia is ashamed of her marriage. She didn't want anybody to know. I had to respect that."

Eric actually smiled at him. "It's not quite a worker's

strike, but not dissimilar. I'm not going to put up a fight or demand the money back."

Hilliard squeezed Conal's shoulder. "Silly twit. You could have told us. We'll help out."

Conal's face lit up. "I don't think I have loved anybody in my life as much as I love Kitty." He stopped and, one by one, he looked at his comrades. "I'm afraid there's more I need to tell you."

"Please don't say more confessions?" said Wilf. "I don't think I can handle it."

Right on cue, there was a sharp rap at the door. As I expected, the visitor was Jack Murdoch. He was with Detective Arcady.

Chapter Thirty-Four

THEY DIDN'T STAY long, just long enough to escort Conal Pierce back to headquarters with them. "For questioning." Detective Arcady was the one who said that, declaring it in a tone of voice that suggested he might be taking Conal to the gallows.

The charge looming over him was assault causing bodily harm. The victims were Arthur Kaufmann and his wife, Katia.

"Do you have anything to say?" Arcady asked.

"Nothing," Conal answered, but it is doubtful if even a naive nun would have believed him.

He looked so fragile that I for one was glad Murdoch agreed to have Hilliard go with them.

When all this had been accomplished, there was no reason for me to stick around at the café, and they didn't want me to. Eric and Wilf closed ranks. Eric nicely; Wilf not so much. Hilliard had asked Jack on what they were basing the pending charge, but he'd responded evasively. "We just want to ask him some questions pertaining to the assault. It's easier to do that at headquarters."

I assumed Jack had investigated Katia's room and

confirmed the telltale connection to Conal. The love triangle as a motive for murder is well documented. Except that he seemed such a gentle sort of man, I wouldn't have been surprised if Conal had clobbered Kaufmann. I wouldn't feel particularly sorry. I simply couldn't believe he'd hurt Katia, but I was beginning to suspect what had actually happened.

I told the two men I'd be in touch and headed home.

I felt exhausted.

As I got close to my house, my heart sank. There was a single light shining in the porch. Everything else was dark. Gramps was either in bed already or he wasn't at home. After all that had happened today, I'd been looking forward to the comfort of a late-night visit and a cup of tea. *Get used to it,* a scolding inner voice popped out.

He wasn't home, and it didn't take a brilliant deductive mind to figure out he was spending the evening with Bertha Johnson.

I got undressed and crawled into bed.

I expected to fall asleep right away, but of course I didn't. I chased sleep as if it were a mosquito, just out of reach. Most of the night, I tossed and turned. When I did finally drop off, I fell into a terrible nightmare.

I am in this house, but I seem younger. I am looking for Gran and Gramps, but they are nowhere to be found. I go into their bedroom, and they are both lying on top of the covers as if they are taking a nap. A woman is sitting next to the bed. She says to me in a cold, unfriendly way, "They're dead. You will have to leave the house right away. They've left everything to their son."

"But he's dead too," I cry out.

The woman shrugs. "You'll have to sort that out. All I know is you can't stay here."

"But I can take my things with me, can't I?"

"No. Nothing can be touched."

I look over at the bed, and the bodies have vanished. Perhaps they weren't dead after all. I experience such longing that it almost chokes me. Perhaps they are alive and I will see them again.

I woke up and stayed awake. I had no desire to return to that particular dream. I listened, but the house was silent. Gramps hadn't come home. Finally, I got up and went to the bathroom to wash. All the time I was listening for the sound of the front door. Nothing. My chest ached. It was hard not to run out to Bertha Johnson's house and see that Gramps was indeed alive.

I went downstairs, made some toast, put a pot on to brew some coffee, and forced myself to come back to the present. There was a running conversation in my head.

Bertha, you should know this about Gramps. He's very fussy about his morning egg. He doesn't like it runny, but not hard either. And the tea. Very fussy about the tea. You must pour in the milk first, then the tea, which has been steeped for five minutes. Don't forget to warm the pot before you put in the tea leaves. Two heaping spoonfuls.

I left Gramps a note saying I'd call later and set out for the office. I had no reason to go by way of Bertha's house, so I didn't. I decided to risk messing up my clothes and got out my bike. It took a lot less energy to bicycle than to walk, and this morning I felt as if I didn't have much in reserve. I looked up at the sky, which hadn't made up its mind at this point. Was it going to play host to an inimical ball of fire or just sit in a cloudy grey sulk of held-in humidity?

It was getting on for eight. Along Yonge Street, various shops were starting to roll down their awnings for the day. I locked up my bicycle to a lamppost outside the Arcade and went in.

In spite of everything, the place lifted my spirits. I loved going to work, truth be told. The glass ceiling allowed light to flood into the open interior space. Even in winter it was bright. Now the air cooling system kept the temperature bearable. A few people looked as if they had taken advantage of this to spend a night even if it meant a wooden bench for a bed.

I headed for the third floor.

The offices before ours were dark, but there was a light on in T. Gilmore and Associates. My heart skipped a beat. With this new angle to the Kaufmann crime, the police must have released Mr. Gilmore. I thought he deserved to have some time off, but I guessed he was keen to get down to work.

I was only partly right about that. He was inside the office, but he wasn't working.

He was tied to my chair.

I didn't realize he was tied up when I stepped into the office. It was very odd that he was at my desk and not his own, but not so strange that I turned tail and ran out.

Actually, I'm glad I didn't. He would have died.

"Mr. Gilmore. Are you all right?"

"Close the door, will you, Miss Frayne? And lock it, please." His voice was unnaturally calm, and he enunciated the words carefully.

I half obeyed. Closed, but not locked.

All of this had taken only moments. When I faced him again, I understood the reason for his unnatural posture and strained voice. His arms were pulled back in an uncomfortable position behind the chair. I could see a trickle of blood coming from his nostril. Before I could go to help him, a man stepped out from the adjoining room. He was holding a nasty looking gun, which was aimed at me.

It was Arthur Kaufmann.

Chapter Thirty-Five

"Good morning, Miss Frayne. I was hoping you would show up."

"What's going on?"

Mr. Gilmore was the one who answered.

"Mr. Kaufmann believes we have a significant amount of money in our safe. He wants the combination so he can help himself. We have not yet agreed on the barter. He says if I give him the combination, he will let me go unharmed. As long as I promise to give him enough time to leave before I notify the police. I am disinclined to trust him. I have also told him that there is no money in the safe. That we keep a few dollars for petty expenses, but no substantial money."

"Bullshit," burst out Kaufmann. "He's a Jew. Of course he's got money stashed away."

I answered with a composure I didn't exactly feel.

"No, he doesn't. It's exactly what he says."

"Why won't he give me the combination, then?"

Mr. Gilmore sighed. "I told you I don't have it."

Kaufmann waved the gun at me. "You do, then?"

I looked at Mr. Gilmore. I knew he could get into the

safe if he wanted to. Clearly, he didn't. What the hell was I going to do?

Kaufmann let me off the hook. "Let's put it this way. If I get the money, I shall leave you both in peace. You will promise not to give the alarm for at least three hours, so I can get out of town. If there is no money in that safe, then I will assume that the Jew here has lied. And I will be forced to take measures."

"What sort of measures?"

"Shall we say some cleansing will be in order?"

Mr. Gilmore tried to turn around, but he couldn't. "I keep telling you I am not a Jew."

"That doesn't matter one way or the other, really. I know you have money because my wife told me."

"What?"

"She said you were slipping her money on the quiet. She was saving it up so she could leave me."

Kaufmann came over to the chair and stood behind Mr. Gilmore. He pressed the gun hard behind his ear. His left arm was still pressed against his chest, but his wound didn't seem to be impeding him much.

"Why were you giving a respectable Gentile woman money, Jew-boy?"

I interceded.

"He wasn't giving your wife money. Somebody else was."

Kaufmann stared at me. "Who?"

At this point I saw no reason to hold back. I actually felt

weirdly calm, and my thinking processes were clear. Thank God for survival instinct. There wasn't a chance Kaufmann was going to let us go. *Keep him talking,* I thought. *Wait for my opportunity. Just don't let him shoot Mr. Gilmore.*

"One of the men at the Paradise Café. An Irishman named Conal Pierce. He and your wife knew each other years ago."

That did give him something to think about for a moment. Perhaps he'd already suspected it. Into that tiny gap of distraction, I pressed forward.

"I tell you what, Mr. Kaufmann. Mr. Gilmore does not indeed have the combination to the safe, but I do. I swear to you there is no money in there. We have about five dollars in my desk, which you can take."

He sneered. "You must think I'm some kind of pinhead. First of all you will give me that five, then you will open the safe. If there is no money inside, then I will start using the Jew here for target practice until he tells me where he's hiding it." Suddenly he slapped his free hand on his forehead. "No. Wait. Better still, I'll use you for a target. I'll wager that when you scream, he will speak."

"These offices aren't soundproof," interjected Mr. Gilmore. "Somebody will hear you."

Kaufmann waved the gun in the air. "You notice this little extra barrel here." There was what appeared to be a metal extension on the end of the gun barrel. "Lovely little invention." He stroked it in a repulsively suggestive way. "It's called a silencer. A sound suppressor. All anybody would hear is a sort of thump, as if you've dropped a box on the floor. Nobody will come to investigate until it's too late."

I kept thinking, *Play for time. Play for time.*

Kaufmann again pressed the gun against Mr. Gilmore's temple. It obviously hurt.

"Let's do the safe first." He smirked at me. "I can tell you're one of those women who think they have balls. In fact, I'm almost tempted to get you to take off your clothes so we can check it out. Balls or no balls." He jabbed at Mr. Gilmore. "His wife thought she had balls. She didn't. She tried to get away like the weak bitch she really was."

"You were the one who attacked her?" It was more of a statement than a question. Neither Mr. Gilmore nor I was surprised.

"That's right, Jew. It was me. Like I said, good thing she died. No more breeding of Jews." Again the smirk. "You got my letters, I presume?"

Mr. Gilmore, with an almost superhuman effort, struggled to get his arms free. Kaufmann gave him a vicious blow across his head.

The major problem was that the desk was between me and Mr. Gilmore, and Kaufmann was standing behind him and the chair he was tied to. There was nothing I could use as a weapon that I'd get to in time.

Kaufmann snapped at me. "You. Miss Smarty-pants. Open the safe. Now."

"I haven't memorized the combination. It's in my desk."

"Okay. There's no hurry." He shifted the gun in my direction. He leered at me in a way that I still shudder about. "It's hot in here. Why don't you take off your clothes?"

I wish I could tell you I was suddenly seized with superhuman strength. That I leaped over the desk and socked the bastard on the jaw. What happened wasn't quite as satisfying, but it worked.

I fainted.

At least, I pretended to faint.

It was a huge risk that tormented me for months after and added to my store of nightmares. Kaufmann could have shot Mr. Gilmore on the spot. He could have shot me. I was relying on his obvious contempt for women.

I had contrived to fall so that I wasn't completely visible from where he was.

I groaned. "Help me. I'll do what you say."

As I dropped into my swoon I rolled on to my back and pulled my arms up underneath me. My legs were bent at the knees. I moaned again. As I hoped, Kaufmann came around the desk. I didn't move. I had to pretend to close my eyes. I sensed rather than saw that he was bending down to look closer.

I shoved myself up, fast and hard, catching him under the chin with my head. There was an intensely satisfying clunk as his lower teeth met his upper teeth. His head jerked back. Before he could do anything, I grabbed his wrist and pulled it downward, snapping his lower arm across my knee the way you do with a piece of kindling. I heard the lovely sound of a bone crunching. He yelled. So did I. The gun went off, the bullet plowing into the floor. He was right about the silencer, but there was a noise.

It was of course an uneven contest, even with these victories. In spite of his injury, he didn't drop the gun. He was a powerful man, and he was enraged. He staggered away from me. Even filled with desperation and fury as I was, I didn't stand a chance.

However, at that moment God intervened.

God was in the form of Hilliard Taylor.

I hadn't locked the door. Good instincts on my part. Hilliard burst in, immediately took in what was happening, and before Kaufmann had a chance to say, "We're just having a friendly discussion," Hill twisted the gun out of his hand and shoved him to the floor. I did my part by kicking Kaufmann hard in the place he seemed so focussed on. He wasn't getting up in a hurry.

Chapter Thirty-Six

THERE WERE A few ends to tie up.

After subduing Kaufmann, Hill rang the police. Detective Murdoch arrived quickly. Kaufmann was carted off by two delightfully rough constables. Among other things, to my mind, Kaufmann had as good as confessed to attacking Ida Gilmore.

"I intend to nail the bastard," said Jack.

I let Mr. Gilmore tell most of the story.

Kaufmann must have followed him when he left his house and, unsuspecting, Mr. Gilmore had let him into the office. Kaufmann had immediately attacked him and tied him to the chair. He had started on his rant about money and the Jews. We weren't sure what would have transpired, probably what he'd threatened, but I had arrived at that point.

Here, Mr. Gilmore had been forced to stop for a moment in his narrative to regain his composure. "Charlotte behaved with the utmost calm and courage. I would be dead if it weren't for her."

Unfortunately, I had a delayed reaction just about then, and I started shaking uncontrollably. All three men were very kind, and after a little blubbering I was all right.

All of this took a while to sort out. Eventually, Mr. Gilmore was taken to the hospital to ensure there were no serious injuries sustained from Kaufmann's beating. I refused to go. I was fine. Hill would have none of it.

I agreed, however, to go back to the Paradise.

Although he almost started a riot among the men waiting outside, Hill insisted on turning out the "Closed" sign. He promised them all a free lunch the following day, gave them each a chit to demonstrate his sincerity, and drew the blinds.

Eric and Wilf were in the kitchen. I wouldn't have minded if Pearl had vanished, but she was there. She gaped at me with wide eyes, but, for whatever peculiar reasons of her own, she suddenly became very solicitous. She made me sit down and even lifted my feet onto another chair.

Eric immediately offered me soup, which I refused. I wasn't hungry. In fact, I felt as if I'd never eat again. He paused briefly, then hurried over to the icebox.

"I know what you need."

He took out a plate. "Bread-and-butter pudding. Sweets always help after a shock."

He placed it in front of me.

Somewhat listlessly, I picked up the spoon. The others watched intently. But it wasn't the quality of the dessert that they were interested in. It was my welfare. The feeling of being so cared about made me a bit teary again. I ate some of the pudding. Eric was right. I ate some more. And some more. When I polished off the last bit, I thought for a minute they might all do a dance. Pearl actually let out a whoop. Eric immediately went and got another slice. I ate that too.

Finally, I started to feel as if I were returning to the human race. Wilf went to make a pot of tea.

"Thank God you did, but I never asked you why you were coming to the office," I asked Hilliard.

He winked. "I had your wages."

I saw the other two men smile at each other, and even I sensed there was more to it than that. I had a warm glow in my stomach that didn't just come from big helpings of bread-and-butter pudding.

"You certainly seemed to know what you were doing."

"Army training. You never forget." He grinned at me. "You seemed to know what you were doing yourself."

"Instinct."

WE MUST HAVE gone over things again, as people do after situations like these, but after an hour I was ready to fall over with exhaustion.

"I'll walk you home," said Hilliard.

"No, thanks. I'll be fine." Besides, there was one more task I had to finish, and I had to do it now.

After some wrangling, Hilliard agreed to get a taxicab for me. I promised I'd come back after a rest.

"Where to, madam?" the taxi driver asked.

I gave him my address. Pearl, together with the three

men, was standing on the sidewalk. They gave me a send-off fit for royalty. I waved goodbye and waited until the taxi had turned the corner.

I leaned forward and tapped the driver on the shoulder.

"I've changed my mind. Take me to the General Hospital."

"Feeling all right, are we, madam?" he asked in alarm.

"Quite all right, thank you. There's somebody I want to see."

I wanted to talk to Katia Kaufmann while I had the chance.

Chapter Thirty-Seven

I WAVED MY LETTER from Detective Murdoch at the woman constable on duty, and she let me through the screen to Katia's bed. She was lying on her back as before, but her eyes were open, staring up at the ceiling. I pulled the chair closer.

"Mrs. Kaufmann, I was here previously. I want to let you know that some things have happened since I saw you last."

No response. There was white surgical tape across her eyebrow, and the green and yellow bruise on her jaw stood out clearly. I knew how it had got there, which emboldened me to speak.

"You have had a dreadful experience, but it is imperative that we talk. I am not the police; I have no authority to arrest or detain you. I would not want to do that anyway. However, you should know that your husband, Arthur Kaufmann, has been detained and is currently under arrest."

Her eyes darted in my direction.

"What for?" she whispered.

"Murder. The police believe he is responsible for the attack on Ida Gilmore."

"How is she?"

"I am very sorry to have to tell you this, but she has died."

A tear fell out of Katia's right eye and rolled down her cheek. She wiped it away. I noticed all of her knuckles were cut and bruised.

"I feared as much."

"Mrs. Kaufmann, your husband also assaulted Mr. Gilmore, and he tried to assault me."

That got more of a reaction from her than she had yet evinced.

"How?"

"He was attempting to rob Mr. Gilmore. I arrived at the office, and he threatened me. He had a gun, and I believe he was prepared to use it."

She lifted her hand to her mouth. "How did you get away?"

"I was able to trick him, and fortunately for us, Hilliard Taylor arrived at that moment and was able to disarm him. I was lucky. Your husband is a very strong man."

An almost imperceptible nod.

"He beat you, didn't he?"

She froze.

"You have nothing to fear. He won't be able to hurt you again. He will be convicted."

She turned her head on the pillow, but I could see she was trembling.

"Katia, the police will come soon to ask you questions about what happened. So far you have not spoken. I am here to ask you to do just that. Innocent people will suffer if you do not."

Again, the slight nod.

"Your husband is a violent and brutal man. He found out that you were seeing Conal Pierce, didn't he? Your old sweetheart? I know that you thought Conal had died in the war, but he never died in your heart. When you met him again it must have almost unbearable to contemplate what might have been."

No response to that. I didn't want to cause her pain, but, as Wilf had said, don't we have to clean out infections for them to heal? There was a lot of infection in this woman, and I was hoping against hope she had the courage that love can bring to clean it out.

"Conal loves you very much. So much so that he is prepared to take the blame for the attack on your husband."

With widened eyes, she turned her head again to look at me.

"He mustn't."

"He will. There was a witness who saw him going into your house. The police are questioning him now. Unless you have the courage to say what actually happened, it is likely he will be convicted. If they do arrest him, he will go to jail, and I don't think he would be able to stand being incarcerated after what happened to him in the war."

Suddenly she shoved herself up into a sitting position. "Will you get me some water?"

Quickly I poured her a glass from the pitcher on the table.

She drank it down thirstily and licked her dry lips.

"You can, of course, continue your silence. You can say you don't remember what happened. A valid defence."

"It is true. I do not remember. I was in the kitchen. Next I knew I was in the hospital."

"The police know that you and Conal were engaged when you were younger. They will soon know that he came to see you regularly. It is not a big leap to assume that there was a quarrel between the two men and that Conal stabbed your husband with a kitchen knife. He might even be charged with assaulting you. That is the theory of one of the detectives."

"No. He did not. Never."

"You can't have it both ways, Katia. Either you don't remember anything or you know for certain that Conal was not your attacker. That implies that you know who was. Which is it to be?"

She drank more water.

I reached over and touched her icy hand. "Shall I tell you what I believe happened?"

"If you wish."

I felt desperately sorry that she had been reduced to such a state of terror, but I felt a wave of impatience. I couldn't bear to think she'd let Conal get washed down the drain.

"Your husband beat you frequently. You still carry the bruises. Then this last February, what must have felt like a miracle occurred. You walked into the Paradise Café and there was your first and only sweetheart. Conal Pierce. A man you thought had died."

She began to weep. Her tears were silent. This was a woman who long ago had learned the danger of crying aloud.

"It was obvious he still loved you. When you eventually confided in him about the state of your marriage, he was determined to get you out of there so you could start a new life. How am I doing so far?"

"Go on."

"He started to give you money. It wasn't a lot, but the idea was when you had enough you would run away from your husband. Perhaps Conal would go with you?"

"Yes," she whispered.

"He came to see you, expecting Arthur would not be at home. He goes to his Swastika Club on Friday mornings. But not only was he at home, you'd had a quarrel. I suppose I shouldn't put it that way. You didn't quarrel with him. He would get angry and then hit you. You didn't have much chance to defend yourself. You must have shouted, because neighbours heard. When Conal came into the house, were you on the floor?"

"Yes." She touched the bandage on her forehead.

"Conal could see what had happened. In a fury, he grabbed a knife from the counter and stabbed Arthur. Then another man arrived, didn't he? A good neighbour. His wife had been very kind to you."

"Ida," she whispered.

"Mr. Gilmore saw the situation at once, and he persuaded Conal to leave by way of the back door. He told you to say you didn't know what had happened. Nothing could be pinned on anybody as long as you stuck to that. Kaufmann was conscious. Mr. Gilmore also talked to him. Nobody was to remember anything. That was to be your story. Your husband was willing to agree because he wasn't going to admit that he'd beaten a helpless woman. That he was a cuckold. And that her lover had got the better of him. Even his Swastika pals might consider him a weakling if they heard that. It was also in his best interests to cast suspicion on an unknown vagrant. The same one who had attacked Ida Gilmore."

I reached for the pitcher and poured her more water.

"Mr. Gilmore didn't know that somebody had seen Conal going to your house. The no-memory story won't ultimately help. Conal will likely go to prison. He is an avowed communist. It will not be a light sentence."

"That must never happen."

I handed her the fresh glass, and she held it, staring ahead, sorting out her thoughts. I waited until she had made a decision. It didn't take long. She did have courage. And love.

"If you like, we can call in the constable and you can make a sworn statement. If you do that, it will make the due process of the law run more smoothly. Shall I ask her to step in?"

"Very well."

She inched herself up in bed. She was very pale, but she actually looked better now that she had decided to take an active part in her own life.

"You've got some of it right, but not all of it."

"Okay."

"Conal wasn't the one who stabbed Arthur. I did." She gave me a wry smile. "But you knew that already, didn't you?"

Chapter Thirty-Eight

WHAT WITH ONE thing and another, it was dusk by the time I got home. There were lights shining in the front. Gramps was home. The night was not as stifling. The forecast was that the weather was going to break. Cooler air was coming.

Katia had given her statement as promised. She said all of it, including that Conal had come to the house. She said Arthur had been in one of his usual foul moods. He'd started to accuse her of being a slovenly whore. "Opening her legs to any man" was how he put it. When she tried to leave the kitchen, he knocked her to the ground. At which point she saw red. She'd finally had it. She picked up the kitchen knife, and when he turned to the sink and stuck his face under the tap to get some water, she stabbed him. He fell to the ground, and she dropped the knife. Ironically, he probably didn't know what had hit him, although he must have had a pretty good idea. Horrified at what she had done, Katia went into a kind of shock. At that moment, Conal burst in. She told him what had happened. Arthur looked as if he was about to give up the ghost. Conal was trying to comfort her when Mr. Gilmore arrived on the scene. He immediately took charge. He told Conal to get the hell out of there. Katia was to say she knew nothing. Remembered nothing. Nothing. Conal fled, and Mr. Gilmore then talked to Kaufmann. He was to say he knew nothing as well.

So Mr. Gilmore must have thought the culprit was Conal. He was the one he was protecting.

I called out to Gramps. "You there? I'm home!"

To my delight he came into the hall to meet me.

"Good heavens, Lottie, you look utterly exhausted. Come and put your feet up. I've made you a cold chicken supper. Are you hungry?"

"No, thanks, Gramps. Just tea would be fine."

I was so happy to see him I could have burst into tears. I let him lead me meekly into the kitchen to make me some tea. I sat down at the table, put my head in my hands, and to my chagrin I did burst into tears. After all, it had been quite a horrendous day.

I told Gramps all that had happened. Good thing Arthur Kaufmann was in custody or else that dear old man would have taken him on with his bare hands. After I had finished my story and drunk my tea, I was almost unable to stay awake. I got ready to say good night.

He patted my hand. "I'm staying here tonight, of course."

"Only if you want to, Gramps. You've got your own life to lead."

He burst out into belly-shaking laughter. "What a little

hypocrite you are, Lottie. I know how you feel about Bertha and me."

"Well …"

"Well nothing. But you don't have to worry. It's over."

"What!"

"I've come to my senses. I was a bit blinded by carnal urges."

"Really?" I hoped he wasn't going to elaborate.

"It's an affliction that we men experience. Especially after a long period of celibacy."

I really, really hoped he wasn't going to elaborate.

"Mrs. Johnson is a very attractive woman. But the more time we spent together, the more I began to see that she was, shall we say, leading me on. She was keen for us to move into a legal arrangement, and in the meantime, perhaps I could help out with some of her expenses."

"The nerve."

"She did this with great finesse and delicacy, but I'm not that stupid. If I had truly fallen in love with her, I might have felt differently. But I wasn't. It was just …"

"Carnal urges?"

"Exactly."

"Does she know you've come to your senses?"

"I think she suspects. She has decided to take a trip to Montreal for a few days. To visit an aunt."

I thought it was more likely she was going to see her legal husband, but I wasn't yet ready to disclose this to Gramps.

"I don't think I will be available when she gets back." He sighed. "One thing she did do, Lottie, which was a blessing. She showed me I could get back into life again. I think Annie would be all right with that, don't you?"

"I'm sure she would, Gramps. It doesn't mean you loved her any the less."

I yawned. He stood up and began to gather the teacups together. "There was one thing that I don't think I could have got over, Lottie. The gap between us is too big. Bertha doesn't like poetry. And she's never heard of T.S. Eliot."

It was my turn to laugh out loud.

That night, just before snapping off my light, I had some thoughts. One was that Gramps would like Mrs. Parker, the sweet, lonely old lady I'd met on Phoebe Street. I'd bet she could quote T.S. Eliot at length, and more importantly, I could tell she had a kind heart. I just had to figure out a way to get them to meet each other.

My final and lingering thought was that Hilliard Taylor was a heck of a good guy.

As Gramps might have put it:

Mary had a little lamb
That thought it'd met The One.
So wherever Mary went
She'd find that lamb was gone.

Acknowledgements

As usual I owe many thanks to people who helped me create this book and / or just plain supported me with a new endeavour. Conan Tobias gave me a boost by asking for a short story for his magazine, *Taddle Creek*. This was where Charlotte Frayne, Private Investigator, first came to life. Ryan Hamilton and Andre DePasqua found me wonderful material from the library. Lynette Dubois shared some of her own experiences as a former private investigator. Sarah Gaby Trotz gave me good advice on likely menus of the Depression era. But I especially want to acknowledge Marc Côté, my publisher and editor. I am delighted and grateful to be under his wing.

It is called, quite simply, The Web.

Its origins unknown, its likes can be found only in the Clypsis system.

In The Web ordinary ships can go faster than light. It is the biggest, the fastest, the most dangerous race track in the history of the universe.

Now something is wrong with The Web. Mike Murray must dare its perils to take his place among the racers of the Clypsis system—and to solve the murder of a friend.

His fate is waiting in The Web.

Bantam Spectra Books in the *Roger Zelazny's Alien Speedway* series.
Ask your bookseller for the ones you have missed

Book 1: *Clypsis* by Jeffrey A. Carver

Book 2: *Pitfall* by Thomas Wylde

Book 3: *The Web* by Thomas Wylde

ROGER ZELAZNY'S

ALIEN SPEEDWAY

BOOK 3: THE WEB

ROGER ZELAZNY'S

ALIEN SPEEDWAY

BOOK 3: THE WEB

by Thomas Wylde

A BYRON PREISS BOOK

BANTAM BOOKS

TORONTO • NEW YORK • LONDON • SYDNEY • AUCKLAND

ROGER ZELAZNY'S ALIEN SPEEDWAY
BOOK 3: THE WEB
A Bantam Spectra Book / June 1988

Book and cover design by Alex Jay/Studio J.
Cover art by Robert Eggleton.
Interior illustrations by Hayashi
Special thanks to David M. Harris, Amy Stout, Kirby McCauley, and Lou Aronica.

For information address: Bantam Books

ISBN 0-553-27166-0

Published simultaneously in the United States and Canada

Bantam Books are published by Bantam Books, a division of Bantam Doubleday Dell Publishing Group, Inc. Its trademark, consisting of the words "Bantam Books" and the portrayal of a rooster, is Registered in U.S. Patent and Trademark Office and in other countries. Marca Registrada, Bantam Books, 666 Fifth Avenue, New York, New York 10103.

PRINTED IN THE UNITED STATES OF AMERICA

O 0 9 8 7 6 5 4 3 2 1

For Dad

INTRODUCTION

I am a longtime fan of science and technology, as are most people in this business. Racing also holds a kind of fascination for me. *And* I am a great admirer of Jules Verne, partly because he was the first science-fiction pro to get rich writing the stuff. And 1870–71 was a particularly interesting period in his career, as you shall see. . . .

Jules Verne spent the summer of 1870 at Le Contoy, knocking about on his yacht, *Saint Michel*. He was enjoying a lot of publicity at that time, from his very successful novel, *Twenty Thousand Leagues Under the Sea*, and he had a great contract for delivering more stories to his publisher, Hetzel, before too long. On top of that, the writing was going well, and he had been proposed for the Legion of Honor. His life was at one of those bright and golden points which would make any character in a classical drama begin a nervous survey of the horizon for the approach of thunderclouds.

Had he done so, though, it is doubtful he could have done much about what was to hit. The Franco-Prussian War began that summer. At 42, Verne was too old to be drafted, and he was in a sufficiently remote part of the country to be out of danger. So he wrote his stories. There wasn't much else for him to do. Paris underwent a terrible winter siege, and the armistice was signed in May of 1871.

And like most writers, Verne discovered before long that he had blown some big advances and was in need of funds. So he decided to deliver his manuscripts to his publisher, on the rue Jacob in Paris, and get paid for them. This, despite the fact that the city still was not considered perfectly safe. Alas, when he got there he discovered that Hetzel had cut out for the Riviera when the fighting had begun, and had not left a forwarding address. (Publishers are sometimes like that. At least Verne didn't get told that the check was in the mail. He

knew that nothing was coming.) This left him in an awkward position. He had four completed manuscripts in his suitcase, and any number of publishers would have snapped them up. But Hetzel already knew their titles and subjects. So if Verne were to hustle them elsewhere, he would be known to be in breach of contract.

Verne realized then that he had to do something most professional writers do when young and try to get away from as time goes on; i.e., he would have to knock something out in a hurry for a quick return. His best bet seemed to be to sell a novel for immediate payment, getting one of the Paris dailies to spring for it and run it in installments. He could then be writing as they went along, staying a few steps ahead of the presses all the way.

He walked through the city, not particularly cheered by its postwar condition, and he sat about in cafés as he had in his youth, trying to come up with the most suitable idea for such a quick piece. Strolling through the boulevard des Italiens, he was attracted by the window of Thomas Cook & Son, travel agency. (Yes, this was the Cook of "Cook's Tours" fame, the originator of packaged travel, complete with little books of vouchers, etc.) He went in, picked up their latest prospectus, and took it back with him to the Café Tortoni, where he was currently taking the temperatures of ideas. Cook's prospectus made an interesting claim: With the establishment of a steamship route through the Suez Canal to India and the completion of the Union Pacific Railroad, linking San Francisco and New York, it was possible, should one really care to hustle, to make it around the world in three months.

Voilà!

At one o'clock in the morning, when the waiters came by to close up the café, they found Verne sitting at his favorite table writing by gaslight, as was their wont in those days. In less than two weeks he'd sold serial rights to *Around the World in Eighty Days* on the basis of the outline he'd begun that night—to the newspaper *Temps*, for a large chunk of change. It became the most successful serial novel ever published. As soon as it began to appear, *Temps* started picking up additional foreign subscribers, and Paris corre-

spondents from numerous foreign papers were obliged to cable home summaries of the contents of each installment, as people were actually beginning to bet money on how far Fogg would get, and, ultimately, whether he would really make it around the world in eighty days.

Verne kept hammering out the installments, leaving his readers with terrible cliff-hangers such as few modern writers would even consider inflicting upon their gentle audiences. The high point of all this was getting Fogg to New York late and having him miss the steamer to Liverpool by forty-five minutes—which on the face of it seemed to lose him his bet.

Then comes the part that really appeals to any author's literary instincts. Four New York shipping firms, including Cunard Lines, cabled Verne, and each of them offered him a large sum of money if he'd find a way to let Fogg make it over on one of their ships.

Had it been me, the book might have taken a different turn about there. . . .

However, Verne had an idea too good to waste.

A story like this fascinates me—the suspense of a race against the clock, and a "Well, gentlemen, here I am!" —especially when the whole thing was coupled at the personal level with Verne's own race to come up with the idea and get the tale written. It does not come as a complete surprise to learn that Verne was a failed romantic poet and playwright who had taken to heart the tough, practical advice of Alexandre Dumas, that he learn his craft well and write every day at a set time, rather than waiting about for inspiration to pay a visit.

Verne, like the rest of us, was a fan of technology. His interest in balloons, submarines, and rockets requires no real elaboration. His race is actually against the clock rather than a field of competing racers in his tale of Fogg's dash around the globe, but it loses nothing of suspense for all that. In fact, I've always thought of it as a classic racing story.

And it intrigues me that one of the most popular works by one of the earliest science-fiction writers should be a racing tale, taking advantage of all the latest in travel technology and pushing it to its limits. I do not believe that its immense popularity was solely a matter of Verne's name and

his writing skills. Rather, I feel that it also had to do with his having hit upon a particularly appropriate vehicle for the time's love affair with the machine, the infinite variety of which age cannot wither, nor custom stale, as we will consider at greater length next time around the track.

—Roger Zelazny
Santa Fe, 1987

PROLOGUE

More than forty standard years ago an astute businessman with a great many small but very clever heads came to Earth and purchased a thousand European silver coins of the seventeenth century. He brought them to the Clypsis racing system, in hopes of selling them to the idle rich, but instead found himself a victim of the underclasses. He and his coins abruptly disappeared. . . .

Twenty years later a racing champion named Speedball Raybo crossed the barrier of the track wall and vanished in a shower of sparks. Upon verification of his death, a holographic matrix of his brain tapes was assembled and lodged in a suitable psyche-vehicle. Twenty years later it came to him that he had been bribed with some of those stolen coins, but they were nowhere to be found. . . .

At that same time a young man named Michael Murray came to Pitfall to become a racing pilot. But after his ship was wrecked during a race, he found—buried in the debris—a tarnished silver coin. His career stumbled, plagued by rumors of negligence and sabotage. Now Mike carries the coin in his pocket—a bitter reminder. Speedball Raybo is still looking for his. . . .

CHAPTER 1

The big Five Star class ship shuddered and bucked with surprising violence as Michael Murray guided it through the turbulence of the velocity shear. All around him stress-shocks hissed and squealed and torsion bars flexed, relaxing with an ominous twang. Mike laughed. "Now, don't come apart on me!"

The ship settled momentarily as it hit the "groove"—the zone of stressed space that flowed the smoothest. To compensate, Mike pressed down harder on the throttle; the massive ship buckled and popped in an attempt to get out of its own way. Warning beepers sang out, and the wraparound panel in the pilot's bay began to light up with engine warnings—HIGH TEMP, FUEL PUMP OVERSPEED, RADIATOR MAX CAPACITY. Mike killed the audible alarm.

"Caution," said the ship, in a scolding feminine voice. "Caution."

The techscreen went dim, accentuating the crucial message: ENGINE OVERRIDE WARNING.

"Damn . . ." said Mike, easing the throttle back. Most of the lights went out immediately.

Mike cruised down the empty center of the speedway test track, anxiously watching the panel. More warning lights went out, but some remained. He smacked the panel with his gloved hand. One light went out; two new ones came on.

"Oh, man . . ."

He could just imagine what the owners would say: "Did you have to wreck our new ship?"

Mike ran a fast systems-diagnostic routine, and the maintenance screen filled with complaints. Number-eight fuel-pump turbine shaft was getting loose, the lower left astronics-bay fire alarm was riding in the yellow (though two other smoke detectors said to forget it), and the rear-looking infra-

red camera had shut itself down pending a memory update. He smiled in relief. This ship reveled in the trivial—there were no real problems.

The commlink stuttered and squawked. "That's it, Murray. Bring her in."

"Already?"

He still had fuel left.

"Your time is up."

Mike considered, remembering what Jass Blando had told him. When one auditions for the position of backup pilot on a speedway racing team, it's not necessarily a bad idea to demonstrate a little aggressive behavior.

"Murray?"

"Be right there."

The question was, Just how aggressive should he be?

Mike grinned and boosted the thrust until all four killer engines were cranked up to maximum.

"Murray?"

The voluminous tanks emptied fast, and the fusion fuel dumped out, boiling away through the exhaust nozzles.

"What are you doing, Murray?"

Faster and faster the ship went, wobbling down the test track's groove.

"Answer me, Murray!" the controller yelled. "What the hell are you doing?"

"Uh . . . fuel economy test."

Mike was pushed back harder and harder as the g-forces mounted. Six g's . . . seven . . . seven point five . . . the acceleration jammed him hard against the seat's plastic cushions. Faster and faster came his breath, fogging up the inside of his pressure-suit helmet. Fuel graphs shimmied and dropped, the display scale suddenly changing as he approached the end. The panel beeped.

LOW FUEL.

He leaned on the throttle till the alarm was steady, grunting when his harness automatically cinched tighter. A smile flickered at the corners of his mouth. Apparently the ship thought a crash was imminent.

"Caution," said the ship. "*Caution*. CAUTION."

"Bitch, bitch, bitch . . ."

The commlink crackled. ''Damn it, kid! Bring her in!''

''Oh, that's right,'' said Mike, checking the position screen. ''You guys are in a hurry.'' The designated test track was close to the bright yellow glare of Clypsis. Pitfall was on the far side, its orbit just biting into the disk of the star. ''Tell you what I'm going to do. I'll take the shortcut.''

Mike wiggled the control stick, then jerked it sideways. The ship plowed through the velocity shear, shivering and squeaking. The forward-looking viewscreen showed a computer-generated image of the yellow star below him, his course and position numbers glowing on overlay.

''Murray! Don't do it!''

Mike crossed the track in seconds and pierced the shimmering warp-tube wall. The ship emerged—impossibly—and he aimed it for the center of the nearby star. ''Let's go, baby. Right on through—''

He never made it.

Before he could touch its writhing surface, Clypsis dissolved with a noise like an adhesive bandage peeled from tender flesh. The ship went dead.

Immediately he felt rough hands grabbing him out of his seat. He started to laugh. ''It's just a joke!''

''A joke? A *joke?*''

''That's all it was,'' said Mike. ''I just wanted to see how far I could get.''

The simulations boss was stacking hard-copy lists of software documentation on a table beside the terminal. ''Well, you dumped the whole computer. Is *that* what you wanted?''

''I'm sorry.''

''*Sorry?*'' the guy yelled, spinning around. He looked like a man impersonating a steamed lobster. Merkeks always did. ''I guess you think that makes everything all right?''

''No, of course not,'' said Mike, thinking, Just a joke, man . . . a joke . . .

The Merkek glared at him a moment, then turned back to the computer. He reset the power and typed a code on the keyboard. Mike watched as the screen fluttered with alphanumeric garbage, then cleared itself.

One of the flat-headed computer technicians said, "You see that, Kirk?" The other nodded and reached for his phone.

Mike said, "I really didn't think this would happen."

The Merkek still looked steamed. "You mean you *planned* this?"

Mike smiled, trying flattery. "Well, I'd heard how good your simulator was." Nothing, no response. Mike kept going, feeling more and more lame. "And . . . uh, I didn't think I was ever going to get a chance like that again . . . I mean, to go superluminal through the warp-tube wall in real life . . ."

The Merkek smiled without humor. "Go ahead, try it sometime."

As Mike waited in the outer office for his appointment, he began to worry that his little trick might come around to land on him. If ever a simulations boss would be reporting every little glitch, this would be it.

Oh, great—he'd discovered another perfectly wonderful method of destroying what was left of his racing career. These days the only time they let him on a speedway track was to suck the trash out with a debris sweeper. Community service for Pitfall Authority: hard work, low pay, and all the haircuts you could eat.

Mike ran a hand over his close-cropped hair. Thanks again, guys.

"Won't be much longer," said the receptionist. She was a striking, ebon-haired Rykell, her shiny red face dusted with silver sparkles. Makeup or skin disease, Mike had no way of knowing.

"Thank you," he said, sinking deeper into the soft leather couch. Something nibbled lightly at his ear, and Mike peered behind him to find a purple plant drooping out of a wall pot. The plant looked hungry, so Mike moved over, sliding along the couch.

Even without the hostile foliage, this joint was intimidating: real wood wall panels and dark hardwood furniture so authentic you could smell the trees, imported—at numbing expense—from Enigma or Palomar-2. Or maybe even from Earth.

Conspicuous squanderment, Jass Blando might say.

Mike wondered how he was ever going to fit in with the Gajira Syndicate. Or why he even wanted to . . . aside from the money and getting to be a master pilot and having a chance to fly one of the Big Ships that made him drool all night long in dreamland . . .

Yeah, right. But aside from that, he had no use for these geeks. So if they didn't like his aggressive style on the speedway, they could just take a flying jump off a—

"You may go in now," said the receptionist.

Mike looked up, startled. "Excuse me?" He ducked out from under the purple plant, which had followed him across the couch.

"Your turn, Mr. Murray." Her face glittered with silver light.

"Thank you."

Mike stood up, and she smiled, nodding toward the inner door. Her teeth were long and black.

Mike stared and stumbled, almost falling flat on his face as the door slid away.

Nice entrance, kid.

"Sorry," said Mike, glancing around. More wood panels, thick carpet, holos of racing ships.

No hungry plants, thank God.

Mike managed to get into his chair without screwing up.

The balding little man behind the desk was not what Mike expected. Somehow he had pictured a whole crowd of snooty rich folk glaring down at him.

"My name is Rinehart Weel," the man said. "I'm the Gajira Syndicate's tax accountant."

Mike nodded, trying to follow this latest twist. "Why am I talking to, uh . . ."

"*I* don't know," said Weel. "If you ask me, they really should have hired some PR people—especially since we got saddled with this jump-to-master thing. The response has been just—"

"Then, it's true?"

"Oh, it's true, uh . . ." He searched the application. ". . . Mike. From apprentice to master in one nauseating leap. *Every*body wants to try out. You know, it's part of the Trike."

Mike nodded and smiled and hoped the guy meant the Clypsis Tricentennial Celebration. He sure as hell wasn't going to ask and look like an idiot. "How do I qualify?"

"Okay," said Weel. He cleared his throat and began to count on his fingers. "There will be three sets of eliminator heats—three different kinds of races. There's a drag race, a solo circle race, and some sort of race they're calling 'dirty environment,' but I don't know what that—"

"And if I make it, I'll get to run in the big one?"

"Yeah, the Tricentennial Classic. Everybody keeps talking about it, but I can't figure it out. Something about the commercial lanes . . ."

"It's going to be run throughout the entire system. First on the track, then out on the lanes between the planets. They're gonna shut down regular traffic for this one all-out race."

"Whatever for?" asked Rinehart Weel. "I thought you racing people were content to run around and around in your little tracks."

Mike smiled.

Little tracks . . . right. Some of them were nearly four billion kilometers across. He said, "We like a bit of variety from time to time."

"I suppose so," said Weel. "Anyway, as you know, the Trike is to be run by Five Star class ships. Have you ever flown one before?"

"Just in your simulator."

"Oh, yes."

Rinehart Weel glanced at the screen imbedded in his desktop. "I see you crashed."

"Well . . ."

"You crashed and died. And what is more important, you utterly destroyed a ship worth ten and a half million interstellar yen."

"It was just a joke."

Rinehart Weel stared at him as if Mike had switched to some alien language. "A joke?"

"It's just a simulation, you know."

"Yes, but what if you should decide to enjoy a similar joke when you're really flying our ship?"

"That's not very likely."

Weel looked perplexed. "How likely is it, exactly?"

Mike sat up straight in his chair and made his face serious. "Believe me, sir. I would never do that." Weel stared at him so long that Mike gave up and laughed. "Well, maybe just *once*."

Rinehart Weel shook his head. "They really should have hired some PR people for these interviews. I simply do not understand pilots."

Mike nodded . . . and laughed again. He tried to bite his lip. This was not going at all well.

Weel's phone buzzed and he picked it up. "Yes, Mr. Gajira." The screen stayed blank.

Mike tuned out for a minute, taking the opportunity to get his act together. Be serious. Don't joke. Look responsible. Don't stare at the man when he's on the phone, even though he does sound like a sniveling cat's-paw talking to his boss.

Rinehart Weel said, "Absolutely, Mr. Gajira," and hung up, frowning. He stared blankly at Mike for a moment, as if Gajira had just kicked over the foundations of his life. "Uh . . ."

"Jump-to-master?"

"Oh, yes, of course. In any case, uh . . . Mike . . . the program to elevate some deserving rookie to master is quite legitimate. I can't tell you that we're *pleased* exactly—getting stuck with providing the ship—but all the entries in the Trike race took a similar risk."

"I understand."

"As to your inexperience flying Five Star class ships—well, I guess we ought to expect a similar level of experience from all our apprentice candidates."

"How many are there?"

"Thirteen hundred and forty-six have signed up so far, and the deadline is still . . ."

Mike stopped listening for a moment. Thirteen hundred and forty-six applicants. He was stunned and sickened.

Weel just kept chugging along. ". . . of course, many will be eliminated long before they attempt the qualifying

races. Background checks, interviews, physical and mental tests, and so forth—they all take their toll, don't they?”

“Excuse me?” Mike was still zoned out on despair. Thirteen hundred and forty-six—with more to come. Finally he said, “I've already passed the mental and physical tests.”

Rinehart Weel glanced at the computer screen again, and his eyebrows went up. “So it seems.”

Mike nodded. The interview and the background check. He was probably blowing the first of them right now. And as for the second, well, he'd left Earth in an awful hurry, underage, and under a cloud, following the accidental death of his guardian aunt. It was like a bomb ticking away in his past.

Well, to hell with it. If the Gajira Syndicate found out, they found out. That was the chance he took. This was simply too good a deal to pass up.

“Are we finished?” asked Weel.

“You don't want to cut through all the red tape and declare me the winner right now, do you?”

“Gee, Mike. I don't think that would be proper.”

“Then, I guess we're finished.”

“That's what I thought.” Rinehart Weel pushed a button on his desktop, then sat up straight and stared nervously past Mike's shoulder. Mike started to get up. “Just a minute,” said Weel. “There's one more thing to do. And I think you're going to like it. Although God knows it wouldn't mean anything to me.”

A few seconds later a guy came into the office. “This the one?”

“Please,” said Weel. “Mike Murray. Fyodor Willingham. One of our pilots.”

The guy was tall with a lot of bushy blond hair. Mike stood up, absently rubbing his hand over his blank skull.

“Come on, kid,” said Willingham. “I gotta show you the *Universe*.”

Mikc grinncd. “Rcally?”

The *Universe* was on display in the Grand Concourse. As Mike stood flat-footed in the swirling crowd, Fyodor Willingham rattled off her specs. Fifty-nine metric tons,

empty—with room in her tanks for five times her mass in fusion fuel. Thirty-eight meters long, seven and a half across her beam, with twin ramscoops like flattened circles in the front, and a cluster of gaping engine nozzles in the back. Dotted about the surface were lumps and crevices and small spiky projections—sensors and whatnot. The ship was painted silver and gold in a radical polymer that reflected the lights of the concourse in so many directions it was hard to focus on her skin.

The *Universe*.

And most astonishing of all, hardly anybody paid the slightest attention to her. Bettors and pilots and dockworkers hurried past or lounged with drinks and sandwiches, talking loudly and slapping the tout sheets in their hands. Occasionally some preoccupied soul would blunder into the velvet ropes; he'd glance up at the ship, and a head or two would drop back, as if momentarily threatened. Then it was back to lunch or counting money or yelling across the concourse at some friend or drinking buddy.

Mike just stood there in the middle of everything, folks banging into him, spilling their drinks on his sneakers. He couldn't move; he was . . . enchanted. And perplexed. Couldn't these people see what was in front of them?

"You wanna go inside?" asked his guide.

"Now you *are* joking."

"Look, kid, if you end up flying this baby, I think you better take a squint inside. Might improve your chances, come the Trike race."

Mike turned to gawk at him. At that moment the idea he might get to race in this ship was entirely preposterous. He thought, I should be back in my room watching it on the homeset. Not flying it. Not *ever* flying it. I'm not fit to scrub the gunk out of her thruster nozzles.

But he said, "Yeah, sure. Let's look the tub over."

Fyodor Willingham just nodded, smiling faintly. "Whatever you say, champ."

"God, you should *see* that thing!" said Mike, before chomping down on a simulated cheeseburger. Half the diners in Quohogs suspended their forks and chopsticks and looked

over to see who was making so much noise. Mike ignored them.

"Nice, huh?" said Jass Blando. His well-worn, star-browned face wrinkled with a smile.

"Oh, man," said Mike, trying to swallow fast so he could talk. "It's got everything. Switches everywhere, panel lights up the yim-yam. *Ten* screens." He took another big bite and chewed furiously.

"Don't hurt yourself," said Jass.

Speedball Raybo's automaton face was blank as usual. "Ten screens. Sounds like a theater."

Jass said, "Probably designed for guys with ten heads."

"Every engine reports fifty parameters," said Mike, waving his cheeseburger. "That's two hundred simultaneous readouts."

"Sounds confusing," said Speedball. "Must have been designed for a tinhead."

"Come on, it's a great ship!" said Mike. Big bite.

Jass winked at Speedball. "I like *my* new ship better."

"Your new—" Mike grinned, showing a mouthful of—

"That's disgusting," said Jass. "Where are your manners?"

Mike swallowed and wiped his mouth. "You didn't tell me you were starting up racing again."

"Another big mistake," said the automaton. "Did you put a deposit on the pit yet?"

"Damn right I did. KZ-7—it's just been renovated. New paint and everything."

"Maybe it'll bring you luck," said Speedball.

Mike laughed nervously, then shut himself up with the last of his cheeseburger. Jass said, "Yeah, I know, last time it didn't work out so good, but I'm getting more money up front this time. I cut a deal with Westinghouse."

"You'll need it," said Speedball. "Prices are going up."

"It's the Tricentennial," said Blando. "The damned Trike is screwing up everything."

"Yeah," said Mike, wondering if Jass had enough money to hire an apprentice pilot. He chugged his Poldavian root beer, hardly daring to look at Blando.

"The thing is," said Jass, "I'm not in the market for any apprentices."

Mike pushed some bread crumbs around the table. "That's all right."

" 'Cause I already got a good one—if you want the job."

Mike's head jerked up. "You mean it?"

Jass said, "Well, you'll need a ship for the eliminator heats, and I guess I owe you something . . ." Mike nodded, looking down. The wreck of the *Slippery Cat* was not a subject they talked about. Jass quickly added, "But I can't take you right away. I won't have the ship set up for another week or so."

Not good enough, thought Mike, running the jump-to-master race schedule through his mind. He felt himself balanced on the moment, excited and disappointed. Opportunities rose and fell in his eyes.

"There you are, you little runt."

Mike recognized the voice even before he saw the guy's luminescent green hair. Dover Bell leaned close, scowling down at Mike. "Alice Nikla took off on me, joined the Four-oh-four team."

"That's not my fault."

"She hit me in the face."

"So what?" said Mike, trying not to smile. "She hit me, too." Alice Nikla had a problem with hitting people.

Dover said, "She'd still be flying with me if—"

"Ancient history," said Jass. "He beat you fair."

"Are you kidding? He got so close I had to scrape his paint off my—"

"I'm tired of you hanging around," said Speedball. "If you think he did anything wrong, file a complaint with the Racing Commission."

Mike held his breath. Oh, man, don't *say* that. I don't need any trouble with the Commission.

Dover Bell ignored Speedball. Fortunately. "Hey, Mike. You're in that jump-to-master thing, aren't you?"

"So?"

"So I'll see you on the qualifying circuit, dwarf."

"Fine," said Mike. "You can keep an eye on my exhaust nozzle for me."

Loud laughter came from across the room, and everybody at Mike's table looked over. It was just a big sponsor's party: order anything, get smashed, tell jokes, sing songs, get hammered, corner the boss and tell him what you *really* think of him—get fired, go looking for oxygen and a brand new job. Yes, it was a way of life.

Mike wondered if there'd be a party when he won the Tricentennial Classic—and then he laughed. Who was he kidding? Thirteen hundred and forty-six eager applicants—with many more on the way. . .

"Go ahead and laugh, squirt," said Dover Bell.

"No, no, it's not that," Mike said.

"This thing's not over yet," said Bell. "I'm warning you, Murray. You better watch your back, 'cause I'm—"

"Good-bye, Dover," said Speedball, his voice hard-edged.

Bell hesitated, his face growing red, then he left abruptly, chewing on whatever sinister exit line he might have had. You don't mess around with a guy in a racing PV.

Jass said, "That man is starting to unravel."

"He just tries too hard," said Speedball. "Nice hair, though."

Mike nodded, involuntarily rubbing a hand over his own short bristles.

Blando was watching. "Ah, God—community service. It's bad enough without having to humiliate you like that."

Mike said, "I'm thinking of having it chromed."

"I know a good place," said Speedball.

Blando said, "I'm just sorry I can't hire you right away, Mike. I'm still lining up sponsors, and I just don't have the money yet."

"I'll live."

"They keeping you busy?" asked Speedball.

"Oh, yeah," said Mike. "Cleaning, mostly. With the Tricentennial coming up, Pitfall Authority is climbing all over itself trying to get the joint fixed up and scrubbed down and everything. By the way, Jass, we got Big Trash Day coming up in a few days. If you've got any old fusion engines lying about, now's the time to get 'em hauled away for nothing."

Speedball laughed. ‘‘If he had an old engine, he’d be flying it.’’

‘‘This place is really gonna get crowded,’’ said Mike. ‘‘I mean, it’s crowded now, but the closer we get to the Tricentennial—look out. We’re gonna have celebrities packed to the rafters.’’

‘‘I know,’’ said Speedball. ‘‘Old Timers’ Day. The Racing Museum’s been after me to participate. Make speeches, give out awards, shake hands—or whatever they got to shake—I don’t know what all. So far, I’ve been avoiding them.’’

‘‘I don’t blame you,’’ said Jass. ‘‘What the hell, it’s just the Tricentennial. Tell ’em you’re holding out for the Quad.’’

Mike said, ‘‘And I guess you’ll be here for it, too.’’

‘‘Not necessarily.’’

Jass said, ‘‘You going someplace?’’

‘‘No.’’

‘‘Then . . .’’

Speedball bonged his metal head. ‘‘Don’t let this fool you.’’

‘‘What do you mean?’’ asked Mike.

‘‘Brain tapes can be dumped.’’

CHAPTER 2

Aboard the space freighter *Swamp Queen,* 105 hours out of Clypsis system, incoming; Josiah Bent, commanding:

Craig Show poured coffee for Mary-All and Vicky Slicky. "I haven't been to Clypsis in two years."

Vicky waved him off at half a cup. "I've never been there."

"You haven't missed much," said Mary-All. "There's nothing to do if you don't like racing."

Craig Show sat back down at the cramped galley table. "Just so long as you know how to get there."

Vicky smiled. "I put a bunch of numbers in the nav computer. That's all I know."

"She'll get us there," said Mary-All.

"On the other hand," said Vicky, "this is the longest line I've ever set for subspace."

"I noticed that," said Show. "It kind of makes me wonder about the engines, you know?"

"They'll hold," said Mary-All.

Show said, "I just can't understand why the captain is in such a damn hurry to get to Clypsis. Did he say—" Show glanced suddenly at the open door of the galley. "Wouldn't want Ferguson to hear any of this." He turned back to Vicky Slicky. "Did Bent say anything when you programmed the ship?"

"Yeah. He said don't talk about it."

Show sipped his coffee. "That cargo must be pretty hot, that's all I got to say."

"It is," said Vicky. "And that's all I know about it."

They sat in silence for a long moment, then Mary-All said, "Hey, Mike Murray is in Clypsis system, someplace."

"I heard he's racing," said Vicky.

"Amazing, isn't it?" said Mary-All.

Show said, "I just wonder what Bent's gonna do when he gets there. You know, he wasn't exactly the happiest man in the galaxy when Mike jumped ship."

"If I remember correctly," said Mary-All, "he wasn't too happy with us, either."

Vicky said, "He couldn't prove we helped him jump. Besides, he can't complain. He had no hooks in Mike."

"Explain that to him," said Craig Show. "I wouldn't want to be there, but I'd like to tape it."

"Our captain," said Vicky, smirking.

"Mike warned him," said Mary-All. "He always said he was going to Clypsis to race on the speedway."

Vicky smiled. "That's right. And he did it, too."

"That's right," said Show.

Mary-All smiled conspiratorially. "I'm proud of Mike."

"We all are," said Show. "I just hope the captain doesn't kill him."

Twyla Rogres ran her hand over the top of Mike's head. "So the Junkyard Dog got a haircut."

"Puh-*leez!*" he said, ducking out of the way. "I'm trying to *drive*."

They were in the warp sweeper, cleaning the junk out of track 65J. Mike had his tunes cranking from the portable, which he'd set up on the control console, so if Twyla wanted to talk to him, she'd best speak up to be heard. He liked his tunes loud.

Mike checked the display on the intake scoops. The warp-manipulating sweeper changed the configuration of the track, making sure all the debris from the last race—decayed exhaust products, chunks of blown engines, nuts, bolts, dust, thruster gas, misplaced speed wrenches—was funneled into the sweeper's maw.

Twyla yelled in his ear over the crackling beat of the music. "You must really like this job. You're out here all the time."

"I'm pulling extra shifts. See, the Authority's gonna lease a ship for the jump-to-master competition. I'm building up points to get a shot at flying her."

"I never knew Pitfall Authority was that interested in their employees' racing careers."

"Yeah, well, that's for the Trike, too. All the hype, the good-guy image, it's all just a little show for the tourists."

"Typical."

Mike glanced over, wondering if she was entered in the jump-to-master competition. If Lek Croveen loaned her the *Slippery Cat*... well, Mike didn't want to be going up against her in any ship.

The fact was, he had a hard time believing he was still in the program himself. The background check must have turned up nothing—neither the trouble following him from Earth, nor the rumors concerning the wreck of the *Slippery Cat*. Mike was pretty much holding his breath...

Twyla said, "I can't believe they let you out on the track alone with this thing. You could warp your way halfway across the universe."

"Are you kidding? If I tried to leave this track, the warp drive would shut down, and the sweeper would return to the hangar automatically. You better believe they got their eye on me. Hell, a guy could go out and rendezvous with a freighter or something and bring in a load of black-market toothbrushes."

"Dangerous stuff."

"Damn right," he said, looking over. His heart skipped a beat, as usual. She wasn't smiling, but then she didn't need to smile to have that effect on him. There had been a time, not long ago, that he sensed she might be moving closer to him. Now he wasn't so sure. She seemed preoccupied.

After a moment she reached out and turned the music way down. "Remember I said I wanted to talk to you? I didn't plan on yelling the whole thing."

Mike looked over at her. "What whole thing?"

She turned to stare out the front port. Mike could see the faint line of regenerated skin making a loop up one side of her throat and down the other. It was an almost perfect match. "You feeling all right? I mean, the accident..."

"I'm all healed, Mike. Hell, I'm doing better than you." Then, for just an instant, her expression collapsed, as if to say, "Yeah, *sure* I am." She smiled again, back in control. "It's Lek."

Of course it's Lek, he thought. It's always Lek.

"What about him?"

"I think he's going crazy."

The sweeper yawed and pitched around as Mike guided it through the portal and into the hollow globe of warped space that was Pitfall. He powered up the attitude thrusters to maneuver inside the free zone.

Twyla had finished listing Lek's peculiarities. Mike frankly couldn't see what the problem was. "He's just down on his luck, Twyla. He'll straighten out."

"His confidence is shot."

"Yeah, well . . ." Mike trailed off as he lined the sweeper up with the entrance to the south maintenance hangar. The sweeper drifted forward through the shimmering airscreen that protected the shirtsleeve environment of the hangar from the cold vacuum of Pitfall's free zone. "Just let him . . . win some races . . ."

Mike fired braking thrusters, then let the convoluted gravity field of the hangar entrance grab the ship and bring it to the faded landing circle painted in orange stripes on the concrete floor. The skids whined and stuttered, sending harsh vibrations through the ship, then they were on the automatic towline, headed for berth 88.

Twyla said, "That was an awful landing."

"Yeah, I know." Mike ranged over the control panel, hitting switches, deenergizing the ship. Exhaust fans began to whine down. "Ever since they made me cut my hair . . ."

"No, I think it's better this way. You never could keep it combed right."

Mike ran his hand over the top, then jerked it away.

Damn! I gotta stop doing that!

He said, "They make me cut it every two weeks. And the worst part is, I gotta pay for it myself out of my community service allowance."

She laughed. "The obscenity of power abused."

"I know! One hundred twenty-five milliyen."

"That's cheap."

"You kidding? I pay less than that each day for my room."

"Yeah, but your room is a certified dump."

"True," said Mike, grinning. "Anyway, I found this old Polaran barber in a tiny shop on the Strip. Noisy as hell in there, but what the heck, he's Polaran, right? Four arms, four hands, four cranked-up buzzing shears—I mean, the guy is done before I can get comfortable in the chair. One hundred twenty-five mills!"

"Oh, my!"

She liked it a lot, though, so he played along. "They make me look like some kind of chain-gang mouth-breather, and I gotta *pay* for it!"

"Poor baby."

"Not everybody on CS has to cut his hair, you know."

"Be fair, Mike. Not everybody has hair to cut. You want 'em to make the Dooners cut all the tentacles off their heads?"

"I know I'd sleep better."

Mike made an entry on the ship's log and pressed the back of his right wrist to the ID reader. If the data matched, there would be no customs inspection. The WORKING light winked amber, then the green lit up. "Okay," he said.

Twyla asked, "Is that it?"

"Yeah, unless there's nobody around to empty the sack."

Mike grabbed his music deck and they climbed down from the sweeper in the hangar's mild gravity field. Something wide and gray was already limping across the floor toward them.

"Here comes Rezzy," he said.

"You have to wait for him?"

"Yeah, I gotta hand over the ship personally. New customs reg. Things are really tightening up."

"He does the bag?"

"Yeah, especially when it's light. I was the third guy around the circuit, so the sack's probably full of pocket lint. Not that it'll satisfy Rezzy."

They drank cool coffee in a shop just down the ring corridor from the hangar. Twyla brooded over her cup, as if searching for secrets in the dark swirls.

Mike watched her, thinking about Lek. If she had been

leaning toward Mike, all that was over—and would remain over until Lek got himself straightened out. Twyla was too loyal to walk away now.

"So," said Mike. "What do you want me to do about Lek?"

"I don't know," she said, looking up. "Talk to him. See what's the matter with him."

"Oh, he'll love that."

"Well, don't announce yourself, for God's sake."

"You want me to spy on him?"

"If that's what it takes."

Mike sipped his bitter cup. He didn't want to have anything to do with this. "I ought to have Jass and Speedball take a look at him. I mean, it's one thing to see that Lek needs a good talking-to. It's another to do the talking. I'm just a fifth-rate pilot, you know? An out-of-work fifth-rate pilot. Why would he listen to my advice?"

"You're his friend."

"If I had any advice . . ."

"But you'll do it?"

"Yeah, eventually. But you gotta remember I'm pretty busy right now. There's Big Trash Day and—" He glanced at the wall clock and spilled his coffee all over the counter. "My God, is that thing right?" He looked at his watch—it was dead. "Oh, no . . . I gotta go!"

"Soon, okay?"

"*What* soon?"

"Lek."

"All right. I'll set something up. I gotta have Jass or somebody else there. Speedball. Lek likes Speedball, doesn't he? Everybody likes Speedball. Look, I gotta go *right now*."

"So take off."

"I'll talk to Lek. I promise."

"I'm counting on you."

Oh, God, don't say that!

"See you later," said Mike, running out. He glanced back in time to see her pitiful look, and that stopped him dead. "Hey, uh, I just thought. I'm gonna need money for the entrance fee. You know, for the jump-to-master heats. Any ideas?"

She looked up, and her eyes went unfocused for a moment. He could see the change on her face as she dropped her problem and went right to work on his. "Your utility p-suit all paid for?"

"Yeah, but it's secondhand."

"Good. Make it thirdhand."

"Then what'll I—"

"Wear your flying pressure suit for everything."

"Yeah, but all the hoses and stuff hanging down . . ."

"Go ahead, it's hip."

"Yeah?"

"Trust me. I know the racing style."

"Okay, if you say so." He wondered how much he could get for his utility suit. Fifty yen? Seventy-five? Mike turned quickly and collided with a big Merkek coming through the door.

"Watch you, navvy!" the guy said, looking positively furious. They always did.

"S'ree," said Mike, pushing past. He looked back through the door panel, through the haze of scratches in the once-transparent plastic. Twyla was laughing at him.

Well, that was something, at least. He pushed the door open and yelled inside. "Hey, cheer up!"

The big Merkek turned to glare at him, and Mike ducked out, the sound of Twyla's growing laughter in his ears.

Mike had the damnedest feeling he was being followed. He was deep in the underside of pit-ring, away from the central corridor, and far from the outer surface, where the pits opened out onto the free zone with hangar doors and airscreens. He was gliding down a narrow zero-g alley behind a row of cheap apartments, pushing a fat old refrigerator toward the nearest disposal tunnel.

It was sweaty work. Something kept shifting around inside the refrigerator, changing its center of mass. Every time he gave it a shove, it started off at some new and unpredictable angle, and he had to hustle to grab a handhold and jerk it back around before it gouged the wall or dinged a passerby.

Mike took a fast look behind him. There seemed to be a shadow fading back into the crowd, but he couldn't be sure.

This is ridiculous, he thought. Who the hell would follow a guy on Big Trash Day?

Mike pulled his baseball cap off and wiped his sweaty forehead on his sleeve. Across the front of the cap it said PITFALL IS CLEANING UP!

The damned thing didn't fit right. Mike needed more hair.

He looked up, saw that the refrigerator was drifting off toward the wall again. "Ah, come on . . ." Mike jammed the hat back on, pulling it down tightly over his fuzzy skull. Then he jumped across the corridor and braced himself to deliver one more correctional kick to the refrigerator.

Wham!

Another dent appeared in the battered metal surface. Good thing it was trash. Mike wondered how guys moving brand-new equipment managed it.

Well, the fact was, *real* movers probably had a robot to do the work. Give the load a series of micropushes, test the angle, realign it, then more micropushes, all coming so fast it looked reckless—but it was, in reality, perfect: a form of controlled chaos.

Mike came around and kicked the refrigerator again. It rattled back at him. He smiled. Mike the robot had his own system.

He grabbed the mag handle he'd stuck to the refrigerator and began bleeding momentum to the walls with his sneakers. He planned to turn at the next corridor intersect.

The refrigerator rattled and scraped the wall, whacking a chunk of plastic out of a hatch jamb. After Mike passed, some big green guy came out to see what was going on. Mike pulled his cap down further and kept on going, not looking back. Getting fired off community service was a one-way ticket to bozoville.

At the next intersection he gripped the mag handle with one hand and snagged the turnpole with the other. Unfortunately, the refrigerator kept right on going, hardly deflected, and Mike's sweaty grip broke loose. The refrigerator floated on across the intersection, nudging startled folks out of its way,

then hammered the projecting corner, spun slowly, and continued on down the alley, tumbling majestically.

"'Scuse me . . . *s'ree . . . s'ree,*" Mike murmured, passing angry pedestrians in his pursuit of the refrigerator. He was beginning to feel like Captain Ahab stalking the White Whale.

Ten meters down the deserted alley, the refrigerator banged into the wall again, shearing through a light fixture. The alley went dark. "Wonderful," said Mike, scratching his ear. There was another loud crash somewhere down the way.

Mike glanced back one more time, but the intersection had filled with large gray aliens chanting "*Hawee Kweeshna*" and plucking their musical teeth. Mike couldn't see beyond them. "To hell with it," he said, sailing into the dark after the refrigerator.

The corridor shrank even further, forcing him to stretch out and go headfirst. His skull buzzed and his stomach gurgled with nausea, as unshielded gravity zones shifted around him. Every time the refrigerator plowed into something, Mike's orientation swapped around: it was *down* there, *up* there, *over* there, *some*where in the dark.

Tiny red and green lights glowed on pressure hatches, but they weren't bright enough to see by. Mike dug around in his pockets for a flashlight, but when he finally dragged it out, he found the beam weak, its batteries discharged. He gave it a shake, then noticed the switch was jammed in the On position. Apparently it had been lighting up the inside of his pocket for hours. "Better and better."

Somewhere out there (*down* there, *up* there) the Great White Refrigerator banged into something new and fragile-sounding. Mike crept along, moving slowly, waiting for the next corridor light. The alley curved slightly and was filled with floating bits of broken glass. So much for the next corridor light. Up ahead the refrigerator had begun to bounce against the outside of the curve. That ought to slow it down.

A hatch snapped open as Mike passed, blinding him in sudden light, and a Polaran woman reached out for him with four hands. "Pardy-pardy?" she asked. "Wanna pardy?"

"No, thank you, ma'am!" said Mike, racing past. The hatch slammed shut.

Up the way, the banging stopped. Had the refrigerator come to rest? Not bloody likely. The corridor must have straightened out again. Mike strained to listen. The faint rattling sound continued—the refrigerator was still tumbling.

Mike saw he was approaching the next dim corridor lamp. He held his breath as the refrigerator passed slowly beneath it, missing the wire cage by millimeters, and plunged back into the shadows. There was another loud crash.

Mike pushed off quickly for the light. Something wobbled out of the darkness and smacked him on the nose. He flinched back (too late), and swatted at the thing. He rebounded, banging into the corridor wall, then floated free, rubbing his face. After a moment he realized he'd been clobbered by the mag handle, which must have been dislodged from the refrigerator. He thought about going back for it, but by then the handle had disappeared into the darkness, clanking off the distant walls.

Mike oriented himself again and pushed off after the refrigerator. If he ever caught up to the damned thing, it was going to be even harder to handle—though that was difficult to imagine.

Up ahead the dented white box spun slowly past beneath a light. All right, thought Mike. This has gone on long enough.

He didn't know exactly where he was, but somewhere up there was another corridor crossing—and he didn't want to be responsible if that monster crashed through and killed some poor sod.

Mike kicked the wall, accelerating after the refrigerator. His path took him across the corridor, where he kicked off again, harder. Down the line, cross to the other side, kick off again, moving faster and faster and—

Suddenly, not far up ahead, there was a loud, rattling impact. End of the line, coming up right now.

"Oh, no!"

He scrabbled along the walls, trying to slow down. Too late. He pulled his knees up, spun around, and stretched out. An instant later his feet hit the end wall, his legs flexed violently, and he banged his chin on his left knee, biting his

tongue. He saw fireflies arcing behind his clenched eyelids, then something warm and alive brushed his cheek—

—a shrill sound filled the middle of his head, and he found himself inside the exhaust nozzle of a humongous fusion engine. His heart was beating two hundred times a minute, his eyes blinking sideways. From far away came a metallic clicking noise, getting louder. A moment of panic—then the engine lit up, pouring the fires of hell into his face. Shadows flitted across his vision—small batlike animals with leathery wings and lizard heads. They were lighting up like torches—

—then Mike was outside the engine nozzle, flapping hard to get there in time, a silver wrench clutched in his small furry hand. The shriek of panic snapped shut in his mind . . . the withering exhaust sputtered and stopped . . . and the scene went blank.

Mike pried at the tiny hands that gripped his face. In the dim light he held the squirming animal at arm's length. His mother called his name, smiling, and reached out to touch his lips.

Mike yelled. His mother had been dead for five years—killed along with his dad in a subway decompression accident back on Earth.

Her image faded, and he saw the little animal, trembling in his grip. *Mike-Mike-Mike-Mike!* clamored a scratchy voice in his head. A dozen images came fluttering to the surface: Mike working on the *Slippery Cat,* reaching back for a stardriver, smiling; Mike lying in bed, his eyes just peeking from under the blanket; Mike holding out a bit of pancake on a fork—and tiny gray hands prying it loose, the smell of syrup making his mouth water; Mike and others in the middle of German's Yard, approaching the *Slippery Cat* where she floated, burned out after the accident, sabotaged by Jass when—

Mike shivered. The animal shivered. Mike blinked, and the animal blinked, its slow lids moving sideways over huge, moist eyes. A Klaat'k, that was for sure—one of the little semitelepathic alien mechanics that had worked with Mike on the Lek Croveen team—but he had never seen one alone. They always traveled in packs.

"Where are your brothers and sisters?"

Again he found himself inside the engine nozzle, and again the engine lit off with furious power right in his face. An accident in a shipyard, obviously. "Are you the only one who survived?"

He saw the animal floating alone in a vast empty chamber, its mouth open in a long, plaintive cry that echoed and was not answered.

"I'm sorry," said Mike. He wondered if a single lizard-bat could survive without his brain-sharing fellows. No wonder this little guy was panicked. Mike relaxed his grip, surprised at the warmth of the alien's body. "All you guys look alike to me."

The Klaat'k touched Mike's face—

—and he saw the black-edged hole that had been burned in the side of the *Slippery Cat*. There was a group of Klaat'x swarming nearby. One of them came forward, and Mike's hand reached out to trace a long blue scar down the animal's face.

"I remember you!" said Mike. "You're the one I called Scarface."

In Mike's projected image the Klaat'k grinned hideously, revealing dozens of tiny sharp teeth. *Mike-Mike-Mike-Mike!* said the scratchy little voice in his head.

"You're all alone now," said Mike. "You wanna come home with me?" His head filled instantly with shrill, happy noises. "Okay, okay! You know anything about moving refrigerators?"

CHAPTER 3

Mike wadded up his sheets and folded the bed into the wall, pushing on it until it latched. On the homeset half a dozen yellow blobs were jiggling through a series of tormenting exercises. Aerobics for aliens of amorphous shape. Mike flopped down on a bulging bag of dirty laundry and watched for a moment. But when pulsing loops of flesh began to extend, he winced and shut it off. He just liked the music on this show, which sounded something like a junkyard full of spaceships rolling downhill . . . and bouncing on the beat.

Scarface fluttered past, squealing.

"You're right," said Mike. "I *am* wasting my life."

It was early in the first shift, and Mike was off until the middle of the second. What to do? He guessed he could clean up this dump, and he looked around for a place to start. In one corner, heaps of dirty clothes flowed naturally into stacks of paperbacks and data cubes (some borrowed, some bought cheap on the Strip, some found in the trash). On a cluttered shelf, the parts from half-constructed plastic spaceship models mixed organically with a busted cube reader some guy had asked him to fix weeks ago. And leaned up against the wall was the entire pilot's control panel from a thirty-year-old Class A racing ship, which Mike had found in the corridor outside a bankrupt maintenance yard. He smiled. Clean this place up?

"Naw. . ."

You don't screw around with perfection.

He focused on his two pressure suits, which slouched together in the corner like a couple of drunks. "That's right," he said, pointing. "I was going to sell the suit today."

Mike whistled while he bundled his utility pressure suit into the carrying bag. Scarface sang along, whining and chattering, somewhat pitifully. "You wanna come too?" The

lizard-bat squealed and gibbered. He flapped to the ceiling and dived through the little room, dodging the model racecraft that hung down on strings, veering away from Mike's head at the last moment. "All right, all right!" said Mike. "I'll take that as a yes."

They hit the street.

Mike's room was in a plastic hotel at the precise sleazoid center of Pitfall. It was so exquisitely squalid that Pitfall Authority, which required folks on community service to take low-rent public housing, could find no fault with it. Mike was already sufficiently humbled.

They started off for the inspection station, the lizard-bat alternately perched on Mike's shoulder or flying ahead with long, smooth strokes of his leathery gray wings. Every few meters he would look back and grin his spiky grin. Mike would nod and wave him on.

The Strip corridor was, as usual, crowded with pilots, groundcrew, dockworkers, repairmen, B-girls, and so forth—in every variety of oxygen-breathing folk—as well as the occasional methane suckers: tall, brick-colored dudes with bright yellow tanks on their backs and superior looks on their faces—as though there did not exist an even sleazier Strip for the methane folk halfway around this very ring.

The air was filled with shouts and cries and exotic stenches from the food vendors, both licensed and black-market. Elsewhere, merchants hawked everything from digital watches to baseball hats. The Pitfall Cleanup Campaign was striking out on the Strip.

Mike stopped to buy a new battery for his watch.

"You sure this is fresh?"

"Guarantee!" said the vendor, waving his pseudopods airily.

Mike pocketed the tiny battery and moved on, pushing through the crowd. Lots of tourists these days, thanks to the upcoming Trike; the generous supply of gullible folks was driving the hawkers into a feeding frenzy.

"'Lectric jelly!" shouted a squat little creature. He had a head like ten pounds of spuds stuffed into a two-pound bag, with meaty things that resembled dried apricots glued inside

out to every greasy bump. Some of them might have been eyes, others ears—Mike tried not to speculate. "'Lectric jelly!" the fellow screamed, waving little plastic cartons of jiggling green muck at the astonished tourists. The goop looked like brains of some sort.

Mike hurried on past.

In front of one quivering yellow businessman, a picket line of Anti-Leather folk chanted slogans of abuse. Mike looked quickly to make sure he wasn't wearing his cowhide belt. He hated to explain the rather tedious lives that cows still led back on Earth. Fact was, he was having a hard time explaining it to himself.

Across the way a flock of black-striped lizard-bats flapped noisily past. Scarface watched them go, then flew back to Mike and showed his teeth.

"You know those guys?"

Scarface squealed and pressed an image into Mike's brain. Purple-striped Klaat'x fought the black in a fury of teeth and claws and small knives.

"Rival gang," said Mike. "Is that it?"

Scarface blinked, fluttered his tongue, and flew on ahead.

Mike shrugged and followed.

Politics.

Just up the Strip a multiheaded alien was selling lunchboxes with the cartoon character *Speedway Sam* painted on the side. Unauthorized, no doubt. Mike knew the licensing rep from Toyco, a very loud and pushy man who once had wanted to market a line of *Mike the Rookie* toys. Mike had turned him down, rather harshly. Too bad; he could use the money now.

Mike stopped and tapped the side of one of the sample lunchboxes. Composite steeloid. It was the same stuff they made the *Universe* out of. He wondered how it would stand up to a superluminal track exit. . . .

"You like? You like?" said the salesman, turning several of his heads toward Mike.

"Not well enough."

"In that case, you want pardy? Woman? Man? Girl? Boy? Nice juicy alien person? Come back later. I fix."

"No thanks."

"I fix!"

"No!"

Scarface chattered and clicked his teeth at the salesman, and several of the alien's heads lashed out, snapping viciously at the air. "Take it easy," said Mike, pulling Scarface back. "All of you."

The vendor was already busy propositioning somebody else. Scarface grabbed Mike's nose and pressed an image into his brain: Mike slicing heads off the guy with a large knife. "Now, stop it!" Mike said, and Scarface fluttered away, grinning.

Bloodthirsty little fiend.

Outside the equipment inspection center Mike stopped to buy a bag of hard candy clusters. "How much, each?"

The vendor was human, but only barely. One eye was sealed off with plastic and tape, and his clothes smelled as if they had been occupied continuously for many months. The better a look Mike got, the less interested he was in buying food from the guy.

"Dis kine?"

"The red ones, I guess. . . ."

"Dis kine?" he said, putting a dirty finger in the pile.

"Uh, no . . . the green ones."

Mike grabbed the guy's hand before he could poke it in there with the green ones—as if it made any difference.

"Five milliyen."

Mike smiled, seeing a way to get out of this. "What? Five million? You're kidding!"

"Five milliyen. *Milli*yen!"

"That's outrageous! Five million yen?"

"*Milli*yen! *Milli*yen!"

"That's way out of line," said Mike, backing off. "I'm really sorry."

"Five milliyen!" said the man, and for a moment Mike thought the poor guy would start to cry. "Okay, okay, *four* milliyen."

Mike sighed.

The guy scooped up a handful of the green clusters. "You take. Three milliyen each."

"I don't know. . . ."

Scarface was growling again.

Mike backed away, shaking his head. Now he felt like a monster, baiting the guy like this. If the man would just keep his grungy fingers out of the merchandise!

"Two for five. You take!"

"Not today. Sorry."

The man began to shiver and blink. Mike stepped back another pace. "I'm sorry..."

The shivers became shudders, and soon the man was shaking violently. A string of shiny drool dropped from the corner of his mouth.

"I'm sorry . . ." said Mike, reaching out to grab Scarface and pull him back.

The vendor's knees popped and buckled, and he slumped beside the spindly legs of his little table, his grubby sneakers skidding on the pavement. One eye rolled up, showing bloody white.

"HIPEr," said a man in a dull black pressure suit. He shook his head at Mike and walked on by.

"Hey, mister, you sure?" The man turned and Mike said, "I mean, I thought HIPE *sped up* the reaction time. He doesn't look sped up to me."

"Weasel dust," the man said. "It only works for a little while, kid. Just a little while."

"Have you ever . . . uh . . ."

The beginning of a stupid question. The man turned quickly and walked away. Mike looked back at the vendor. Had this guy really been a racing pilot in the old days?

Impossible. Impossible.

It only took half an hour for the techs to put Mike's utility pressure suit through the safety tests. One of the refill-hose connectors leaked a little, and had to be regunked, but other than that, the suit was in pretty good shape. Mike left it at the center on consignment, along with his bank input code.

"How soon do you think . . ."

The clerk looked up from her screen. She was a gray-skinned Poldavian, and her hair was cut just as short as Mike's. Another community-service worker, no doubt. Mike wondered if she was also a pilot, holding out for a job flying.

She said, "Check your balance in the next shift. With the Tricentennial, any kind of suit goes fast."

"Thanks."

She pointed at Scarface. "Orphan?"

"Yeah, I guess. His clan got"—Mike lowered his voice—"uh, got all burned up inside a main engine nozzle."

"You wanna sell him?"

"Are you kidding?"

She shrugged. "Orphans are nonsentient."

"Who says?"

"Pitfall Authority. Without his clan for brain-sharing, he's below the limit. He's classified an animal."

"I don't care. He's no animal."

"That's a fine line."

Mike remembered the Anti-Leather folks he'd seen demonstrating. She was right; the line was pretty fine . . .

The clerk stuck her finger in front of Scarface. He sniffed at it, then snapped. The clerk snatched her finger back, unhurt. "I wouldn't trust him."

"You don't have to."

"He sharing with you?"

"What do you mean? Sharing my brain?"

"Yeah."

Mike stopped and listened. Was there anything going on inside his head? "I don't know. I don't think so."

The clerk shrugged. "I'd be careful if I were you. They aren't like us, you know."

By the time Mike got outside in the street again, the vendor was gone and there were men in shiny green p-suits wandering around, kicking candy in all directions. Pitfall Police. Mike didn't want to know what they had done with the guy. The news was full of stuff about HIPE these days, and it sounded as if the cops were losing patience.

Scarface flew back with a handful of sticky green candy clusters.

"Thanks," said Mike, looking them over. He thought, Better have 'em steam-cleaned.

But Scarface was already gnawing happily on his. Biting down *hard*.

* * *

When he got back to his hotel room, he found a note shoved into the crack of the door. It said, *Spake to Zarathustra.*

The shift manager didn't know what it was about, which didn't surprise Mike. Some alien resident must have taken the message. Mike went back upstairs and opened up his little bed. He lay there for some time before figuring it out. Then he came down to the lobby again and called Zara Treva, the homeset reporter.

What do you know?

Shc wanted to put him on the air.

From an interview with Michael Murray, conducted by Zara Treva on *Good Morning, Pitfall:*

TREVA: I love your haircut, Mikc.

MURRAY: Don't rub it in.

TREVA: But you're keeping busy. . .

MURRAY: Oh, yeah. Pitfall Authority sees to that.

TREVA: And you're still looking forward to getting back on the track.

MURRAY: Absolutcly.

TREVA: What about the Tricentennial Classic?

MURRAY: Well, as you know, one of the teams is sponsoring a jump-to-master program.

TREVA: And you've applied?

MURRAY: Absolutely. In fact, I have a qualifying race in four hours. The first of three. I'm flying the Authority's wild-card ship.

TREVA: Well, you know everyone here at *Good Morning, Pitfall* wishes you the best of luck.

MURRAY: Thanks.

TREVA: And speaking of luck, you don't seem to have had a lot of luck lately. . . .

MURRAY: I'm hanging in there.

TREVA: Your accidcnt in Croveen's *Slippery Cat*—

MURRAY: I know.

TREVA: —which some folks still think was no accident.

MURRAY: I've heard the rumors.

TREVA: The way I understand it, the incident was in-

duced by a silver coin that caused a premature firing of the main engines.

MURRAY: It was a thruster jet, Zara. The jet stuck on, and the ship got sideways in the velocity shear. When the ship ahead of us lit off its main engines . . .

TREVA: But what a freak event. A silver coin jammed across an electrical circuit.

MURRAY: It won't happen again, I don't guess.

TREVA: Are you sure?

MURRAY: Well . . . how could it?

TREVA: Maybe it might . . . with this. [Treva holds a tarnished silver coin to the camera.]

MURRAY: Where'd you get that?

TREVA: Is it like the one you found on the *Slippery Cat*?

MURRAY: Yes . . . it is. Where'd you get it?

TREVA: Would you be surprised to find out this coin was sucked up into the ramscoop of a ship while running on track Monza?

MURRAY: You're kidding.

TREVA: It's not the only one, either.

Mike had very little time to think about what Zara Treva had said. As soon as he got out of the studio, he rushed his entry payment to the Racing League, then confirmed the use of Pitfall Authority's wild-card ship in the first series of qualifying races.

His utility suit had brought a good price on the market—over 150 interstellar yen. That was even more than he'd paid for it—a tribute more to the swollen population of Pitfall than to his meticulous upkeep. Still, it was a good suit. And now all he had to wear was his flying suit, which required an add-on backpack if he wanted to use it around town like a utility suit.

At first it didn't make any difference, though. He was going flying right away.

Mike was shocked when he got down to the south maintenance hangar and saw the ship. It was old *Ninety-nine*, the same hard-luck ship Lek Croveen had leased following the wreck of the *Slippery Cat*.

Ninety-nine's ancient reactors fused hydrogen-boron pel-

let fuel to vaporize and expel deuterium in the exhaust. Today her tanks were just about empty, the ship set up for maximum acceleration on the straight track. In effect, a drag race.

"Just don't embarrass the shop," said his section boss as he strapped Mike into the forward-facing pilot's seat.

"I won't."

Mike settled back. There were new cushions on the seat, and the harness straps smelled fresh. The quick-release was sluggish, though, and he worked it, opening and locking and opening it again, over and over.

"I mean it," said his boss. "And leave that thing alone." He reached across the seat and snapped the harness lock shut.

Mike said, "You don't want me to get trapped in here, do you?"

"That depends on whether you win or lose."

Everybody cleared off the ship, and Mike closed his helmet faceplate. He checked the tiny airlock's sensors, making sure he was alone, then set the electric latches and blew the ready horn in the hangar. He could see workers backing away to the safety zones. His radio crackled: "Good luck, Mike. Peel the skin off those guys."

"Okey-doke."

Another voice: "Gravity coming down."

"Copy."

The hangar grav field dialed back, and the ship creaked, stress-shocks relaxing. Mike was too tightly strapped down to notice a sense of weightlessness. He tapped the stick and brought the ship around, facing out through the shimmering airscreen.

When he glanced in the rear-looking viewscreen, he saw folks covering their ears and protecting their eyes from dust and exhaust. He grinned. Power, babe. That's what it's all about.

Mike pushed forward on the stick, and the ship floated out of the hangar and into the dark vacuum of the free zone.

The ships were paired off in a series of elimination heats. Mike's first race was almost his last, as the ship wobbled

badly coming off the line. Fortunately, the engines overcranked for him, and he beat a guy named Ren Ren Chow.

Mike returned to the hangar for a fresh load of fuel, amounting to about one eighth the ship's capacity. The actual mass of the ship was regulated by Race Control, as measured by a thruster of known rating and a calibrated accelerometer.

His second race was against Hideo Wanatabe, and *Ninety-nine* beat him easily. Mike started to relax.

The third race, however, was much too close. *Ninety-nine* clearly showed her age, as fuel plasma puffed out of her engines from a hundred microleaks.

Mike limped back to the hangar, glad there was only one heat to go. Out of 1280 ships that started, 160 were left. Eighty would advance to the next round of qualifying heats, less than a week away. And the other 1200 would take a hike, the pilots going back to scrounging for a ride and trying to stay active.

Mike checked the standings as he waited to be fueled. Alice Nikla was still in it, flying her new team's AAA-class racer: *404 Flying Circus*. Mike watched her fourth race on the monitor. Nikla beat the guy, but an immediate protest flag went up. Excess fuel.

Mike winced. He didn't want to be the one to tell her. His face still hurt from that time she punched him.

As Mike left the hangar for the fourth time, a voice boomed on the radio. ''So far so good. Don't screw it up.''

''Speedball!''

''I been watching ya, kid.''

''Any advice?''

''Yeah. Try not to crash.''

''Thanks.''

The field assembled on the screen, as the Racing League made another listing of matches. The first name he saw was Twyla Rogres, who was going up against Foatilizer J. Mike hadn't been too surprised when she called to say she had entered the contest, and he smiled to see she was still hanging in there. He was just glad his name hadn't come up opposite hers.

Then he saw the name of his last opponent. Dover Bell. Oh, great, he thought. If he beats me, I feel like a jerk.

If I beat him, he goes nuts and tears my head off. This is perfect.

Mike maneuvered *Ninety-nine* back across the free zone. The lights of Walltown looked like stars in a black sky—but were actually just porchlights on the houses of the crazy folks who lived on the inside of Pitfall's warp surface, plastered to the humming ground with cheap but unrelenting spin-gravity.

Mike slowed the ship as he approached the entrance of the spin-up circle. Red beacons lined the dark warp entrance. He stood off a kilometer or so, waiting for his call, and brooded.

He was thinking about the coins. Silver coins from Earth. Coins minted in Europe in the seventeenth century. Coins like the one he had in his pocket right now. His unlucky charm.

He told everybody he had sucked the coin up off the track, that the deal with the thruster solenoid had been a freak accident. Nobody really believed him, but that didn't matter—nobody could prove Jass Blando had put the coin there. Speedball and Twyla had spent a lot of time on the datanet, erasing all possible evidence.

But now here came Zara Treva, saying there *were* silver coins on the track, coins getting sucked up into the ramscoops of racing ships, coins just appearing on the track out of nowhere, exactly the way Mike had said. The difference was, Mike had been lying.

What the hell was going on?

Where were the coins coming from?

"*Ninety-nine,* this is Race Control."

"Yes, sir."

"Report to the spin-up circle."

"Roger, Control."

Mike tapped his mains out of habit, then screeched in horror.

What was he *doing*? This was a drag race, and he needed all his fuel for the acceleration.

"Oh, man . . ." There wasn't time to go back to the maintenance hangar for more fuel. Besides, his ship had already been weighed. He was due at the starting line. Dover Bell was waiting for him.

Mike used his attitude thrusters to maneuver into the warp zone that circled the inside equator of Pitfall. Instantly his ship appeared on the spin-up circle, shunted by the warp control to his assigned track. The circle blurred, then he was drifting toward a cluster of lights in the middle of a long straight chunk of empty track. The transparent sidewalls were dull, the track practically at rest relative to the fixed stars of distant space.

Mike tapped his thrusters again, looking out toward the circle of lights. He was late. One fat black ship was already there, standing by. Dover Bell.

"Line up, *Ninety-nine*."

"Roger, Control."

Mike settled in between the starting zones and checked his fuel graph. It was already so close to the bottom it was hard to read. Three seconds on full, and the low-fuel light would start to flicker.

"Signal when ready."

Mike ran the preheat diagnostic, then set the fuel pumps on 125 percent of max rate. "*Ninety-nine,* ready."

The ship began to vibrate, jiggling lights on the control panel, as the pumps built up pressure in the plenum. Mike clenched his teeth to keep them from rattling.

Race Control said, as it had three times earlier, "Ignite your mains when the light sweeps past."

"Roger, Control."

Somewhere on another track Twyla Rogres was facing the Foatilizer. Mike hoped she would win—but that only meant he'd have to race against her in the next two rounds. If he beat Dover Bell, that is.

Mike stared down the track.

"Come on, come on . . ." he muttered, watching for the light.

There!

Far down at the end of the warp-tube he saw a ring of white light begin to flicker. Mike's hand tightened on the stick, his foot raised above the engine-start switch. As the circle of light rippled toward them, moving faster and faster, Mike's ship rattled and creaked, eager to be off. The first amber warning light was already flashing on the panel. FUEL

PUMP OVERHEAT. *Ninety-nine* hummed louder and louder, producing low-end harmonics that bypassed the ambient sound microphones plugged into Mike's helmet. He could *feel* the noise inside this ship. "Hold together, baby. . ."

The ring of light swept past, turning green. Mike stomped the switch, lighting off the main fusion engines. The ship jutted forward, accelerating swiftly to ten g's, pushing him back into the new cushions, air sighing out.

The ship hammered and shook, and all the screens and lights went blurry. In his ear the accelerometer spoke cheerfully: "Eleven g's . . . point one . . . point two . . . point four . . . point seven . . ." The lighter the ship, the bigger the boost, and the fuel was running out faster than design specs.

"Caution. Caution."

ENGINE OVERHEAT.

Mike ignored the warning, his right hand clenched painfully around the control stick. The ship wobbled and wiggled and tried to fly sideways down the track.

"Twelve g's . . ."

Up ahead, a wide yellow band marked the end. Mike leaned forward on the stick, adding thruster jets to his speed until the low-thruster fuel alarm shut him down automatically. He didn't bother to reset, not wanting to be disqualified on a safety gig.

MAIN ENGINE SHUTDOWN.

"Reset!" yelled Mike, without thinking. Pointless—he didn't know the override code. It didn't matter—fusion fuel was gone. All the way up in the cockpit he could hear the pipes twanging and crackling as they cooled.

He passed through the yellow end ring, and the ship decelerated automatically in the programmed warpweb. He took a deep breath and managed to pry his aching foot off the main-engine firing switch. Fuel pumps off, cooling pumps pushing the reserves around at 110 percent of max, breakers reset, cabin fans high. Mike glanced at his p-suit readouts. Everything was fine,

"Home on the red-red beacon," said Race Control.

Mike scanned the screen, found the lights flashing at the track exit. He flicked the control stick, heading over. If he was lucky, he'd have enough reserve thruster fuel to get off

the track. (Thank God for automatic shutdowns.) Beyond the exit circle, a glittering tube of warped space would lead the way back to Pitfall.

"Uh . . ." He sequenced all the outside cameras, looking for Dover Bell's black ship. "Race Control, this is *Ninety-nine*."

"Go ahead, *Ninety-nine*."

"Uh . . . how'd I do?"

Something drifted past outside, shiny and jagged, tumbling quickly end over end—a large hunk of reactor shield metal.

"You won, *Ninety-nine*. The *Wild Weekend* blew an engine coming off the line."

"Off the line? Why didn't you—" Mike stopped, staring at the white abort light glowing on his race-status panel.

"Say again, *Ninety-nine*?"

"Never mind. Anybody hurt?"

"Negative."

"Thank you."

"Exit the track, *Ninety-nine*."

"Roger, Control."

Mike wiggled the abort light and it blinked. Loose wire, no doubt—and the acceleration had kept it stuck in the off position. All that work for nothing. He started to laugh. "Dover Bell's gonna kill me!"

CHAPTER 4

Mike dropped into a chair at the low-g end of Quohogs. "I can't stay long. I got to take a load of VIPs on a tour of the racing system."

"Sounds like fun," said Speedball.

"I was looking for Jass."

"He just left. I think he went back to his pit to work on the ship."

"That's what I need to know. Is the ship going to be ready for the next qualifying race?"

"He's trying."

"I know." Mike wondered if he was taking advantage of Jass's sense of guilt.

Speedball said, "Your little friend Dover Bell has been by, looking for you."

"Hey, *I* didn't blow up his stupid engine."

"Takes a lot to convince some people."

"No doubt."

"Seriously, Mike. He really looked mad. I think you better stay out of his way for a while."

"How long?"

"Six or seven hundred years ought to do it."

"That mad, huh?"

Speedball shrugged, his steel shoulders bunching up in a somewhat menacing gesture. "By the way, I saw you on the homeset. *Good Morning, Pitfall.*"

"I bet I looked bald."

"Yeah, but I like the bald look."

"You would."

Speedball's shiny head sparkled with reflected light. He said, "Did you get a good look at that coin she had?"

"Not really. It was kind of melted, you know? But I

think it was the same sort of coin the mob gave Jass for sabotaging my. . . uh, Lek's ship. Do you really think it came off the track?''

''I'd like to find out. All my coins disappeared sometime during the week before I died—after my last braintape update—so I don't know what the hell happened to them.''

''The coin didn't just materialize out there.''

''I've been thinking about Clypsis,'' said Speedball.

''Clypsis?''

''It's going through a hot cycle, which it does every twenty years or so. You may recall I conked out twenty years ago—during a hot cycle.''

''What does that have to do with anything?''

''Tracks get weird during the hot cycle, Mike. I've been checking the records. You get variation in velocity and cross-section. Things just sort of kink up. And I happen to know the sweepers pick up more junk during hot cycles.''

''I haven't heard anything, and I've been working out of the maintenance yard for months.''

''You're hearing it now.''

''How would it work?'' asked Mike. ''What's the mechanism?''

Speedball leaned back in his chair. ''Suppose there was a pocket of old debris, locked up in some twisted hunk of warped space.''

''Like a miniature version of Pitfall.''

Speedball nodded. ''Now suppose a webtube just swelled out—pumped up by the heat of Clypsis—and intersected this hypothetical pocket. It might tear open, spilling its contents onto the track.''

''Okay, I like that. What are you going to do about it?''

''I want to go to the maintenance hangar and examine the junk they're bringing off the tracks right now—concentrating on track Monza.''

''That's a good idea, and I wish I could go with you.''

''Why can't you?''

''I got work to do.'' Mike sighted beyond Speedball, to

where a brown-haired young woman was looking out across the tables. ''That's Helen DeSitter. She works for the Racing Museum.'' Speedball's head swiveled alarmingly. ''Now she sees me,'' said Mike. ''She's coming over.''

''Oh, God,'' said the automaton. He started to climb under the table.

''Hey, take it easy,'' said Mike. ''She's looking for me.''

''There you are!'' said Helen DeSitter, coming up.

''Is it time?''

''Yes, it is.'' She watched Speedball climb back into his chair. ''Aren't you—''

He grumbled. ''I used to be.''

''But we've been trying to get you for weeks.''

''I know.''

''It's the Tricentennial,'' said Helen.

''I know. Old Timers' Junk.'' Speedball looked at Mike. ''I'm a museum piece, you know?''

''You're a priceless historical resource,'' said Helen DeSitter. ''Why, with your memories—''

''I know. I'm sorry. I'm just too . . . crotchety . . . or something.''

Mike kept his mouth shut, but a smile was leaking out. Crotchety old Uncle Speedball, thought Mike. Somebody ought to glue a long white beard on him. Somebody really brave. And really stupid.

Helen said, ''I wish you'd change your mind. There's still lots of time.'' She looked at Mike. ''But not for you. Maybe you'd better come with me right now.''

''Okey-doke.''

Mike got up, and Speedball said, ''Hurry back. I'll wait for you.''

''Right.''

As they left the restaurant, Mike told her, ''First, I have to go back to my room.''

Shc gave him a peculiar look. ''Really?''

He laughed. ''I have to get my flying suit. But if you want, I'll meet you at the museum—or whatever.''

She thought that over. ''No, we're late as it is. I better keep an eye on you.''

* * *

When he slid open the door there was a blur of leathery wings and a squealing noise. ''Scarface!'' Mike tried to shut the door on Helen. ''Don't let him touch your—''

But it was too late; the Klaat'k had landed on her face. Her startled yelp cut off abruptly, and her arms dropped limply to her sides. Mike gently pried Scarface loose. There were tears in Helen's eyes.

Mike tossed the lizard-bat into the room and pushed Helen outside into the hall, shutting the door. ''God, I'm sorry. I should have remembered . . .''

She took a deep breath. ''It's all right.''

''I guess I should take him out more often. He gets so lonely in there.''

''I thought they lived in flocks or something.''

''He did. But his people . . .''

''I know.'' She squeezed his arm. ''I saw it.''

''Sometimes I think he whines too much.''

Helen waited in the hall while Mike changed into his flying pressure suit. He tried to explain to Scarface what he'd done wrong, but didn't have the heart to get angry. Before Mike left, the lizard-bat hummed, stroking his face—and Mike caught the scent of Helen DeSitter buried in the images of forgiveness. ''Okay,'' he said. ''I'll tell her.''

When they got to the Racing Museum's dock, Mike found out his copilot was Alice Nikla. ''What are you doing here?'' he asked, standing several meters away.

''Relax, Murray. I'm not going to hit you.''

Mike touched the bone beneath his left eye. ''Damn thing still hurts.''

Alice grinned, moving closer. ''Anyway, I'm out here working off a fine.''

''Oh, yeah. You messed around with the fuel quota on your last jump-to-master drag race.''

Nikla stared at him, smiling faintly. ''Yeah, something like that.''She reached out swiftly and touched his cheek. ''Does it really hurt?''

"When it wants to," he said, flinching back. "I'm probably marked for life."

She laughed.

He said, "I hear you left Dover Bell."

"Yeah, I finally got smart."

"What made you decide?"

She looked at him so long he was about to back off. Perhaps it was too personal. "You don't have to—"

"No, I'll tell you," she said. "Dover Bell is no longer kidding around."

"Yeah?"

"Dover Bell is getting . . . dangerous."

"How come?"

"Frustration, I guess. He wants very much to succeed at racing."

"So do I."

"Yeah, but for him it's serious."

"Hey, *I'm* serious."

"No sane person is *that* serious."

Mike started to make some joke, but stopped when he saw the look on her face. Conversation complete.

He said, "Let's go to work."

The ship had cleared customs and was waiting for them. Mike was expecting a busload of middle-aged tourists. He couldn't have been more wrong.

Mike took all he could take, then he banged his harness release and turned around to face the back of the bus. "We're not going anywhere until you little girls settle down!"

"Space Rangers! Space Rangers!" they all yelled back.

"Shut up and stop throwing things!" said Mike.

"Space Rangers! Space Rangers!"

Mike looked at Alice Nikla, who was strapped into the copilot's seat. He said, "I'm not going to live through this."

Alice laughed, and put the preflight checklist away. "Let's go, Mike."

"Space Rangers! Space Rangers!"

One of them floated forward and got right in Mike's face. "My name's Margie! Margie Phillips!"

"That's fine, Margie," he said. "Now go back to your seat and buckle up!"

"This is not a rental," she said. "I own my own space suit."

"I'm impressed."

Mike looked at Alice Nikla, pleading. "Come on, Margie," she said. "Sit down and we'll go."

"My mommy's a race pilot," said Margie. "I'm gonna be a racer, too."

"Not if I see you first," muttered Mike.

"When I'm old enough, I'll wax your butt."

"Sure, kid. Go sit down. Don't you wanna tour the system?"

"I've seen it."

"Sit down, Margie," said Alice. "Maybe some of the other girls haven't seen the speedway."

"I've seen everything," said Margie. "Twice."

"Maybe you'd like to fly this bus?" said Mike.

She looked over the controls. "I could do that."

"Do you know how a harness interlock works?"

"Of course."

"Then you know I can't even undock until every one of you little women sits down and buckles up."

"I know where the override is," she said, reaching under the panel.

Mike smacked her hand away.

"Go back to your seat, Margie," said Alice.

"I wanna ride up front."

Mike said, "How'd you like to ride outside? I'll fix you a seat in one of the main engine nozzles."

She shook her head. "Too dangerous."

"Yes," said Mike. "But do you have any idea how dangerous it is for you to stay where you are? Within my reach?"

Margie smiled at him. "I know you like me." He lunged at her and she pushed off, screaming happily. She slapped the backs of the seats as she went, flying a corkscrew pattern to the rear of the bus.

"Space Rangers! Space Rangers!" yelled the girls. They began to sing:

Space Rangers! Space Rangers!
Blasting through the night!
Space Rangers! Space Rangers!
What a lovely sight!
Space Rangers! Space Rangers!
Masters of the void!
Space Rangers! Space Rangers!
We're all humanoid!

"Bunch of racists," muttered Mike.

"Let's go," said Alice.

"Sure." He watched the screen, waiting for Margie to buckle up. When the light went green, he locked his own buckle and got a start-enable light on the panel. "About time." He disengaged from the dock—and the girls cheered like shrill banshees.

Mike flinched, thinking, I should have expected that.

He lowered his faceplate and locked it down. His suit green-lighted in muffled silence, and he kept his outside microphone dialed way down. There, that was better. Now all he had to do was open a hatch and evacuate the bus. See how fast the little monsters could get their suits sealed up . . .

Mike radioed Pitfall Port Authority and requested permission to exit the station. His flight plan was reviewed and approved, and Mike brought the ship around and aimed it at the portal. More cheers, barely audible. Mike hit the warp zone dead center, and in a few seconds they were popping out into real space ten million kilometers from the surface of Clypsis. Bright light streamed into the bus through the ports.

Pitfall was creeping down the side of the star, dragging its plume of glowing gas. Mike got on the intercom PA. "Try not to look directly at Pitfall." He could see in the rearview mirror that every head turned to look directly at Pitfall. Fortunately the glass in the ports was ray-shielded.

"Actually," said Mike, "you couldn't see the real Pitfall if you tried, but you can see the diamond glow at the tip of the Dragon's Claw, where stellar hydrogen is beating on the warp field. Every time Pitfall dives into the star, it charges up the energy field—and dumps the trash."

Alice said, "They really need to know about the trash."

Mike ignored her. "Pitfall's outer shell is not a physical structure, of course. Or it would never survive the close orbit of Clypsis."

Someone tapped his shoulder, and he turned. It was Margie. She knocked on his faceplate, and he reluctantly opened up. She said, "It's a sphere of warped space."

"I know that," said Mike. "And why aren't you in your seat?"

"You just said buckle my harness, so I did."

Mike checked the mirror. Floating in Margie's empty seat was a buckled harness. She grinned at him.

"How old are you?" he asked.

"I'm eight and three quarters, standard."

"How'd you like to be nine, someday?"

"Tell them what Pitfall really is."

"Don't they listen to you any more?"

"Tell them, Murray. They need to know everything, 'cause they're all very stupid."

Mike keyed the PA. "For your information, ladies, Pitfall is a hollow spherical shell some twelve kilometers in radius. It's about a kilometer thick, and the warp machines that hold it up are over three hundred years old."

"Tell them how the warp engines work."

"A warp engine is made of a whole bunch of very mysterious junk that nobody knows a damn thing about."

"Tell them about the aliens who left the first warp ship here."

"Nobody knows anything about them, either."

"You disappoint me, Murray."

"What a shame."

Alice started laughing.

They reentered the speedway warpweb and popped out at the terminal of a new experimental rally course. From here, over a billion kilometers from Clypsis, they could see the whole spiderweb pattern of glittering tracks. Spread out at a right angle was the plane of the ecliptic, where a number of reconstructed planets chugged along, linked by the paths and the sliding interchanges of the commercial warpweb. Several

tenuous rings looped about, remnants of dust and gas and rock left over from the work that had been done to the planets.

"Tell the Rangers what happened to all the original planets," said Margie.

"The consortium fixed them," said Mike, smiling. Soon all this would be over, and he could meet Speedball at the maintenance hangar. Mike was also curious about the debris coming off track Monza.

Margie said, "Tell them!"

Mike glanced in the mirror. All the little girls were singing and laughing and yelling and throwing candy wrappers. "I think one of us is boring them."

"They're all so stupid."

Mike turned to Alice. "What exactly is it you're supposed to do?"

"I'm the referee."

Mike nodded, but he kept his eye on her. In the next two hours Alice broke no clinches and took away no points. Some referee.

One final stop: a visit to a regular speedway track. When Mike filed his flight plan they had given him a choice, so he had picked track Monza, hoping he might find something interesting to make this stupid trip worthwhile.

The track was temporarily shut down, the fabric of space still, unstreaming, quiescent. Mike maneuvered the bus down the centerline, barely moving.

"We call this the groove," he said. "After the pace ship goes by—and the warp is set—this is where the track moves the fastest. It's sort of like water running through a pipe. The warp-tube itself is a standing wave vortex, but it slowly loses energy, so it has to be pumped up from time to time."

Mike used his thrusters to nudge the ship sideways on the track—feeling awfully vulnerable—and lit the main engines for a few seconds. The bus glided off toward the edge of the tube. "Believe it or not," he told them, "I've never had a chance to see the edge up close."

"Me, neither," said Alice.

Mike spun the ship and tapped the mains again to slow down, stopping the ship a few hundred meters from the twinkling edge of the track.

"What's the big deal?" asked Margie, looking out a porthole.

"I don't know," said Mike. "Where's your curiosity, your sense of adventure? Think of this as a learning experience."

"If you say so. Let's get out and have a closer look."

"No way!" said Mike. "Nobody's leaving the ship!"

Margie said, "Where's your sense of adventure?"

Before Mike could answer, Margie yelled back into the bus: "Who wants to go out on the track and look around?"

"No!" said Mike, but by then everybody was cheering and checking one another's suits and getting ready to hit the airlock. Mike turned at Alice. "Okay, ref. Tell 'em to stay where they are."

Alice looked back at the girls. "But they're so excited," she told Mike. "Don't you think it might be fun?"

"Now *wait*!" said Mike.

Alice popped her harness release and turned to address the girls. "I'm going to look at every suit, so you better all have a line of green lights."

The Space Rangers cheered, comparing status lights. "Green light! Green light! Me, too! Green light! Green light! I'm all set! Green light! Green light! Space Rangers! Space Rangers! Let's go!"

In an instant, everybody was crowding around the airlock hatch.

"That's it!" said Mike. He keyed the PA and boosted the volume. "Nobody move and I *mean* it! *I* am the pilot and *I* say nobody leaves the ship. There must be about a million safety regs that'll back me up, so I don't want to hear any discussion. We will not debate. We will not vote. *Nobody* is getting off this bus until we're hard-docked back at the Racing Museum. And that," he said, surveying the frozen young ladies, "is that."

An alarm chimed on his panel and he turned back to the console.

AIRLOCK INNER HATCH OPEN

Followed by

AIRLOCK INNER HATCH CLOSED

And

AIRLOCK CYCLING

Somebody had defied him.

Take a guess.

"Oh, jeez," said Mike. "This is a nightmare."

CHAPTER 5

Mike jumped from his seat. Suit hoses jerked him back, and he had to grab his EVA backpack. "Now *you* are in charge," he told Alice Nikla, getting hooked up.

"I'm going with you!"

"No, you're not!"

"You just want the glory," she yelled at him.

"Are you serious?"

A crowd of Space Rangers was clogging the aisle of the bus. "Come on, ladies! Make way!" he yelled, scattering Rangers left and right. At the airlock he dropped his faceplate and sealed his suit.

By the time he had cycled through, Margie was gone. He keyed his radio. "Where the hell are you?"

"Over here," she said, her voice half buried in static.

Mike climbed over the ship to get a better look. He scanned the glittering track edge for navigation lights.

"No, idiot. Over *here*!"

Mike swiveled, looking in toward the middle of the track. There she was, drifting slowly away. "Oh, no . . ."

"It's like flying," she said.

"Come back here!" he yelled, feeling like an idiot. How could she come back? She had no reaction system, no thruster jets. She couldn't do anything but drift.

Mike scrambled down the side of the bus and ducked into the open airlock. He grabbed a length of rope and hooked a small air tank to his suit utility belt. He searched frantically for any kind of thruster pack, but found nothing. He thought about going back inside the bus and looking, but this big airlock took too long to cycle. He'd have to make do with what he had.

He pulled himself outside and checked his watch: [2] 0928. "Alice, this track goes live in half an hour. If I'm not

back in ten minutes, key the emergency comm-line transmitter: Code Red. I don't know how this is going to work out."

"Good luck."

"You mean it?"

"Of course I mean it."

"Okay, thank you. Now stay off the air. I'm going to be busy."

"Prima donna," muttered Alice, setting a countdown timer to ten minutes. Proper procedure would be *not* to wait, but apparently Murray was trying to get out of this without an official inquiry—just grab the little bitch and drag her back inside. Obviously, a cover-up.

Alice considered keying the Code Red right away—just to see what Mike would say. Then she remembered she was the one who had encouraged the girls to leave the ship. If there *was* an inquiry, that wouldn't look good.

The timer said nine minutes and thirty-two seconds.

So Murray expected her to just sit here and sweat it out. What a twerp. Then she thought, wait a minute—if *he*'s in trouble, we're *both* in trouble.

Alice reached out and disabled the ship's radar transponder.

If you're gonna cover something up, then cover it up all the way. . .

At Race Control a track controller kept one eye on the schedule and one eye on the time and one eye on the pending file. Images stacked and floated across his sensorium. Track Monza was going hot soon, and his pending file was flashing with some mickety-mousy tourist bus.

The controller scanned for transponder returns—nothing. The track was clear.

He called Pitfall Port Authority, but they had no record of the bus leaving the speedway.

"Well," said the track controller, "he's gone now."

He made another radar sweep while the Port Authority guy thought it over—again, no transponder code painted on his screen. Damn it, the track was clear.

"Now," said the controller, "I gotta do skin-track look-see, check out the groove."

"Sorry," said Authority. "We'll chew him for you, don't worry."

"Chewing's too good for him," muttered the controller, keying off.

He tapped the pending file with a long, slender finger. "You in trouble big time plenty," he said, scanning the personnel datascreen. "Michael M. Murray, ex-pilot (if I am having my way). Next time, call in your clearance, Mr. Slime."

Humans.

Mike spotted Margie's flashing lights again, much farther down the track than he'd have thought. Damn.

He nervously checked his watch: [2] 0928. The track was supposed to come alive at ten hundred, so that left him . . . uh . . . Mike checked his watch again: [2] 0928. He tapped it with a thick, gloved finger: [2] 0928. He tapped it again, harder: [2] 0927. "Oh, no . . ." Again and again: [2] 0923 . . . [2] 0P35 . . . [2] ZAJH . . . until the display simply flickered out.

Nice fresh battery, that amorphous geek had sold him.

Mike's stomach got hot and floated away. He keyed his radio. "Uh, Alice . . . what, uh . . . what time do you . . . uh . . ."

The speedway glimmered faintly, white, yellow, green . . . then the track shuddered in a confusing blur, the pace ship having passed at superluminal speed.

"Oh, man . . ."

Margie's navigation beacon was drifting away now, caught in the stream of moving space. Mike groaned and pushed off for the center, aiming to get himself in a faster lane and overtake her. "I'm doomed . . ."

Why was she doing this to him?

He could see what career remained turning to dust.

The farther inward he went, the faster he moved. The lights of the track shined through the glittery walls and floated across his view, making it difficult to concentrate. And there was another problem. He kept wanting to look behind him.

If the track was warping up to speed, would the racecraft be long in coming?

"Say something, Margie."

"I see you," she said, her voice stronger in his earphones. "Are you coming out to get me?"

"What do you think?"

"Well, I'm not ready to come in yet. It's fun out here."

"Fun?" Mike glanced back nervously, wondering if he should tell Alice to call in the emergency right away—if only to cancel the injection of racers. When he looked forward again, he had a devil of a time finding Margie's beacon. She had jumped along the track even farther.

"Are you still accelerating?" he asked.

"Of course. I want to get in the groove. That's the best part."

"How can you maneuver like that?"

"I swiped an oxy bottle from the airlock. I'm using it for a thruster jet."

"My God," muttered Mike.

"You think I'm stupid enough to come out here with no way of getting back?"

"Beats me, little girl. I don't know what to think anymore."

Mike unsnapped his oxygen bottle and blasted directly for the centerline. If she was maneuvering, the only chance he'd have of catching her would be to get in the groove before she did. He'd have to race the little darling.

As an afterthought, Mike turned off his navigation beacon. If she noticed what he was doing, she'd certainly beat him to it.

"Hey, where'd you go?"

"I'm right here, babe . . ." he said, his eyes fixed on her nav light. If she got wise and turned off hers . . .

He was beyond her now, moving faster, closing slowly. Mike gave the bottle another squirt, his body wobbling with the slightly off-center thrust. Fortunately, the warpstream itself tended to stretch things out in line with the direction of travel.

Margie's light drifted closer, and now he could see her suit. Of course, that meant she'd be able to see him, too. He could only hope she'd be looking toward the edge of the track. "I see you," she said.

Wrong again. Mike frowned and gave his makeshift thruster another squirt. He felt himself jerked about, almost

losing his grip on the oxygen bottle. He was in the velocity shear now, so he pulled his legs up close, making himself smaller. The shear could pry loose panels right off a racer, but ships were wide and subject to a greater force. Soon the tugging smoothed out, and Mike found himself really zipping along. He was in the groove.

"Hey!" yelled Margie. She reacted just a hair too slow, and Mike swept up behind her as she was still wobbling her way through the last of the shear. He reached out and snagged her ankle.

"Let go!"

"Drop dead," said Mike. "Just as soon as I get you home." He turned, looking back, and wondered how far away the bus was now. "Alice? Can you read me?"

No response.

If he knew exactly where to aim, he could point his directional antenna at the bus. He looked around. They had just passed through the ecliptic, headed north. By now he had to be a couple hundred kilometers ahead of the bus, and every second he stayed in the groove was another ten klicks. His suit-to-suit radio had a range of a couple of kilometers. No wonder she wouldn't answer.

Mike tied one end of the rope to his belt and knotted the other end around Margie's suit. "We're gonna work this out."

That was when the racecraft hit the track.

They seemed to come from nowhere, a dozen or more of them, joining the raceway groove in front and behind them, converging swiftly, closing the gap.

"This is great!" said Margie. "Let's race 'em!"

"They'd win," said Mike, watching the ramscoop of the ship behind them edge forward. It was like looking down the throat of inchoate hell.

"Can he see us?"

"I doubt it. His radar is designed to track ships, not space suits."

"Can't you call him on the emergency freek?"

"I could, if I wanted anybody to know we're out here. I don't think you understand how much trouble we're in."

"Hey, I'm just a kid. *You're* responsible!"

"Okay, the trouble *I'm* in. I'd rather just get you back to the ship and forget this whole thing ever happened."

And he thought, Fat chance, with her mouth.

Margie said, "You sure he can't see us?"

"Naw. He's probably watching his tac screen right now, looking for a chance to light off his main engines."

Which reminded him. The ship to worry about was not the one coming up from behind. Mike looked forward—and groaned. They were only ten meters from the blackened main engine nozzles of the guy ahead.

"Let's drop back a bit."

Mike pulled Margie close, then aimed his oxy bottle to the side. He gave a long squirt, and they backed up into the velocity shear. He gripped the rope tightly. "Hang on!"

The ship behind was moving up faster now, and in seconds was alongside, just a few meters away. "My God," said Mike. "It's the *Slippery Cat*—my old ship!"

Mike shoved his oxy bottle behind him and opened the valve. They jerked forward, matching speed in the warpstream, and ran smack into the ship. Mike snagged a safety latch and threaded a loop of his rope through it, making a loose knot.

"What are we doing?"

"Hitching a ride."

"That's no fun," said Margie. "I wanna fly all by myself." She jerked the line and the knot came undone.

"Hey," said Mike. "Leave that alone!"

As he reached for the rope, the ship quivered and jumped and swung wide, its blasting main engines filling his ears with radio static.

Margie hollered, "Yay!"

Mike grabbed for the safety ring, catching it with his gloved fingertips. He could feel the vibration of the coolant pumps, just beneath the panel. He held on as the ship accelerated around the ship in front, trying to pass on the right. As they got out in the velocity shear, the force built up, and his grip weakened. "I can't hold on!"

"Good!"

"You wanna *fry*?"

Mike leaned forward to grab the loop with his other

hand, but the shear got worse—then the ship twisted and shimmied as the boosters came on. The *Cat* zoomed up beside the guy ahead, who had finally caught on and lit off his own mains. Mike's eyes filled with violet glare, and he nodded sharply, flipping down his sun visor. The *Slippery Cat* boosted again, trying to get around, engines on max, shaking and wobbling in the turbulence.

"I can't—"

Mike's grip gave way, and they slid back, bouncing against the side of the ship. He snagged a projecting radio antenna, but it snapped off in his hand. "Damn . . ." He grabbed Margie, swung her up over his head, and kicked off as hard as he could. They drifted away quickly. Mike brought the oxygen bottle around, pointed it at the ship, and dumped it all.

They accelerated sideways, dropping back faster and faster in the slower warpstream. The aft end of the ship approached, fusion engines flaring.

"Scrunch up!" he yelled, pulling Margie close to him. The glare of the exhaust blossomed around them—and shut off. His suit temp peaked, alarms whining in his ears, then dropped. The ship had shut down, diving back for the groove.

Mike and Margie continued to drift farther and farther back. Ship after ship sped past.

Mike looked around. They were high above the plane of the ecliptic, having peaked over the north celestial pole, and were moving down again. In another few minutes they'd be back down among the orbits of the planets.

"That was great!" said Margie.

Mike took a breath, aimed the oxy bottle, and hit the valve. It was empty. "You got any juice left?"

"Not much."

"Give me the bottle."

"No, it's mine."

Mike jerked it out of her hand.

"Hey!" she said.

"You'd probably just use it to get back in the groove."

"So what? It's fun in the groove."

"Yeah, but I feel safer with a ship around me."

"You're no fun."

"Sue me."

They were still drifting sideways across the track, moving slower and slower. Mike estimated they could easily drop below the ecliptic before hitting the wall.

Then the track went yellow—and ten seconds later the pace ship sped past, cutting the warp down to practically nothing. No forward motion, but they were still drifting sideways toward the wall.

Alice must have transmitted the Code Red. At the worst possible time.

Mike pointed Margie's oxygen bottle at the edge of the track and emptied all the gas. He watched for a long moment, but it was obvious they were still drifting outward.

"Okay," he told Margie. "Here's the thing. We're going to hit the wall."

"Then what?"

"I don't know."

He checked his suit status lights, then looked hers over. They had consumables for another half hour. If the wall didn't kill them, a little sloppiness on the part of the rescue squad would do the job.

"Is it a real wall?"

"Never been there, kid."

"Is it a force field?"

"Something like that, I guess."

Whatever it was, the wall was very near. Mike looked around, searching the track for moving lights. He set his radio on the emergency frequency and keyed the transmitter: "Code Red, Code Red. Man on the track!"

No response.

"They'll find the bus first," he said. "They've got the big beacon."

"But nobody on the bus knows where we are."

"Nope."

And there wasn't time for an extended search—the wall was just a few dozen meters away. Mike threw the oxygen bottle at it, but there was little change in the rate of drift.

"The bottle didn't have enough mass," said Margie. "I already thought of that."

"How much do you weigh?" asked Mike. "Maybe I ought to throw you."

"Very funny."

Mike turned to see how close they were, then looked away, not liking the view. He dropped his head, aiming his directional antenna at where he hoped the bus was floating. "Alice, do you read me? Alice? Come in, Alice." He switched to the omni antenna. "Code Red, Code Red. Man down on the track, near the outside wall, just below the plane of the ecliptic. Can you read me?"

He made a RAM loop of that message and put the emergency transmitter on automatic. He thought, I should have done that about a year and a half ago.

His suit cooler went up two notches. He looked over his shoulder. It was too late. They were at the wall.

Mike blinked. The glittering wall shimmered with unfocused patches of light. The closer they came, the harder it was to look at. Then, when it seemed as if they would never actually reach it . . . they pushed softly against the light. Mike held his breath.

Margie grabbed tighter, wrapping her arms around his waist. They began to roll against the wall, bouncing gently along. All the lights in Mike's helmet readout flickered, the letters and numbers turning to garbage.

"It tingles!" said Margie, her voice filled with static. Her helmet was half an inch from his, but she seemed to be calling from a billion kilometers away.

Mike took a breath. The air tasted sour, and he looked automatically to see if his tanks were going empty—but the readout was just a hash of nonsense. Still, if the actual circuits were really this screwed up, the suit would have failed by now.

A garbled voice squawked on his radio, ripped by static and squeals. It didn't sound like Margie. He looked down the track and saw a fuzzy red beacon approaching. It was the crash ship, cruising upstream.

He started to yell—

—and the beacon went out.

Everything went out: the track, the glittering walls, the starry sky, the planets and the web of warp-tubes that

connected them. Margie squeezed so hard he could hardly breathe, sour air or not. "I'm scared!" she said, her transmission flawless.

"It's all right," he said, but he had no idea how it was. There was nothing to see, just a velvety darkness all around them. He noticed his suit readouts had cleared; everything was green light. He could even hear the tiny voice of the recorded RAM loop repeating his emergency message on the crash frequency, but he would have bet anything it wasn't getting out.

"Where are we?" asked Margie. "Where'd everything go?"

"I don't know."

He turned on his wrist light and watched the beam die out in the distance. Bits of dust sparkled all around them, and shiny points of light slowly winked, like silver coins flipping end over end.

He no longer had any sense of motion, so when he saw the misty zone of light go by, he couldn't tell if he was passing it or it was passing him. There was no way of knowing how far away it was. Half a meter or a billion klicks, it didn't matter: the light drifted past and disappeared into the darkness.

Then, from the opposite direction, there came another light, which grew steadily until it filled half of everything with a hazy golden shimmer. In the center was a blurry red glow, and as the shimmer spread out, growing thinner, the red glow shrank down to an intense dot of light.

"It's coming this way..." said Margie.

Abruptly the golden incandescence swept past, engulfing them—

—and they were back out on the track, at the center of a spreading swarm of dust and pebbles. The red light became the beacon of the crash ship, which floated in front of them a hundred meters out.

"—read you loud and clear," said a voice in Mike's helmet. "Would you please turn off that damned loop."

CHAPTER 6

"You're gonna have to stop asking me that," said Mike. "I don't *know* what happened."

"Okay, okay," said Speedball. "I just wanted to show an interest."

Mike laughed until he heard how loud the echo sounded. They were in the Racing League's south maintenance hangar, walking down a row of shiny black sweepers. In a quiet voice he said, "You should have seen the way Alice Nikla climbed all over me. She's convinced I discovered the Holy Grail or something—and she just *knows* I'm holding out on her, trying to grab all the glory."

"What glory is that, exactly?"

"Beats me. I'm just glad they didn't fine me."

"Wasn't really your fault."

"I know." After a moment Mike added, "It *was* pretty weird in there. . . ." He watched the light glint off the curved bodies of the warp machines. "It's funny. I'm really kind of glad I got stuck with community service, 'cause it gave me a chance to hang out here and fly the sweepers."

"I know," said Speedball. "I used to work here, too."

"What, before you got famous?"

"Yeah. And after I got dead, too."

"You know, that's one thing I still haven't figured out. Why do you have to work, being dead and all?"

"There are lots of good reasons for working, Mike. Money is only one of them."

"Then, you don't need the money?"

"Of course I need the money. Everybody needs money."

Mike nodded and said, "Mmmm." He wondered if Uncle Speedball would ever give him any straight answers.

The automaton stopped in front of one of the sweepers, which was still smoking from the cold of the speedway.

"This guy," he said, "has just come back from a sweep of track Monza. I know, 'cause before we got here, I sent him out special."

"They let you do that?"

"I'm well connected."

"Has it been through customs?"

"Ain't been through nothing."

The sweeper clicked as it warmed, and puffs of gas drifted away on the gentle current of the hangar's filtered air. Mike said, "I don't know the key code for this one."

"No problem."

Speedball plugged one finger into a hole on the flank of the sweeper, and a compartment whined open at the rear. "Dig in."

Mike looked back to see if anyone was watching, then he moved around behind the sweeper. The collection bin was several cubic meters big, lined with a plastic trash bag. The bag was bulging. "This is more junk than I usually get." Mike gathered up the top of the bag and pulled, hefting its weight in the low-g field. "It's heavy, too."

"It should be," said Speedball. "This is the first sweep since they hauled you off the track."

"Really?" Mike pulled the bag the rest of the way out of the bin and laid it out on the hangar's concrete floor. He crouched down and spread the neck of the bag wide, then reached in and began raking stuff out to the opening.

There was lots of fine dust and tiny dry pebbles and bits of melted rock, some of it pulled into tight round spheres, like rusty ball bearings. A shiny new Craftsman screwdriver rolled out and Mike grabbed it. "Hey, I lost one just like this!"

Speedball said, "You and half a million other guys. Keep digging."

Mike used the screwdriver to paw through the debris. More fluffy metal flakes. "Pretty much the same stuff throughout." Then the blade of the screwdriver tapped something hard. Mike looked at Speedball, then scraped slowly through the gravel. A blackened silver coin rolled out, singing on the concrete.

And another one.

And another.

Speedball crouched down beside him, his steel limbs whining softly. "Keep going."

Mike reached way inside the bag and pulled out something long and straight, swelling to grooved knobs at each end. It was scoured white and pitted, coated with chalk. He held it up for Speedball to look at.

"Thigh bone," said the automaton, taking hold of it. "Human, I think."

Mike wasn't ready for bones. He looked away, losing interest in the bag of junk. Bones made him think of all the pilots who had gone over the high side and disappeared off the track in the last three hundred years. Pilots who were never seen again. Pilots like . . .

Speedball tapped the bone lightly against his steel forehead, *clink, clink, clink*. "It just occurred to me. This could be my thigh bone."

"Oh, no, don't say that . . ."

"Put it down!" said a gruff voice, and Mike twisted around. There were half a dozen men in green pressure suits standing behind them. Cops.

"I knew this would happen . . ." muttered Mike. His racing career was over—again. "I . . . uh, work here," he said, standing up. And if a shaved head wasn't enough ID, he had the community service badge pinned to his shirt.

"What about him?" asked the man in charge.

Speedball stayed in his crouch. "Go away, I'm busy."

The cop leaned closer. "What have you got there?"

"None of your business."

Mike winced.

The cop's face got red. "Give me that bone!" He tried to snatch it out of Speedball's hand, but the automaton had yanked it a long way back before the guy could even begin to reach out. Racing reflexes.

"This is mine!" said Speedball.

"It's League property, tinhead. Give it to me!"

"Drink my lube oil, fleshface!"

After that things got ugly.

* * *

Outside in the corridor Speedball said, "I really think it could have been one of my thigh bones."

"They'll check it out," said Mike. "If it's yours, you'll get it back."

"You really think that's how things work around here?"

"Doesn't it?"

"We need evidence, Mike."

"We *got* evidence."

"Like what?"

Mike pulled a dull silver coin out of his pocket. Speedball seized it, his hand moving faster than Mike could see. "From the collection bin?"

"And I'd appreciate it if you didn't tell anybody. I really don't need to go to jail right now."

"But they searched us."

"I know."

"And you just stood there."

"With my mouth shut."

The automaton's blank steel head rotated up to stare at Mike. "I'm grinning," said Speedball.

"I'll take your word for it."

Scarface chattered raucously when Mike and Speedball came in, flapping from one side of the tiny room to the other, scattering books and knocking over heaps of dirty clothes.

"You ought to let him out more often," said Speedball.

"I know."

"What do you feed him?"

"Whatever I eat."

"And where does he . . . I mean . . ." Speedball's head swiveled around the room. "Is he housebroken?"

"So far."

"Take my advice. Shake your sneakers out before you put 'em on."

Mike laughed. "I do that anyway, force of habit. This joint used to have roaches the size of—"

"*Used* to have?"

"Scarface earns his keep."

Speedball nodded. "I get it."

"I think he's reverting to more primitive behavior. He's . . . lonely."

"I imagine so."

Mike rubbed some of the tarnish off the coin. On the front was the profile of a wavy-haired young man with a prognathous chin. Ferdinand III of Austria, the coin said. On the back, a crest of arms surmounted by a crown. Dated 1629.

He held it up to his exuberant friend. Scarface took the coin and fingered it delicately, then sniffed around the edges. After a moment he stuck his tongue out and tapped the coin against it. He began to hum, and the tip of his tongue flicked over the surface of the coin. Finally he put the whole thing in his mouth, closed his eyes, and began to rock his head back and forth, as if he were listening to the quiet music that leaked out of the distant ends of the universe. With his free hands he began climbing up the front of Mike's shirt.

"Oh, God . . ." said Mike. "This is the part I hate."

When Scarface reached Mike's neck he jumped suddenly and grabbed hold of Mike's face. The lizard-bat's large eyes opened wide, startled, then drifted off, going unfocused. Thick sideways eyelids slowly closed.

Afterward, Mike could only remember the pain and the flare of scorching light and the desperate sound of Speedball Raybo's last words: "For God's sake, help me! Anybody! *Anybody!*"

Dover Bell ducked back into the alley's entrance, knocking the black baseball cap off his head. He grabbed for it, missed, and watched it drift off down the zero-corridor. "Steaming platters of meat," he said.

He ran a hand through his bright green hair, then swore again when he realized he'd have to chase down the cap. He took a last look at Mike, who was dodging folks up ahead, then pushed off down the side alley. The delay might mean he'd lose Murray in the crowd, but that would be better than getting caught following the guy.

He pulled hard on a handhold, careening off center toward the far side of the alley. Up ahead the black cap drifted toward the wall, caught in a residual grav field from

one of the unseen rooms beyond. It turned away as the field diminished, darting off in some new direction. The same badly shielded grav fields were also doing work on Bell, and his stomach was beginning to rotate on a schedule all its own. "Mother of meat."

Dover caught up to the cap twenty meters from the main corridor. He half crushed the stupid thing getting a grip on it, then pushed off again, headed back to see what Mike was up to.

By the time he hit the intersection again—the black cap jammed down tightly on his head—Mike had disappeared.

Dover cursed and pushed off recklessly into the traffic, bouncing off guys and gals and geeks of every stripe, taking the occasional swat on the butt as he squirmed his way past. He was too busy to yell back at them, his eyes scanning restlessly for Mike's well-clipped head.

There!

No, just a chrome-headed robot.

"Damn," said Dover Bell, reaching up to pull his cap down tighter. His bushy hair pried at the cap like expanding green foam, rising to announce his presence.

A Merkek momentarily blocked his way, and they danced and dodged for a moment, until the genetically red-faced alien shoved Bell aside, yelling, "*Kwazz, skweeledd!*"

"Same you, tomato-face."

Up ahead the back of a close-cropped skull bounced into view.

"Finally," said Dover Bell. He grabbed a handhold to slow down, and kept his eye on Murray's head. Eventually, Bell knew, Mike would turn off and go down some deserted corridor.

And then, Lord help him.

Bell's knuckles ached to become acquainted with the face of the kid who had blown him out of the jump-to-master competition.

He saw his chance coming up. The crowds were thinning out, and that made Dover Bell smile. Then he noticed something annoying. Somebody else was following Michael Murray.

At first Bell doubted his discovery, and he kept a close

eye on the big human in the yellow-and-black Goodyear pressure suit. The guy had his helmet off, plugged into the rack on the backpack. He kept ten meters behind Mike, even farther back when room opened up. In fact, when the traffic in the corridor between them became too light, the guy actually hung back and pretended to examine a door address or a lurid anti-HIPE poster.

"Amateur," said Bell.

But there were times when Dover himself had to slow down to keep from running into the big guy who was following Mike.

What was going on here, anyway?

It occurred to him that Murray had beat three other squealheads to get the privilege of flying against the *Wild Weekend*. What if one of them wanted to beat up on the little guy too?

Hey, man, get in line.

Yeah, but he already *was* in line. And he was in line *ahead* of Bell. Dover didn't like that.

The big guy in the Goodyear pressure suit loitered in the corridor again, brushing past a pair of Laats, who left a slimy smudge on the wall. Suddenly the man took off fast.

Dover Bell looked up forward, saw Mike disappearing around a corner. Oh, great.

The big guy hit the corner, grabbed a turnpole, and whipped himself out of sight, right on Mike's heels. Bell snagged a handhold of his own and yanked himself forward at high velocity—right into the broad green stomach of an oversized Chaibol.

"S'ree, s'ree," said Bell, trying to shove his way between the alien and the wall.

The Chaibol's skin was pulsing blue-violet—probably not a good sign. He seized Bell by the throat. "You seem to be in an awfully big hurry for a man with green hair."

"What?"

The Chaibol's face went pale pink, the top of his head glowing with the same shade of iridescent green that Bell dyed his hair. Dover flinched. It was like looking into a haunted mirror.

The Chaibol said, "You making fun of me?"

"Making fun of *you*?" Dover sighed, face-to-face with the illogic of a bully. Beyond the rippling colors of the alien's shoulder, Bell could see the intersection where Mike had vanished. Every second counted . . .

"I am *talking* to you," said the multicolored alien.

Dover Bell snarled. This Chaibol was well over two meters tall—half again as big as they usually got. It must have gone to his head.

Bell said, "Out of my way, geek!"

The Chaibol smiled. Each long tooth had been filed to a point.

Dover Bell said, "Oh, shit . . ."

Mike caught the turnpole and whipped himself into a shortcut to the ring crossover, on his way back to his hole-in-the-wall flophouse room. As he had figured, the alley was deserted.

When he heard someone round the corner behind him, Mike looked back to see who it was. Just some guy wearing a glossy yellow-and-black pressure suit and a determined look on his face. A salesman, no doubt, late for an appointment.

Mike took the next turning, down a long ventilator shaft about one meter square. Something whanged the wall behind him, and Mike looked back. Same guy. He'd knocked his helmet loose from the backpack, and was chasing it down the alley.

Mike frogged his legs and kicked both sides simultaneously, maintaining his course down the precise center of the shaft. Off to the sides were warehouses, all in zero-g. The grav field was pure and empty down this way.

He heard another scrabbling sound behind him, like armored gloves against plastic. Mike carefully dropped his head and looked back down along his belly. Same guy, coming this way, his neck arched to see forward. What the hell . . .

"Excuse me," the guy said.

"What?" said Mike, not slowing.

The guy reared back to answer and smacked the top of his head into the wall of the shaft. His body pitched downward and he crashed face first into the opposite side.

Mike ducked into a branching shaft as the guy hurtled past. He dragged the toes of his sneakers on the plastic walls, grinding himself to a stop, and looked back to see what would happen. After a moment the fellow appeared at the mouth of the shaft. "Got a minute?"

There was a bubble of bright red blood at the end of his nose. Mike felt sorry for him, and waved. "Follow me." He didn't feel comfortable meeting the guy in a ventilator shaft. Too cramped. Too noisy. Too dangerous.

"Hey, where are you going?" the man yelled.

"You'll see."

A short way down the tunnel Mike came to the opening of a fair-sized corridor. The man followed Mike out there, glancing around furtively.

Now what? thought Mike.

The man said, "I think I can help you."

"How so?"

The guy came to a stop half a meter away. He was a lot larger than Mike had thought. He was breathing hard, and the bubble of blood at the end of his nose blew out big and popped. He wiped at it with his reinforced p-suit glove, somewhat clumsily, and as soon as he lowered his hand, another bright red bubble appeared.

"Banged your nose, huh?" said Mike.

"Nothing serious."

Mike waited.

"Glad I caught you alone," the guy said.

Mike nodded, not especially liking the sound of *that*.

"Got a little . . . proposition for you."

"Okay."

"You're a race pilot, aren't you?"

Mike smiled noncommittally, but didn't answer.

"Aren't you?"

"Sometimes."

Did this goon just want his autograph?

"Dangerous business, that," the guy said.

"Yeah, I guess."

Oh, Mike. You are so cool.

The big man dabbed again at his slowly bleeding nose. "I mean, a guy could get killed."

"That's something I'd like to avoid."

"Yeah, but sometimes you just can't, right? Guy cuts you off, or torches your ship with his exhaust, or knocks you right off the course—over the high side and into the history books. Know what I mean?"

"I've heard about it."

What was the guy going to do? Offer him money to stay out of races? Mike waited.

The big man winked. "You're a young guy, right? Got your whole life ahead of you? I'm guessing a guy like you would like a little guarantee."

"Didn't you just say there wasn't any?"

"Oh, don't get me wrong. I can't stop you from getting killed."

Mike tensed. "Is that right?"

"But I can see to it that getting killed ain't so permanent."

All of a sudden Mike knew exactly what the guy was talking about. "Brain tapes," he said. "You're selling brain tapes."

The big man looked up and down the empty corridor. He smiled at Mike. "Brain tapes. You got it."

Mike grinned. This was intriguing. There wasn't a pilot in Pitfall who didn't have brain tapes—or dream of someday owning them. In a line of work where the smallest mistake can shred your life, having brain tapes on file was like knowing a secret road back from the dead. How could you put a price on that? The Brain Bank could—and did. A nice fat one.

"I can't afford 'em," said Mike.

"That's the beauty of it, friend. I'm in a position to make you a deal you can't refuse—a deal that'll mean a whole new life."

Now Mike was very interested. "Bootleg tapes?"

The man took exception to the term. "Let me tell you something about the way the Racing League controls the Brain Bank."

"I don't need anyone to—"

"Just hear me out, will ya?"

Mike took a deep breath while the man went through a well-rehearsed spiel. Mike tried to interrupt from time to

time, but the guy just kept pushing. He was wasting his time—Mike was already sold. An opportunity like this didn't roll around every day.

"Here's what I'm going to do for you," the man said. He had a deal. A very sweet deal. So what if it was the black market? *Every*body did business on the black market. Mike didn't need to think about it another second.

The man was typing into his notepad. After a moment the pad chimed. "How's this?" he asked, showing Mike the screen. "You available?"

Mike thought vaguely about his schedule. The taping appointment was two days away, in the middle of the first shift. He was supposed to be sweeping a track or something for Pitfall Authority, but he knew he could work something out.

"I'll be there."

The man nodded solemnly. "If you do—you'll live forever."

"I'll *be* there," Mike repeated.

The man just grinned.

CHAPTER 7

Speedball and Twyla on the datanet:

SPEEDBALL: What are you doing here?

NET: *Image of a robot with question marks radiating from its head.*

TWYLA: What do you mean? I never left. I think they must have forgotten about me.

NET: *Image of Twyla standing all alone in a candy store.*

SPEEDBALL: Somebody screwed up. Even if your tapes were to be permanent, they should have dumped your matrix onto storage when you got out of the growth tank.

NET: *Image of storage bins lined up forever.*

TWYLA: Which is like being dead.

NET: *Amid the bins, a coffin.*

SPEEDBALL: I guess. I know my tapes stayed inactive for a long time before my body conked out, but I can't remember what it was like.

TWYLA: Speaking of your death . . .

SPEEDBALL: Must we?

TWYLA: Aren't you still investigating?

SPEEDBALL: There are so many discrepancies.

TWYLA: You wanna know one more?

SPEEDBALL: What?

TWYLA: You weren't killed in a race.

SPEEDBALL: What do you mean? My ship didn't go over the high side?

TWYLA: Oh, you crashed all right. We've all seen the tapes of that.

NET: *The racer* Relativity *plunges into the glittering track wall and explodes in a shower of blue sparks.*

TWYLA: But that didn't happen during the race. It happened before, during a test run.

SPEEDBALL: I'll be damned. Are you sure?

TWYLA: Here's the official record.

NET: *Data strings—patched and partly scrambled.*

SPEEDBALL: This is the original, isn't it? It's never been copied.

TWYLA: No, and it's coming apart. That flutter-charge matrix crap is fragile as hell.

SPEEDBALL: They should be archiving it—with periodic recopies.

TWYLA: It got lost.

SPEEDBALL: Or somebody buried it. Damn, this makes me mad. This is my life we're talking about, and somebody's letting it rot.

TWYLA: What about your own brain tapes?

SPEEDBALL: Oh, hell, they're about half shot, too. Every time I go in there, I have to fight the librarian to get something copied. Don't they understand? My memories *are* my life! I need a certain threshold of material to maintain a sense of my self. When that goes, I might as well be a book on a shelf, turning to dust.

TWYLA: I found out something else about your death.

SPEEDBALL: Oh, God, I'm afraid to ask.

TWYLA: Your copilot was not reported killed in the crash.

NET: *Data strings.*

TWYLA: You always assumed you died in a race—and that your copilot died with you. But this was a practice run, and you were apparently flying alone.

SPEEDBALL: I don't believe it. What happened to Russell?

TWYLA: I don't know.

SPEEDBALL: But he's dead, isn't he?

TWYLA: I'm still trying to track that down.

SPEEDBALL: I'll help you.

TWYLA: Good. I'm sure you know your way around the datanet better than I do.

SPEEDBALL: I'm beginning to wonder.

TWYLA: What's that mean?

SPEEDBALL: Pitfall is a dangerous place.

NET: *The robot walks on an empty plain—a shadow passes over.*

TWYLA: Don't do that.

NET: *Image goes dark.*

SPEEDBALL: What if I just *think* I'm in control? What if somebody got in here and programmed me to be harmless?

TWYLA: Is there any way to tell for sure?

SPEEDBALL: I don't know. I never had to think about it before. It may be I'm not capable of figuring it out. There may not be enough left of me to get the job done.

Mike followed the numbers down the corridor, looking for Jass's new pit. KZ-7 was the one, but the number on the last set of double doors was KZ-5. Now what?

The corridor stopped abruptly, blocked off and sealed, the welds burned black and sloppily made. Mike backtracked to the last alley and found a handwritten note taped to the wall. It wasn't in English or any of the pidgins used by humans, but at least he knew somebody was telling somebody else that things had been changed around. Mike followed the alley to another scribbled sign, then down a narrow, unlit passage.

He saw double doors, hanging ajar. The numbers had fallen off, but the smudged white metal kept no secrets—there were clean places shaped out where the address KZ-7 used to be. If there *had* been a KZ-6, it seemed to have been eaten by the detour.

Mike started to put his ID wrist to the monitor, but noticed the ready light was out. In fact, the green plastic cover was missing, and the bulb was just a naked filament. "Big-time racing at its best."

He knocked on one of the doors, and it swung open slightly. "Hello?" There was a lot of noise in there—metal being pounded, tools ringing as they bounced on the floor, guys yelling, motors whining, robots croaking out numbers. Nobody was going to hear his polite greeting in the middle of all that, so Mike pushed his way inside—

He froze in the doorway.

Dock KZ-7 was wide open to the vacuum of Pitfall.

As he stood there, holding his breath, face all scrunched up, eyes clamped shut, his brain kept saying, The door was open, there was no suction, the door was open, there was no rush of air . . .

He squinted through one eye. The scene was chaotic, as

nearly a dozen men and aliens and robots swarmed over the ship. Beyond the racer Mike could see clearly the hard bright lights of Walltown—without the gray shimmer of the airscreen to obscure his view.

Yet nobody was wearing a pressure suit—and the air was not blowing like a hurricane through the doors and out into the vacuum of the free zone.

Mike stumbled forward, looking around.

"Hey, Mike!" someone yelled.

He looked at the ship, finally prying loose the image of a man. Tall, skinny, and human—blond hair combed back in a DA. My God, it was Andy Veekle. Mike grinned, and took a breath. "Andy! Hey! I didn't know you were back working for Jass."

"You kidding? I never miss a chance to work my butt off for peanuts."

The ship was silver and green, a thick bundle of packed tubes—ramscoops in front, exhaust nozzles out the end. *Bad Momma* was the name, written in stylish script along the side.

"Looking good!" said Mike, but he couldn't help thinking that Jass's last ship had looked good, too—but it had crapped out during its first qualifying run. "I just hope it flies!"

Andy said, "It flies, all right. Brand new Westinghouse engines."

"I'm glad. Jass here?"

"Inside."

Mike looked at all the guys and aliens and robots that climbed over the ship, reading off instruments and closing motor shields with speed wrenches and air tools. "You got a lot of guys working for you."

"Just a smoke screen," said Andy. "Most of them are factory men—they just finished the engine replacement, and now they're running coil-alignment tests."

"They put 'em in right here?"

"Yeah, I was amazed, but they had a swivel-tug shove the pair of them right through the screen. Saved us a bundle in dockyard costs. No overhead, see?"

"Speaking of the airscreen," said Mike. "Where the hell is it?"

Andy turned, looking past the ship. He grinned. "Oh, that. It's new. A low-distortion suppressor field. It's experimental. See the ring of green lights? That means it's on."

Mike frowned. "It's gonna take some getting used to. I just walked in and thought I was dead."

"How'd you—" Andy looked past Mike to the open doors. "Oh. Uh, do me a favor and close those doors."

"Okay."

Mike went back and swung them shut. There was a new ring seal, and a bunch of locking hardware that looked rather permanent. He started to turn when Andy slammed into the doors and began setting the locks as fast as he could.

Mike watched for a moment, then latched some of them himself. "We in a hurry?"

"Something like that."

"Gonna be hard getting out again."

"That's the idea." Andy's face was dripping with sweat. "See, this ain't the door anymore. It's supposed to be sealed and locked."

"Oh."

Andy pointed through the side wall glass. "That's the new control room."

Mike looked, nodding. Apparently KZ-6 had given way to a doubling of pit volume. Now that he looked, he could see where the old control-room wall used to go, subdividing the hangar floor. "I was wondering why—"

He stopped and looked back at the locked doors. "Wait a minute. What if the new airscreen happened to fail?"

Andy wiped his wet forehead. "I guess this end of pit-ring is happy it didn't."

"But the doors were open. I just—"

"Well, they should have been locked and sealed," said Andy. "The new entrance is around the corner. KZ-5."

"But I thought—"

"We're gonna change the numbers, eventually."

"Oh."

"Let's not tell Jass about the open doors, okay? He has enough to worry about."

"You got it."

Mike didn't want it to get around, either. He already had a nice working reputation as a jinx.

"Hey, Mike!" yelled Jass, popping up through the ship's airlock hatch. "What do you think?"

"Looks good."

"And it'll run good, too."

The engine reps were hauling their tools off to the side and going on out through the control-room airlock, four at a time. Mike saw a pair of small maintenance robots trembling at the airlock hatch, waiting for their turn.

Jass slid down the side of the ship, landing softly in the low-g field. "We're knocking off for an hour or so."

Mike looked at the men and machines headed out. "They coming back?"

"Nope, just me and Andy. Some of those guys will be back tomorrow—for the acceptance run. Other than that, the ship is tight." He smacked her smooth skin. "*Nawquood*, as the Poldavians say."

Mike looked at the *Bad Momma* and smiled. "You really gonna win some races this time?"

"I better. I'm getting too old to keep making comebacks."

Mike nodded.

Andy was up inside an engine nozzle, whistling without constraint of tune. The airlock cycled, and the hangar was cleared of all but the three of them.

Mike said. "Is this it? Just you and Andy?"

"Well, we got a computer to do the tac, and we're hiring another guy to help out with maintenance. Oso will be back after—"

"Andy's little robot?"

"Right. Coming out of the shop in a day or two. He got pinched between the ship and the rollout cradle."

"Oh, great."

"He'll survive."

"Good."

Mike noticed the sponsor's cap Jass was wearing, and he read off the name. "Koestler's Authentic Meats."

"Yeah, well, it pays the bills," said Jass. "Some of 'em."

"Koestler sponsored Lek for a little while, but he dropped them."

"*He* dropped *them*?"

"Real meat is getting . . . controversial."

"Don't I know it," said Jass. "This big ol' green fella like to take my head off the other day. I think he wanted to eat *me*. Since then, I kinda don't wear the hat out to restaurants, you know?"

"Maybe you can do better, find another sponsor."

"Yeah, maybe. Speaking of meat gone bad, your friend Dover Bell was in here a little while ago."

"Looking for me?"

"I guess."

"*Scroom*, as the Poldavians say."

"You haven't seen him?"

"Nope."

"Somebody's been tap-dancing on his face."

"That right?" said Mike. "Wasn't me."

The hangar shook once, groaning. Mike looked around.

"What the hell was that?"

"Beats me."

"Must be a party next door."

Jass nodded and smiled and looked at the ship. He looked at the walls and he looked at the floor. He looked at Mike, then back at the ship, nodding toward the nozzle end, where Andy whistled off-key. Jass grinned and Mike smiled back and they both stood there in a silence that was becoming more and more uncomfortable.

Jass cleared his throat, but said nothing.

Mike nodded.

Andy whistled.

Now Jass nodded.

And they both smiled.

Finally Mike said, "What about Koestler? Does he know I'm getting involved?"

"I told him."

"But he doesn't like it."

"He'll get used to it."

Mike wondered.

"The funny thing is," said Jass, "now that a few of those

damned coins have come zinging off track Monza, he feels better about hiring you. I mean, you came out and said it had been an accident—and now, by God, it's beginning to look as though it *was* an accident."

"Lucky me."

Jass exhaled explosively. "Yeah, lucky you."

Mike nodded. There was no proof now either way. Jass had paid off his debts—and the gamblers who had bought up his paper. As far as everyone was concerned, the matter was closed. All that remained was for Mike to get on with his stalled career.

Andy's meandering whistle lost its echo as he dropped out of the engine nozzle. "Hey, Mike. You still here?"

"He works here," said Jass.

"Yeah?" Andy looked at Mike. "That's great."

"He's my backup pilot."

"That's great."

"It *is* great," said Jass. "I don't care *what* you've heard."

Andy frowned at Jass. "I *said* it was great, you old fart. Now take it easy." Then he grabbed Mike around the shoulders and grinned. "This time we win!"

Twyla caught Mike just as he was leaving his room. "Can't talk now," he said. "I gotta go."

"It'll just take a second, Mike."

"Then, walk down with me."

The hotel clerk glanced over without interest as they dropped out of the tube. This was the sort of dump where they didn't care who (or what) you brought up to your room—a policy Mike had never had a chance to take advantage of.

He and Twyla went out into the strand, where folks were busy being weird just as hard as they could. "Happy happy people," said Mike, "with no place to go."

"They're out looking to score some dope, if you believe all the stories on the newsnet."

"Yep."

"You headed into work?"

"No. You mean Jass's pit?"

"Jass's pit? No, I meant your community service job."

"That's over—for now."

"You're working for Jass? Really?"

Mike stopped and looked at her. "What's the matter with that?"

"I think it's great."

"So does everybody. Come on, I'm late."

They headed on down the Strip, dodging vendors and cretins and cops rousting HIPErs.

"What's on your mind?" asked Mike.

"I told you before. It's Lek. He's driving me crazy."

"Oh, yeah. And you want a meeting."

"I really think he's whacked, you know?"

Mike smiled. "Whacked?"

"It's not funny."

"No . . ." But Lek was about the most straight-arrow kind of guy Mike had ever known: a tall and skinny young man with short blond hair and a shy grin—the poster boy for Innocuous Earthlings. "It's just hard to imagine Lek whacked."

"I don't want you to imagine it. I want you to *see* it."

"All right . . . uh, tomorrow. Quohogs. Sometime in the second shift. Late."

"How late?"

"I'll call you when I've talked to Speedball."

"Good. I want him there."

"Fine. I'll call you at Lek's pit. You're still there, in your old room?"

"For now."

Mike glanced at her. "What's that mean?"

"I'm trying for the jump-to-master thing."

"Yeah, I know. You really think you'll win?"

Her expression was serious as she calculated her chances. Mike watched the breeze from a nearby ventilator lift her long red hair and let it float. He had to smile.

"What?" she asked, smiling back.

"Nothing. What did you decide? Can you win?"

"I don't know anyone who could beat me. Do you?"

"Not personally."

* * *

The address the big man had given him turned out to be the sleaziest tattoo parlor Mike had ever seen—just a crusty little back room subdivided from somebody's junk shop on an alley off the Strip. Was he really going to trust his one and only brain to these guys? Did he have a choice?

"Just relax, honey," the woman said as she wheeled the equipment over to his chair. She looked like an ex-callgirl who had studied brain surgery by mail. Everything would be fine, as long as she didn't smear her mascara or break a nail.

Mike said, "I guess you've done this before, right?"

"Sure, honey. Give me your hand."

Mike pried his arm loose. The plastic chair was sticky with something he didn't want to know anything about. She snapped a wide metal cuff over his left wrist. Mike felt a sudden rasping as the cuff closed down and lit up. Blood monitor. He held his hand perfectly still, for fear the cuff would slip and tear open one of his favorite arteries.

Mike looked up at the wall in front of him, where examples of the tattoo-master's art were displayed. Images of death and sentimentality predominated: skulls and hearts (of both human and nonhuman design), pierced by bloody swords and underscored by slogans of contempt in a half-dozen arcane languages. The art of intimidation . . .

Mike shivered and wondered where the big guy had gotten to. He'd taken his cut and split. "How many of these do you do a day?"

"Oh, you'd be surprised."

That few, huh?

Mike took a deep breath.

"That's the way," she said, adjusting the slotted metal cap over his skull. "Just relax and let it happen."

Mike closed his eyes and remembered what the big guy had said. Live forever.

Right now he felt as if he were about to be executed by mistake. What if the lady had misunderstood? God knows, there were nonhumans in Pitfall who liked a little recreational brain burning now and then.

"Uh . . ."

"I said, *relax*!"

"I'm *trying*!"

"Don't be an Earthling."

Mike started to tell her he *was* an Earthling, but changed his mind. "Brain tape, right?"

"What?"

"That's what we're here for, right? Brain taping?"

She came around from wiring up the back of his head and smiled greasily. "What did you think you were getting, honey?"

"Uh . . ."

She winked. "We can discuss it afterwards, okay."

No!

"Fine . . ."

He simply wanted to get it done and get the hell out of there. Just make me immortal, please. And snap it up—I'm in a bit of a hurry to get to forever.

The taping smelled like peppermint, and when it was done all he could remember was getting his head squashed between one of the big ships and somebody's docking cradle. " 'Lectric jelly!" the vendor cried. Mike could still feel the ripples wobbling through his fragile brain. The ripples tasted like peppermint.

CHAPTER 8

The Anti-Meat League was sitting at a banquet table, looking grim. It was early in the third shift, and Quohogs was mostly empty.

Mike passed the table, barely glancing at the league. Humans and Poldavians and Rykells, uniformly sour and sleepy-looking. The sit-in had been going on for days, but because Quohogs never closed and always had a table available, nobody complained and Pitfall Police stayed out of it.

The Anti-Meat folks were drinking Rigellian coffee, which—for all Mike knew—may have been a violation of the league's precepts. It was awfully difficult to figure out what was ethical to eat and drink these days.

By the time Mike returned to his table, Jass and Speedball were leaned way back in their chairs, arms folded across their chests. Jass wasn't wearing his meat hat.

Lek Croveen laughed and wiped his eyes and chuckled and grinned and spilled his Coke and laughed again. "That's not all. This is great. The other day I'm out running test heats and somebody busted off one of my curb finders."

"Your what?" asked Mike.

"My tac-comm antenna," said Lek. "Busted it right off."

"I don't get it," said Jass. "You mean somebody flew past your ship so close that—"

Lek laughed. "No, no, somebody was *out* there. Somebody was out there flying around on the track. No ship. Just this guy, flying around on the track."

Mike cleared his throat, said nothing. Forget it, man. He wasn't going to be the one to tell him.

"Somebody on the track," said Speedball. "Just flying around without a ship."

Lek laughed. "I think there were *two* of them."

"Two of them," said Jass, winking at Mike.

Lek laughed and wiped tears off his face. "And that's not all. You know that guy, the homeset cameraman—he's suing me for negligence, right? He won't settle it. Or rather, he *will* settle it, but he wants fifteen thousand interstellar yen." Lek laughed. "You believe that? Guy's suit leaks and he blames *me* for setting fire to the maintenance hangar."

Mike smiled weakly. Lek hadn't even been in the pit when it happened.

Lek said, "And the kicker is, Mike saved the idiot's life." He laughed again, as if he couldn't help it. It seemed to Mike that Lek's blond hair was thinning faster than ever these days. "Oh, brother," said Lek, reaching for his Coke.

"That's some bad luck, all right," said Speedball.

Lek broke out laughing again, accidentally snorted some of the Coke into his nose. He gagged, coughed, laughed, choked, and pounded the table. The Anti-Meat League looked over.

Lek gasped. "Oh, this is great. I *love* it." He grinned. "All part of life's rich pageantry, huh, guys?"

"I guess," said Mike.

Lek nodded, spinning his glass on its edge, tipping it, catching it, spinning it again, faster and faster. Coke rose up the inside walls and splashed out gracefully in the low-g field.

Jass said, "How's that deal coming with Frank James?"

Lek laughed sharply, Coke spilling as the glass spun away off the table. Lek snatched it out of the air on its way to the carpet. "Frank L. James," he said, straightening up. "He's the first guy who ever put money on me, you know that? He's the first. I started my team with his money. Me and Bob Hand and a Class A ship with hot coils that wouldn't superconduct on a bet—leaked more plasma than a supernova."

"Bob Hand?" asked Mike. "How long ago was—"

"He's dead now."

"Brain tapes?"

"Nope. Couldn't afford 'em. He's gone—completely gone."

Mike shivered, remembering his session in the cracked plastic seat.

Lek said, "The James Syndicate put me on the track. And now. . . well, they're phasing out."

"They're not the only guys with money, Lek," said Speedball.

"No, I guess not."

Lek stared at his sticky glass. Quohogs got very quiet. Mike watched an ice cube slide slowly across a cold puddle.

After Lek had gone home, Speedball said, "Happy guy."

Jass grunted.

"It's not that bad," said Mike. "He just needs to get something going again."

Jass said, "What did Twyla say?"

"She's overreacting," said Mike. "I think she's just feeling guilty about looking for a chance to get her own ship."

"It's worse than that, Mike," said Speedball.

"That's right," said Jass. "It's weasel dust."

"No!" said Mike.

Speedball said, "The man's on HIPE."

"I don't believe it."

Jass said, "Mike, he's squeezed. How could he *not* know you and Margie were the ones flying around out there on track Monza?"

"He's been busy."

"Oh, hell," said Jass. "Everybody in Pitfall has heard the story by now."

"I don't know. . ."

"And what about his eyes?" said Speedball. "You notice the size of his pupils?"

"What about them?"

"Pinhead pupils, Mike. Hypersensitivity to low light."

"I don't believe it."

Jass laughed. "I'll bet he could read a newspaper inside a fuel tank."

"It's a side effect of his enhanced reaction speed," said Speedball. "Didn't you see the way he spun that glass? The way he caught it before it could hit the floor?"

"I could have caught it, too," said Mike. "He just waited so long to start reaching for it."

"That's the point, Mike," said Speedball. "He's got the reaction time, but his judgment is shot."

Mike shook his head.

Jass said, "HIPE don't work that good, after you been into it for a while."

"But it seems to get better and better," said Speedball. "Doses go up, the brain gets squeezed."

Mike still couldn't believe it. "What am I going to tell Twyla?"

Jass said, "I think she already knows, Mike."

Speedball asked, "Has he got brain tapes?"

"No, I don't think so."

"Too bad," said Jass.

"You mean it's too late for him?"

Jass shrugged.

"What do you expect?" asked Speedball. "He's a human being."

Mr. Langley, Mike's sixth-grade teacher, rapped the blackboard with his oversized wooden compass. "Come on, people. I've got three dots marked on the board, now how do I construct a circle that passes through all of them?"

Mike knew how, but the others in the class squirmed around in their seats and stared at the tops of their desks. Mike was amazed. All these eleven-year-old kids—kids he remembered from school—and here he was: seventeen, and a race pilot on the Clypsis circuit. How'd he get back to Earth? And what was he doing in the sixth grade?

"Mike?" asked Mr. Langley. "What do you say?" He used the chalk to darken the three dots. "Can you do it?"

"Yes, sir."

"Then, come up to the board."

Mike climbed carefully out of the tiny desk-seat. Nobody seemed to notice that he was bigger than his classmates—but then, he wasn't *that* much taller . . .

He went to the front of the room and took the oversized compass. Mr. Langley cocked his head at him, as if to say, "You sure you know what you're doing?"

Mike picked a pair of dots for centers and drew equal sized arcs above and below them. He used the meterstick to connect the intersects, drawing a line that was perpendicular to the dots. Mr. Langley nodded.

Mike drew another perpendicular line, pairing up the third dot with one of the others. He put the rubber tip of the compass where the two lines crossed, spread the legs to touch the chalk end of the compass to one of the dots, then drew a circle through all three. Simple.

"Not bad," said Mr. Langley. "But where'd you learn geometry?"

Mike almost said, "In the ninth grade." Instead he cleared his throat and mumbled something about his dad showing him.

"You may sit down."

Mike went back down the aisle and squeezed behind his desk. He snuck a look out the window. The sky was blue and the breeze blew fresh off the Atlantic Ocean. Down the coast a rocket lifted on a plume of steam, the laser beam invisible in the bright sky.

Now this was very strange. Mike had done the sixth grade in Cleveland, but now he was down in Florida—as if he'd already gone to live with Aunt Anna.

The class murmured on, and Mike lost interest. He started thinking about going home. He had an urge to just get up and walk out.

Was this a dream or what?

Would it fall apart if he left the school? Would he wake up if he tried too hard to turn the dream to his own purposes?

Mike took his pencil and began writing on the back of a piece of scratch paper. He wrote:

I am asleep in my room in Pitfall.

He looked up. Mr. Langley was using his compass to square a triangle.

Mike read his note:

Time flows like a river.

He turned the pencil around to erase the sentence, but ended up scribbling through the words. The eraser had migrated to the other end of the pencil.

"Whatever," he muttered.

He wrote:

You can't keep me here.

He looked at the wall clock, but it was one of Pitfall's ten-hour shift clocks, and he couldn't figure out when this class was suppose to end.

But why did he have to wait?

Mike stood up, and the feet of his desk sang out on the hard plastic tiles.

"What is it, Mike?" asked Mr. Langley.

"Uh . . . I have to leave now . . ."

"Sit *down*, Mike."

"Uh . . ."

Mike backed down the aisle toward the door. Langley's brows bunched up. "I said, *sit down*."

Mike grinned nervously.

This isn't real . . .

Mr. Langley started toward him, and Mike took off, banging through the door, and pounding off down the endless hall. Where the hell was the way out of this stupid place?

"Michael Murray!" shouted Mr. Langley, the authority in his voice taking the breath from Mike's lungs. He began to sweat. Where's the damned door?

He skidded around a corner, his sneakers squeaking on the polished floor. Sunlight flooded through a translucent door panel. *Finally!* Langley was right behind him.

Mike hit the door and burst out into the sunlight. He could feel its warmth on his face. He ran down the concrete steps, leaping over two girls who sat at the bottom comparing oven mitts.

Mike turned to gape, saw Langley in midair, his pantlegs blown back, revealing a pair of red-and-green argyle socks that looked just like the ones Mike had given his dad for Christmas last year.

Last year, when Mike was ten . . .

He stared at the man, afraid there would be some sort of transformation, but Langley stayed Langley. Mike bent forward and kept on running.

Half a block from school he could still hear Langley's shoes crunching in the sandy dirt, but eventually the footfalls faded out. Mike kept running until he noticed he was headed

in the wrong direction. He cut to the right, saw some houses that belonged someplace else, then got turned in the proper direction. He looked around. Langley had given up.

Sooner than he expected, Mike rounded a corner and saw his house. His dad's car was in the driveway, although it was the middle of the day.

Mike slowed to a walk, his heart pounding. He could taste the sour spit of his heavy breathing. Everything felt so real.

He stumbled over the curb and caught his balance without losing sight of the house. He was afraid it would mutate away.

My old house . . .

He stopped to listen. The house was quiet. Insects buzzed through the flowering grass. The hot sun drew sweat from his forehead, and he wiped it off with his hand. It felt oily.

This is real . . .

He could see in through the windows, but there was no motion. He came closer. At the corner of the garage he saw under the door that his mom's car was inside.

They're both home.

He moved closer, his sneakers plopping on the asphalt driveway. His legs felt rubbery.

This is real . . .

He came to the front door and stopped. His folks were inside. It was a year before the accident in the shuttle tube, a year before they . . .

He touched the doorknob.

This is real . . .

Now he could hear their voices, inside the house. She said something, his dad replied, and they both laughed. Mike could feel the hardness of the doorknob.

This is real . . .

He opened the door. The entryway was deserted, the voices louder. He stepped forward, turned the corner, walked down the hall toward the family room. The homeset was on. Baseball from the Lunardome. " . . . Ridley's going back . . . waiting . . . waiting . . ." He heard his dead parents laugh.

This is real . . .

His sneakers scuffed on the carpet, and beneath the nap the floorboards creaked faintly. Light from outside lit the hall, and a slanting beam of sunlight glittered with dust. He came to the wide arch. The homeset was loud. He could hear his parents shifting on the vinyl couch. Mike was hypnotized by the view through the sliding glass door out into the backyard. The Atlantic was deep blue, flecked with whitecaps.

"He's home," said his mother.

Mike turned, stepped down helplessly into the room. They were looking back over the top of the sofa at him. Smiling. They looked so young.

Mike took a breath. He could hear his pulse hissing through his head. They smiled at him. He stepped forward. His mother held out her hand. His dad grinned, opened his mouth to say something, and Mike caught the image from the homeset. He stared at it, confused.

Not the Lunardome, not a baseball game, but a long dark tunnel, through which the camera rocketed noiselessly. The shuttle tube.

Mike blinked. His mother smiled. On the screen, a flicker of light.

The walls of his house groaned and bulged outward, then the glass blew out and everything came apart. Explosive decompression.

From the homeset came the withering exhaust, burning outward in savage heat. Mike screamed, feeling that awful flame burn through his skull.

"No!"

He woke suffocating, with Scarface hunkered down on his face, tiny hands gripping hard, lizard teeth chattering. Behind Mike's aching eyes, Scarface's brothers and sisters perished in the engine's brutal flame, leaving two orphans crying in the dark.

The first thing Dover Bell recognized was that big old yellow-and-black pressure suit. He moved closer, his head pushed forward, and got a look at the side of the guy's face. Oh, yes. Same guy that had been following Mike. Bell hung back, keeping the man in sight as they floated down the

pit-ring corridor. After a while, they came through a ring-connect and hit light gravity. The guy kept on going.

Another ring-connect, moving into the heart of Pitfall, then out on a main thoroughfare.

The Strip.

Yeah, this was the right amount of sleaze for a guy like this. A salesman or something. Bell could tell by the way he looked at everybody—that predatory squint, followed by a friendly wave.

Dover Bell grinned.

What you want with my pal Michael?

The big man turned into an alley. Bell stepped up, looked down, and followed. It wasn't long before the guy went through a door with a magkey. TATTOO said a buzzing neon sign over the door. Bell crept closer. Lettered crudely on the door itself, MUIR INTERPRIZES.

Dover Bell nodded and smiled to himself.

Gotcha!

It was a small item, buried in a twenty-year-old back issue of the *Pitside News:* RAYBO'S COPILOT FOUND DEAD, PRESUMED SUICIDE

Speedball and Twyla on the datanet:

SPEEDBALL: I don't believe it. He never would have killed himself.

TWYLA: They say it was an overdose of HIPE.

SPEEDBALL: He was clean, the whole time I knew him. He *hated* drugs.

NET: *Image of Russell climbing out of a fusion engine—he waves and smiles.*

TWYLA: But after you died . . . isn't it possible he . . . I don't know . . . trying to compensate or something.

NET: *Image fades.*

SPEEDBALL: No, I don't think so. I think somebody killed him. I think they tied him down and injected his body with HIPE to make it look like an overdose.

TWYLA: Anything's possible.

SPEEDBALL: What drives me nuts, where the hell was I?

This happened two weeks after my ship went over the high side. By then, I should have been back on the street in a psyche-vehicle of some sort. Why don't I remember this?

TWYLA: Your old copilot . . .

SPEEDBALL: Yeah, I think it would have interested me, but my memories are blank. Either they hid it from me, or somebody has erased the data subsequently. Damn it, this makes me mad.

When Vicky Slicky came up onto the bridge, nobody was on duty but Mary-All, who was reading data off one of the computer screens. The *Swamp Queen* was 58 hours out of Clypsis system.

"What are you playing?" Vicky asked.

Mary-All jumped back, her head snapping around. "Don't *do* that!"

Vicky sipped her coffee and nodded at the screen. "That's cargo lading."

"I know. I got curious about our shipment to Pitfall."

"Probably toilet paper."

Mary-All glanced back at the hatch. "Cap'n Bent still in his cabin?"

Vicky said, "I don't know. It's not my day to tuck him in."

Mary-All stared at the screen. "There's something interesting here."

"Yeah?"

"We're not going to Pitfall."

"We are if I did my math right."

"I mean, we've got nothing in the cargo bay for Pitfall."

"One of the planets, then. My program just gets us within two billion klicks."

"Not one of the planets."

Vicky lowered her mug. "What else is there?"

"Clypsis."

"Right. Clypsis system. That's the designation. But they mean Pitfall, or one of the—"

"No," said Mary-All. "It's very explicit. The whole cargo is slated for Clypsis—the star Clypsis."

Vicky's smile faltered. "Wait a minute. We're gonna dump our cargo off into a star?"

"That's what it says."

Vicky leaned over to study the screen. Mary-All said, "And look at the instructions for special handling."

"Check procedures, diagnostics . . . Excuse me. Hold this." Vicky Slicky handed Mary-All her coffee mug and leaned across to type on the keyboard. A window formed an overlay, and new data jumped onto the screen. "It's a live load."

"Alive? You mean—"

"No, I mean it's powered up. Or will be, when we release it into an intercept orbit of Clypsis."

"It's going *into* the star, right?"

"Yep."

Mary-All sipped Vicky's coffee, then handed it back. "Here."

"You leave any for me?"

Mary-All lowered her voice. "I don't like it. What's in that cargo?"

"I don't know, but—"

A loud, gruff voice exploded behind them. "Can't you girls find any real work to do?"

They turned quickly. Josiah Bent stood in the hatchway, his hairy chest erupting from his half-opened long johns.

CHAPTER 9

MIDNITE prepared his news report and fed the five thousand words directly into the net.

HIPE USAGE UP ONE HUNDRED TWENTY-FIVE PERCENT. MAJOR NEW SUPPLIER SOUGHT BY PITFALL POLICE. TENSIONS RISE.

Then he went into the data and layered dozens of spurious files onto the net, backing up his bogus statements.

Inside Pitfall, tensions rose.

Speedball on the datanet with the Master of Integrated Data Networks and Intelligence Transfer Engineer:

SPEEDBALL: What happened to Russell?

MIDNITE: It wasn't an accidental overdose.

SPEEDBALL: I know that.

MIDNITE: Nor was it suicide.

SPEEDBALL: Then it was murder. They killed him because he knew something—or they *thought* he knew something.

MIDNITE: Apparently.

SPEEDBALL: How come *you* don't know more about all this? Where the hell *were* you?

MIDNITE: I can only analyze data that comes to me. When people deliberately hide the truth . . .

SPEEDBALL: What happened to his tapes? I know he had tapes—I helped pay for them.

MIDNITE: I checked that out. They were defective. Apparently they couldn't be salvaged.

SPEEDBALL: Apparently?

MIDNITE: They were transferred to a memory technician, who subsequently destroyed them.

SPEEDBALL: He—

MIDNITE: Accidentally, he says.

SPEEDBALL: I want to talk to him.

MIDNITE: He's dead.

SPEEDBALL: All right, load his tapes. I'll talk to *them*. I'm not proud.

MIDNITE: His tapes never turned up.

SPEEDBALL: Oh, this is great. I get murdered, my copilot gets murdered, his tapes are lost, the guy who lost them is dead—maybe murdered—and *his* tapes are missing. Meanwhile, my tapes are full of junk and I feel like a stranger to myself—whatever the hell *that* means. It's all coming apart, I tell you. There are times when I think it would be better if I were just dead, like folks are supposed to be.

MIDNITE: Who'd keep me company?

SPEEDBALL: I'll tell you what makes me crazy—and this'll give you a laugh. I'm afraid all the time now. I don't know what's going to happen to me. I no longer feel safe being dead.

MIDNITE: You're sicker than I thought.

SPEEDBALL: I can't stand the idea they could kill me again, that it might even be *easier* this time.

MIDNITE: A sense of injustice.

SPEEDBALL: Yeah. That's the emotion I'm running on these days.

MIDNITE: Then, let me tell you something that might make you feel better—it's my contribution to Pitfall's Cleanup Campaign.

SPEEDBALL: What?

MIDNITE: I'm setting a trap for *the* major HIPE supplier.

SPEEDBALL: Who is it?

MIDNITE: I haven't found out yet, which is why I'm setting the trap. But if I did know, I wouldn't tell you.

SPEEDBALL: Why the hell not?

MIDNITE: Are you kidding? The way your brain is leaking, you can't even keep secret the stuff you *don't* know.

A clerk in the Brain Bank put Mike's bootleg tape on the monitor, took one look at the garbage that skittered across her screen, and shook her head. Improper format.

She filled out a rejection report and dropped the tape canister in the OUT slot. The tape was routed back to the holding deck.

Her rejection report went to the tape's place of origin—a tattoo parlor just off the Strip—where it attempted to enter the message memory of an unplugged comm unit. Not happening.

By the time the notice of the report's nondelivery reached the Brain Bank, the first clerk was off duty and another clerk handled the matter. An additional urgent notice was filled out, and a hard copy was dispatched by mailbot.

The mailbot rapped at the door of the tattoo parlor and waited with machine patience for ten minutes. It rapped again, waited twenty more minutes, then received a recall transmission and returned to its pickup point for another load of junk mail.

By the time the notice of the urgent notice's nondelivery reached the Brain Bank, yet another clerk was in the saddle. A follow-on report was filed, and the disposition of Mike's nonstandard tapes was placed in the computer's holding window, listed under the only name on the package: Muir Interprizes.

Alice Nikla keyed her transmitter. "I'm still here, Control."

"Stand by, *Four-zero-four*, we're waiting for clearance on an inboard test track."

"I told you, Control. I don't want an inboard track. I want track Monza. It has the exact characteristics for my engine test."

"Copy, *Four-zero-four.* Let me see if Monza is occupied."

"It's not. I checked."

"Copy. Stand by."

Nikla fiddled nervously with her transmitter switch, which seemed to be sticking. She took a deep breath. If she couldn't get track Monza, there was no point in going. Something strange was happening on that track, and if Murray wouldn't talk about it, well, she'd just have to go there and find out for herself.

Because if it *was* important, why should *he* get all the credit? He wasn't the only pilot in Pitfall who needed a little career boost.

"Uh, *Four-zero-four*, this is Race Control. Be advised, track Monza is holding at trans two point seven five."

"That's fine."

"I can let you have it for thirty minutes."

"That'll do, Control. Thanks."

"*Four-zero-four,* please enter the spin-up circle in the next two minutes. If you are unable to accomplish this maneuver, please advise Control at once."

"Roger, Control."

"Have a nice run, *Four-zero-four.* Control, out."

Alice Nikla wasted no time plunging between the red beacons, and the darkness of the warp exit drew its shadow over the smooth white flanks of *404 Flying Circus*. A moment later she was on the track.

For half an hour she cruised near the wall, looking for signs of irregular patches, finding nothing.

"Son of a bitch," she muttered.

Then, about the time Race Control was trying to coax her off the track, the ship began to go sour.

TELEMETRY AND CONTROLLER TAPE
3/07.33.12 – 3/07.37.29
Ship: *404 Flying Circus*
Pilot: Alice Nikla
Track: Monza
Activity: engine test

RACE CONTROL: Be advised, *Four-zero-four*, your time is up. This track is closing. Proceed to the nearest pit lane for transport back to Pitfall.

NIKLA: Roger, Control. My . . . uh, tests are nearly complete. But . . . uh . . .

SHIP: PROXIMITY ALARM—FRONT.

NIKLA: What?

SHIP: "*Collision. Collision.*"

NIKLA: Oh, no . . .

SHIP: RAMSCOOP INACTIVE. STAND BY.

NIKLA: Come on, you stupid . . .

SHIP: STAND BY. RAMSCOOP FAILURE.

RACE CONTROL: *Four-zero-four*, you are requested to exit this track—

NIKLA: In a minute, Control.

RACE CONTROL: Now, *Four-zero-four*. This track is closed.

NIKLA: Copy, Control. Understood. But something just plowed into my—

SHIP: ENGINE FAILURE—STARBOARD ENGINE.

NIKLA: Damn.

RACE CONTROL: Say again, *Four-zero-four*?

NIKLA: I just lost the [garbled]

SHIP: COOLANT LEAK #6. LASER OVERHEAT #6. ENGINE ABORT.

NIKLA: Great.

RACE CONTROL: Do you require assistance, *Four-zero-four*?

NIKLA: No, Control. Thanks.

SHIP: "*Caution. Caution.*" RADIATION HAZARD—STARBOARD ENGINE.

NIKLA: Steaming meat.

RACE CONTROL: Say again, *Four-zero-four*?

NIKLA: Disregard, Control. [garbled] key was open. I think it's stuck.

RACE CONTROL: Be advised, *Four-zero-four*. This track is closed. Please proceed to the nearest pit lane.

NIKLA: I heard you the first time!

SHIP: "*Caution. Fire.*" FIRE ALARM. LASER BAY #6.

NIKLA: Oh, shit. Extinguishers . . . eight, nine [garbled] fifteen . . . uh, nineteen . . . let's go, let's [garbled]

RACE CONTROL: Come in, *Four-zero-four.*

SHIP: "*Ship in distress. Ship needs assistance. Home on my beacon. Ship in—*"

NIKLA: *Can it!*

RACE CONTROL: Come in, *Four-zero-four.*

NIKLA: I'm *busy*, Control. Call back later.

RACE CONTROL: Do you need assistance? Your beacon cut off.

NIKLA: I *shut* it off. [garbled] all right.

SHIP: "*Caution. Fire.*" FIRE ALARM. LASER BAY #4.

NIKLA: I don't believe this . . .

RACE CONTROL: Come in, *Four-zero-four.*

NIKLA: Leave me alone, Control.

RACE CONTROL: You're drifting toward the edge of the track, *Four-zero-four.*

NIKLA: No shit, Sherlock.

RACE CONTROL: Say again, *Four-zero-four*?

NIKLA: [garbled]

RACE CONTROL: Say again, *Four-zero-four.*

SHIP: ENGINE FAILURE—PORT ENGINE. SAFETY ABORT.

NIKLA: What [garbled] piece of junk.

RACE CONTROL: Be advised, *Four-zero-four*, your track is closed. You must exit track immediately. If you need assistance leaving the track, inform this Control at once.

SHIP: "*Caution.*" APPROACHING TRACK PERIMETER.

NIKLA: Shut up! I see the [garbled] perimeter!

RACE CONTROL: Come in, *Four-zero-four.*

SHIP: "*Ship in distress. Ship needs assistance. Home on my beacon—*"

NIKLA: *Off*, I said!

RACE CONTROL: Come in, *Four-zero-four.*

NIKLA: [garbled] a minute. I see a ship. I see [garbled]

RACE CONTROL: Say again.

NIKLA: [garbled] ship at the perimeter. I have a radar lock-up.

RACE CONTROL: Uh, *Four-zero-four*, we show no other traffic on this track.

NIKLA: I'm headed for the ship. [garbled] thruster fuel, but I think I [garbled]

RACE CONTROL: Say again, *Four-zero-four.* Your transmission is breaking up.

NIKLA: [garbled]

RACE CONTROL: Be advised, *Four-zero-four.* We have no ship under control. Can you give us a visual—

NIKLA: Oh, no . . .

RACE CONTROL: Say again.

NIKLA: It's not a ship . . .

RACE CONTROL: Can you describe—

NIKLA: [garbled]

RACE CONTROL: Say again, *Four-zero-four.*

NIKLA: [garbled]

RACE CONTROL: Come in, *Four-zero-four.*

NIKLA: [static]

RACE CONTROL: Come in, *Four-zero-four.*

NIKLA: [static]

RACE CONTROL: Come on, Alice. Talk to me, babe.

NIKLA: [static]
RACE CONTROL: Oh, my God . . .

At the time of the last transmission from *404 Flying Circus* a robot astronomy probe turned to lock on a source of x-radiation coincident with the outer edge of track Monza. Source subsequently vanished. No data taken.

Approximately seventeen minutes after the final transmission from *404 Flying Circus*, someone in Race Control center called Dover Bell to tell him his ex-copilot—and ex-girlfriend—had disappeared off track Monza during a routine engine test. Bell's phone took the message, saying, "Mr. Bell is not at home right now, but I'm sure he'll be delighted to return your call at his earliest convenience."

"I'll bet," the man said, hanging up. He had never known Dover Bell to be delighted to do anything that didn't involve inflicting great damage on somebody.

Dover Bell grinned in the dark. The service corridor was empty, and his scanner told him there were no security beams, either above or below the visual spectrum.

He listened for a moment to the crackling hum of grav fields and the distant whine of an exhaust fan. There was nobody in sight, and nobody just around the corner out walking his hippopotamus—or whatever creature passed for pets in this devioid section of Pitfall.

Dover crept to the back door of the tattoo parlor, flicked his dim white light around, checking it out, then dialed back to the red blackout beam. It was hard to imagine Michael Murray going into a joint like this, but stranger things had happened.

"First . . ." he said, studying the lock. He pulled the logic probe out of his jacket and plugged it into the lock. The lights cycled through once and went red. Dover reset the probe and ran it through again. Red lights.

Either this lock was ultrasophisticated—or it was busted.

Dover hummed to himself for a moment, then turned the probe around and swiftly banged the doorknob. The case cracked, the lock squealed, the knob turned.

He was in.

Dover stood at the door and listened. Nothing. He quietly closed the door and turned into the darkness. Dialing up the flashlight's beam, Dover stepped slowly forward. He was grinning again.

So easy . . .

The back room was filthy, complete with rust-stained washbasin and a rumpled cot. Cardboard boxes leaned on one another in crooked stacks, full of black-market alien toilet paper and poisonous scouring powder.

"Must be saving it for somebody else . . ."

He pushed open the plastic curtain and poked his head into the main room. Through the dirty glass he could see the gloomy lights of the alley outside. It was deep in the third shift, and the street was quiet and still—quieter than he would have expected.

Dover flicked the flashlight this way and that. He saw several fat plastic chairs, and, off to the side, a rack of electric needles. One of them was still plugged in, buzzing softly in the dark.

"Cheerful place . . ." said Dover.

What the hell did Murray *do* in here?

He wasn't the sort of guy who could appreciate the works of art that were plastered all over the wall. Such marvelous tattoos: rocket ships piercing hearts, daggers dripping green blood, bulging skulls grinning with alien teeth, "Mother" entwined with black roses, a selection of hard-core comments in alien script, and the ever-popular EARTH SUCKS.

Dover grinned. This was great stuff. "I ought to get a tattoo . . ."

He moved closer to the buzzing needle, his sneakers crunching on the gritty floor. This corner of the room stank of burned flesh. Nonhuman flesh. He peered closely at the needles, fascinated by the smell. After a moment he reached over and unplugged the one that buzzed. He touched the tip to his palm. It was hot, but left no mark. He smiled and put it down, wondering if Alice liked guys with tattoos.

In the silence of the shop he listened. Water dripped in the basin. Air hissed from a duct that echoed with distant whistles. Outside in the street a drunk was singing four-part

harmony with himself. It was a love ballad, a song of regret and longing, of desire and of the failure of desire. Dover smiled, a bit sadly, and thought again of Alice. Somehow, *damn it*, he was going to find a way of getting back together with her.

"Like that song, do you?"

He whirled, and the light was in his face, hiding the man who had spoken. But Dover could see from the backscatter there was only one of them, and that made him smile.

One was no problem.

CHAPTER 10

NOTICE TO ALL PERSONNEL:
UNTIL FURTHER NOTICE, TRACK MONZA IS CLOSED TO ALL TRAFFIC. BY ORDER OF PITFALL AUTHORITY AND THE CLYPSIS RACING LEAGUE. *NO EXCEPTIONS!!*

Mike felt someone rapping on the top of his head. "Just a sec," he said, carefully pulling his hands out of the live circuit. He looked up. It was Jass.

"Speedball's here. He wants to talk to you."

"Uh . . ."

"It's all right. Take a break."

Mike nodded, then looked down beneath his feet. He was standing on Oso, Andy's monkeylike maintenance robot. "Back in a while."

Oso squeaked and whistled.

Mike climbed out of the pump sequencer bay, then slid down the side of the *Bad Momma* to the hangar floor. Speedball was standing by the old blocked-off corridor hatch.

"What's up?" asked Mike.

"They closed track Monza."

"Yeah, I know. Alice Nikla never came back."

"Something's happening out there, Mike. And I think it has something to do with what happened to me twenty years ago. I gotta get out there before the League destroys it."

"How you gonna—"

"I'll need something with warp engines. Like a track sweeper."

"Where you gonna get—"

"From the maintenance hangar."

"But how you gonna get into the—"

"I was hoping you'd help me with that part, Mike. You work there. You've got clearance."

"Not anymore. I'm off community service. Got a job with Jass."

"Son of a bitch."

"Sorry," said Mike. But he was thinking, Why is this guy always trying to get me in trouble?

"It's not just the hangar," said Speedball. "I also need somebody with recent experience with sweepers. Somebody I can trust."

"When?"

"Right away."

Mike frowned. "I got a race coming up, you know? It's the second qualifier—for the jump-to-master program."

Speedball didn't say anything. Mike looked around. Jass was off by the ship, talking to Andy. The team was still a man short, and Mike wanted to get back to work. He said, "Does it have to be right now? I mean, you really can't get to a sweeper, and you can't get on that track without one."

Speedball remained silent.

Mike felt guilty for not helping, then he got angry for being put in this position. "I'm trying to get some kind of career going here," he wanted to say. "Don't ruin things for me, man. You've *had* your career." But he kept his mouth shut.

Finally Speedball said, "Okay, I'll work something out. Go back to work."

"I know how much this means to you . . ."

Speedball nodded.

"Anytime but now. . ."

"I don't think I can wait."

Mike shook his head. "I'm sorry."

"Don't worry about it. I'll find somebody. I'll get Twyla to search the datanet."

"Twyla? Is she still on the net? I thought sure they'd put her tapes back in storage."

"I guess somebody in the Brain Bank screwed up. But it's all right now—I got MIDNITE to authorize it. She's doing research for me."

"Yeah, but I thought it was impossible to have two versions of the same person at the same time."

"What made you think that?"

"Well, when Twyla came out of the tank, her tape-carrier PV fell apart. Twyla told me its mind disintegrated *because* she was back on the street."

"She's talking custom, not metaphysics. It is legal—under certain circumstances—to have copies active."

"Does the real Twyla know?"

"They're both real, Mike."

"You know what I mean."

Speedball hesitated. "I don't know what the other Twyla knows."

"Isn't it kind of . . . I don't know, unethical?"

"I never thought about it, Mike. But put me down on the side of tapes' rights."

"Naturally."

"Don't look now, but unauthorized brain tapes are pretty common. There's lots of weird things happening out there on the datanet."

"I can imagine."

"Actually, you probably couldn't. For instance, did you know everybody on the net sees it differently?"

"Yeah? How do you see it?"

"It looks a lot like Miami Beach."

"Really?"

Mike wondered if Speedball was kidding him. He said, "You might take Scarface with you. He could probably sniff out the workings of a sweeper—if you get hold of one."

"That's a good idea. I will."

Mike turned and yelled, *"Klaino-vor!"* The lizard-bat peeped out of the ship's airlock, a stardriver in his mouth. He blinked. *"Klaino-vor!"* said Mike.

Scarface pushed off and flapped over to them, landing on top of Mike's head. He took the stardriver out of his mouth and used it to poke Speedball's shoulder, as if to make an adjustment. The Klaat'k chattered happily.

"He likes to joke around," said Mike.

"I'll remember."

"Um . . . I just thought. I don't know enough Poldavian

to tell him to go with you. And I don't guess he can read your mind."

"Thousands have failed," said Speedball. "Fortunately I know Poldavian quite well. I used to have one for a girlfriend."

He chanted a string of words that Mike couldn't follow, and Scarface walked down Mike's face to look into his eyes. The creature seemed sad.

"It's all right," said Mike. "He's a nice man."

Scarface began to squeal. He reached out and touched Mike's face, planting images of sorrow and abandonment. The engine nozzle flared with awful light. Mike winced and pried the little guy loose. "*Seezee!* I *mean* it!"

Scarface pushed off and fluttered in the air above them, his teeth clicking. Then he lighted on Speedball's ovoid skull, skittering for a purchase on the smooth metal.

Speedball said, "I may have to glue him down."

"Right."

"I'll let you get back to work now."

"Okay."

"Good luck in the race."

"Thank you."

Speedball turned, and Scarface scrabbled around, looking back with his huge dark eyes. Mike called after them. "Keep me informed, okay?"

"Sure."

They disappeared through the airlock into the control room, and Mike turned back to the *Bad Momma*. There was so much left to do—but all of a sudden he didn't want to do any of it.

Mike was back in the pump bay when he heard someone moving around in the ship above him. "Jass?" No answer, but the noises stopped. A moment later they were back, closer. Mike said, "Andy?"

More silence, then, "That you, Mike?" It was a voice he couldn't place. The guy said, "Where the hell are you?"

"See the open maintenance hatch?"

"Oh . . ."

More weird noises. It sounded like the guy was wres-

tling alligators or something. Then a blond-haired head poked down through the hatch, looking around.

"Over here," said Mike.

The head turned, and Mike recognized him. It was Fyodor Willingham, the pilot for the Gajira Syndicate who had shown him around the *Universe*. What the hell was *he* doing here?

"There you are!" said Willingham, smiling. "Blando just said you were in here someplace."

"Last-minute stuff . . . you know."

"Yeah, right. So . . . how's it going?"

"Fine, I guess."

"Mr. Gajira asked me to wish everyone luck."

"Thanks."

"How's it look?" Willingham reached down and smacked a pump housing. "No problems, right?"

"We'll be ready."

"Great."

Mike nodded back and smiled, not sure what to say.

"Well, Mr. Gajira just wanted me to check up on everybody. Not many left, you know. But I got a feeling we may be seeing a lot more of you."

"I hope so."

"Chance to hit the big time." Willingham grinned. "So to speak."

"Yep."

"Can ya handle it?"

"We'll find out."

An hour later, while Mike sat alone strapped in the *Bad Momma*, waiting for permission from Race Control to move away from the pit and test engines, somebody on the speedway blew an engine. The homeset monitor showed it all: the tumbling ship disintegrated, its pieces hitting the track walls in a shower of blue sparks.

Mike closed his eyes and took a deep breath. Jass was saying something on the ship comm, but he couldn't make it out.

I'm going out there in five minutes, thought Mike. In ten

minutes I could be dead, blown all over the track, pieces of me sucked up in somebody's ramscoop. Seriously *dead*.

He opened his eyes, blinked, looked around. Jass had shut up, thank God.

Race Control asked for and got a ready-light transmission. Mike touched the controls lightly. *Bad Momma* moved away from the pit and drifted out to the edge of the safety zone.

All Mike could think was, At least I got those damned brain tapes. My mind is on record. In death, I will live.

Hurray for sleazy black-market gangsters . . .

Race Control said, "Pilots, test your engines."

"Roger, Control."

Mike grinned, tapping the mains.

Whatever happened, he was *covered*.

At that moment, several kilometers away in the center of Pitfall's clustered rings, an event was taking place that would have interested Mr. Murray exceedingly.

In a package of nonstandard tapes identified simply with "Muir Interprizes," some as-yet-unknown persona was coming apart, memory by memory, data bit by data bit, emptying out into the nothingness of disorganized electric charge.

Speedball came into the enormous globe of the Racing Museum with Scarface on his shoulder and a bona-fide sweeper expert stumbling along at his side. There was a party going on. They passed under a banner that read OLD TIMERS' DAYS.

Speedball whispered, "Thank God for media hype."

The sweeper expert didn't know how to answer him. He was having enough trouble just walking.

They went directly to the registration desk and Speedball announced himself. There was a bit of happy confusion, because the distinguished speedway champion had not been expected to attend—something about the crotchety factor.

But here he was, in the metal, and everybody fell to ostentatious rejoicing. Inside, the old champion just grinned and grinned, and the image of a wolf came easily to mind.

The woman slapped a stick-on nameplate to Speedball's

gleaming chest. "And who's your friend?" she asked, frowning at the junky-looking racing PV that loitered unsteadily beside him.

"Nobody special."

The woman nodded, rummaged about on her table, and came up with a GUEST nameplate. She held it out, and Mike made several tries before he could get his new steel fingers to take hold of the damned thing. Once he had it, he couldn't figure out how to rotate his wrist. Finally Speedball had to grab the nameplate and smack it to Mike's corroded chest.

Thanks, said Mike on their private radio frequency. They moved on inside the museum, with Scarface flapping along in front. "I feel so strange," said Mike.

Keep your voice down.

I didn't know "it was on. Hey, is that me?" *Hello.* "Hello."

Speedball spun Mike around and ripped open his back. Mike sensed a tingling surge of electricity, then the empty feeling he'd been trying to get used to went away. Now he felt . . . "alive" . . . or something . . .

This is a body-simulation mode, said Speedball. *It'll help you get used to running the PV.*

Kind of like training wheels.

Speedball slammed Mike's back shut.

"Ow!"

"Be a man!"

Or whatever, said Mike.

Hey, it was the best I could do on short notice.

It's a piece of junk.

Speedball turned on him. "What's the last thing you remember?"

I was sitting in a sticky plastic chair in a sleazy tattoo parlor, getting ready to have my head exploded.

You wanna go back?

"No."

Then, stop complaining.

They circulated through the museum, wandering through the crowd. Speedball waved and pounded the backs of old friends—some of which thumped meatily, while others gonged like empty oil drums. By the buffet table several PVs were

having an argument, poking one another with hard steel fingers. Mike got close enough to read the nametags—Mario Andretti and Richard Petty. Artificial constructs, obviously.

Mike kept moving, looking around. The curved floor inside the vast globe seemed as flat as always, courtesy of the museum's notorious grav field. Above him—in the empty center of the sphere—floated famous racing ships.

While staring at the paint job on one big old brute, Mike noticed that if he "squinted" he could see where they had painted over part of the ship's name. "Look," he said, pointing. Scarface climbed out to the end of his arm and looked at Mike's hand. "Not *that*." The Klaat'k howled, and tested his sharp little teeth on Mike's extended finger.

Speedball said, *Try to behave, Mike. You're embarrassing me.*

"Sorry." *I mean, sorry.*

Speedball paused beside a Junior Johnson construct to be photographed beneath the replica of *Relativity,* Speedball's old ship, lost—as it turned out—not during a race, but on a test run through the speedway. Mike noticed that Speedball said nothing to taint the dubious glamour of a racing death.

All the while, as he talked, joked, flicked the rims of champagne-filled glasses with his titanium fingers—in lieu of toasting—Speedball kept his sensors focused on the ancient alien warp machine they called the *Spider.*

That's our target, he said, transmitting the image to Mike.

Will it even fly?

Of course it flies. They take it out on publicity runs every four or five years. They're sure to have it spruced up for the Trike.

Mike looked at it. Today the *Spider* wore a fresh coat of bright yellow paint on its ugly, rather-flealike body. The cockpit sat like a swelling head atop its fat, rounded frame, and a half-dozen fragile legs hung down, joints flexed.

Looks decrepit to me.

What do you expect? said Speedball. *It's a museum piece.*

The alien machine had been used to create the first of what became the speedway tracks, and later its mysterious engines were copied to propel all the sweepers and pace ships

and rescue craft in the system. Nobody really knew how it worked, even less how it had gotten here. It was rumored to have been in the neighborhood long before the Consortium formed to organize the tracks and build Pitfall.

The stupid thing was hundreds—perhaps thousands—of years old and very possibly unreliable. But it was the only warp machine in town not under armed guard at this moment.

I hope you know what you're doing, said Mike.

He watched while Speedball leaned close to the wall panel at the entrance of the Racing Museum. When nobody was paying any attention, the automaton casually stuck his control finger into the interface. A moment later alarms commenced to ring—and folks not comfortable living in a vacuum started running for the museum's huge airlock doors. Speedball moved nonchalantly away.

Mike just stood there and watched, feeling vaguely uneasy that none of this seemed to bother him. They were here to steal an immensely valuable warp ship, so why didn't he feel . . . anxious . . . or guilty . . . or *some*thing?

Had Speedball done a little editing on Mike's moral circuits?

The museum was emptying out quite nicely as the automaton strolled to Mike's side and looked up at the belly of the *Spider. Do you remember your data cubes, Mike?*

There's a hatch in the middle, said Mike, helplessly cooperating in his role as sweeper expert. *In the space between where the legs come together. See it?*

Yep.

We're really going to do this, aren't we?

You bet.

Okey-doke.

And Mike was thinking, Yep, he's been messing with my mind . . .

There was nothing to do but ride it out.

The air pressure in the museum dipped drastically, cutting in half the din from the alarm bells. Lights continued to flash—although anyone not aware of the problem by now probably didn't have a problem.

Scarface came flapping like mad from a corner of the

museum, beating his leathery wings against the thinning air. Klaat'x were extraordinarily tough little bastards, and they could survive a vacuum for quite a while. But flying without air to push against was impossible, without being rude.

Speedball snagged the lizard-bat out of the air and tossed him at the *Spider*'s belly. A moment later Speedball bent his knees and jumped up to grab one of the half-dozen spindly legs. It flexed with his momentum.

Get up here!

Mike looked around at what was left of the panicked crowd, shrugged (sort of), and jumped. He banged his head on the bottom of the *Spider,* but Speedball snared him before he could rebound. Fortunately, the grav field in this part of the Museum was nil.

Very graceful, Mike.

Stuff it.

Speedball swung over and grabbed a handhold beside the hatch. Scarface, acting without benefit of a sweeper expert, had already figured out how to get the hatch open. Speedball looked inside, then gestured to the Klaat'k to get in there. Scarface was blinking furiously as his eyes dried out, and seemed only too eager. Up he went.

You're next, said Speedball. *Hurry up!*

Mike climbed into the tall, narrow airlock. At intervals there were sealed hatches leading into the interior of the ship—maintenance crawlways, no doubt. He met Scarface at the top of the dark column, then something banged into Mike's feet. *I'm closing the hatch,* said Speedball.

Scarface popped the inner hatch and climbed inside the cockpit. Mike scrambled after him, with Speedball crowding his heels as before. Mike said, *Take it easy!*

Speedball slammed the inner hatch and sealed it. The light was rather dim inside the cockpit, but Mike found a way of turning up the amplitude of his vision. The place was amazingly spacious, bigger even than his room in Pitfall. Mike floated over to the curved wall, which was studded with obscure alien gauges.

Get over here, Mike! said Speedball. He and Scarface were already jerking the plastic cover off the main control

console. Speedball very carefully plugged his finger into the command access port.

Mike drifted over, colliding with a couple of human-designed seats, which had been bolted to the deck in front of the console. *How's it feel?*

Like my guts were hung with Christmas lights.

The panel was an add-on, built to fit right over the original alien controls. For hundreds of years this machine had been in service on the tracks—first as a pace ship, then a rescue pod, and finally as a backup track sweeper. The control panel looked old, hastily slapped together, frequently repaired, and falling apart.

Speedball turned to Mike. *Come on, plug in here.* Mike looked at the end of his finger. It was filthy with the slow leak of corrosive oils. *Come on, Mike! I need your help.*

Mike reluctantly plugged his finger into the panel. *It tingles . . .* A cacophony of data buzzed around his head like a swarm of wasps. *I don't know what I'm doing.*

You better just think about that, said Speedball. *You're the sweeper expert, remember?*

Yeah, right.

Mike leaned into the data swarm and tasted the flow. Some of it he recognized, some of it would take more study, and some of it—a lot of it—was alien nonsense that had never been translated.

How's it look?

It looks like I feel, said Mike. *But I've found the oxygen circuits—and the tanks are nearly full.* Switches glowed on the panel, indicating a sequence of actuation and control. Mike couldn't tell if the switch plaques were really illuminated, or if the datastream just made it look that way. In either case, he was getting a lecture on sweeper operation. He started the oxygen pumps, then said, *I'm going through the power circuits now.*

'Preciate it, said Speedball. *Getting this thing moving is high on my list of priorities.*

In another minute Mike knew enough about the *Spider*'s control to dump a concise tutorial onto Speedball's memory. Now there were two sweeper experts on board.

Two thirds of a charge, Mike said, jerking his finger out

of the panel. *We could open a warp-tube halfway to the next star.*

All I need is to get onto track Monza.

Air pressure was coming up fast in the cabin, and Scarface had begun to fill his lungs and test his wings.

"See," said Speedball. "I told you they kept this thing in great shape."

"Just our luck." Mike pushed off to look down through the porthole. He saw that the museum was nearly empty—only a few tinheads moving about with disdainful slowness, stepping around the serving robots, whose champagne foamed extravagantly in the low-pressure environment.

Then Mike detected strange metallic scrapings beneath the floor. *Feel that?*

Speedball checked the panel. *The outer hatch is open. There's somebody in the airlock.*

Mike heard a jumble of voices and tones as Speedball scanned the popular suit-radio frequencies. Abruptly there came a horrifying voice:

"—you think you are?" demanded the voice. "I mean, *really*! You come out of there *at once*!"

It was a voice stunningly familiar to Mike: Margie Phillips, girl monster. *Now we really* are *in trouble.*

Speedball got on the same freek. "Get out of the airlock, kid. We're leaving."

"I absolutely *forbid* it!"

"You forbid it?"

"I'm a docent of this museum."

She's a docent, Speedball said to Mike.

I'm not surprised. Remind me to look that word up.

Speedball said, "Come on, get out of there, kid. I mean it."

"I won't! I'm responsible for this ship."

"I'm not going to argue with you," said Speedball. "Get *out*!"

Mike checked the port. Half a dozen humanoids in green pressure suits were coming through the airlock. *Cops are here.*

"I'm not budging," said Margie.

"Oh, hell," said Speedball.

"I told you she's trouble," said Mike.

Now the cops were homing in, pointing at the *Spider*, surging forward, shoving robots aside. "I guess we can't wait," said Speedball. He hit the switches that closed and locked the lower hatch.

What are you doing?

We have no choice. She's coming with us. Speedball ran the airlock cycle, then swiveled his chair, reached out, and jerked the inner hatch open. "Get in here and shut up."

Margie crept out of the airlock, looking around. Scarface fluttered past, squawking, and she swiped at him.

"*Seezee!*" said Mike, and Scarface flapped over and landed on his shoulder.

Margie hesitated, then closed the hatch. She grabbed the back of Speedball's chair and pulled herself closer. "Who are you?" she asked, craning forward to get a look at his nametag.

"Speedball Raybo, ex-human."

"What about the other guy?"

"That's Mike Murray."

Quiet! said Mike. "Forget he said that."

"I remember you!" She floated over beside him and looked down through the porthole. "You'll never get away with this, Michael Murray. Look."

He looked. Cops crowded around under the *Spider*, staring up at them. Apparently they could see the lights inside the cockpit, but couldn't figure out what was going on. That wouldn't last. Mike said, *I think it's time to get moving. You want me to fly?*

That's okay. I'm on it.

Then, what am I doing here?

The ship began to make churning noises, and lights on the panel flickered. Speedball gripped the control yoke, and the *Spider* shuddered.

You're the expert, Mike.

Yeah, but now you know as much about this tub as I do.

Then, you're here to keep me company, said Speedball. *And because there's no escape.*

Good point.

The *Spider*'s navigation lights flared, then it drifted away

from its holding slot in the museum's grav field. Mike felt himself pulled to a spot on the wall of the cockpit, and Speedball had to fire thrusters to keep the *Spider* from dropping into the gravity detent of some other museum exhibit.

The *Spider* drifted toward the entrance to the museum's maintenance gravity tunnel. Mike looked all around beneath them, scanning the floor for slowpokes. *Clear.* Speedball keyed the transmitter code and the tunnel doors broke seal and opened.

Margie said, "I'm gonna give you one last time to go back."

"Sorry," said Speedball. "I got work to do."

He aimed the ship into the deenergized grav tunnel, shining the headlights on the curving walls. Up ahead Mike could see what looked like a scattering of stars—the lights of Walltown shining at the mouth of the short tunnel.

"We're coming out," said Speedball.

CHAPTER 11

Mike was fidgeting in the hot seat, waiting for the ship to be refueled, when the news broke that madmen had stolen the ancient alien track sweeper.

"Oh, man," he muttered. "He really did it . . ."

Mike felt anxious and relieved and a little guilty. He wondered who Speedball had gotten to take his place.

Jass came on the voice comm. "You know anything about this?"

"Not really."

His fuel gauge chimed, and Mike got ready to go back out on the track.

The *Spider* entered track Monza by warping right through its inner wall. Immediately the control panel blinked, as a recall order swept through the ship. It was ignored. The screen lit up with targets. They were after them already.

"I don't get it," said Speedball. "Who the hell knew I was coming here?"

"Are you kidding?" said Margie. "Everybody in Pitfall knows you're obsessed with finding the rest of your stupid bones."

Speedball looked at her. "*Every*body knows that?" His steel head turned toward Mike, who was strapped into the right-hand seat beside him.

"Don't look at me," said Mike. "I didn't tell anybody."

Five fast-moving targets were fanned out behind them, and converging. The speedway track flickered rapidly, stuttering the screens and throwing shadows through the cockpit glass. "Pulse transmission," said Speedball. The *Spider* didn't respond.

"They must really want you back," said Margie. She was behind Mike, with her arm hooked around his neck. Scarface was on the other side, perched on Mike's shoulder,

trying to dig his claws into the steel. "You guys mind?" said Mike. "I'm trying to—oh, jeez!" Another blip had appeared on the screen at the edge of the screen. "Patrol ship in front of us!"

"Where?" asked Speedball.

"At the wall."

After a moment Speedball said, "That's no ship . . ."

They watched the target for several seconds, as it slowly became more distinct. "I've never seen anything like that," said Margie.

Mike said, "Now I *am* worried."

The target swelled, gradually forming a hazy, tear-shaped plume. "Those are microtargets," said Speedball. "It looks like a load of gravel."

It's all coming from the same place, said Mike. *Like there's a hole in the track.*

You know that warp-pocket of junk I was talking about? said Speedball. *I think the bottom just busted out.*

Before Mike could answer, everyone tipped sideways as the *Spider* whipped around toward the plume and began to accelerate. Margie lost her grip, falling away. Mike reached out and snagged her boot, hauling her back.

"Thanks."

"Grab the chair, okay?" he said. "Not me."

The ship tilted again, and Mike said, "Hey, Speedball, watch what you're doing!"

Speedball said, "Uh . . ." Titanium fingers fluttered over the panel, flicking switches. "Um . . . we seem to be out of . . . uh, control."

"I blame *you* for this," said Margie, closing her helmet's faceplate.

The *Spider* hissed and pinged as it plowed through the litter, moving faster all the while, aimed for the exact spot on the wall where the dust came in—the precise spot, in fact, where Mike and Margie had found their dark cul-de-sac.

When Mike reentered the track he was running third, behind Mishima and Twyla. Three laps to go.

Jass's voice crackled on the tac comm. "You're gonna have to do something, Mike. And fast."

"How's their fuel look?"

"Mishima's not your problem. If he's challenged for first, he's screwed, 'cause he hasn't pitted for fuel in half an hour. Twyla's your target. She's topped off and flying tight."

"Naturally," muttered Mike.

He checked the tac board, which displayed symbols of all the ships. Twyla was a hundred and fifty meters ahead, in the groove, floating easy. "Can I pass her in the shear?"

"Don't try it. She's got the fuel to wear you out."

"Copy."

He'd have to use the pipeline. Mike lit off his main engines, then tipped the control stick to the side, guiding *Bad Momma* out of the groove and into the velocity shear. The ship bounced around, squealing with stress. He broke through and eased back, approaching the fat red gravity beacon that guarded the entrance to the pipeline. He keyed the tactical computer for a lane insertion.

The ship shook and wheezed and rocked about as it dived through the turbulence toward the "chute"—the fastest gravity-assisted path around the spinning beacon. In the engine bay behind him, pumps whined and pounded, keeping the fuel flowing and the plasma magnets superconducting.

"You're on the path," said Jass.

"Thank you."

Panel lights blinked, and the note of the pumps stuttered, dropped, regained their pitch. Mike's eyes flicked over the controls. Power surge?

Ahead of him the entrance to the pipeline rose up, and he boosted the thrust. The ship broke away, trying to twist itself into a knot. Stress-shocks adjusted to the dynamic load, hissing and twanging. The pipeline was right there. He jerked the control stick, then shut down the mains. The pipeline took over, the ship accelerating automatically to match the faster track.

"I'm in!"

Bad Momma careened through the twisting pattern, and Mike fought the controls to keep the nose of the ship headed down the center of the narrow groove. This pipeline was *hot*, and he could see on the tac screen how his ship moved up against the leaders. Both Mishima and Twyla had lit off main

engines. Either they had engaged in a passing duel, or they were reacting to Mike's sudden move. After a moment, one of the blips peeled off, and Jass yelled in Mike's earphones, "Mishima's coming in!"

"Great!"

Now Twyla shut down and dropped back into the groove. Had she forgotten that *Bad Momma* was in the pipeline, moving up?

Mike looked at the race-position screen. They were high above the south pole of Clypsis, rising up toward the plane of the ecliptic. In three quarters of a lap he'd be dumped automatically out of the pipeline and back onto the track—right in Twyla's face.

It was going to be close. Should he risk lighting the mains? Mike keyed his transmitter. "Jass, I—"

The panel lights blinked again, and Mike said, "Stand by." This time it took longer for the pumps to resume their high-pitched wail. He said, "Something's happening . . ."

"I read power spikes," said Andy Veekle, who was monitoring *Bad Momma*'s maintenance computer from the pit. "Give me full telemetry, Mike."

"Stand by." The ship skipped and shuddered through the turbulence, and Mike had to fight the controls with both hands. "Look, I'm kinda busy, okay? Can't you do it yourself?"

"I tried, but the computer's not answering the prompt."

"Terrific."

The manual switch was about half a meter out of reach, located on the auxiliary maintenance control panel, which was designed to be operated by the copilot.

Mike lined everything up in the corner of his eye, then made a lunge for the switch. No way, his harness was too tight. "Help . . ."

"I'm still waiting," said Andy.

"I haven't forgotten you."

Mike popped the quick-release on his harness, pulled his coolant hoses tight, and tried again, leaning sideways across the copilot's seat. He had to take his eyes off the forward viewscreen to find the switch, then fumble with the safety interlock. "Damn . . ." His gloved fingers were about twice

as thick as he wanted them to be, but he finally got it done. "There you go!"

When he looked up, he found the ship had twisted sideways, aiming itself at the glittering wall. "No, you don't," said Mike as he kicked the control stick over.

The ship straightened up. Mike snapped his harness together and pulled the straps tight again. "I'm all set now."

Then the panel lights blinked again, and the viewscreen filled with fractal junk. He hit the camera-reset switch. The screen cleared, went blank, then flashed into life.

Mike was ready to compensate for drift during the blackout, but he was still right there, flying straight down the middle of the narrow groove. "Talk about luck . . ."

Then everything in the cockpit went south. Thrusters fired at random; the ship shimmied, pitched downward, and began to roll. Mike jerked the control stick, but it was dead.

"I can't . . ."

Abruptly the main engines lit off, all by themselves, and he was shoved back into the seat cushions.

"Mike!" yelled Jass.

Bad Momma accelerated at max, heading right for the track wall.

The *Spider* was practically singing by the time it hit the hole in the speedway wall. In it went, shuddering, purring, clamoring; penetrating and enlarging. Its power circuits cranked up and set themselves to requirements only the *Spider* understood.

Mike tried to grab the yoke, but was tossed off with a shrug and a mild electric shock that nearly wiped his memory. He said, "I think we're just here for the ride."

Margie was pressed up against the front porthole, grinning into the darkness as the *Spider* accelerated toward the shimmering distance. She turned, eyes wide, and keyed her suit radio. "I *love* it!"

The path faintly glowed, the narrow warp-tube just bright enough to reveal the closeness of the walls, the tightness of the turns, and the horrible speed of the ancient ship.

Speedball said, "None of the new instruments are working. The ship's gone rogue."

The hull rattled with debris, then the tube went dark. Mike watched the alien panel lights flicker across Speedball's smooth face. Here is where we die, he thought. He looked at Margie and wondered what dying meant to her. Had her mommy bought brain tapes for her?

A moment later the ship broke through into the light, brighter than before; the walls backed off some distance, and glistened like wet stone. Margie turned from the porthole, grinning. Even Mike tried to smile.

The ride smoothed out, then nothing at all happened for a long time.

The warp drive had shut itself down. Apparently the *Spider* had only used it to gain entrance to whatever it had found out there on the edge of track Monza. There was no telling how fast they were going, but Mike guessed it was extravagantly superluminal. He said, "This track is not supposed to be here."

"It's somebody's main line," said Speedball. "That's obvious."

Margie hinged her faceplate upward and took in some air. "Where are we?"

"Better you should ask, Where are we going?" said Speedball.

She did.

"Beats me," he said.

"Ha ha ha," she said, in a precise, ironic tone that made Mike's steel spine crawl.

He said, *This warp-tube is either very very new or very very old.*

I vote for old, said Speedball. *The interesting thing is, it can't be seen from the outside.* "You know, folks have wondered for hundreds of years who built the *Spider.* I got a feeling we may find out today."

Margie said, "If this line doesn't just dead-end."

"That's a pleasant thought," said Mike.

Abruptly the *Spider* whined and bucked, and lights flickered on the panel. The warp-tube narrowed and darkened, began to stutter.

Mike told Margie, "You just had to say it, didn't you?"

"Don't be superstitious."

The tube widened again, and passed a number of dark openings. The screen filled suddenly with targets. Rocks banged against the skin of the ship, tumbling away into the hazy darkness.

"Looks like a warpweb interchange," said Speedball.

"All that rock and junk," said Mike. "Where's it coming from?"

"My guess is, somewhere out there the web's got itself wrapped around a planet—cutting it open, chopping it up, dragging the pieces inside."

"Like a meat grinder," said Margie.

"Or a construction crew," said Mike.

The *Spider* picked one of the dark entrances and plunged inside. In a few minutes they were back out on a main-line track, cruising at top speed.

A lot more time went by.

"No more talk about dead ends," said Mike. "Okay?"

"I got another idea," said Margie. "What if it never ends?"

"You are a well of cheerful predictions."

It wasn't long before the *Spider* slowed again, choosing another narrow line from the selection at the interchange. This one stayed dim, its walls a mottled gray blur.

Speedball said, "I got a feeling, folks. Get your tickets ready."

Without warning the tube flickered brightly, becoming transparent.

"That's it," said Speedball. "We just went sublight."

I can see stars! said Mike, looking right through the walls of the web.

Speedball moved his head in small, precise jerks. *I can't get a fix. We're nowhere near the Clypsis system.*

Then where—

"I don't know, Michael."

The *Spider* rotated nose down.

"Look out!" said Margie.

The star was right *there*, close enough to touch, it seemed, and dim enough to look at, despite its proximity.

A red dwarf, said Mike.

The *Spider* turned again, shifting the dim red globe away from the center, and followed the warp-tube out toward a swiftly growing dot.

"It's a planet," said Margie, pointing.

"Yeah," said Mike. "We noticed."

The *Spider* sped toward it, and the cool, reflected light of the planet blue-shifted to a haze of violet fluff. The *Spider* reached the globe and began to circle, grazing the atmosphere in a glow of red and yellow fire that never quite touched the ship's fragile skin. The planet swung by beneath them, full of purple water and dark green continents and pink clouds. It looked ugly and dead.

The ship began to drop, steeper and steeper, toward the uninviting cloud tops. "I think you better check your pressure suit, kid," said Speedball. "It looks like we're coming down."

"Abort! Abort!" Jass was yelling in Mike's ears. "Full abort!"

Mike felt the ship shaking itself to pieces, crashing through the turbulence, accelerating toward the edge of the track. The forward viewscreen was full of sparks. How far away was the wall?

"Abort, Mike. *Right now!*"

If Jass was telling Mike to do it, that meant they had already failed to do it from the pit. The computers must be screwed up. Mike reached overhead for the main breaker. Power spikes hadn't tripped it, but there were surge protectors to take care of the small stuff. He hesitated.

"Come on, Mike! Full abort!"

"No."

He swiveled the main exhaust nozzles, and felt the ship turn. Which way had he been headed when the screen went dead? He tried to figure it out, but the damned attitude thrusters kept firing at random, throwing him around in his harness. It was confusing.

The only safe place in the pipeline was in the groove, where the turbulence dropped off. Could he feel his way back to the centerline?

"Abort! Damn it!"

"No! If I trip the main breaker I'll lose all power."

If he *was* headed for the wall, without power he'd just keep right on going, unable to maneuver.

Mike reached up and selectively killed the thruster circuits. The main engines continued to stutter intermittently, but he needed them to steer the ship. They only fired in one direction—and he still had some control over the nozzle angle.

Mike looked at the stress-shocks, noting which were compressed, which were stretched. He aimed the nozzles to the right. The mains came on, fired for several seconds, then shut down. The ship floated free for a moment, shocks relaxing partway. The rest of their stress had to be coming from the track's turbulence—its natural desire to twist any physical object into a shape of least resistance.

Mike got an idea. "I'm going to . . . oh, forget it!" Too complicated to explain in a hurry.

He tried another camera-reset, but the view remained scrambled. He keyed the rear- and side-looking cameras, but the screens they presented were all full of seething fractal garbage. Obviously it was an image-processing problem, not a camera problem.

"Mike! Mike!"

"Leave me alone. I'm busy!"

"You've moved back away from the sidewall," said Jass. His voice was full of static, radio interference from stuff exiting the track at superluminal speed—the reaction products from Mike's fusion exhaust, probably.

"Backing away?"

"It's hard to read," said Jass. "The resolution is poor."

The mains started up again, and Mike groaned as the acceleration jumped on his chest. If the g's were up, the ship was light—fuel was running out. At the moment, he couldn't decide if that was a good thing or not.

He centered the engine nozzles, saw the vertical shocks compress, and angled the engines down. The compressing shocks hissed louder, and banged against their stops. "Whups . . ." He angled the nozzles up, and the shocks relaxed. He held them there until the shocks reacted again,

counted slowly to five, then reversed the nozzle angle, counted three, and centered them again. The shocks relaxed—then the mains shut down.

Mike took a breath, looked instinctively at the fuel-graph screen, but it was full of garbage. "Damn." How the hell much fuel did this tub carry?

Mike keyed his transmitter. "Can you talk me through?"

"No," said Jass. "I can't see you well enough. I might send you into the wall or something. Just keep doing what you're doing till you get dumped back out on the track."

"All right, but I gotta tell you something."

"What?"

The mains lit off again.

Mike said, "Your new ship sucks."

The *Spider* hit the ground hard, screaming. Mike jumped out of his seat, headed for the window—and nearly collapsed when his full-g weight landed hard on tefloid knee joints. Speedball wobbled forward, grabbing onto the wall, and pressed his blank steel face to the glass.

Margie was already there.

Scarface climbed up Mike's back to his shoulder. They all peered out the window together. *Oh, my God . . .* said Mike.

The sun was going down on what looked like the biggest junkyard in the universe. Spaceships, large and small, ripped apart, pried open, rusting, battered with rock and dirt, overgrown with purplish-green vines and shrubs—all of it spread out across the plain as far as Mike could see, a plain strewn with huge boulders of melted iron and nickel, sharp-edged chunks of glittering black glass, and moldy-looking clumps of dark earth.

"Not a very cheerful sight," said Speedball.

Margie's radio coughed. "It looks just exactly like hell to me."

In the distance a chunk of smooth, twisted metal plowed into the field, sending up dirt and shiny pieces of some old ship's side panels.

What was that? asked Mike.

Then the *Spider* gonged with the impact of a hunk of rock, hissing as a cloud of dust broke over them.

"I get the idea this is not a safe place," said Speedball. He went back to the controls and tried to persuade something to work.

"It's like the elephants' graveyard," said Margie. "All those old ships, coming here to die."

Several more rocks thudded to the dirt, and the *Spider* vibrated.

Any luck? asked Mike.

Controls are still dead—but the Spider'*s alive.* "Hey, you feel that?"

"It's trembling," said Margie.

Should we get out?

Well, Mike, I *can't get the damned thing to move. Why don't* you *give it a try.*

Mike plugged in—and got out in a hurry. It seemed that chunks of alien data were breaking up and coming at him in a most unfriendly way. *It's gone haywire.*

That's right, said Speedball. *And the longer we stay here, the more likely it is we'll get clobberd by something coming down.* "We seem to be at the terminus of the warp-tube, Margie. I think we'll have to get out."

"That's easy for you," she said. "But I don't have that much air left. What if we have to stay a long time?"

"This ain't no tech ship," said Speedball. "We got no way of testing the air out there—except your spacesuit. It has sensors."

"It only tests the environment for oxygen," said Margie. "All the toxicity monitors are on the inside."

"That's all right," said Speedball. "Give it to me. I'll wear it inside out and tell you what it says."

Another rock smacked the ground, just missing the *Spider.* The inside of the cockpit commenced to tingle.

"C'mon, kid," said Speedball. "There's not much time."

"All right, all right," she said, popping her faceplate. She gave the helmet a quarter turn and pulled it off. Next the gloves. She was just working the side latch when the *Spider* shrilled. "What's that?"

Then the sidewalls zippered apart along unseen lines—

and the cockpit split wide open, exposing them to the evening air.

Margie grabbed for her helmet, but it went bouncing away, landing on the ground below them. She looked up at Speedball, her eyes wide, breath in check, cheeks bulging.

CHAPTER 12

Bad Momma suddenly stopped bumping around, and the stress-shocks relaxed, sighing. Mike guessed he had passed the start/finish line, and that the pipeline had dumped him back out onto the main track.

"*Now* will you abort?" asked Jass. "There's traffic all around you."

Mike's viewscreens were still scrambled. "All right, I'm ready!"

He reached overhead and hit the main breaker—just as the fusion engines ignited. They shut down immediately, along with all the ship's systems. He rode in silence for a moment. Without power, the microphones that brought him cabin noises were shut down. Somewhere out there cooling pumps were winding down, and had the instruments been working, he'd have seen the engine temps swiftly rising.

Mike popped his harness release and ducked under the maintenance console, which faced the copilot's station. He flicked on his wrist light, then pulled the access panel and isolated the computer power board. Everything looked all right—no smoke or burned components—but that didn't mean anything. Mike counted down through the circuits, trying to read the markings through the vapor haze inside his helmet.

"Damn it . . ."

He actually felt queasy. Nearing the end of the most crucial race of his life, and here he was, stretched out across the center console with his head under the dashboard, fiddling with a bunch of switches he couldn't even see. Finally he had to lift his fogged-up faceplate.

The change in pressure banged his ears, and he yawned, trying to clear the tubes. The ship was full of ominous creaks and clicking noises, and the air smelled of hot metal and soft

plastic. Coolant pumps had been shut down for too long. "Burning up . . ." he muttered.

Mike wiped his sweat-drenched face with a stiffly gloved hand and blinked the sting out of his eyes. It took another ten or fifteen endless seconds to locate the right row on the power panel, then he flipped a sequence of tiny switches, specifically disabling the tactical computer. He straightened up, dropped his faceplate, and reset the main breaker.

His earphones filled with a confusion of noise—the rattles and sighs of a buffeted ship, the start-up growl of pumps, the ringing and hooting of alarms that warned of imminent disaster. Jass and Andy simultaneously shouted at him on separate radios:

"—no circumstances light your mains because the track has just gone yellow and the pace ship is due onto the web at any—"

"—running more parallel computer checks to determine if your telemetry can be trusted as long as the system is compromised by fluctuations of—"

"I'm back," said Mike, ignoring them both.

He hit the camera-reset for the third time. The screen filled with static, blanked, and cleared—revealing the smoking exhaust nozzles of a sleek black-and-white ship ten meters ahead. It was Twyla's ship—the *Slippery Cat*—rapidly falling back and rocking in the turbulence.

Mike tensed, firing thrusters to maneuver out of the way. *Bad Momma* responded perfectly, as if nothing had happened. He checked the position board: a lap and a half to go. Incredibly, he was running second.

"I've still got a chance!"

"Negative," said Jass. "They just black-flagged you for the control problem."

"But it's fixed! I shut down the tactical computer. Power spikes had screwed the program. But now—"

"It doesn't matter. They—"

Race Control got on the line: "*Bad Momma*, exit the track on the next pit lane. Stand by in your pit maintenance hangar, pending inspection by a race marshal."

"But that'll take—"

"Exit the track at once, *Bad Momma*."

He was approaching a pit lane, but Mike made no preparations for exiting the track. It just wasn't fair. After all the trouble he'd gone through staying alive in the pipeline...and now the race was almost over. There wasn't nearly enough time to get through an inspection and still make it back out on the track. How could they do this to him? Didn't they know how important it was for him to win this race?

The entrance to pit lane swept past, unused. Mike keyed his transmitter. "Race Control, this is *Bad Momma*. Will you please explain how—"

"*Bad Momma*, you are disqualified. Exit the track immediately, or your pit will be fined."

Mike couldn't believe it. He was so close, and the ship was running just fine now, and—

"Come on, Mike," said Jass. "We'll talk about it later."

"Oh, you can count on that."

He savagely wrenched the stick, and *Bad Momma* twisted away from the groove in an ironic victory roll.

Margie's eyes were starting to bug out.

"You might as well go ahead and breathe," said Speedball, peering over the side of the *Spider*.

"Scarface seems to like it," said Mike. Margie shook her head violently. "Then again," said Mike, "he might be holding *his* breath, too. Waiting for you . . ."

Scarface chattered loudly, bobbing his little lizard head. Margie took a swipe at him, groaning. Finally she gave up, expelling the dregs of her air. She filled her lungs in a spasm, then turned red blowing it all out. She sniffed cautiously.

"How is it?" asked Speedball.

"It smells . . . rusty . . . and sour . . . just like a real junkyard." She took several deep breaths, returning slowly to normal. "In fact," she said, "it stinks."

"That settled," said Speedball, "let's get out of here."

"I'm not going!" said Margie.

Speedball picked her up and heaved her over the side. "And so forth," he muttered. *C'mon, Mike. You're next.*

Together they climbed over the side and dropped down to the soft, well-turned soil. Scarface fluttered down and landed on Mike's shoulder. Speedball dusted off Margie's helmet and handed it to her. "For what it's worth."

She snatched the helmet out of his hands and checked the clamping ring for dents. "If my seals are broken . . . "

"You're . . . all right . . ." said Speedball. He seemed distracted.

"I haven't turned green yet, if that's what you mean."

Speedball didn't appear to be listening. He took several steps forward and stopped. "Oh, no . . ."

What do you see? asked Mike.

"Oh, my God," said the automaton, running off into the dump.

"What's he doing?" asked Margie.

"I don't know," said Mike, following Speedball to a nearby crater full of twisted metal. *What is it?*

They stood over the wreck, looking in. A chunk of scorched metal stuck up. In small letters it said *04 Flying Cir.*

"That's Alice Nikla's ship," said Speedball. "What's left of it." He descended into the crater and began to pry at the wreckage. Scarface flew down and lighted on the twisted surface, touching and sniffing and tasting. He started to growl.

Mike hesitated a moment, as a chunk of rock crashed down ten meters away, then he got in there beside Speedball, tearing at the blackened metal.

"What's going on?" asked Margie, standing at the rim.

"Friend of ours," said Speedball, without looking back. His arm motors whined and stuttered as he worked. *I can see into the cockpit.*

Is Alice . . . ?

Speedball stopped digging, then pulled Scarface off the metal. *She's there, all right. You'd be better off not looking.*

But—

"I mean it!" said Speedball, grabbing Mike's elbow. He yanked Mike out of the wreckage, and they stepped back together. Scarface skittered around on Mike's head, whimpering.

"She's dead, isn't she?" said Margie.

Speedball said, "She never made it through the entrance

tunnel. By the time her ship hit the main line, it was just a melted piece of junk.''

But the Racing League reported blue light.

Parts of the ship must have blown clear and disintegrated, going through the warp-wall. The rest came here.

Another rain of small stones rattled across the junkheap. Speedball looked up. ''It's not safe out here.'' He helped Mike up the crater's slope. Mike looked back. *Forget it*, said Speedball. *There's nothing anybody can do.*

We could bury her.

She'll be buried soon enough.

They joined Margie at the rim. ''It's getting dark,'' she said. ''Did anyone bring any sandwiches or anything?''

''Uh-oh,'' said Mike.

''That's just perfect,'' said Margie.

More rocks slammed into the plain of rubble. Mike turned in time to see a dim cloud of dirt billowing out of the violet evening sky, about five hundred meters up. ''There's the warp exit,'' he said, pointing.

''And there goes our ride,'' said Speedball.

Mike whipped around. The *Spider* had snapped shut and was lifting straight into the air. Suddenly it shot off low to the ground, and disappeared behind some stunted trees at the edge of the dump.

Scarface chittered and flapped his wings.

''When's it coming back?'' asked Margie.

Mike looked at Speedball, and Speedball said, *She's your little friend. I'll let you tell her.*

After the race Mike reported to Pitfall Hospital as ordered, and was shunted off to a waiting area. He arrived in time to see Rosenberg, who had finished second, disappear through the door on the far side of the room. There was one other guy in the waiting room, but Mike didn't recognize him.

''Have a seat,'' the man said. ''This won't take long.''

Mike sat down. ''Is this what I think it is?''

The guy nodded vigorously, then reached up to flick long red hair out of his eyes. Mike fought an impulse to paw through his own meager crop of bristles. Joining Blando's

team *had* saved him from another scheduled haircut—not that it made much difference.

The red-haired guy looked at the doors, then leaned closer to Mike. "I only ran fifth, so you know this doesn't make any sense to me. Hell, they didn't even inspect my ship. How'd you do? You're not Mishima, are you?"

"No."

Mishima had come back on the track to finish third.

"I wouldn't know," said the redhead. "Never met the guy."

"He's Japanese."

"What's that?"

"You know, Oriental. He doesn't look a bit like me."

"More hair, I guess."

"At least. You're not from Earth, are you?"

"Hey, give me a break. I was born on a ship, going from one place to someplace else. Japanese, huh? I never studied history."

Mike nodded.

The guy said, "So how'd you do?"

"I was disqualified."

"And they got you here? What the hell for? They're not testing everybody, are they?"

"I didn't know they were testing *any*body."

"Yeah, well, Pitfall's gone to hell, lately." He looked around the room, checking out the ceiling corners, then leaned close again. "Hey, man, I know a way to fix the test. Clean results, no matter what. Blood, brain, and piss—the test is clean. You could be jumping like a—"

"No thanks."

"Whatever you say." He looked Mike over. "They got you once, they could get you again."

"What do you mean, they got me once? I don't do drugs."

"But you been in the slammer, I see."

Mike smacked his shorn skull. "This is not for jail, man. It's community service. I was between rides, and I had to do *some*thing. That's the law."

"Whatever you say."

"I've never used HIPE. Never."

"Then, why are you here? Why did they disqualify you?"

"It was mechanical, man. A safety gig."

"Whatever you say."

The inner door banged open and Rosenberg came out, looking ticked off. Beyond him Mike caught a glimpse of stainless steel apparatus and wicked-looking brain probes. Rosenberg whirled and shouted back into the examination room, "Sorry to disappoint you, *Doctor.*" He turned, fixed his eyes on Mike. "This is insulting!"

"I know just what you mean," said the red-haired guy.

The doctor appeared at the door, and several eye-stalks rotated about, scanning the room. The voice box around his neck hissed with static. "I am taking the next body now, please."

Mike leaned back in his chair and stared at the ceiling. Finally the red-haired guy said, "I guess that's me . . ."

"I'm cold and I'm hungry," said Margie.

"Don't be an Earthling," said Speedball.

"Don't you call me that!"

It was pitch dark on the hillside. All around them lay the ruins they'd found—fat stones of ancient granite, with wrinkled bars of shiny blue steel holding them together. This was an old, but not a primitive site.

Speedball said, "Somebody worked on this planet."

Terraformed? asked Mike. "Really?"

"Think about it," said Speedball. "Habitable planets are rare around red dwarf stars, yet this one is not only habitable, it just happens to be a remarkably close copy of Earth—gravity, atmosphere, temperature."

"It's too cold," said Margie.

"Cut it out," said Mike. "You don't hear Scarface complaining."

"He's already asleep," said Margie.

"Another thing," said Speedball. "This planet isn't nearly as big as you would expect, considering the gravity field. What have they put in the core, platinum?"

"Who's they?" asked Mike.

"You know what I think?" said Speedball. "The folks

who worked this place over were the ones who did a number on Enigma."

"Nobody worked on Enigma," said Mike. "They found it like that."

"Right, along with the *Spider.* You think it's natural, too?"

"Well . . ."

Margie said, "Okay, I'm ready for my bedtime story now."

"Is that right?" said Mike.

"I don't know any stories," said Speedball.

"Weren't you ever a kid?"

"Yeah, but my memories are a bit scrambled. What about you, Mike?"

"I'm afraid to look."

So far he'd been running his PV without thinking about his own past—he was afraid maybe he might not be all there. What if that sleazy woman had made a mistake when she taped him?

"You're gonna have to look sometime," said Speedball. "This is a great chance to test your tapes. I mean, I wish I'd paid more attention to mine."

"Maybe some other time."

"Come on," said Margie. "Just one story."

Mike said, "I'm not going in there."

"What if I just sort of poked around?" said Speedball. "I won't break anything."

"It's the least you can do," said Margie. "Considering you stranded me out here without so much as a cheese sandwich."

"I don't know . . ." said Mike.

"Oh, *pleeeeeez* . . ." she said, in a whiny voice that could scrape the rust off a hundred junkyard spaceships. "*Pretty* please!"

"All right, all right!"

"It'll be fun," said Speedball. He quickly pried open a small door on Mike's shoulder.

Be careful . . .

I'll keep it out of the front, said Speedball. *You won't even know I'm in here.*

Mike cringed, as best he could. He felt something warm and wet wash over his body, smelling of peppermint. Vaguely he could hear Speedball saying, *Oh, this should be good—a little adventure you had with a refrigerator.*

It's boring.

Wait a minute—not so boring. I see you got propositioned.

Yeah, well . . .

Mike heard a husky voice saying, Pardy-pardy?

Four hands reached out from a haze of light. *A Polaran,* said Mike. *I seem to remember.*

You turned her down.

Hey, I had my refrigerator to worry about.

Of course.

"How's that story coming?" asked Margie.

Find something else, said Mike.

Let me just watch a little more of this; see if there are any more chicks popping out of the walls.

I don't remember any.

Wait a minute. What the hell is this?

What is what? More chicks?

Did you know someone was following you?

Really? It's a funny thing. I thought maybe—

It's true, and it's no joke. Look at this.

Mike "blinked." The darkness of the night was replaced by the darkness of a narrow corridor in Pitfall. Something tickled his ear, and he reached up to scratch. Ahead of him was the sound of a heavy crash.

Yeah, so?

Let me crank it up, said Speedball.

The scene got bright and grainy, then Speedball played it through again. This time Mike could see the dented white refrigerator sail off down the corridor, having just demolished a light fixture. Something flicked his ear again as it whizzed on past. "What the hell was *that*?"

"What was what?" asked Margie in a sleepy voice. "Where's my story?"

Somebody was shooting at you, said Speedball. He played the scene again, slowing it down. The spinning green pellet was obvious, now. It wobbled right past Mike's ear, ruffling the tiny hairs with its shock wave.

That's a bio-pak, said Speedball. *It gets in you, the next day your guts turn to mush.*

Mike started to reach for his ear, but his steel head was a blank. "Oh."

Another pellet whizzed past, sparking faintly off the side of the shaft. The sound dialed up, and he could hear it smacking into something way down there where the dim corridor boiled with amplified light.

Why would anybody want to shoot me?

I don't know. I'm running a search.

"Where the hell's my story?" asked Margie. She yawned.

Here's something weird, said Speedball. *Somebody left a security door open.*

You mean the one at Jass's pit?

Yeah. That could have proved fatal.

You think it was deliberate?

No way to tell from here. Maybe if I check around, I'll get lucky.

Speedball submerged again. While he was gone, Mike ran the refrigerator sequence backward until he found the part where he had first gotten the feeling he was being followed. Up and back he went, through the crowded corridor, with that damned refrigerator always in his way. He finally managed to locate a moment where he was squinting at a shadowy figure behind him. *Hey.*

What?

Enhance this for me, will you? I think this is the guy who was following me.

Speedball brightened the image and manipulated it every which way he could but the man never became clear enough to recognize.

Nothing, said Mike.

It takes time.

But why didn't the guy finish me off? I was all alone down there.

He probably thought he had, said Speedball. *Look.*

In the playback Mike turned from the corridor wall, holding his hands over his face.

For a moment Mike was puzzled. *Oh, I remember that,*

he said. *There was this loose mag handle floating around, and I got smacked in the nose. Hurt like hell.*

There you go, said Speedball. *Looks convincing to me.*

I guess.

Speedball showed Mike how to enhance the images for himself, then went back to his own search. To Mike he seemed awfully casual about it all.

Mike zoomed forward to relive the moment when the first bio-pak zipped past his ear. Over and over, he played it, and each time it gave him the creeps. He froze the pellet in midair and tried to stare it down. Death in a capsule . . .

Stop playing around! Speedball was back. *Okay, look—I found something. There was a homeset playing in the commissary that day while you ate lunch.*

I know I wasn't paying any attention.

Doesn't matter. You could still hear it in the background. Listen.

Speedball played it back: a report of a pressure-door blowout in a utility shaft just off Jass's corridor. For twenty minutes there had been hard vacuum right outside that safety door.

I don't remember any blowout.

Speedball ran the scene back. Mike was talking to Jass in the pit when the room vibrated. Mike said, What was that? Jass said, Beats me. Mike said, Must be a party next door.

That was it?

The time matches, said Speedball.

I don't believe it.

Believe it.

My God, I feel like such an idiot. That's twice somebody tried to kill me.

Three times, said Speedball. *I just found another one.*

A new scene came to life. Mike was bargaining half-heartedly with a weird old candy vendor in front of the pressure-suit inspection center. Suddenly the man shuddered and began to drool. Soon he was ready to collapse on the street. *A reaction to HIPE, apparently,* said Mike.

Speedball ran the scene back and slowed it down, zooming in on the man's face. *See that?* The man jerked

in slow motion. Speedball backed it up again, searching the line of his head and neck. *There!* He ran the scene again, ultra-slow, as a dart the size of a gnat nailed the man in the back of his neck. *That's what set him off. I'll bet it was meant for you.*

Mike watched the man start to shake. *For God's sake, turn it off!*

Might have been HIPE, said Speedball. *It put him on the ground, but from the look of him, he had a tolerance. Probably would have killed you.*

Who the hell is doing this?

I'm still looking.

Mike searched on his own for the day the big man in the Goodyear suit chased him down the ventilator shaft. First he ran it back to see if the guy had taken any shots at him. He hadn't. Then Mike searched through blurry shots of the corridor crowd, brief images glimpsed from the corner of his eye or captured innocently as he glanced back to see why someone laughed.

All those faces: blue and red and yellow, wide and fat or scrunched down to nothing; wobbling or erect, eyes staring or drooping or missing altogether . . .

There!

In the middle of this impossible clutter, he found a mass of green hair peeping from underneath a black baseball cap. The man had his head turned away, and Mike waited for him to face forward. But when he did, something exquisitely ugly leaned out to block the view. Mike zoomed in and fiddled with the picture, running it backward and forward, but there was simply not enough of the face showing to be sure.

On the other hand, how many people did Mike know who wore green hair and held a grudge against him?

Something tickled his memory. Back he went to the scene in the pit, to a time shortly before the muffled explosion. Jass crinkled up his eyes and said, Speaking of meat gone bad, your friend Dover Bell was in here a little while ago.

Son of a bitch.

"None of that," said Margie. "I want a clean story."

* * *

Mike was back in darkness on a cold slab of granite. *I know who's after me now. It's Dover Bell.*

Of course!

What do you mean, of course?

Uh, Mike, I guess I'd better show you something I picked up off the datanet before we left. It's restricted access material, so there's no way you could have known.

The darkness vanished, and Mike found himself moving . . .

. . . along the crowded Strip, dodging traffic, down an alleyway and through a busted door beneath a sign that says TATTOO . . . beyond the back room, parting the curtains, into the filthy shop, where chairs are overturned . . . green-suited Pitfall Police angrily shout, pushing back, making way . . . and on the floor, stacked up in a rotting heap, two bodies lie in mysterious pose beneath the glare of the homeset lights . . .

(Mike stared in disbelief. The black-market man, dead. The woman who made his tapes, dead. It made no sense.)

. . . the camera zooms in as a cop pries open the woman's hand . . . green hairs in her fist . . .

And Mike thought: Dover Bell.

Oh, no, he said. *Now we've* got *to get back. Somehow I've got to warn . . . myself.* It made him feel strange, thinking about that other Mike. The *real* Mike . . .

"*I,*" said Margie, "am still *waiting*."

"Oh, hell," said Speedball, plunging back into Mike's memories. Eventually he found a story Mike's mom had told him when he was eight, something about three smug little pigs building condos in the woods. Speedball even told it in the voice she had used, but Mike couldn't bear to listen. Death was already on his mind.

By the time Mike returned to Jass's pit, Andy Veekle had already finished checking out the ship. "You were right," he said. "The tactical computer went nuts, started firing off thrusters at random. All the other computers got scrambled by inputs from the tac."

"How could this happen?" asked Mike.

"I don't know yet," said Andy. "Voltage spikes from someplace."

"Tough break," said Jass.

"I could have won that race!"

"Don't whine."

Mike looked at Andy. "What's he mean, don't whine? Am I whining? I just said I could've won, that's all. Is that whining?"

Andy shrugged. "All I know is, that was great flying in the pipeline, Mike. I don't know how you stayed off the walls. I really don't."

"You should have died out there," said Jass. "You should have gone over the high side. I don't know a master who could have flown blind through the pipeline."

"With random thruster firings," said Andy. "And the mains just lighting off any old time they wanted."

"You should be lying on a slab somewhere," said Jass.

Mike looked away, feeling chills. He wished they'd stop saying that. He had tapes, damn it. He was going to live forever . . .

"Great flying, Mike," Andy said again. "Really."

"Great flying, huh?" Mike tossed his helmet at Oso. "Well, it wasn't good enough, was it?"

"It's just one race, Mike," said Jass. "You'll get 'em next time."

"Just one race! Don't you realize—"

"It wasn't even a *real* race," said Jass. "This whole jump-to-master junk is just show-business hype."

"Is that right? Hey, excuse me for dreaming, but I'm trying to put my career back together here."

"You got a job."

Mike looked around, and he couldn't help the contemptuous smirk on his face. "I don't mean to be rude, but—"

"Don't say it, Mike," said Andy. "It *is* a job. And I don't think you're in a position to—"

"Yeah?"

Jass said, "It's a *real* job, Mike. Not some stupid showbusiness—"

"I could be a master," said Mike. "Just like that—a *master.* What difference does it make if it's just a con for public relations? It's a certified master's ticket. I checked on

that. They can't tear it up without going through a League hearing.''

''They'll figure something out,'' said Jass. ''You don't know the kind of people you're—''

''Oh, and you're the expert on how folks should behave?''

Andy said, ''Mike, that's—''

''There are better ways to get a master's ticket,'' said Jass. ''Those people—''

''What about 'em?''

''Gajira doesn't care about you.''

''You don't know what you're talking about.''

''I want you to forget about the jump-to-master program.''

Mike laughed sharply. ''I guess I'll have to. After today—''

''Don't misunderstand me, Mike,'' said Jass. ''You're still alive in the program. With your points from the drag races, and your position at the time of the disqualification—''

''I'm still in?''

''Officially.''

''That's great!''

''Damn it, Mike—''

''Hey, it's my life.''

''But it's *my* ship.''

Mike started to answer, then stopped. Jass wouldn't look at him. ''What are you saying? You won't back me for the last eliminator?''

Jass didn't answer.

Mike looked at Andy. ''Is he serious?''

''Looks that way.''

''I can't have the ship?''

Jass wouldn't say.

Mike said, ''Then, I guess there's no point in staying here, is there?''

Nobody would answer him.

''I don't believe you guys,'' said Mike. He felt crushed—and what was worse, he had the horrible feeling that this time it was all his fault.

He walked slowly toward the door. Nobody stopped him.

CHAPTER 13

Not since his episode with the refrigerator had Mike experienced so strong an impression that he was being followed through the corridors of Pitfall. After looking back several times, and seeing nothing unusual, he was beginning to feel absolutely paranoid. But then, as he squirmed his way through a crowded ring crossover, Mike caught sight of someone lurking behind him—just a flash of green hair, really.

"Dover Bell . . ."

That made sense; Speedball had mentioned that Bell was looking for him. Mike stopped to let the man catch up . . . but then he thought, Wait a minute, I haven't got time to listen to one of his stupid tirades. Maybe later.

So he ducked into a greasy-spoon diner, pushing past a large yellow alien who flowed out into the aisle. "You, hey!" the guy said. "Spillum soups, you."

"S'ree, s'ree," said Mike, glancing back. The yellow blob of an alien had six bowls of soup lined up on the counter, and he was dipping or slurping or gargling with them all simultaneously. Mike said, "Don't hurt yourself."

He locked the bathroom door behind him and climbed onto the driptank. Scrub brushes swayed and clinked in their rack, bouncing against a thick coil of suction hose. There was a loud crash, and he looked down at a jumble of sluice nozzles he'd knocked over. "Oh, hell . . ."

Mike kept going. He pried open the vent grille and climbed into the air duct. In five minutes he was back out in a corridor, on the other side of the ring, grinning like a fool. Take that, Dover Bell.

Mike hesitated at the door to Lek Croveen's pit, mentally pumping himself up. It's going to work, he told himself.

It *had* to work.

Mike pressed his ID wrist to the reader. "I will announce you, Mr. Murray," said the door.

A moment later Lek was on the line, laughing, and telling him to come on through to his office. The door hissed and popped away from the seals, swinging inward.

Mike stepped across the lip of the sill. The control room was deserted, though piled with junked control panels, wire harnesses, and half-squashed boxes full of rusty parts. Out through the safety glass he could see the maintenance hangar, where the *Slippery Cat* floated in near freefall, swaying in slow harmonic oscillation against the spindly arms of the rollout carriage. There was nobody out there, either. Mike crossed the control room toward Lek's office. He could hear voices and laughter inside. It sounded like there was a party going on.

"Hey!" he said, smiling, as he stepped in front of the open door. The impression of a party died out quickly. The whole team was there: Andru the Merkek, and Dwaine (a female Polaran), and Twyla Rogres—all looking grim and uncomfortable. Lek was the one doing all the laughing.

"Mike!" said Lek. "Get in here!"

Andru nodded, addressing Mike in the calm Cambridge tones that contrasted so strangely with his angry-looking, brick-red skin. "We haven't been seeing much of you, Michael."

"You know how it is . . ."

Dwaine wrapped her four arms around him. "Missed ya, babe."

Twyla glanced at him nervously, but said nothing. Her long red hair was braided and pinned tightly to her skull—racing mode, she called it—so her helmet would fit. Mike liked everything she did with her hair.

"This is great!" said Lek. "The precise moment my copilot comes to tell me she's had enough, an absolutely perfect replacement pops his hairless little head through my door. Is that luck or what?"

"I didn't *say* I was quitting," said Twyla, her voice quiet but clearly exasperated. "But I have had enough of this crap."

"Exactly what crap is that?" asked Lek. He winked at Mike.

"You know what I'm talking about."

Andru said, "We are all of us quite concerned, Lek."

"Concerned about what?"

"The problem that everybody can—"

"There *is* no problem, Twyla," said Lek. "You wanna pull out, fine. You wanna jump-to-master, fabulous. Mike can take your place. Can't you, Mike?"

Twyla said, "No, he can't. Mike's got a job with Jass."

"Actually, I quit," said Mike.

"There you go!" said Lek.

Twyla gave Mike a look that made his head jerk back half an inch. "Hey, don't blame me."

"It's perfect," said Lek.

"Boss . . ." said Dwaine.

"What? You leaving, too? Great, there's plenty of good ship's mechanics out there. Some of them even got more arms than you."

"I didn't say anything."

"Maybe I should come back some other time," said Mike.

"No, no, stay!" said Lek. He laughed. "We're celebrating Twyla's recent victory!"

"Yeah, but—"

"What can I do for you?"

Mike's smile flickered, and he peeked at Twyla. "Actually, I was looking for a ship."

"Oh, Christ," she said.

Mike looked at Lek. "See, there's one more qualifying heat for the jump-to-master deal, and Jass . . . well, he decided he'd rather not . . . uh . . . well . . ."

Mike smiled, and Lek smiled back, his eyes glittering—on his lips, the whispered word, "Perfect."

Twyla caught Mike's eye. "Can I talk to you for a minute?"

"No need to talk," said Lek. "It's settled. Mike's come back to fly for me. Twyla, you can go sulk someplace else."

"Lek, I only said you should—"

"Get out!"

A cruel smile came instantly to his lips and disappeared just as quickly.

Twyla stood stunned for a moment. Lek said, "Mmmm?"

"Fine," she said, pushing past Mike. She stopped, looking into his eyes, her face so close to his she made him dizzy. "Don't be blinded by ambition, kid."

"What?"

But she was gone. She didn't look back.

There was silence in the office, as Andru and Dwaine exchanged glances. Lek said, "Now's the time, folks. You staying or what?"

Neither answered. Mike heard the corridor hatch break its seal, but when he looked, it was already closing. Twyla was gone.

"Go back to work," said Lek. "If you're going."

They left, carefully easing past Mike in the doorway. He thought he could see on their confused faces the torment of decisions unmade. But theirs were alien faces, and one never could be sure what they were masking.

Lek laughed, and Mike was astonished by the sound of it—so light and happy, without irony or bitterness. It was as if he had forgotten all about the confrontation with his team. "Hey, pal!" he said. "Welcome back! It's gonna be great!"

Mike smiled back, and it occurred to him a face didn't have to be alien to hide the thoughts behind.

The trail led through the brush and trees a kilometer or so to the top of a small hill, where they stopped and looked back. Mike collapsed on the dirt. "This damned gravity!"

"Oh, get up!" said Margie.

Speedball peered down at him. "You don't hear Margie complaining—"

"I'm hungry!"

"—about the gravity," finished Speedball. "On the other hand, I might have your body-simulator program cranked up a little high."

Mike's heart was pounding like mad and he could hardly get his breath. "Gosh, you think so?"

"I hate sarcasm," said Speedball.

"You can see the whole junkyard from here," said Margie.

"That's the point," said Speedball.

Mike looked at Margie. "How come you're not exhausted?"

"I work out in the playground—during the high-g hours."

She must be nuts.

Can it, Mike.

Speedball was tracing the shape of the cratered zone with his finger. "Adjusting for the angle of view, I'd say the junkyard is just about exactly circular, with the biggest heap in the center. In fact, if you plot junk against the diameter, it looks like a normal distribution curve."

Scarface climbed onto the top of his head for a better look.

Mike said, "That stuff must have been coming down for centuries."

"All those ships," said Margie. "Where were they going?"

"Maybe they were coming here," said Mike.

"To do what?"

"To exhaust themselves hiking up these stupid trails."

Speedball was still peering at the junkyard. "There are many layers," he said. "When I scan in the infrared band, I can see ships buried under the dirt."

"What are you looking for?" asked Mike.

"Two things. First, and pretty unlikely, we might find a ship less damaged than the others, something we might fix up."

"Fat chance," said Margie. "Why don't you look for something to eat, instead."

"And the other thing," said Speedball, "is even more unlikely. Just a dream, in fact."

What is it?

"I mean, the chances I might actually—Oh, my God, I don't believe it. There it is!" Speedball took off back down the trail, running toward the junk zone.

What did you find? yelled Mike.

I'll tell you when I know for sure, said Speedball. *And by the way, there's no need to shout.*

"Where's he going?" asked Margie.

Mike watched the shiny steel man disappear into the tall weeds. "Come on, kid. We got more hiking to do."

They found Speedball digging through the dirt with a flat chunk of blistered steel. He looked up and waved. "Help me, you guys."

Mike could see a cleared spot, where Speedball had thrown back pieces of wrecked ships. There was a lip of metal, its paint a faded amber color, rising out of the dirt. It was the corner of some ship long buried by incoming debris.

"What's he doing now?" asked Margie.

"Digging out some old ship."

"Come on," said Speedball. "Find something and help me dig."

"He's crazy," said Margie. She went over to sit on a jutting shelf of pitted meteorite.

Mike looked around. They were close to the edge of the blasted earth, far enough from the warp opening that no rocks or pieces of alien junk were falling nearby. "Okay," he said. He grabbed a chunk of twisted steel and got down on the dirt beside Speedball. "Where should I dig?"

"Down along the orange thing."

Speedball had already uncovered another corroded meter of it. "What is it?" asked Mike.

"*Relativity.*"

"Whatever you say." Mike began to scrape the soil away from the warped and dimpled metal. He stopped abruptly. "Relativity. You mean, it's *Relativity,* your old ship? The one you were in when you went—"

"Shut up and get to work," said Speedball.

"Damn," said Mike, getting back to it. "Your old ship. After all these years . . ." Then he remembered what they had found in Alice Nikla's ship. "Oh . . ."

It took hours of work, and then, when they reached the ship's cockpit, they found it crushed flat under the soil. Without heavy equipment, there was no way to get a look inside.

Speedball stood beside the wreck, looking down, his once-gleaming metal caked with dirt. Mike waited. Off to the

side, Margie sat on her meteorite and swung her legs. She said, "What about the black box?"

Speedball's head jerked up. "You're a genius!"

She shrugged. "Everybody knows that."

Speedball went around to the other side of the wreck and began digging a new trench. "C'mon, Mike!"

Mike limped over to Margie. "Thanks a lot."

It took another hour of digging to uncover the inspection plate. Speedball produced a stardriver finger and undid the screws. The plate hinged open and he reached inside.

Margie came to the edge of the hole to watch. Mike crouched in the dirt, his simulated heart pounding from fatigue. If he'd known how to sweat, he would have been squatting in a puddle.

Speedball rose up out of the hole. "A waste of time."

"Wrecked?" asked Mike.

"Missing," said Speedball.

"But who—"

Just then a voice came from behind them. "What are you doing here?"

They turned, found a gray-bearded, rather ratty-looking black man standing there. He pointed his walking stick at them. "Get away from that ship."

Speedball climbed out of the trench, stumbled forward a few steps, and dropped to his knees in front of the man. "Son of a bitch," said Speedball. "It's me."

Mike leaned back against the junked ship, and Margie knelt by his side. "It must be a shock," she said, nodding to where Speedball and the man jabbered rapidly, comparing notes.

Mike said, "I think at least one of them better hire a good lawyer."

The bearded man brought Speedball over to where Mike and Margie sat. "Didn't mean to be rude. Name's Larry Raybo—I used to be a race pilot."

"I know," said Mike. "You're famous. I remember—"

"How long have you been here?" asked Margie.

"Thirteen hundred and forty-five years."

"More like twenty," said Speedball. "Standard."

"Is that all?" asked Raybo. "The years are real short around here." He nodded past Speedball. "It's all right, babe. Come on over."

A tall blond Poldavian woman came up behind them. Mike stared helplessly at the way the tatters of a space suit draped over her statuesque form. She looked about twenty—and gorgeous.

Raybo said, "We got guests."

The blue-skinned woman nodded at everybody. "My name's Tanya Vir."

"Hi," said Mike.

"Hello," said Margie.

"Who're the metal men?" asked Tanya.

Raybo said, "The one on the ground I don't know. This one's me. Just ignore him."

The woman grinned at Speedball. "You're Larry's matrix? Do you know me?"

"I don't seem to. Perhaps you came after my last update."

"By a matter of days, probably," said Raybo.

"You always did work fast," said Tanya.

Speedball said, "That's why they call him—"

"Knock it off!" said Raybo.

Tanya nodded at Speedball. "I know what you mean, believe me."

"I don't," said Margie.

"I'll tell you later," said Speedball. "In about ten years . . ."

That night they spent in Raybo's camp—more high-tech alien ruins, near a stream. He had banged together a lot of sheet metal off old ships, roofing over the spaces beneath the tumbled stones. Spitted above the fire was a large rodent, crackling and smoking and stinking up the place. Raybo didn't seem to notice. He dragged out a couple of badly used flight seats for his guests.

"Don't get many visitors," he said.

"I'm surprised you get any," said Speedball.

"What's that supposed to mean?"

Mike said, "He means, you must be very isolated here."

"Sometimes there are crashes," said Tanya, "right out in the junkyard. In fact, just the other day—"

"It's a warp exit," said Raybo.

"Yeah, we figured that out," said Speedball.

Raybo scowled in the light of the fire. "There may be lots more, dumping out all over the planet. We see blue flashes sometimes in the night."

"Cerenkov radiation," said Margie, chewing on a hunk of bananalike root.

"Yeah," said Raybo, looking at her. "I guess."

"You're very smart, Margie," said Tanya.

"I know."

Oh, man, thought Mike. Don't get her started.

Raybo said, "You never told me what you were doing around my old ship."

"Looking for the black box," said Speedball.

"Oh, that. I pulled it out the second day I was here, back when the ship was lying on the top of the heap."

"You still have it?"

"Yeah, somewhere. I can't play it for you, though. I don't have the equipment."

"Get it out," said Speedball. "I *am* the equipment."

COCKPIT TAPE OF THE *RELATIVITY*
1/8.22.09 – 1/8.23.44
Pilot: Larry Raybo
Passenger: Tanya Vantage Vir
Track: Monza
Activity: engine test

SHIP: THRUSTER MALFUNCTION.

RAYBO: What the hell?

VIR: What is it, honey?

RAYBO: Controls are screwed up—and *now* the main engines have just lit off. What the hell is going on?

SHIP: HIGH TEMP—ENGINE BAY #2. HIGH TEMP—ENGINE BAY #4. "*Caution.*" RADIATION HAZARD.

RAYBO: They won't shut down!

SHIP: HIGH TEMP—ENGINE BAY #3. COOLING PUMPS AT MAX. PUMP FAILURE—ENGINE BAY #3. ENGINE ABORT.

RAYBO: So abort, abort! Abort yourself!

SHIP: ENGINE OVERRIDE—ACKNOWLEDGED.

RAYBO: Override? I didn't authorize [garbled]

SHIP: *"Caution. Caution."* TURBINE OVERSPEED—ALL ENGINES.

RAYBO: Son of a bitch.

SHIP: MAIN POWER ABORT WARNING. MAIN POWER OVERRIDE—ACKNOWLEDGED.

RAYBO: No override! Abort, abort!

SHIP: PROXIMITY ALARM—SHIP AT THE PERIMETER.

VIR: My God, Larry! We're going to crash!

SHIP: *"Ship in distress. Ship needs assistance. Home on my beacon. Ship in distress. Ship needs—"*

RAYBO: Code Red, Code Red; come in, Race Control. All systems failure, ship out of control, headed for the wall—

SHIP: WARP ENGINE ACTIVATED.

RAYBO: Now what's it doing?

VIR: Warp engine? Do you have a—

SHIP: PROXIMITY ALARM—FRONT. COLLISION WARNING.

VIR: What's *that*! The speedway's coming apart!

RAYBO: Oh, shit . . .

VIR: We're going inside!

SHIP: *"Caution."* EXPLOSION—AUX POWER BAY.

VIR: The ship's coming apart, Larry! I can see the [garbled]

RAYBO: [garbled]

SHIP: *"Good-bye, Raybo. Next time play by our rules."*

RAYBO: Gajira, Gajira, you son of a— [GARBLED]

[STATIC HISS—TAPE ENDS]

CHAPTER 14

"Did you say Gajira?" asked Mike. "*Tadashi* Gajira?"

"Yeah," said Raybo. "That's the guy. A real crook."

Speedball plugged in and played the cockpit tape again, but Mike was too stunned to pay attention. Gajira a crook?

"What was that about a warp-something?" asked Speedball, jerking his control finger out of the black box.

"Warp engine, warp drive, whatever you want to call it," said Raybo. "Gajira had it installed for me—thought we were going to do some smuggling or something."

"But you didn't," said Speedball. "And you never meant to."

"Naw, but I surely did wanna get me a warp engine. Unfortunately, I let it slip I was stringing him along—which is probably why he programmed my ship to go haywire. Who told you? Russell?"

"Russell's dead."

Raybo looked confused. "Dead?"

"Who's Russell?" asked Margie, her voice somewhat muffled by the chunk of burned rodent in her mouth.

"My old copilot," Speedball and Raybo said simultaneously.

"Oh, that sounds weird," said Margie. "Do it again."

"No," they both said.

Margie looked at Mike. "Doesn't that sound weird? You try it."

"Shut up and eat your rat," said Mike.

She smiled. "I know you like me."

"I think," said Raybo, "we're straying from the subject."

"That's right," said Margie. "Did you go over the high side or not?"

"*I* didn't," said Raybo. "But the warp engine must have

been blown free by the explosion. It probably went through the wall into real—"

"*That's* what caused the blue sparks!" said Mike. "I've seen the pictures. *Every*body in *Pitfall* has seen the—"

"Glad to hear it," said Raybo.

Speedball said, "So your ship got sucked into the hole in the track."

"Obviously," said Raybo. "We stumbled onto some old webtube that was left over when—"

"The *Spider*-makers," said Speedball. "This planet is one of their way stations."

"Hey, pal, don't tell me. I've been living here on Fantasy Island for thirteen hundred and forty-five—"

"Yeah, yeah," said Speedball. "You're a monster of survival."

"Very funny," said Raybo. "Just tell me when the bus leaves."

"It don't," said Speedball.

"We flew here in the old track sweeper," said Mike.

"The *Spider*?" said Raybo. "I thought that hunk of junk was in a museum."

"It was," said Margie, "until just a little while ago. And I'll have you know it's *not* a hunk of—"

"So where is it?" asked Raybo, ignoring her.

"It took off," said Mike.

"There was a recall order on the program stack," said Speedball. "Maybe it went back to Pitfall."

"We're screwed if it did," said Raybo. " 'Cause we're gonna need a warpship to get back on the web."

Tanya said, "Too bad they can't fix the old one."

"Old one what?" asked Margie.

Raybo laughed.

"The old spider," said Tanya.

"Another piece of junk," said Raybo. "Forget about it."

Mike looked at Speedball. *Interested?*

You bet.

The next morning the bunch of them went hiking through the brush, up an overgrown trail. Scarface flew on ahead.

The pale red star looked fat, nearly five times wider than

the sun as seen from Earth. (Sunrise this morning had taken eleven minutes and twenty-three seconds; Margie had timed it.) According to Speedball the star was only about five million kilometers away—close enough for a natural planet to become face-locked. But the day here was only a few hours longer than a day on Earth—more evidence of terraforming, in Speedball's opinion.

At this distance, even a dim star felt hot. Mike noticed Margie was sweating, and that seemed to amuse him.

Raybo was telling them what to expect. "Through these trees there's a wide meadow full of purple grass. Nothing else will grow there."

"The old spider is right in the middle," said Tanya. "Rusting in a heap. Like me."

"A most delicious heap," said Speedball. "If I may say so."

"Ooooo," she said. "I like him!"

Raybo turned to glare. "Back off, brother. I know where your off button is."

Speedball laughed. "Be the last thing you ever touched."

Margie said, "Something's been bothering me, Tanya."

"What, darling?"

"How come you look so young?"

"She's Poldavian," said Raybo.

Tanya said, "I shed my skin, honey, every year or so."

"It's worse than crackers in bed," said Raybo.

Mike studied Tanya's blue skin with curiosity until he saw Raybo glaring at him. Mike turned away, embarrassed, and caught sight of something sparkling through the trees. "Hey, isn't that—"

"Thc sweeper!" said Margie, running ahead.

"Something's wrong . . ." said Mike. A few more steps, and they broke through into the clearing. Scarface came flapping over and landed on Mike's shoulder.

"There's *two* of them," said Tanya.

There were. The *Spider* rested beside a corroding hulk—its disintegrating twin.

Raybo said, "You came here in that thing?"

"We were shanghaied," said Speedball.

When they had gotten within ten meters Mike noticed

the two craft were not simply sitting there, side by side. There were a number of steel-ribbed connections running between them.

"What are they doing?" asked Speedball.

Tanya said, "I'm not sure I want to see this. It might be . . . personal."

"Don't be silly," said Raybo. "They're just machines."

"I resent that," said Speedball.

"We'll talk about *your* case later."

Margie said, "It looks to me like some sort of jump start."

"Maybe that's why the *Spider* took off like that," said Mike, "running through the leak in the track. Maybe it was coming here. *Right* here."

"It's kind of romantic," said Tanya.

Raybo said, "Can you really control that thing?"

"Not exactly," said Speedball.

"Well, can't you do something? You know, machine-to-machine."

Speedball laughed. "I don't think so. It doesn't like me anymore."

"But you know how it works, right?"

"Maybe you'd better talk to Mike. He's the sweeper expert."

Raybo turned and squinted at Mike. "Do you think you could fix it?"

"Which one?"

"Take your pick."

Mike moved closer. There was a faint growling noise coming out of one of the machines. "I don't know."

"Yeah, well, I feel like an idiot even asking," said Raybo.

Mike stared at him. No doubt about it, he liked Speedball better. "Let me give it some thought," he said. "I might be able to come up with something."

Twyla snuggled down into the pilot's seat. Jass asked her how it felt. "Not bad." She looked over at him. "*Slippery Cat*'s a tandem three-A class, just like this. I've spent time in both seats."

"Well, the one you're in now is available for that last eliminator heat—if you want it."

"I want it—but I don't understand. I thought you were against the Gajira people."

"I am. And I trust you to figure it out for yourself."

"But you don't trust Mike."

"It means too much to Mike."

"You think he'll make the wrong decision?"

"Let's just say, I hope you can knock him out of the race so he won't have to face it."

Twyla touched the controls lightly. "I think it can be done."

"Good."

"But what makes you think being a master doesn't mean that much to me?"

Jass smiled. "You're a better pilot than he is, so you have more chances."

"He's not that bad."

"No, but he's too eager. He can't let this opportunity pass by. His confidence is . . . well, let's just say I feel responsible for his desperation."

Twyla looked over, then quickly away. She recognized that pitiful expression from the time Jass visited her in the hospital growth tank—following the near-fatal accident he'd caused. She didn't want to think about the way he looked. It was like watching her father cry.

Mike worked with Dwaine on the maintenance of the *Slippery Cat*, going over the ship until it was absolutely tight. She didn't say much, and he got the impression that she blamed him for Twyla's exit.

It was the same with Andru. He and Mike went through the tactical programs in great detail, but the Merkek never showed much enthusiasm.

During a lunch break, Mike said, "I hear Twyla's got a ride with Jass Blando."

"Should be interesting," said Andru. "You two haven't flown one-on-one since your sessions in the simulator." He turned to Dwaine, who was stirring sweetener in her iced tea with one pair of hands and peeling the tough blue skin off an

Ooloovian apple with the other. "On the intercom they called themselves Alley Cat and the Junkyard Dog. You sort out which was which."

"Thanks," said Mike.

Dwaine said, "I remember." She smiled briefly at Mike. "You two were pretty evenly matched."

"Right," said Andru. "Twyla knew what she was doing, and Mike did what he didn't know was impossible."

"I know a little more now," said Mike.

"And so take fewer risks," said Andru. "It's a toss-up whether you've moved ahead or not."

Mike shrugged, and snagged a bit of oily lettuce with his chopsticks. A taste for green salad was a little something left over from Lek's old team evaluator, S. Richardson Eddington. He asked them what had happened to the guy, but neither Andru nor Dwaine knew.

"I hope he found his way to a planet," said Mike. "That's what he always wanted."

Thinking about Eddington reminded him of the old days, when they were all waiting for Twyla to get out of the growth tank. Only difference was, this time she wasn't coming back.

Mike turned around and saw everybody watching him. He waved, felt like a fool, and turned back to stare at the alien warpships. Obviously there was no point in trying to fix the old one—it looked as if it would crumble to dust in the next five minutes. He approached instead the bright yellow *Spider.*

The closer he got, the louder was the purring noise. The heavy ribbed cables that connected them hung down in gentle curves. He half expected to see bulges of strange fluid pumping through the hoses, like some cartoon version of a refueling. But the hoses—or cables (he really didn't know what they were)—hung motionless.

Mike walked slowly all the way around the two ships, trying to remember just one thing he might have picked up from his visits to the Racing Museum. At this point it might not even matter *what* fact he remembered—just so he could make a start at remembering *some*thing.

The *Spider*'s twin was dark and rust-stained, with skinny

legs so hobbled and knee-sprung its belly actually touched the dirt, where even the purple grass refused to grow. Its cockpit windows were pitted and streaked—though not so badly as he had thought, seeing it for the first time through the trees. Even the paint looked brighter. Maybe the sun had come out from behind a cloud.

Mike finished his circuit, and looked back at the others. They were still staring at him.

This is ridiculous, he thought. Do they really expect me to fix the damned thing?

How's it look? asked Speedball.

How do you think? said Mike. *It sucks.*

The *Spider*'s cockpit had sealed up again, so he ducked to crawl under its belly, where the airlock hatch was. But when he reached for the skin a bright arc of electricity jumped out at him.

Zzzzzzzwhap!

Mike fell back and rubbed his tingling metal hand. Several hundred jumbled memories orbited his head for a moment, then faded away. "My goodness . . ."

Speedball knelt beside him in the purple grass. "Maybe you ought to try the other one."

"That's ridiculous."

"Why?"

"For one thing, I can't even get inside the damned thing."

"What's wrong with belly hatch?"

"Well, just look at—" Mike stopped. The legs of the ancient machine had flexed, and now there was room beneath it. "Something's happening," he whispered.

"I know," Speedball whispered back. "It seems the *Spider* is pumping new life into the old guy."

"But what does that mean?"

"I don't know. Why are we whispering? Do you think it can hear us?"

"You think it can't?"

"Interesting point."

Twyla sat strapped in the pilot's seat, watching the screens as the rollout carriage shoved *Bad Momma* through

the airscreen. Jass sat beside her, manning the tactical computer and the antijamming console.

"Stay alert," he said.

"Okay."

After a moment he said, "That was a stupid thing for me to say, wasn't it?"

She laughed. "Couldn't hurt."

She tried to relax, but the seat just wasn't as comfortable as her old one in the *Slippery Cat*. She took a deep breath.

It was to be a short race. Ten laps at a distance of eighty million kilometers, with the groove set at three and a half times the speed of light. The press was playing it up big for the Tricentennial. The race favorite proclaimed by most of the tout sheets was some guy she'd never heard of. Pitfall was a big place.

Race Control got on the line: "Pilots, test your engines."

Twyla was about to tap the main-engine start switch when she stopped to check her position. "Damn . . ." she whispered. She was still a hundred meters inside the one-kilometer safety zone. "These are tricky people . . ."

She boosted with thruster jets until she was clear, then tapped the main engines at ten percent thrust.

"Looks good," said Andy Veekle on the tech comm.

"Copy," said Jass.

Twyla shut down the mains, adjusting her speed with the forward thrusters. She looked over at Jass. "Was I late or did they really hope to catch me lighting off inside the safety zone?"

"Hard to tell." His face was hidden behind the reflective sun visor of his pressure-suit helmet.

Twyla checked her viewscreens, running through the cameras one by one. A number of ships approached the starting-line warp zone that circled the inside of Pitfall. One of them was the *Slippery Cat*.

She wondered how Mike was getting on.

"Settle down, damn it!" said Mike.

Lek squirmed around in the right-hand seat. They were at the entrance to the spin-up circle, waiting for a go light from Race Control.

Lek said, "I'm all right, Mike," then laughed. "This is gonna be great." He grabbed the disconnected copilot's stick and whipped it back and forth.

"Please," said Mike. "If you accidentally got control, I'd be dead in this race. You're just here to—"

"Oh, yeah. Computer op, right? Sorry, Mike."

Race Control keyed its transmitter, filling Mike's ears with static. "Pilots . . ."

"Let's go!" said Lek, grabbing the stick again.

"Leave that the hell alone!"

"—light, enter the spin-up circle," said Race Control.

"Which light?" said Mike. "The white light? Did they say—"

"I don't know."

"Normally it's the white light," said Mike. "For a controlled lineup. They wouldn't change it, would they? Just for this one race?"

"I don't know."

"Wait a minute, if it's a racing start, I'm looking for a green light. What did the guy say?"

"Beats me." Lek's hands continued to paw the controls. "Come on, come on, come on . . ."

Mike watched the panel. It was too late now to ask Race Control to repeat the instructions—he'd look really lame. But which was it, white or green? He decided to go on the first light that lit up.

"Come on, come on, come on!" said Lek. He suddenly broke out laughing. "God, I love flying!"

"Get your hands *off* the controls!" said Mike.

"I love this, I love this . . ." muttered Lek. His fingers ran lightly over the panel.

Mike couldn't look.

"Stand by," said Race Control. "We're waiting for a timer reset."

"Come on, *come on*." said Lek.

The tech-comm light flickered. The radio hissed, then Dwaine said, "Hey, Mike, I'm reading shutdown on a main coolant pump."

"Oh, no . . ."

Mike checked his board, then looked over at Lek. "Could you—"

"What?" asked Lek.

Mike swore and reached across to reset a circuit breaker Lek had inadvertently flicked off.

"It's back on now," said Dwaine. "What's the deal?"

"Stand by," said Race Control.

Lek looked at Mike. "They make us wait. This is the part I hate."

"Yeah, me too."

After about a million years the green panel light came on, and Mike sent the ship through the warp zone and into the spin-up circle. A racing start.

Lek began to laugh hysterically.

CHAPTER 15

Margie said, "You on a break or what?"

"I'm just gathering my wits," said Mike.

"Well, it couldn't possibly take *this* long. Get to work."

Mike stood for a moment, looking at the two machines. The more he stared at the ugly old spider, the more depressed he got. There was simply no way he was ever going to get that thing running. He said, "You know, maybe we should wait a bit, give the *Spider* a chance to calm down. I mean, that's the ship that got us here. I don't see why it can't be the one that—" He stopped, his imaginary mouth hanging open.

The museum's *Spider* had begun to scream. It gave a shudder, snapped back its steel hoses, and rose straight into the air. It was out of sight before Margie could finish saying, "What in the hell is it doing now?"

Mike sat down in the purple grass and looked at the piece of junk that was left. Yes, things were really starting to work out.

Vicky Slicky was in front of the nav computer, watching the numbers as the ship neared the exit point into real space. In her earphone she could hear Mary-All in the engine room, arguing with Dixie Jewell and Craig Show about the cargo pod.

Vicky keyed the intercom. "I don't care how you do it, Mary-All, just get a consensus—anything I can take to the cap."

She looked up from the screen. The first mate, Bowker Ferguson, was staring at her. "Problem?" he asked.

"Nope. Just checking the engine readouts. Got some fluctuation in the cataform field."

Ferguson nodded. Captain Bent was in his cabin, but due on the bridge for the transition to real space.

Vicky let her eyes go unfocused, listening on the intercom. Dixie Jewell wanted to say nothing about the cargo—just business as usual. Craig Show told her to wise up.

"What's that supposed to mean?" asked Dixie.

"Just that not every cargo Bent might take on is equally safe and proper."

"It's safe," said Dixie. "I inspected the launch pod myself. You saying I don't know what—"

"Oh, sure," said Craig, "*we're* safe—maybe—but that doesn't mean the cargo is safe for—"

"That's not our problem!" said Dixie. "We just deliver what folks—"

"What folks *want* ain't always what they *ought* to have."

"What, you their mommy? You gonna tell 'em what they can and cannot—"

"Dixie, I'm just saying there are limits. There are lines we shouldn't cross."

Again Vicky Slicky spoke softly into the intercom. "Come on, Mary-All, make 'em—"

"All right, all right," said Mary-All. Her voice became slightly muffled and distant. "Come on, you guys. Vicky wants to know what we're gonna do. The captain will be on the bridge in five minutes."

"Sooner," said Vicky.

Mary-All ignored her. "All right, Dixie—you say hands off, do our job. Craig—you say . . . what? Dump the stuff? Refuse to deploy? What?"

"I say, let's sit on the capt'n till he tells us exactly what is in the pod. Then we decide what to do with it."

Dixie said, "And if he won't tell you?"

"Then we assume the worst, and destroy it."

"You're crazy! First of all, Capt'n Bent won't tell you squat—not because the cargo is really bad, but because that's the kind of guy he is. He doesn't like getting pushed around."

"We could *make* him like it."

"Oh, big man," said Dixie, her voice pitched well into the ironic. "Look, it's *his* ship and he can do any damned thing he pleases."

"Yeah? Well the Union of Freighthandlers and Ship's Mechanics might have something to say about that."

Not after they find out what we've already agreed to transport. Not after their accountants get a look at the bonus system we got going here. We'd be lucky to stay out of jail. And I don't know about you, but I don't want any wires in *my* head."

"Come on, come on," said Vicky Slicky. "We only got a few minutes. He's gonna—"

"The numbers, missy," said a booming voice behind her. "How do they look?"

Vicky didn't turn from the computer screens. "On the nose, *Cap*." She heard Mary-All telling the others that Bent was on the bridge, and subsequently the argument in the engine room got so loud Vicky was afraid the captain would hear it leaking out of her earphones.

She said, "We're at Clypsis Gate, Cap," then keyed a recorded warning that played on the PA throughout the ship: "Attention all personnel—prepare for transition into real space. Observe all health and safety regulations. Transition in ten seconds . . . nine . . . eight . . ."

" . . . four . . ." said Vicky, cutting in with the live update. " . . . three . . . two . . ."

She stopped to grit her teeth against the vibration. Her stomach crawled up and down her windpipe like a trained snake; then viewscreens cleared, and Clypsis burned like a hot yellow spark in the black sky. The computer locked onto the datastream from Pitfall beacon and compared the star's image with its measured output.

"Two point oh eight gigaklicks," said Vicky.

"Very nice," said Bent.

Ferguson was busy messing with the display. The star dimmed, and the web of speedway tracks grew bright. The computer plotted the positions of the planets, marking them on the screen in perspective.

"Very nice," repeated Bent. He sounded sleepy.

Vicky said, "I've got a course set for the nearest Pitfall portal." She kept her voice neutral. "Permission to run it, Cap." Her hand went to the keyboard.

"Uh, no, Vicky, we're not going to the portal right away."

"Sir?"

"Our first business is with Clypsis."

"Clypsis?"

"That's right, honey, so tell your friends in the engine room." He was halfway through the hatch when he turned. "Incidentally, when I want those clowns to know what's in that pod, I'll bloody well tell 'em—and not before."

Mike directed his eyes across the grid, found the fuel symbol, and blinked twice. The techscreen flipped through the displays, one by one. It didn't look good. The race was nearly over, and Twyla was out front in *Bad Momma*. The *Cat* was a few hundred meters back.

Fuel was low, especially in the fusion tanks. If it got much worse, he wouldn't have enough to pump through his outdated electromagnets. It only took a five-degree rise to hit the superconducting threshold.

Lek was playing with the ECCM console, laying out random targets and sending pulses of radar jamming in every direction. As long as he stayed amused, he was out of Mike's hair (what there was of it).

The ship crossed the plane of the ecliptic from the north. Last lap. A few ships dropped onto the track from pipelines, but nobody was close enough to threaten the results.

Twyla first, Mike second.

If the race ended like this, she'd get the jump-to-master bid, and Mike could get another haircut and go back to sweeping tracks.

Damn.

"Put more targets on her screen," he said, but Lek was humming to himself, making the bogies fly in formation. Mike lit his mains and edged up, but shut them down when he caught sight of the fuel graph dropping.

Twyla never budged. She might have fuel, or she might not. It didn't matter; Mike was too far back to challenge. On the other hand, if he could nose up a bit and use the ramscoop, he might be able to conserve his fuel—while forcing Twyla to dump her hot exhaust through his engines.

"I got an idea," said Mike. "When I say, put one big target on the screen, coming right at her. We'll panic her into lighting her mains."

Lek wasn't paying any attention.

"Come on, man!" said Mike. "Help me!"

"Mmmm?"

Mike could see only a confusion of lights reflected in Lek's visor. "Never mind." Mike leaned over and programmed the ECCM deck. "Now, don't touch anything."

"Mmmm?"

Mike lit his mains and started dumping his reserves. When he was fifty meters back he keyed the ECCM program and cut his engines. But the tac screen reacted to the false radar target, so it looked as if Mike was charging like a maniac right at Twyla's exhaust nozzles.

"Coming to getcha, babe!"

The target swept up through the distance between them—and kept on going, plowing right through her ship in simulated collision. Mike was stunned.

She never even *twitched*.

He ran a fast diagnostic on the ECCM deck, but it was fine. The signals were getting out, painting on her tac screen.

"Is she *crazy*?" he asked. "If that had really been my ship . . ."

Then he remembered.

The last time he used this trick, *she* was the one running the ECCM board. She knew it was the sort of thing he'd try, and she just wasn't buying it.

"Son of a bitch . . ."

Half a lap to go.

Lek was leaned way back in his flight chair. According to his suit monitors, he was asleep. More good news.

Suddenly Mike's tac screen erupted with a dozen targets. Jagged streaks of yellow light swept across the screen, obscuring everything. It was just Twyla's way of saying, "We got our own ECCM deck, sucker. Pick a target."

"All right," said Mike. "Pick one of mine."

He set the target deck to mimic his ship—coasting meekly behind *Bad Momma*—then keyed the same evasion program, with the same fat target blasting right up the middle

of the groove. Other bogies spun and twiddled, breaking through the velocity shear in electronic bravado.

Mike lit off his mains and kicked the control stick over to set the ship spinning. He left the groove, allowing the slightest wobble to develop. On the screen he looked like the most bogus target imaginable, so incredibly anonymous that when he got close to Twyla she ignored him completely.

What the hell, she knew this trick, and she could see he was still floating behind her in the groove, trying to look inconspicuous.

Mike eased over toward the groove, fighting the shear, the last of his fusion fuel gushing into the plasma tubes. Stress-shocks hissed and engine warnings bleeped as the final seconds ticked down. He held his breath. The ship bucked and creaked, fuel tanks depleted and growing hot.

Come on, come on!

The start/finish line flashed by, and Twyla shut down her jamming. Mike did the same, and when the screens cleared he was fifteen meters in front.

He couldn't believe it. Twyla had been so flummoxed by the electronic blizzard she had never even lit her mains.

Mike stared at the screen to make sure. He was concentrating so hard he almost missed the announcement from Race Control. The results were official—he had nailed the Alley Cat's hide to the wall.

His laughter woke Lek up.

Mike rolled onto his back and shoved himself under the drooping belly of the alien machine. Scarface climbed up onto his face and squealed at him. "Not now!" said Mike, prying him loose. *"Seezee!"* Scarface crawled away, teeth chattering.

Mike reached out for the lip of the hatch, then jerked his hand back. He turned his head to look at Speedball, who was crouched down in the shadow of the ancient ship. "If *this* guy bites me, that's it. I'm done. We go looking for a place to build a nice cottage or something."

"Try it," said Speedball.

The machine creaked and groaned, raising up a bit higher. Mike saw one of the knee joints quivering, and he

wondered how long before the whole thing dropped down and squashed him into scrap metal.

He reached out again, hesitated, then thought, Go ahead and touch the damned thing. Get it over with.

He lightly tapped the old spider with one steel finger. Nothing. Encouraged, he slipped his hand into the latching hole and felt around for the switch. It was stuck. He pushed hard against the corrosion, then heard it clunk into place. The hatch began to squeal and hiss, scraping open in noisy spasms.

Mike yelled, rolling out from under. The air that blew over him smelled flat, and the dust drizzling from the hatch was like the finest talc.

"He's in!" shouted Speedball.

"Oh, good," Mike said to himself. "An optimist."

It was a tight fit, of course—but he was expecting that. He just hadn't guessed how hard it would be going up that slippery tunnel in a one-g field.

At the inner hatch he extended his steel toes, braced them in the slots, and toggled the switch. The hatch popped, whining as it lifted, then slid out of the way. The air that hit him now smelled like the nether end of Death—and he didn't know how to tune it out.

Mike peered into the reddish light coming through the windows—ports that now sparkled, clean and polished, though no one had touched them. He raised up slowly and looked around. "Damn . . ." he whispered.

Sitting in the control chairs were heaps of bone and skin, collapsed into rotted piles.

A metallic scraping noise startled him, and Mike leapt out of the hatchway and into the cockpit. Speedball said, "Now are you in?"

"Completely."

A shiny steel head rose above the hatch's lip. "Uh-oh. Who are they?"

"Just another pair of troubleshooters," said Mike. "Only I get the feeling they couldn't figure it out."

"Spidermites," said Speedball. "Do you think they built this thing?"

"Or raised it from a pup, do you mean?"

"Whatever."

"I don't know. But I'll tell you one thing: I'm not even *looking* at this tub of junk until they're out of here."

"Done."

When Speedball dropped the first package of blackened bones down the entrance tube, Mike heard Margie scream his name. He raised up and waved at her from the cockpit. She stood for a moment, eyes wide, holding her hand over her mouth, then sat down abruptly in the grass.

"I guess she thought it was me," he told Speedball.

"Plenty of time for that."

Speedball dropped the other parcel of corruption to the ground, and Mike said, "This doesn't mean a thing to you, does it?"

"You're in a position to answer that one."

"Yeah, but what happens to me when we get back to Pitfall?"

"What do you mean?"

"Well, there'll be no reason to keep *me* alive on the datanet, will there?"

"I guess not."

"I just keep remembering what happened to Squib when Twyla came out of the tank. You know, I can't help but wonder what it's going to feel like to have my mind disintegrate right in front of me."

"Don't worry about it. I'll buy you a dream-meld."

"What's that?"

"You'll go back on the net, then I'll bring Mike into the Brain Bank to take a little snooze. When he wakes up there'll just be one of you—and he'll have all your memories . . . and all his, too."

"Will I be him, or will he be me?"

"Everybody will be everybody. Don't you have work to do?"

"Tell me something."

"What?"

"Did you ask . . . me . . . Mike . . . if you could copy him and . . . uh, check me out of the Bank?"

"What's the matter? You bored?"

"Just curious."

Speedball hesitated in the hatchway. "Mike, I would never do anything to hurt you."

"Yeah, but—"

"We'll talk about it when we get back. Okay?"

Speedball then dropped out of sight, down the entrance tube, to see to the burial of the alien remains. Mike watched him through the porthole, saw the way the automaton knelt with care to place the bones on the ground. It was really rather touching.

Mike brushed the pilot's seat off and sat down at the main control console. Those switches and lights that were labeled were, of course, labeled in mightily strange script. Under the add-on panel, the *Spider* had had the same layout, but as far as Mike knew, nobody had ever tried to operate the ship with the alien controls. Not recently, anyway.

He tentatively tapped the panel, probing for electric zaps, but the ship was so far unarmed. Okay, nice start.

Mike flicked off all the switches he figured ought to be off when main power was applied, then put his steel thumb under a big red toggle he hoped was the power-on switch.

He hesitated, without knowing why. Everybody was waiting for him to do the impossible, and it suddenly occurred to him how ridiculous that was—and how disappointed everybody would be if he threw the switch and nothing happened. Or worse—if the old spider just got up and flew away like its brother, leaving Mike's friends on the purple planet forever.

Not that Mike would be in such good shape, stuck inside. How long had the dead pilots flown helplessly through the warpweb? And more important, had their fatal error begun by flipping up the power-on switch?

Interesting question, that—well worth a bit of a think.

So Mike took his thumb off the red switch and leaned back in the alien chair. After all, there was plenty of time . . .

"Hurry up!" said Speedball, poking his head back inside. Mike jumped, his mechanical heart banging like crazy. "C'mon, Mike. Folks are counting on ya!"

Mike got off the chair and paced around the cockpit,

thinking, I'm too human to operate one of these damned things.

"Have you found the main power switch?"

"It's got to be this one," said Mike, pointing at the red toggle.

"Then, let's go," said Speedball, reaching for it.

"*No!*"

"What's the matter? You nervous?"

Mike laughed without looking at him.

"Sorry," said Speedball. "Don't mean to pressure you."

"Then, leave!"

He did. After another minute, Mike got down on his hands and knees and peered under the control panel. He didn't know what he was looking for, but it occurred to him that if there was nothing unusual to look at on top of the panel, maybe it was time to take a peek inside.

He popped the latches and swung the doors apart. For a moment, as he gazed blindly into the dark compartment, things seemed to flow and squirm and shift back out of sight.

Mike cautiously moved forward, sliding slowly on his knees, until he was crammed halfway inside the bay. His eyes adjusted themselves by degrees, and after a moment he reached out to touch—

"What's in there?" asked Speedball, and Mike banged his head on the bottom of the control panel. He backed out and lay down on the floor. "I thought you were leaving."

"Whatcha doing?"

"I don't know. I just remembered something from an old lecture or something. Aren't there some switches inside? Maintenance switches of some sort?"

"Could be," said Speedball. "That'd be where I'd put 'em."

Mike nodded. "I was going to look for them, but it was dark in there and I had to wait for my eyes to adjust—then you came back and I banged my head."

"Yeah, I saw that. You ought to be more careful." Speedball turned on one of his fingers and knelt down, focusing his beam inside the console. "How's this?"

Mike rolled over and crawled back to the bay. "Shine it over here." The innards glistened and quivered in the light.

"Looks like the guts of a spaghetti squash," he said. "Wait a minute, here's something." A line of toggle switches stuck out, looking rather like finger bones. All of them were down but one.

An image popped into Mike's brain, something from his studies of the museum's *Spider.* "I *know* those switches," he said. "They're maintenance test switches."

"I would have guessed that," said Speedball. "What about the one that's up?"

"I think it's the switch that dumps control to the maintenance data buffer, where the test routines are supposed to be stored. Trying to fly like that would have been fatal, I'm sure." Mike reached out and flicked the one switch down. Nothing happened.

"Is that it?" asked Speedball. "Is it fixed now?"

"How should I know?" Mike kept looking around inside the bay, but he could see nothing else to mess with. As they crawled out and buttoned up the panel, he wondered if that could have been the whole problem. Mike stood up and banged his hands together in a wiping motion. "I guess the next thing to do is search the rest of the ship for strange switches."

Speedball said, "No time for that," and flipped the red toggle. The control panel beeped and lit up. "Perfect," he said.

Mike just stared at him and listened to the alarms going off inside his artificial body.

Jass caught up to them in the corridor at Pitfall Hospital, on the way in for the mandatory drug tests.

"Just hear me out, Mike. I've been doing some checking."

"Not interested."

"They're the wrong kind of people," said Blando. "Believe me, I ought to know."

Mike kept on walking. "I won the race, and if they offer me the job, I'm gonna take it. I earned it."

"You can't do that!"

"Try and stop me."

Mike turned to give Jass the benefit of his superior smirk, and got tangled up with Lek's feet.

"I shouldn't even *be* here," said Lek, giggling. His eyes looked haunted. "I mean, *I* wasn't flying, was I?"

Jass reached out and grabbed one of the coolant hoses that dangled from Mike's pressure suit. Mike whirled and jerked the hose loose. "Hands off, all right?"

"At least you could listen to me."

"You think they're crooks, right?" said Mike. "Okay, prove it. What do they do? Do they hang out with gamblers? Do they fix races? What? Do they shave lap times? What do they do that's so bad?"

"I can't be sure," said Jass. "But I think Gajira is the man who paid the bookie who put me in that bind a few months ago. I think he's the one behind the . . . deal . . . with the *Slippery Cat*." Jass tried to look at Mike but failed.

"The truth is," said Mike, "you can't be sure, can you?"

They stopped in front of the waiting-room door. A couple of other pilots were out front, talking nervously in quiet tones.

Mike told Jass, "If you'll excuse us . . ."

"I shouldn't have to take the test," said Lek.

One of the pilots looked him over. "Get a lawyer, friend. You're gonna need one."

Jass leaned close to Mike and spoke softly. "Don't you think I owe you a little good advice for once?"

Mike's voice was a little louder. "Look, you sabotaged my career once already. I'm not going to let you do me again. This is my chance to get on the map around here, and if they even *hint* at making the offer, I'm gonna be there with a big fat grin on my face. Now why don't you just take a hike?"

"Mike . . ."

"I mean it, old man."

Mike pushed the door open, then held it for Lek Croveen. "Hurry up!"

"Yes, boss!" said Lek, grinning broadly. His frivolous tone was a transparent lie, but Mike was too worked up to notice.

CHAPTER 16

Mike looked down through the spider's windows to where Speedball was reporting to Raybo about the machine's status. The bearded man smiled, and yelled at Tanya and Margie. "Pile on, everybody!"

Hey! said Mike. *Don't you think we ought to test this thing first?*

Speedball stood alone in the meadow, looking up at him. *I think they're in a hurry to get back. As a matter of fact, so are we.*

Oh, yeah—Dover Bell is trying to kill me . . . It sounded so strange to say someone was trying to kill him—and still feel perfectly safe. It's not really me, he thought. But it *is* me.

He heard noises in the airlock shaft, then Margie poked her head inside. "I don't believe you really fixed it."

She climbed inside, making way for Tanya. Next came Raybo. He nodded at the lights on the alien console. "Very good. I like it."

Raybo climbed into the cockpit, then Speedball poked his head through the hatch. "Room for one more?"

"Are you kidding?" asked Mike. He pointed to the copilot's seat. "I want you—" Then he noticed Raybo already getting settled in there. "Well, either one of you . . . I guess."

Speedball's blank steel face hung for a long moment in the hatchway. "Maybe I'd be better off staying here."

"Aw, come on!" said Raybo. "I'll hold your hand."

"Please," said Mike, and Speedball got inside without a word and closed the hatch. Mike climbed into the pilot's seat, thinking, The dude's right—neither of us have much to look forward to in Pitfall.

"Everybody find something to grab onto," said Raybo,

and Tanya put her arms around his neck. "Somewhere else, darling."

Mike said, "I hope this thing holds the air long enough to get back."

"Maybe it'll make more," said Speedball.

"Oxygen?" said Raybo. "Is that likely?"

"If the same folks terraformed this planet—yes, it is likely."

"We'll see." Mike pulled back on the stick and the spider lifted from the ground. He let it drift sideways, across the ruddy landscape. "So far, so good."

Speedball said, "All right, Raybo, show him the place where you throw the coins."

"It's beyond the junkyard."

"What coins?" asked Mike.

"Yeah, that's right," said Speedball. "You've been busy."

"See, I had all these silver coins," said Raybo. "And I used to—"

"Oh!" said Mike. "The coins!" He slapped his steel thigh where regular folks had pockets. "I've got one . . . somewhere."

"I had lots of 'em," said Raybo. "A little something from my old pal Tadashi Gajira—to seal the deal, he said. I'm not sure where he got 'em, but there were rumors floating around Pitfall that—"

"Pitfall is always full of rumors," said Speedball. "What we need right now are directions."

"Over this hill and to the right."

"Thank you."

Mike nudged the ship's control yoke, and the spider picked up speed along the ground. "What about the coins?"

Raybo laughed. "Just to amuse myself, you understand, I'd stick a coin to my forehead and concentrate real hard, sort of mentally merge myself with the metal."

"Like a message in a bottle," said Tanya.

"Yeah," said Raybo. "Whatever. Anyway, I'd toss 'em at this little warp entrance I'd found. You know: trying to send 'em back to the speedway. 'Course, most of 'em just dumped out in the junkyard."

"A cul-de-sac," said Speedball.

"Obviously."

"But some of them were getting through," said Mike.

"Yeah," said Raybo. "So I gathered." He pointed through the cockpit glass. "There it is."

Mike looked. A tiny chunk of sky glittered and swirled above him.

"Vary the warp field as you go up," said Speedball. "Close off any warp-tubes you might start."

"Why?"

"I don't want the atmosphere of this planet to follow us us back to Pitfall. Folks there are paranoid enough as it is."

"Gotcha."

I just hope we're not too late, said Speedball. *For Mike's sake.*

But Mike was thinking, What about me?

The big office was filled with the Gajira folks. Fyodor Willingham was there, and so was Rinehart Weel, the tax accountant who'd first interviewed Mike. There were also a couple of Merkeks who headed the maintenance team, and four more assorted aliens who were not introduced, so Mike didn't know what they did.

Larouse, the team leader, sat behind a fat brown desk and smiled a lot, and behind him stood the meanest-looking goon Mike had ever seen. Dark blue skin with green splotches and hands like catcher's mitts. He stared through Mike with two pairs of bright yellow eyes.

Larouse said, "I'm afraid Mr. Gajira couldn't be with us in person today. He's stuck in a teleconference, but he hopes to check in from time to time."

"Fine," said Mike, squirming around in his hard chair, despite the rather low-g gravity field.

Larouse just kept grinning at him like a used-spaceship salesman. "I guess you know why you're here."

Fyodor Willingham smiled and winked at Mike. The big blue guy just kept staring, as if he were trying to dissolve the skin off Mike's face.

Mike figeted some more, thinking, That guy's got coherent light coming out of his eyes . . .

"Mike?" said Larouse.

"Yes, sir."

"We like the way you handle a ship."

"Yes, sir."

"Now, God knows we weren't the happiest folks when we drew the jump-to-master promotion."

"No, sir."

"But now that we get a look at the talent unearthed by the competition . . . well, let me just say we're delighted."

Willingham winked again. The big blue guy seemed stone dead—except for the hot yellow eyes.

"What do you say?" asked Larouse. "You want the job?"

Mike hesitated. No one in the room moved a millimeter, smiles frozen on their faces. Who *were* these strange people? How was it going to be, working with them, living with them, going out for pizza with them?

He thought of Jass, his oldest friend in Pitfall—now against him, thanks to Mike's own bullheadedness. He thought of Speedball—missing and presumed dead (again). He thought of Twyla and Lek—bound by ropes of error and loyalty, drifting away. Mike sensed he was at a crossroads in his life. This could easily be the worst decision he ever made.

Mike cleared his throat. "Damned right I want this job!" Might as well sound like you mean it . . .

Still no one moved. He wondered if they had heard him. His own ears seemed to be filled with static—the sound of blood crashing through his head. He felt positively dizzy.

Was it too late to back out?

Larouse began to nod vigorously. "Yes, yes, yes! Welcome aboard, Mr. Murray. Welcome aboard."

The big blue guy just stood there, burning holes through Mike's skull.

Quohogs was almost deserted. The Anti-Meat League had dispersed and gone home for dinner. Twyla sat with Jass Blando at a clean table. Neither of them had ordered, or wanted to.

"I don't know what he's going to do," said Twyla.

"He shouldn't have gone in there."

"Are you kidding, he was so whacked he probably thought it wouldn't show up. I don't think he thought he'd ever be tested. He wasn't flying, you know."

"It's the Tricentennial," said Jass. "The Racing League doesn't want any hint of impropriety."

Twyla laughed without humor. "Well, it's too late for that. This town is full of HIPErs, and always has been."

"Yeah, but it seems to be getting worse. The price is going down. And I've been told the stuff is stronger, full of unpredictable impurities, something like that. Every day the news is nothing but HIPE, HIPE, HIPE."

Twyla stared at the empty table. "They suspended him, Jass. They took his ticket. The ship's been impounded."

"Ah, jeez . . ."

"He'll go nuts," said Twyla. "If he can't race . . . I don't know *what* he'll do. He doesn't have brain tapes, you know."

"Have you talked to him?"

"Talk to him? I can't even *find* him."

Mike was in Lek's deserted pit, gathering up his junk, when the call came in for him. He thought it might be Mr. Gajira, welcoming him to the team, but he was wrong. It was Dover Bell.

"How ya doing, dwarf?" said Bell. "Staying alive?" As he laughed, a power fluctuation distorted his image on the comm screen, making him look disturbingly evil.

Mike said, "What do you want, Dover? I'm running a little late."

"Hey, you're a hard guy to get hold of, you know? I'm sure I saw you the other day on the Strip, but the next thing I know, you're gone. You avoiding me, or what?"

"I'm just busy, that's all."

"Yeah, I heard of your good fortune."

"Thanks."

"I didn't say anything that requires thanks."

"You're right. I guess I was reading between the lines. What do you want, Dover?"

"I found out something you might want to know."

"What?"

Dover giggled. ''It's a secret, Mike. Not the sort of thing I want to blab out on a comm screen, you know?''

''So what do you want to do?''

''Let's get together, someplace where nobody will disturb us.''

''I can't right now. I'm late.''

''Soon, okay?''

''Sure.''

''I'll be in touch.''

Mike broke the connection, feeling pissed off. But then he thought, Oh, what the hell, maybe I ought to be nicer to the guy. He's never actually *done* anything but talk big.

Mike decided that the next time Bell called, he would meet him and get it over with.

Mike stood off to the side in the Gajira pit, waiting for the *Universe* to finish fueling. He'd never been inside one of the big Five Star pits, and he was wearing himself out just trying to see it all. The joint was purely bloated with wide-track lifting robots and derricks and rollout jigs and racks upon racks of gleaming spare parts. In the spaces left over, serious-faced workers hurried from job to job. Mike stayed near the door and tried to keep out of folks' way. He was afraid of getting trampled.

Willingham came up, swaggering in the low-g field. ''How ya getting along, Mike?''

''I keep expecting somebody to hand me a broom.''

''Wait till you get strapped into the pilot's seat. You'll remember what you're doing here.''

''Are you kidding? I can hardly remember my name.''

Willingham grinned. ''The first time I saw you, I knew you'd be our guy.''

''Yeah?''

''You got that look.''

Mike rubbed a hand over his bristly head. ''I *used* to have that look.''

Willingham said, ''Be sure to talk to our accountant. He's got some tricks that'll come in handy at tax time.''

''I never made so much I had to *pay* taxes—beyond the standard utilities fee.''

Willingham laughed. "Mark my words, kid. You're gonna be rich someday."

After he left, Mike noticed the big blue guy watching him from across the hangar. He just kept staring . . . and staring . . . and staring.

What the hell did the goon want?

Mike vowed to stay out of the big guy's shadow . . .

Not long after, Mike was relieved to be called aboard the *Universe* for his check flight. Defoe, one of the junior pilots, took him out. "Where's Willingham?" asked Mike.

"Where do you expect?" said Defoe. "Back in his office."

Mike nodded. It was good to be reminded of his true status on the team. Naturally Willingham was too busy for stuff like this.

They slipped out of the hangar and confirmed their request for an empty test track. Race Control kept them waiting for a few minutes, while the spin-up circle cleared out. Pitfall was building to the Tricentennial Classic with a flurry of small-scale races.

"*Universe*, be advised you're next in the gate."

"Copy, Control," said Defoe. He looked at Mike. "I guess you've read the specs."

"Yeah, and I've logged some hours on your simulator."

"That thing hasn't been the same since some clown crashed it into Clypsis."

"Tough break," said Mike, trying to sound nonchalant.

When they got the word, Defoe aimed the huge ship into the equatorial warp zone. The darkness spread over them—

—and they were in the spin-up circle, quickly accelerating.

The nose of the ship wobbled around erratically. Mike's hands were poised over the controls, but not quite touching. "You want me to take it?"

"You'll be the first to know, Murray."

In less than a minute the spin-up circle had dumped them onto an empty track. Defoe keyed a series of automatic diagnostic programs. The ship twitched around in the groove, thrusters firing, numbers flashing on the many techscreens. A warning chimed, then two of the main engines lit off, and

Mike felt a mild surge. The engines shut down, and the screens filled with numbers and graphs. Next, the other two engines ignited, held thrust, and shut down. More numbers.

Defoe said, "The ship's been off the track for weeks—on display, or some stupid thing. I don't want to open her up till I'm sure nothing shook loose."

Mike nodded, said nothing. The ship sure looked tight to him.

Lights on the engine computers flickered, as tuning instructions came in from the pit. Back in the control room a team of technicians were busy poring over the telemetry, and watching even bigger computers for suggestions.

"Number three's running a little hot," said Mike. "And I see one of the coolant pumps is off the revs profile."

"I know," said Defoe. "But that's not something you have to worry about. We have techs for that sort of thing."

"Yeah, but—"

"They see everything we see and a lot more. Just let 'em do their jobs, okay?"

"Fine."

Mike relaxed in his seat, with nothing to do but talk to himself.

Big mistake, man.

This was a *big* mistake.

Eventually Defoe let Mike fly the *Universe* around the main track—but would not allow him to go into a pipeline. Mike felt as if he were back in speedway kindergarten. It was degrading, man. Rules up the yim-yam, the hours sucked, and hey, Defoe was a definite *squealhead*.

The checkout run proceeded at a pace so slow it was almost boring. Trust a big team to take the life out of flying.

Off-shift, Mike stretched out in his tiny plastic hotel room, staring at the computer print-out of his master's certificate, which he'd taped to the wall. The Gajira Syndicate had come around with some money for better lodging, but Pitfall was so booked up with Tricentennial visitors Mike counted himself lucky to be able to stay where he was.

After a while he doused the light and let his mind wander. He saw himself at the controls of the *Universe*,

blasting like a maniac through the speedway, zipping nimbly through the glittering corridor of the pipeline, scorching the skins of ships so big he could hardly get clearance to pass.

He saw himself standing beside the ship after the race, its sides streaked and burnt, his own face running with sweat, all smudged and heroic-looking, as he accepted the swollen silver trophy, bright lights of the homeset cameras glaring in his half-closed eyes . . .

"Grand Champion Michael MacAlister Murray . . ." the announcer was saying.

Jass was there, and Twyla, and Lek Croveen, all of them smiling and nodding and looking proud just to have known Mike in the hectic days before his hour of triumph.

Speedball was there, his racing PV polished and gleaming, with Scarface perched on his shoulder, chattering and whining, looking lost and pathetic—

Mike broke out of his reverie, troubled by thoughts of Speedball and Scarface. What in the hell had happened to those guys? Where *were* they? And when—if ever—were they coming back?

Mike filled his lungs with the stale air of his dark little room. Suddenly it didn't matter what happened out there on the track in two days. Winning was nothing, if he couldn't share it with his friends.

Mike flew the spider all the way back to the purple planet, ignoring Raybo's insistent whine. "I don't care *what* you say," Mike said. "I'm not leaving him behind. He's already been orphaned once."

Mike guided the warp ship past the dumping ground and followed the faint paths through the purple grass. Nobody else said anything, and he knew this was torture for them. They had thought they were on their way home.

Just a little while longer, he thought. Just a little while . . .

He located the meadow and landed the craft in the same bare patch where it had lifted off. "I'll be right back."

Speedball popped the inner hatch for him, and Mike climbed down without a word. He opened the lower hatch and dropped to the ground. As he stepped out from under the

spider, all he could hear was the buzzing of insects and the hiss of the wind ruffling the pink trees that surrounded the meadow. He clapped his hands—a loud clanking sound. "*Klaino-vor!*" he yelled. "*Klaino-vor!*" Nothing, no response.

He thinks I abandoned him.

"*Klaino-vor!* Damn it!" Mike scrutinized the treeline, searching for the crazed flap of the lizard-bat's wrinkled gray wings. "Come on, you rotten little monster! I'm not leaving without you!"

Hurry up, Mike, said Speedball. *We got places to go and people to see.*

Mike ignored him. He started out across the meadow, trying to scan in all directions at once. Nothing moved, or chattered, or squealed.

"Damn it," he whispered.

After a few more minutes Speedball trotted across the meadow to him and grabbed his arm. "Come on, Mike. He must have gone off somewhere."

"He's here," said Mike, jerking free. "I *know* it."

"He might like it here, Mike. Maybe that's why he wasn't hanging around when we left."

"He wasn't here because *I* sent him away—and didn't call him when it was time to go."

"You don't know that for sure."

Mike said, "You're in a hurry, go on ahead."

"I can't do that."

"Well, damn it, I can't just leave—" He stopped. "What's that?" He ran clumsily toward a dark mound in the meadow. "Scarface!"

That's not him, said Speedball. *That's where I buried those guys we found in the spider.*

Mike wasn't listening. He saw the heaps of dirt, but that wasn't all. Something stirred there, moving slowly, as if in pain. "Oh, no . . ."

It was Scarface. He was lying face down on the open patch of dirt, his wings quivering. He'd been digging into the grave, trying to reach . . . *some*body.

Mike dropped to the ground beside him, calling his name. He lifted the animal, saw the slow, sideways lids close halfway, his huge, dark eyes staring out, dull with disinterest.

"I'm back," said Mike. "I didn't mean to leave you."

Scarface didn't move.

"What's the matter with him?" asked Margie, who had come over from the ship.

"I don't know," said Mike. He held the Klaat'k to his steel face, but could feel no psychic surge. "He's stunned."

"He's an orphan, Mike," said Speedball. "They never live very long away from their families."

"*I* was his family!" said Mike, pressing the animal to his face. "Why won't he—"

"You're not Mike, that's why," said Margie. "Give him to me."

She grabbed Scarface out of Mike's tender steel grip and brought him to her face. "Come on, baby." The Klaat'k reached in through the helmet's open faceplate and touched her chin with his little paws. "That's right," she said, as he stroked her cheeks. With a small cry, she went rigid, her eyes squeezed shut. Scarface clung to her helmet and squirmed around eagerly to get a better grip on her face. His eyes were also closed. Then Mike heard a sound the animal had never made before.

Scarface was purring.

Lek Croveen was all suited up, floating through the wide tunnel in the dark. The ribbed walls were grainy in his HIPEd-up eyes. At the inner lip he pressed through the airscreen and into Jaleel's shipyard.

It was dimly lit, deserted in the third shift, and crowded with junked ships. Dark shapes swung slowly in the null-g docking slips, scraping shiny arcs in their neighbors' rusty hulls. Dirty oil floated by in convoluted mists, collecting randomly in globules, red and green and glittering yellow, caught spinning in midair by some eddy of the artificial gravity.

Down at the end was a fenced-off area—one of dozens of police impound yards. Just outside the chain-link, a victim of the overflow, was the *Slippery Cat*.

Lek giggled, moving closer.

* * *

The track was dark and empty, ripping along at twice the speed of light. The ship glided down the groove in perfect trim, alone and silent.

Inside the cockpit, screens and instruments painted their frenetic displays across his naked face. He flew with his helmet stowed behind the seat. He wanted to experience the track without interference. For the first time. And the last.

CHAPTER 17

Mike was just bringing the *Universe* off the track. This time Defoe had let him do some real flying, although he held back on the turbo version of attitude control, saying Mike wasn't ready to whip the ship around that recklessly.

Mike was allowed, however, to pilot the ship back through the entry portal. He had just entered Pitfall through the north-pole warp zone, and was looking for the Gajira pit's beacon amid the jumble of worklights and welding sparks and multicolored signal lights, when the proximity alarm honked.

The incoming ship passed within five meters of the *Universe*, radio-silent, tumbling badly. Chunks of it clanged off the skin of the racecraft, sharp pings that echoed through the cockpit. "What the hell was that?" asked Mike.

Defoe was already on the commlink to Race Control, reporting a flagrant near-miss. Mike locked a radar-assisted camera on the object and zoomed in. "Oh, no . . ."

It was the *Spider*—scorched, blackened, trailing gas and debris. "Speedball is back . . ."

Mike could only guess what he had encountered out there on track Monza, but from the look of the wrecked *Spider,* it wasn't good news.

When the workers in the maintenance hangar saw the *Spider* coming in like a runaway rocket, they scattered to the bunkers. At the last moment, the warp ship lit off a dozen thrusters, killing the tumble and slowing its forward motion to about twice the legal entrance speed.

As it penetrated the airscreen, firing off emergency braking rockets, the workers clamped hands to their ears. Automatic exhaust fans came on in the hangar, blowing the poisonous fumes back through the airscreen. Alarms rang

out, and the workers grabbed their oxygen masks, strapping them over the appropriate orifices.

Meanwhile, the *Spider* pranced and skidded on its delicate feet, knees bent, sparks flying, gouging the hangar's concrete floor. It thudded into the side of the bunker and lay there hissing and ticking and wheezing.

The workers rose up slowly, making nervous jokes. A robot was dispatched to sniff the ship for poisons and radioactivity. Alarms bleeped, and the workers sank back into the bunker and waited. Fans stepped up in pitch.

For twenty minutes nothing at all happened.

Then the fans dropped down to normal, and the robot went back for another sniff. The workers rose up and moved cautiously to the *Spider*'s burned flanks. It was still bobbing slowly on its spindly legs.

The workers walked all around the craft, poking and sniffing and measuring. Someone banged on it with a wrench. They all listened. No response.

The robot returned, crawled under the belly of the *Spider,* and opened the hatch. A stench dropped heavily to the hangar floor, and a portable fan was wheeled over and set a-blowing.

The robot whined and clicked and went up the shaft and opened the inner hatch. More corruption and nastiness. The robot sniffed around, while the workers watched on the video screen.

The interior was shattered, burned, gutted, and uninhabited.

Mike pushed against the crowd, wishing he were a foot or two taller. In one corner of the hangar was the burned-out *Spider,* surrounded by armed cops in green pressure suits. The guy in front of him squirmed halfway around to face Mike. "Hey, kid, what are you trying to do, climb up my back?"

"Sorry."

"Anyway, there ain't nothing to look at. Damned thing's empty."

"It just flew in here on its own?"

"You sound like it was haunted. They were running a recall beam, you know, since that idiot took off in it."

Mike stood on his tiptoes. "It sure looks screwed up."

"Must've hit something on the way back. There was that guy who went over the high side a few hours ago. Maybe they collided in never-never land."

Mike did not reply. He was not ready to think about Lek Croveen. Somebody jostled Mike from behind, and he rebounded into the guy in front of him. *"S'ree."*

The guy shrugged. "My fault for being here. I should've stayed home and watched this on—"

The rest of his words were lost under the blare of alarms. The crowd surged; forward, back, to the side. Nobody knew what to do, but Mike recognized the alarm: incoming.

A voice came on the PA and delivered a garbled message that filled the hangar with perplexed faces. Arguments broke out over what the message had been. Fights broke out over what language it had been.

Mike felt himself shoved around by a powerful surf. He lashed out with elbows to keep upright. Folks could die under that mass of—

"Ahhhh!" the crowd said, in one voice, as the gravity dialed back to almost nothing. Somebody was on the ball in the control room. Now the hangar was vast and loosely packed, as folks floated into the empty space over their heads. The incoming alarm continued to bleat, but the sense of panic had evaporated. Mike felt cool air on his face. The fans were on high.

"That's better," he started to say to his companion, but the man had drifted away.

Someone caught Mike's eye. It was Fyodor Willingham. "Hey, Mike! What brings you here?"

"Just curious." He decided he better not mention his friendship with Speedball. The Gajira Syndicate might not approve of his fraternizing with thieves.

"What's that damned ringing noise?" asked Willingham.

"Incoming alarm," said Mike, and he pointed toward the shimmering airscreen.

Indeed, something *was* out there, edging closer. Folks were pushing off one another, trying to clear a zone. The gravity dialed up slightly, with the back wall designated as the floor. The crowd began to fall slowly away from the airscreen.

''Somebody in the control room really knows what he's doing,'' said Mike. He braced himself to keep facing the hangar's opening. The incoming ship drifted through the airscreen and became distinct.

''What in the hell . . .'' said Willingham.

Mike gaped, and everybody began talking at once. It was another *Spider*-like warp ship, unburned, undamaged, pristine. In fact, this one looked brand new.

The strange ship floated to the hangar floor right above a locking point, and grapplers took hold of its tiny feet.

Gently, the gravity field angled toward the concrete floor, and folks commenced to settle together, like cards being shuffled. Green-suited cops pushed through the noisy crowd. A roar rippled back from the front, and Mike jumped to get a look. Something was coming out of the ship, slithering metallically down from its belly.

''It's some kind of robot,'' said Willingham.

''It's a racing PV,'' said Mike.

Cops struggled to reach the automaton, but were held back by the crowd—perhaps even intentionally. Another roar rippled back, and a second PV descended to the concrete—a decrepit device of old design and bad abuse. Next came a tall blond Poldavian woman in a skimpy pressure suit, the material of which was ripped open in a heart-stopping manner. Her blue skin gleamed through the gaps.

''I like that,'' said Fyodor Willingham.

Next: a gray-bearded black man—another decrepit device of old design and much bad abuse.

''Who the hell is that?'' asked Willingham.

A final figure dropped from beneath the flexed legs of the ship. Finally, somebody Mike could recognize. ''Oh, my God, it's Margie Phillips.'' And perched on her shoulder was a battle-scarred lizard-bat, which squawked and flapped its wings and clicked its teeth in vigorous protest. Suddenly it was obvious what personality manned the superior racing PV.

''Speedball!'' yelled Mike, and the crowd took up the chant.

The automaton stepped foward, raising his arms. Then the bearded man reached out to jerk them down. He pushed in front and raised his *own* arms, grinning broadly. The

automaton turned to look at the big blonde. She shrugged. Mike wondered what *that* meant.

Suddenly the ship uttered a shrill cry, forcing the spectators back in fright. A moment later the *Spider*-like machine shivered and rose into the air. Mike heard the double clank of hatches closing, then the warp ship floated away through the airscreen and was gone.

By now the cops had penetrated the astonished inner crowd—and the shiny automaton took off running. The mob shrieked as he dived right through the airscreen and out of the hangar.

"Oh, Speedball . . ." said Mike. "What have you done?"

Forthwith Speedball reappeared, peeking up over the lip of the floor. He reached out, and the other automaton, the one in the junky PV, darted forward, just ahead of the cops.

"Who the hell is that idiot?" Mike wondered aloud.

Speedball succeeded in yanking the other guy over the edge and they both disappeared. Cops got on hands and knees to peer over the side after them, but nobody ventured out in pursuit.

Mike would have followed if he'd had a pressure suit. As it was, he had to fight his way through the crowd back to the corridor entrance to the hangar. The crowd continued to surge forward, cheering and chanting Speedball's name. Mike looked back. They were surrounding the bearded man, ignoring Margie and the blond Poldavian.

At the door Mike caught sight of the other ship, now abandoned in the corner of the hangar. He noticed the name "Spider" painted just below the cockpit glass. If the beat-up ship was the one from the Racing Museum, where the hell did the other one come from?

And where had it gone?

Mike thrust himself through the crowd. The corridors and ring-connecting flyways of Pitfall were choked with happy tourists and off-duty workers. It wasn't even shift-change traffic; it was the damned Tricentennial—as if some vast interstellar party had been sucked into Pitfall and plated out on all its inner surfaces: loud, frenzied, colorful, reeking folk, all with about a dozen elbows zeroed in on Mike's nose.

He prowled the walkways and freefall drop chutes and arm-wrenching beltways, hoping to spot Speedball or his rusty companion. Several times he thought he caught sight of the pair, but either it turned out to be someone else or he was turned back by the crowd and never found out who it was.

After a while Mike noticed there were an awful lot of cops milling about. Sure, they were looking for Speedball, but it occurred to Mike they were keeping an eye on *him,* too. If he found Speedball . . . or if Speedball came looking for him . . .

"Sneaky bastards . . ."

Eventually Mike went to a Brain Bank terminal and plugged himself into Twyla Rogres. "Hi. Remember me?"

"Of course, I do," said Twyla. "How ya doing, Junkyard?"

"Oh, I'm okay."

The sound of her voice made him sigh. He didn't care what rules had been bent to keep her on the net. He had the distinct feeling that *this* Twyla liked him better than the other one. He wondered if they got together and talked about him.

"Here's the thing," he said. "I'm looking for Speedball."

"Well, he's not in here. I haven't heard from him since he consulted me on the *Spider* deal. I'm the one who suggested he take you along."

"When? What do you mean?"

"You were too busy to go, remember? So he went down to the Brain Bank and struck a copy of your tapes."

"How did he even know they were there?"

"I keep my eyes open. Did you know they've been erased?"

"Are you kidding me?"

"Nope. First they were rejected, then something just swooped out of the datanet and pulled your plug."

"My God . . ." Mike remembered what Speedball had said about brain tapes being vulnerable. The idea made him sick.

Twyla said, "Pitfall is a dangerous place, kid."

"What about Speedball?"

"Which one? The news I'm getting on the net right now

is that the real Speedball Raybo just came home, along with some bimbo who was flying a test run with him when he went over the high side."

"That was Raybo?"

"Reports are still sketchy—"

"But, Twyla, we found Raybo's thigh bone in the sweeper bin."

"Obviously not."

"Then whose—"

"Wait a minute. Okay, I'm reading a report . . . says the bone wasn't even human . . . they think it belonged to an alien businessman . . . who disappeared out of Pitfall forty years ago . . . right after getting robbed. Oh."

"What?"

"He's the guy who brought all those silver coins to Pitfall."

"Well, I'll be damned."

"Anyway, I'll know more about Raybo in about fifteen minutes. He's going on the homeset."

"Where's—"

"His steel counterpart is still missing."

Mike was exasperated. "I don't get it. Where the hell *is* he? Why doesn't he check in?"

Speedball rose slowly from behind the crates, waiting for the man to leave the datascreen. "Come on, buddy," he whispered. "It must be obvious by now your girlfriend's not home."

Finally the guy flicked the off button and slouched away. Mike eased up beside Speedball. "I don't see why we have to run."

"We're running because they're chasing us."

"Yeah, but—"

"I'll explain it later."

Speedball jumped over the boxes and stepped quickly to the deserted datascreen. He plugged in, and Mike saw the screen flash and fill with junk. Speedball danced around quite alarmingly for a moment, then leapt up and planted his feet on either side of the screen. With a strangled scream he

pushed off, ripping his finger from the interface, and skidded across the floor in a stream of sparks.

Mike hopped the barrier and ran to his side. "What happened?"

"D-d-d-d."

"Excuse me?"

"D-d-drag m-m-m."

"What?"

"Drag me! Drag m-m-me out of h-h-h-here!"

Mike grabbed a tow loop on the back of Speedball's neck and pulled him behind the crates. "F-f-f-farther!" said Speedball. Mike towed him all the way to the mouth of a zero-g alleyway and pushed him in. They floated off into the semidarkness.

What's this all about?

They were waiting for me on the net. If I hadn't pulled loose, I'd have been sucked inside.

"Who'd do that?"

"Cops, I guess. They must think we kidnapped Margie Phillips."

"We did."

"Or went out there to smuggle something in."

"I know we didn't do *that,* so can't we at least warn Mike about—"

"If we go to the cops now, they'll put our brains on hold. They're very methodical, very precise, very slow. By the time they get to the part about warning Mike, it might already be too late."

"Okay, we'll just have to find him ourselves."

"They'll be watching him to get to us."

"So we find somebody to give him a message."

"Who do you trust?"

"Well, I guess I—"

"Wait a minute," said Speedball, reaching out for the wall. He grabbed Mike, and they rotated in the dim corridor, slamming into the heavy plastic and scraping to a stop. "I know somebody you can trust. You."

"Me?"

"You."

"Aren't they looking for me, too?"

"Yeah, but they'll never recognize you—after I get through fiddling with your datanet signature."

Speedball was already digging into Mike's access port. "Wait a minute," said Mike, jerking upright. "You can't just—ow!"

"Sorry."

"Fiddle with your own damned datanet signature!"

"What if I screw myself up? Are *you* gonna fix me?"

"How can I? I don't know how!"

"Exactly."

An electric wave of giddiness swept over Mike, hissing loudly. Light blossomed from pinpoints in the darkness, filling his eyes. For a moment he could see all the way around behind him, then a couple of million memory images flickered past, exploding in his face.

"Jesus Steaming Christ!" said Speedball. "You crashed their simulator into Clypsis."

"Yeah, I just thought it'd be—"

"You idiot! Look at this."

Mike saw himself yanked in exaggerated speed from the cockpit of Gajira's simulator, saw the angry computer tech, his crimson Merkek face turning jerkily to glare at him. He saw the computer screen, blank, gray, and lifeless. And he saw the technician lean swiftly to type a code on the keyboard. The screen flashed with junk, then cleared.

"I don't get it," said Mike.

"Look at that flash again."

The scene backed up and replayed, slower. The flash stuttered, screens of data flickering past. Again, slower: the screen pulsed with page after page of data—text, equations, diagrams, code words, everything.

"That's it," said Speedball. "That's why they've been trying to kill you."

"*What's* it?" said Mike, struggling to read the flickering screens. "I don't even know what it means! And how could I have seen it, going by so fast? It was just a flash of light."

"You're seeing it now, aren't you? And all it took was a brain tape and a little manipulation. A third-grader could have done it."

"But how could they be sure this got into my brain? How do they know I didn't blink?"

"All they had to do was get your tapes and look 'em over."

"But they couldn't tape me without—" Mike remembered the big guy in the Goodyear pressure suit. Black-market tapes, he offered, real cheap—*far* too cheap to pass up. "That guy was working for them."

"No doubt."

Mike ran the screens again, slowly, reading the words this time, absorbing the data. It was a plan to smuggle in a vast cargo pod full of HIPE during the Tricentennial Classic.

Raceships were not subject to customs inspection—they just went round and round. But this race was different, moving off the regular tracks and cruising through the commercial warpweb. Gajira had found a window of vulnerability—and he was driving a truckload of HIPE right through it.

Okay. The Gajira Syndicate was just a bunch of crooks. And they wanted him dead. "But what about Dover Bell?" asked Mike. "How does he fit into this?"

"Maybe they hired him to do you. God knows he has plenty of motivation."

"That bastard."

The blazing globe of Clypsis filled the screens with a sheet of yellow light. The *Swamp Queen* was fifty thousand klicks above its trembling surface, stationed outside Pitfall's innermost portal. Another ship angled in, closing up the distance.

Mary-All pointed at the small screen in the galley. "Here they are."

Vicky Slicky studied the image. "It's just a crazy-looking runabout."

"I told you before," said Craig Show. "They're not taking delivery now. They just want to look it over."

"What?" said Mary-All. "Make sure we haven't shot up all their valuable dope?" Ever since Bent had told them what was in the cargo pod, Mary-All had been burning up with sarcasm.

"I don't like it either," said Vicky. "Why don't they just take it with them?"

"Won't fit," said Mary-All.

"Let 'em get a bigger ship."

"They can't bring the stuff through Pitfall portal," said Show. "Everybody's getting searched by customs—now more than ever. Even a small cargo—"

"—which this is not," said Mary-All.

Alarms buzzed in the galley.

"That's me," said Craig, getting up. He took a final gulp of warm coffee, then went out.

From far away came a series of metallic scrapes and bumps. Vicky looked at the screen. The runabout had docked with the *Swamp Queen*'s auxiliary airlock. "I feel lousy about this."

"Join the club," said Mary-All. "I keep thinking about all those race pilots with their brains pumped up on HIPE."

"I know, I know. If it weren't for a chance to see Mike Murray again . . ."

"Be ironic if he's one of them."

"Oh, God, don't say that. Not even as a joke."

"Wasn't a joke, Vicky. You know how ambitious he was, how important it was for him to make good."

"Yeah, but—"

"Ain't no pilot ever took HIPE planning to fly worse."

"He wouldn't do it, Mary. He's not that stupid."

Mary-All shrugged. "Everybody makes mistakes. The universe is a dangerous place."

Three men had come aboard to inspect the cargo, and while they were in the hold, all nonessential personnel were kept out. That was fine with Vicky Slicky. After a while she left the galley and went up to the bridge. When Bowker Ferguson saw her, he put her on watch and went below.

Vicky stared for a while out the big screen. As a result of a slight velocity mismatch during the docking, the *Swamp Queen* had begun a slow rotation. Now the yellow glare of Clypsis was behind them, and the screen was full of stars. She fooled around with the display, and soon there were several circles painted on the screen with dull colored dots riding the lines—planets of Clypsis system.

She was reading about the Earthlike planet called Enig-

ma when the shouting began. It got louder, moving her way. Captain Bent was mightily pissed off about something.

Vicky turned as the men came onto the bridge. Bent and Ferguson and two strangers. The captain's face was red, Ferguson's white. The strangers were cool, barely interested.

"This is my ship, *my* ship," said Bent. "And if I take it into my mind to—"

"You will not visit Pitfall," said one of the men. His voice was calm, and he was smiling quite pleasantly.

Bent laughed. "You seem to think—"

"You will leave the system immediately after the cargo is correctly placed."

"This," said Bent, slamming his wide palm on the nav console, "is my *ship*."

The smiling stranger nodded vigorously. "Correct. Absolutely correct."

"In that case—"

"Nevertheless, you *will* exit Clypsis system as instructed."

Captain Bent was strangling with anger.

The stranger glanced at Vicky, then stepped close to whisper in Bent's ear. The captain listened, reluctantly and with contempt for several seconds. Then his expression changed abruptly, and his gaze jerked about the bridge in sudden fright. The stranger stepped away, slipping something back into his pocket. "Good," he said. "I see you are convinced."

Captain Bent stood without moving, as the color faded from his face. The stranger turned and left the bridge with his partner.

After a long moment, Bent cleared his throat and instructed Ferguson to see to the deployment of the cargo capsule. When the mate had left the bridge, Bent turned to Vicky. He had trouble meeting her eyes. "Prepare a course for Dylstra. Have the numbers ready in half an hour."

"I thought we were going to hunt up some cargo in Clypsis system?"

"We'll deadhead out of here. There'll be something for us in Dylstra—there always is."

Vicky thought about seeing Mike Murray. It was annoying to miss this chance, but the excitement of leaving the

system in a rush blunted the disappointment. What did that guy say to Bent?

The captain went to his chair and sat down with deliberate care, as though the gravity had been cranked up.

For several minutes Vicky worked on the cataform numbers for the subspace jump. When she looked up, the runabout had undocked and slipped away toward Pitfall. She glanced behind her to where the captain sat. He was visibly more relaxed.

Vicky buzzed Mary-All in the galley. "Go grease the engines, babe. We're dragging our butts out of here in twenty minutes."

Naturally Mary-All wanted to know what it was all about, and why they weren't going into Pitfall to see Mike.

"Maybe it's better this way," said Vicky. She lowered her voice. "I don't think Mike will miss not seeing Bent."

"I heard that," said the captain, right behind her.

"Uh . . ."

"We'll be back someday," he said. "And if that little ship-jumping sneak is still around, he'll wish he'd never been born. I promise you."

CHAPTER 18

Mike hesitated outside the door to Jass's pit. He'd been surprised by the call, and even more surprised that he'd agreed to meet Jass here. Mike touched his wrist to the scanner. The monitor stuttered and tweeped, then said, "Hi, Mike. Come on in." The hatch clunked and hissed and swung open. Mike stepped through and let it close behind him. Jass was standing on the other side of the control room. "Come over here, Mike. I wanna show you something."

"Does this have anything to do—"

"It's not about the Gajira Syndicate," Jass said, walking away.

Mike followed, looking around. The pit was deserted, the maintenance bay empty. Jass waited at the entrance to his office. "In here."

Mike immediately saw the old racing PV, slumped in a dark corner of the room. Jass rotated his desklight, shifting shadows across the PV's dented blank face. "Is it . . . ?"

"Yeah, it's empty," said Jass. "I found it outside my utility airlock."

Mike moved closer and squatted down beside the crumpled steel body. It smelled acrid. "This is the one I saw today."

"Where?"

"In the maintenance hangar. It was there with . . ." Mike trailed off, thinking. Twyla had told him Speedball made a copy of his brain tapes. Had this PV been the carrier?

"What's it doing here?" asked Jass.

"I don't know. Maybe he was looking for me. Would the Brain Bank tell us who was inside?"

"If it's listed. Why don't you check the serial number?"

Mike pulled the PV away from the wall and turned it

around. The back of the unit was a gaping hole that dripped black plastic. "My God."

"That's a problem," said Jass. "No serial number."

Mike rolled the PV back against the wall. Now the smoky stench was sharp in his nostrils. "When did you find it? Exactly."

"Twenty minutes ago, I guess."

Mike got up and left the office, Jass following. Mike looked through the safety glass into the hangar. "You found it outside your airlock?"

"Yeah."

Mike popped the hatch and went through. "You coming?" Jass got into the airlock with him, and Mike ran the cycle. The hangar was already pressurized, so the outer door green-lighted immediately, and Mike pushed it open. "Where's the ship?"

"Andy's got it out running tests with Twyla."

"She work here all the time now?"

"We haven't decided."

Mike walked across the empty hangar to the airscreen. It was dark out there in the free zone, and he could see the navigation lights of ships and robot freight pods. "I guess anybody in a suit could have just floated in here." He stepped closer to the nearly invisible airscreen.

"Careful," said Jass.

"I think that was me in the PV."

"You?"

The laser pulse hit the screen and scattered, sweeping across. Mike dropped to the floor, eyes darting. "There!" he said, pointing. A figure in a pressure suit glided off into the darkness. Mike felt his hand burning, then Jass yanked him back from the airscreen and dragged him deep into the hangar. Mike kept looking back. "Did you see him?"

"He's gone now," said Jass.

Mike held up his right hand. It was red and puffy, cracked by a network of fine lines. "I've been hit."

"No, you weren't," said Jass. "That's vac-bite."

"What?"

"You put your hand through the screen."

"Did I?" Mike stared stupidly at his hand. The next

thing he knew he was on the floor, looking up at Jass. "Maybe I ought to have somebody check this . . ."

His eyes were open, but he could not control their motion. The corridor was dark and deserted and pounding with the throb of unseen ventilators. He was walking down the corridor, paralyzed, his legs numb. He felt disconnected, helpless. He came to a hatch and stopped. A metal hand reached out to touch the latch. Was it his hand? He couldn't feel a thing.

His eyes zoomed in close and focused on the latch. A finger lit up, and shadows rotated around the latch as the finger moved. Behind a tiny sliding metal door was a probe jack. The tip of one of the fingers peeled back, revealing a multitiered plug. The finger pushed into the jack.

The world lit up, buzzing. Diagrams flickered in front of him, detailing in three dimensions the routing of wires and conduits. Voltages chattered, light beams flickered, frequencies shifted. He could *hear* the color of the light.

The latch clicked, and the door swung slowly open. It was even darker inside. He saw himself step through and close the hatch. He waited in the darkness, listening to the ventilators. After a moment he tried to speak. *"Nmmena . . ."*

Shut up, Mike.

"Uhhma . . ."

Look, I'm glad you're awake. Now shut up, I'm busy.

They stood by the door in the dark room. Slowly he began to make out details—conduits, pipes, air ducts. There was another door across the room. He sensed light out there, and people. "Awake . . ."

Damn it!

He saw a glowing hand rise up swiftly, then a violet light exploded in his face with a shriek. *Ow!*

Sorry, but you needed that.

What's going on?

You're with me.

He started to ask who "me" was, and he got a bright image of Speedball, the man and the machine, blended. The image faded. *Speedball? I'm inside you?*

Yeah. I thought it'd be safer. The cops are looking for us, you know, and it's twice as hard hiding two PVs.

What happened to—

I sent him back to Jass's pit to warn Mike, but I don't think he made it. The last thing I saw was some guy homing in on him.

You mean the cops—

I don't know.

Mike heard the words and knew what they meant, but he couldn't feel them. He couldn't feel anything. It was as if the knowledge was in code.

Okay, said Speedball, *here's the deal.*

A solid block of information expanded through a series of new dimensions. Mike saw it all and knew what it meant, grasping the intricacies of the plan immediately. But he couldn't have told you if it was a good idea.

Speedball brought them to the door on the far side of the dark utility room. Mike could hear voices now, approaching close, making his head itch. Speedball waited until the voices died out, then he turned the doorknob. Mike heard the innards of the lock grind and snap. The door opened and they looked out.

The corridor was empty. Mike caught a whiff of floor plan, then Speedball stepped out, walking quickly to a closed door. This one wasn't locked. Mike watched the room rotate across his vision. One man sat behind the desk, and another stood nearby, leaning on it. They both looked up from the comm screen, where Mike saw the blurry face of a third.

"Who are you?" asked Larouse, reaching out to blank the comm screen. "What do you want?"

Rinehart Weel stepped forward. "We're busy, you mind?"

"This won't take long," said Speedball, introducing himself. "I'm looking for Tadashi Gajira."

Larouse smiled. "You have business with Mr. Gajira? I just had him on the phone."

Mike heard a high-pitched whine. It came and went three times, then Larouse put his hands on the desk and smiled.

Cute, said Speedball. "Nothing personal," he said out loud. The room shifted, and Mike realized Speedball was

backing up to the door. "It's just that I don't like to leave loose ends hanging about."

The door burst open, and Mike saw nothing but a blur as Speedball turned and swatted the big blue alien into a corner, where he landed unconscious in a heap. Speedball kicked the door shut and turned back around.

The men at the desk hadn't moved.

Speedball said, "Keep your fingers off the buttons, if you don't mind."

Larouse smiled sweetly. "Why don't you tell me what this is about?"

"Just trot Gajira in here, okay?"

Rinehart Weel said, "You don't seem to understand. Nobody sees Mr. Gajira."

"Shy man, is he? Just tell him we know all about the HIPE shipment."

Weel looked sharply at Larouse, and the team leader said, "HIPE shipment?"

"That's right, so there's no longer any reason to kill Michael Murray."

Mr. Larouse managed to look perplexed. "I don't understand. Mr. Murray *works* for us."

I do? said Mike. *Does that mean I won the jump-to-master competition?*

Shut up, Mike.

"What I don't understand," said Speedball, "is why you guys are doing all this. What's the point of this big shipment? There can't be that many HIPE users in Pitfall."

The two men looked at one another, then Larouse said, "I simply do not know what you're talking about."

Speedball took a step toward them.

"Oh, please," said Larouse. "We all know you're not going to harm us."

"What makes you so sure?"

"First," said Weel, counting on his fingers, "you're inside a racing PV, and while you may not feel it, there *are* built-in prohibitions against doing anything violent—unless attacked. Second, whatever the hardware you inhabit, you're still a human being, and a pretty good guy despite your ugly mood. You simply aren't capable of killing us. Third, even if

you *were* to go nuts, there is no way you could cross the space between us. The slope of gravity prevents it."

Speedball took another step forward, and found that the grav field shifted abruptly. It was like an invisible wall between him and the men.

"And finally," said Rinehart Weel, "you won't want to move any closer—even if you could—when I tell you there's a man with a gun right behind you."

Speedball turned quickly, and Mike saw the room spin past. The big blue guy was still out, lying in the corner, but standing at the open door was indeed a man with a gun. "Don't make me use this thing," he said. Mike relaxed. It was only Fyodor Willingham, looking nervous.

Just then a spindly wooden table leg swatted the top of Willingham's head, and he crumpled to the floor. Lurching up behind him, drunk out of his mind, was Larry Raybo. He stumbled into the room, nearly tripping over Willingham, and bounced off Speedball's chest. "Outta my way!"

"Oh, for Christ's sake," muttered Speedball, as Raybo pushed past him to confront the men at the desk.

"Where's Gajira!"

"He's out," said Rinehart Weel, peering with curiosity at Raybo's bearded face.

"Well . . . get him in here!" said Raybo, weaving about in the middle of the room. He turned, rediscovering Speedball. "You work here?"

Willingham was groaning and crawling around on the floor. Raybo fixed the man with a bleary, red-eyed stare. "You better stay down there, buddy. I'll whip your ass." He spun around, lost his balance, and fell forward, bouncing off the vertical grav field that surrounded the desk. Raybo slapped at it angrily. "The hell is this?"

"Go home," said Speedball. "You're drunk."

Raybo leaned casually against the grav field and sneered at the automaton. "What are you saying?"

"I'm saying you're drunk."

"Yeah? Who are you?"

"Speedball Raybo."

"Well, so am I, buddy. And if you're me, that makes you just as drunk as I am. So watch it!"

We should have left him in that junkyard, said Speedball.

"Stop wiggling around," said Raybo, though Speedball was standing rock-steady. He turned again, backing clumsily off the grav field, and addressed the guys at the desk. "Is Gajira here yet? I got something to settle with him. Little thing called murder. Won't take a minute of his valuable time."

He turned to grin at Speedball, and his eyes widened in alarm. Speedball swiveled his head. "Oh, shit."

Willingham was up on his feet with the gun in his hand. He looked different now—less harmless, more cold-blooded. The gun's rotating beam was shining on Raybo's face.

"Keep watching the light," he told Raybo. "It gets more and more interesting."

"You idiot!" shouted Speedball, turning on Raybo. "How could you be so stupid, wandering in here like this?"

"You're here, aren't ya?"

"But I'm not drunk."

"Drop dead!"

"Oh, yeah?"

Speedball reached out and shoved Raybo against the grav field. The man bounced and staggered back, swatting Speedball on the lower half of his smooth, ovoid head.

"Scrapheap!"

"Meathead!"

Speedball shoved Raybo back against the grav field. The man bounced off and fell to the floor.

"Hey!" said Willingham. "Let's get organized here. *I'm* the guy with the gun."

"Stay out of it," said Raybo. He rose up shakily and smacked Speedball across the chest with the table leg he'd found lying on the floor. Wood splinters sprayed across the room.

"Missed me," said Speedball, pushing Raybo back against the field.

"You tinhead bastard!"

"Better man than you'll ever be!"

"Oh, yeah?" Raybo was looking for something else to hit Speedball with.

"Gentlemen, please," said Larouse.

Speedball snagged Raybo by his jacket and began to shake him up and down so hard nothing the man said made any sense.

Leave him alone! yelled Mike.

Stay out of this!

"I mean it!" said Willingham, moving closer.

In a blur of accelerated motion Speedball swung around and propelled Raybo at the door. "Run, you stupid hunk of meat!"

Willingham's gun turned to follow, lighting up Raybo's back. The beam tightened, shrinking down to an angry red dot. In just that instant Raybo's jacket began to smoke.

"Me first," said Speedball, advancing on Willingham. The gun came around, and the light was there, flickering in Mike's eyes, going violet. Speedball reached out and Willingham started to yell. The light grew hot in a microsecond.

Mike felt his face flare up and explode. Speedball kept coming, sightless, wordless, diagrams sketching across the darkness, as he calculated the intercept vectors from his last sighted moment. Mike felt the world rotate upward, then they landed heavily on the man, pinning him to the floor. Willingham went limp beneath them.

The universe rotated again as Speedball got to his feet. He turned toward the door, and Mike could see its outline superimposed on a shifting image of the room. Willingham stood in front of them, the gun in his hand bright with frozen light.

Mike tried to flinch back, but Speedball just walked right through the image. It wasn't real, only the last full view of the room before Speedball's face went to pieces.

They stood in the doorway, and a new image formed, showing the hallway as it had looked on their way in. It was deathly silent, and Mike wondered about that until he realized they had no sound sensors.

Speedball shut the office door hard, jamming it into the frame, then he walked down the hall.

Where are we going? asked Mike.

Back the way we came. If they don't know how we got inside, they might not cover our exit. If we can get out in that service corridor, we might make it to a datanet terminal. No

reason now not to plug in and broadcast everything. I got my proof.

The images shifted clumsily as they moved down the hallway toward the equipment closet door. The silence was unnerving. Mike had to ask. *Are we going to get out of this?*

How the hell should I know?

Can you at least tell if they're following?

No, I can't. But if that guy burns through my back plate and boils away the brain—you might feel a little something.

They were nearing the door. A few more meters . . .

Mike asked, *Do you think Raybo got out all right?*

That idiot? Hell, he probably went back to see what happened. He's so—

Speedball stopped. The hallway floor had rotated upward into a wall. This was something new—the memory image showed nothing. Speedball backed up, turned to the left, and reached for the corridor's wall. It was right where the image predicted. He turned back and probed the air in front of him. The invisible wall was still there, blocking their escape. *This doesn't look good.*

He turned, the image spinning, and moved back down the deserted hallway. Another unseen wall rose up in front of them. *Uh-huh.*

Speedball backed up slowly, and bumped into the first wall, which had moved closer. Soon it was apparent the sidewalls of the corridor were moving in as well.

We're caught in a gravity trap.

Did they—unh! Mike felt Speedball's body collapse in a heap, as the ceiling dropped. *Did they find us?*

I don't know. This could be an automatic intruder response.

I hope it is, said Mike.

It made him sick to think of the gunman standing a few meters away, watching them crouch helplessly in the invisible trap. He said so.

I hope they are *right in front of us,* said Speedball. *'Cause if this system is automatic, then Raybo is caught, too. The idiot!*

By the time the walls stopped moving, Speedball was sitting on the floor, his knobby steel knees up around where his head used to be. They waited.

Now what? asked Mike.

It's up to them. Just remember we have tapes on file. If they kill us . . .

Is it going to hurt?

I don't remember.

They waited.

Mike said, *Why don't they* do *something!*

Relax. They might not even be out there.

But they *were* out there, arguing. And when the argument was over, and Willingham had gotten his way, the white heat of his weapon filled Mike's imaginary face.

Jass/Lek/Scarface/Twyla: the images were rapid, compressed, and achingly desperate. It's not *me* dying . . . not *really* me . . .

A comforting thought, but look—if not him, *who*?

Gajira was speaking from the screen. "I've combed through the datanet and we're still clear. Speedball never made a report, so anything he knew is gone now. Our plans may proceed without change."

"What about Mike Murray?" asked Larouse.

"Coming to that. If we hesitate much longer, we'll have to wait until after the race. Put our man on it right away. I want Murray dead."

The screen went blank.

The medibot was just starting to spray the bandage onto Mike's hand when word came there was a phone call. It was Dover Bell. "Someone is trying to kill you."

"I'm beginning to figure that out," said Mike.

"I happen to know who it is and why they're doing it. Interested?"

"Tell me."

"Not on the phone. Meet me at your room. One hour."

"I'll be there."

* * *

Mike was a little late getting to his room. He discovered the lock had been busted and the door was off its track. "Dover Bell, you maniac!" He kicked the door open—and nearly choked. Bell was sitting on the bed, waiting for him with a blaster in his hand. Mike froze in the doorway, his heart double-thumping in runaway fright. The worst part was that he felt like such an idiot. How could he have walked right into this!

"Come on, man," he said. "Nothing I've ever done to you on the track was so bad you have to . . . to . . . uh . . ."

About the time he noticed Dover Bell wasn't paying much attention to him, someone tapped Mike on the back. He jerked around with a squeak.

"Hi," said the automaton.

"Oh, God, Speedball!"

"No, I'm sorry. My name is MIDNITE."

Mike's head whipped around again. Dover Bell still wasn't moving. Mike turned back to MIDNITE. "What in the hell is—"

"I'm afraid I've busted up their little game," said MIDNITE. "There was supposed to be a man in there whose job it was to burn a hole through your skull. He was then going to put the blaster in your hand. And so forth. Whoever it was, I scared him off—coming up the stairs like a herd of pigmy dinosaurs."

"Yeah, but . . ." Mike looked at Bell again, noticing for the first time the extra eyehole in his forehead, just beneath a glistening lock of green hair. "There are ice crystals in his hair."

"He's not done defrosting."

"Defrosting? How long has he—"

"Oh, he's been dead for quite some time," said MIDNITE. "Somebody's been saving him just for this."

"But he called me on the phone. I saw him!"

"A video replicant, obviously. I saw it too, which is why I'm here."

"But who's doing all this?"

"I don't know."

"Why are they after me?"

"My guess is that you know something they're trying to suppress."

''What?''

''I don't know yet. I *can* tell you that your friend Speedball . . . has been found.''

''Is he all right?''

MIDNITE hesitated, and Mike wondered how long a moment could be to a computer program. ''His PV was found,'' said MIDNITE, ''in a scrap yard. Wrecked, burned out, empty.''

''But he's safe . . . in the Brain Bank.''

''His tapes are gone, Mike, erased. I thought I could protect him, but I couldn't. The man is gone . . . utterly gone.''

Mike stared blankly. ''Gone . . . erased . . . dead . . . are you sure?''

''Trust me,'' said MIDNITE. ''I don't make mistakes.''

CHAPTER 19

For three hours Mike had smiled and winked and laughed and grinned until he thought his face would crumble to dust. Now, finally, it was over: the ceremonies and the press conferences, the handshaking and the bogus photo opportunities. Only the race was left, and it seemed downright anticlimactic.

He crossed alone onto pit-ring through a maintenance causeway, having ditched his more enthusiastic followers in a maze of forgotten air ducts. He floated to a stop in the dim tunnel and listened to the pulse of ventilators. "Not a good time to get lost," he muttered. "So pay attention."

He turned left into the next zero-g duct opening and drifted past locked hatches with burned-out status lamps. He was thinking of turning back, when he heard something coming down the duct behind him—it was an ominous, thumping sound.

Mike grabbed a wobbly handhold and launched himself down the shaft to a deserted corridor nexus. For a moment he didn't know which way to go, then he recognized a pattern of lights in the distance, and pushed off toward them. At the next turning the sound was closer, but he knew he was near the back entrance to the Gajira Syndicate's sprawling pit complex. He checked his watch and silently swore. He was already late.

At the hatch he pressed his ID wrist to the scanner and banged the switch with his left hand. "Come on, come on!" Mike looked back into the dark tunnel. Something moved in the shadows, coming this way. The scanner asked him to say a few words for voice analysis. Mike said, "Open this damned door before I chew off the hinges!"

The hatch chimed and began to swing slowly open. He pressed eagerly against the door, looking back down the tunnel. Here it comes . . .

Without warning the door swung wide, and he fell

forward into a heavy grav field. Somebody grabbed his tender right hand, yanking him inside. Then the lights came on and he saw Willingham standing there with a pulse-beam gun in his hand. "Look out, kid! It's a bloodsucker!"

Mike was thrown to the deck. There was a sizzling sound and the light flared. Something thudded against the wall, just opposite the hatch where Mike lay, half in and half out.

Willingham stepped over him, into the corridor. The light shifted again as Mike twisted around. Willingham held up a large limp bag of—

Oh God . . . it's Scarface.

His guts were half blown out.

Willingham grinned, looking goofy. "Hey, talk about a lucky shot!" He waved Scarface in front of Mike for a moment, then tossed the body down the empty shaft. "Scavengers will get it." He stepped over Mike again, then held out his hand. "Come on, kid. The race starts in a few minutes."

Mike got into the pressure suit provided by Team Gajira, a suit so new it still reeked of solvents from the cold welds. Willingham was right beside him in the locker room, entangled with his suit cooler. "Help me with this stupid thing!"

Mike got him straightened out, working automatically, his head still buzzing. He kept seeing the limp body of Scarface dangling from Willingham's grip. "Hurry up, Mike!"

He nodded, feeling hollow and sick. He wanted to go off by himself and work this horrible thing through in his mind, but there was no time now to think about anything.

He drifted in the darkness. He was so very cold, and the pain in his stomach was riding up his spine and throbbing with every beat of his slowed-down heart. His mouth was dry, his brain a swirl of confused longing for death.

He could still see the light spinning from the gun's lens—a glittering blossom of light that reminded him of hot fusion exhaust, but he no longer remembered why.

He felt so alone . . . so cold . . . so lost—

The darkness twanged and clattered and shrieked, echoing with vague menace. He welcomed the danger and waited for death.

Death in the fluttery light.

He thought of friendly voices, voices stopped by the insistent light. He was alone, as he had always been. Where had those voices come from?

His body tightened painfully, instinctively sealing off his aching wound.

Mike-Mike-Mike-Mike, he cried.

Strange images flickered: a young man smiled, reaching out to take him home—

—when the light came, cutting him off, sending him to the empty cold darkness, waiting to die, wanting to die, willing his body to give up its pointless life-sustaining efforts.

The image of the young man came again, confusing him.

He collided helplessly with the unseen wall, bouncing off in silence. A skewer of pain pierced his belly. Let me die, he thought. Let me die.

The young man frowned. Why?

Mike-Mike-Mike-Mike, he cried.

It was a prayer.

He became aware of noises in the dark. They were coming this way—marauders, scavengers, a pack of them, coming to eat him.

Over here! he thought.

The noises stopped. Cautious scavengers.

Come on! I'm ready! Get over here and do your job!

The noises resumed, coming near. He heard—no, he felt—*felt* voices, saw symbols, tasted images of welcome. His body warmed, tingled, began to glimmer—he could *see* the light growing all around him. He blinked in the light, his eyes brimming with tears.

The tears sang to him, asking, What is your name?

Warm hands touched, gentle tongues tested his skin, tasting his pain and devouring it whole.

His mind unfurled, doubling and redoubling, and was filled once more with friendly voices.

Oh, my brothers and sisters, he said, weeping. I am called Scarface. And you are all my brothers and sisters . . . my new brothers and sisters . . .

* * *

Just before the race the ready room was full of pilots and techs and business-suited guys with diamond-studded teeth. After the start, the place was still crowded with relief pilots and backups. It turned out Mike was only scheduled to run a small part of the race.

He sank down in a leather chair and carefully placed his gloved right hand on the armrest. He had peeled the bandage off, prematurely. He didn't want anybody to know how much it still hurt, lest they jerk him from the track today.

Mike watched the videoscreen as dots of colored light chased themselves around the speedway. Interspersed were shipcam close-ups of desperate passing duels, complete with the hysterical commentary Mike used to find so exciting. All around him folks talked and laughed and drank and smoked and handed bowls of dip back and forth. The girlfriends of the suits giggled and tossed their hair, as did a number of the boyfriends.

Mike sat in his pressure suit with his helmet on and his faceplate open. He noticed all the other pilots had their helmets off. Mike smiled ironically. It was true, he didn't belong with these people. They were all strangers, and to Mike's relief, they all pretty much ignored him.

The first part of the race was a simple high-speed course that circled Clypsis at two billion kilometers, a lane warped to travel at seventy-five times the speed of light. Lap time: a little over nine minutes.

It was nearly an hour into the race before they grabbed Mike and hustled him out to the control-room airlock. "Third fueling," the tech said. "End of the seventh lap."

"I'm going in now?"

"That's right. Laps eight, nine, and ten." The tech grinned and said sarcastically, "Think you can handle it, kid?"

Mike was mentally flipping through a list of inane retorts when Willingham stepped up beside him and slapped his faceplate shut. "Get on your horse," he said, over the suit-to-suit radio. "I don't want to be late."

The *Universe* emerged abruptly out of the darkness of Pitfall's free zone, activating heat lamps and spotlights in the vacuum dock. The ship was instantly seized by grapplers and

fuel nozzles, and a man in a utility pressure suit darted out at the end of a tether to spray coolant on the radiator fins, hiding half the ship in a cloud of foam that boiled in the light and froze in the shadows.

Mike and Willingham clung to the outside of the pit, just beyond the vibrating airscreen, with their suits plugged into the standby emergency box. As soon as the ship's airlock hatch popped, Mike felt Willingham's fist in his back, prodding. *"Hit it!"*

Mike uncoupled, feeling his ears pop, then slapped his rider on the safety line and triggered the motor. The rider took off, jerking the breath from his lungs, and in two seconds he was at the end of the bow grappler, reaching for a handhold on the ship. Willingham was right behind him.

A pressure-suited man rose out of the airlock, his visor down. He waved vaguely at Mike. "Watch the temp on number three. Who's the pilot?"

Mike glanced at Willingham's blank visor. "Me, I guess."

Another man popped from the airlock. "Better work that out pretty soon."

"Me," said Mike. "I'm the pilot."

"Okay," said the first guy. "Make sure your suit couplings are tight. We got a little leak or something."

"All right."

The two men were already crawling past. Mike felt Willingham's fist in his back again, and pushed off for the hatch, ignoring the ladder rungs that had emerged from the ship's smooth surface. He dived headfirst into the open airlock, accidentally banging his right hand on a control lever. He grunted in pain, thinking, Smooth move, Mike.

Willingham joined him, closing the hatch over them. Mike filled the airlock from the tank, checked the pressure, and popped the inner hatch.

It was raining inside.

"Small leak," said Willingham. "Right."

Mike settled into the left-hand pilot's seat, plugging in his hoses and hooking up his communication and power cables. Instantly the ambient sounds of the ship began to twang and crackle and hiss in his ears.

The hiss, it turned out, was from his cooler connection. Mike grabbed a wrench from the box under the seat and torqued the nozzle locking ring until the hiss damped out, then he checked to make sure the dehumidifiers were set on high.

A glance over the screens and readouts told him what he needed to know. The ship would be fully fueled in another forty or fifty seconds. Mike threaded up his harness and locked himself down.

His radio crackled. "Thirty seconds."

"Copy."

Willingham said, "When they give you clearance, take her out. I'm just here to back you up."

"Right."

Mike's heart was pounding like two guys with sledgehammers, taking turns.

"Twenty seconds."

"Copy."

Willingham said, "You don't have to acknowledge anything that comes in on that line."

"What about tac?"

"Tac, you talk to. They like to know you're paying attention."

Mike nodded.

"Ten seconds. Start your preheat."

"Roger . . . uh . . ."

Damn!

Mike coughed and swore again under his breath. Willingham said, "Tac comm is the *blue* light, Mike. And anyway, you won't hear from them in the pit, unless it's important. And in that case they always announce themselves."

"Okay."

Mike heard scrapes and vibrations behind and above him. From the pit crew: "Fueling complete."

He reached for the controls, then caught himself. He leaned back and waited. More clunks and metallic scraping noises, then: "You're clear. Have a nice day."

Mike scanned the ship all around, then peeled away from the pit with his thrusters. He used maximum chemical thrust until he was out beyond the one-kilometer safety zone, then

pulsed the mains at fifty percent of max, aimed at the equatorial exit band.

The ship surged sluggishly, the mass of her topped-off fuel tanks holding her back. Mike upped the throttle until the cockpit creaked, then eased back as the ship hit the zone. His code was read, and the ship routed to the return pit lane. The *Universe* bounced and shook and rocked through the accelerating tube of light, then a dot of blackness spread out in front of him, glimmering faintly.

The darkness swiftly wrapped around him, then lit up with the exhaust of ships in his path. The console chimed as the start/finish line flashed past. For Mike, the Tricentennial Classic had begun at last.

The blue light came on.

"*Universe,* this is tac. You are now in eighth place. Make no tactical moves without permisson."

Mike said, "Is he kidding?"

"I don't think so," said Willingham. "This is a very conservative team."

The blue light flickered.

"*Universe,* acknowledge."

"Roger, tac."

"Close it up to one hundred meters *precisely* and maintain that position."

"Roger."

Mike stroked the mains, and the ship jerked and wallowed and swayed forward until the proximity alarm tooted. He shut down the engines and waited for the ship to match velocity with the speedway, then he read the numbers from the high-resolution radar: 99.066 meters.

He smiled, expecting a reprimand, but none came. "You're wrong," he told Willingham. "They're regular daredevils."

For the next thirty minutes Mike was bored half into a coma by the wimpy tac advice, and so angry at the team's unwillingness to do any real racing—including their flat *refusal* to authorize turbo attitude controls—that he almost forgot what it was he'd come out here to do.

As the ship dropped toward the plane of the ecliptic, tac said, "Bring her in."

"Roger."

The next phase of the race was already under way, as an inner track filled with ships completing their tenth lap on the big speedway. The entrance to the transfer lane was just opposite the nearest pit lane.

Mike glanced at Willingham. "Getting a little turbulence here."

"No problem."

He approached the start/finish line.

Mike said, "Here, take it a second. I wanna make some adjustments to my harness."

"Wait a minute!"

"Go ahead." Mike let go of the stick and the *Universe* began to bounce in the wake of the ship ahead.

Willingham grabbed the stick, and immediately the *Universe* started to roll over like a sick whale. "Mike!"

"You're doing fine," said Mike as he rummaged around in the toolbox under his seat.

"Watch that roll rate, *Universe*," said tac.

"Copy," said Mike.

The ship continued to roll, but now it had also started to wobble from side to side.

"Murray!" shouted Willingham. "Damn it, don't mess around!"

Mike reached overhead and popped the shipcam circuit breakers. Almost immediately he got a call from Media Control: "*Universe*, we've lost your cockpit video. In fact, we've lost all—"

"Must be a glitch," said Mike. "I'll check into it, if I have time."

Tac said, "Uh, watch your stability, *Universe*."

"Copy."

"Don't screw around!" said Willingham. "I mean it! Take the stick, Murray!"

The ship's shock absorbers began to wheeze. Alarms lit up and beeped. Mike feigned astonishment. "Are you telling me you can't fly this thing?"

Willingham sputtered out some stupid excuse, then Mike said, "All right, I'll take over. Here, put your head forward."

He helped the man lean over, said, "This is for Scarface, asshole," and whacked him hard across the back of his neck with the flat of the nozzle wrench. *"Ow!"* yelled Mike, his hand quivering in pain. Willingham slumped in his harness.

Mike patted him down, holding the wrench cocked and ready. He found no gun, which surprised him, because MIDNITE had warned him that while Willingham might talk a good game, he was no pilot. But it was all right: the guy was definitely zonked out.

Mike put the wrench aside and pulled Willingham away from the control stick. His right hand was throbbing like hell, but there was nothing he could do about that now. He stabilized the ship, checked his screens, then lit the main engines. Mike peeled off across the track to the transfer-lane entrance, muttering, "So much for my new career."

The blue light lit up at once.

"Wrong exit, *Universe*! Take the next pit lane and report home."

"Blow it out."

He hit the entrance dead center and boosted his mains to 110 percent of max. The seat cushion wheezed as the acceleration mounted, and the transfer tube blurred with speed.

The blue light flashed repeatedly.

"Exit the track at once!"

"Ha!" said Mike.

As the *Universe* dropped sunward, Clypsis blue-shifted through gamma rays, disappearing altogether. The tube narrowed and the ship bumped across invisible ribs of turbulence, then Mike was out onto the "dirty" track—his tac screens filling with electronic junk.

Clypsis was back, but the track wobbled so much, the radial component of his speedway velocity was enough to send the star red- and blue-shifting in a slow, stuttering pulse. An interesting effect, but Mike was too busy flying to pay much attention. Half the ships on the course were lining up to fly through his cockpit.

"*Universe, Universe*, do you read?"

"Drop dead," said Mike. "You copy that?" He killed the tac-comm radio. "Never mind."

He resisted the opportunity to crank up his ECCM generator and give these guys a little race. He still had work to do.

Mike grabbed a screwdriver from the tool box and pried open a section of control panel, revealing the hidden keyboard behind it. As MIDNITE had discovered, reviewing the data flash hidden in Mike's freshly taped memory, the *Universe* was an unusually versatile machine.

He tapped in the release code—the cipher computer wasn't programmed to clear his voiceprint—and got control of the ship's illegal warp drive. He pushed the micro data cube MIDNITE had given him into the receptacle, and—as long as he was in there—flipped the turbo-enable toggle. ("Take that, tac!") When he dropped the panel, he saw that switches on the control board were lit up with new designations, reprogrammed by MIDNITE's chip.

"Okay," said Mike. "That's encouraging."

He took hold of the stick and was about to get things rolling when somebody crossed overhead and dropped down in front of him, spewing electronic garbage in his face. The screens wobbled, images breaking up and coming back together.

"Who the hell is . . ."

Mike checked the tac board for the ship's code. It was the *Shrike*. Pilot: Louise Phillips—who just *had* to be Margie's mother. "I don't believe it. She really did sic her mommy on me."

Mike whipped the stick to the side, lighting his mains as he went. The *Universe* growled and whined and shimmied as Mike hammered the big ship through the turbulence of the velocity shear. He nudged the stick and rolled the *Universe* over, flying a corkscrew loop around the ship as he passed.

Turbo control, eh? Very nice.

Mike sat grinning for a moment, his fusion exhaust boiling the pretty paintjob off the *Shrike*'s gleaming hide, then he continued on out of the groove and blasted down the throat of a pipeline entrance.

The pipeline twisted and kinked up, trying its best to

squash the ship into a crumpled pile of trash. Mike kept the nose centered and watched the forward viewscreen.

Willingham nodded against his harness, groaning on the suit-to-suit radio. Mike fingered the wrench in his lap, then let it go. There wasn't time to mess with Willingham now.

Mike energized the warp field.

The light on the panel came on, but the track looked just the same. Maybe the cameras weren't sensitive enough to pick it up. On the other hand, if the warp field *wasn't* there . . .

Well, he'd never know what hit him.

Mike saw Clypsis start to blue-shift as the undulating speedway turned inward. This was it. He swung the stick to follow, and the ship cocked sideways in the narrow pipeline.

Mike took a deep breath, muttered, "Hope it works," and shoved the stick forward, triggering the warp drive as he went.

The ship lurched like a demon toward the coruscating wall of the warp-tube. Mike had time to think, This is no simulation . . .

Then he pierced the awful barrier, going over the high side for real.

It felt like . . . well, it felt like nothing at all. The ship simply floated through the track wall, whisper-silent. Clypsis—which was centered in the screen, fifty million kilometers away—turned blue and disappeared so fast Mike thought he had accidentally pulled the plug on the universe.

The screen went blank—no sun, no speedway, no stars beyond. A cryptic scrawl of numbers and glyphs marked the computer's notion of where things had gone. Mike could only follow.

Willingham groaned again, his head bobbing. Mike watched him out of the corner of his eye.

The computer's circular symbol for Clypsis spread out and disappeared off the edges of the screen. Mike panicked and released the trigger.

Clypsis swelled out of nothingness, going from gray to violet to blue to green to yellow—all in one near-blinding

flash. He jerked the stick. The star dipped into the orange, then yellowed out, filling the screen.

Mike took a fast hot breath.

The star's surface was just below him; it churned like boiling oatmeal.

"What the hell is that?" said Willingham. He sounded drunk.

"You just sit there," said Mike, "or I'll hit you again."

"I'd rather you didn't."

Mike scanned for the first beacon, then activated the warp engine again, easing forward on the stick. The *Universe* tilted and dropped and glided toward the designated entry point on the surface of the star. The screen flared brightly, then dimmed as protective circuits cut in. The ship quivered slightly, and Mike checked the display. "We're inside."

Willingham kept his mouth shut.

The second beacon twinkled in the distance, indicated on the screen by the computer. There was nothing to see in there but plasma glowing blue-white, and the deeper they went, the brighter it got.

Then, buried in the brilliant glare of the star, Mike saw the shadow. At first he thought he was looking at Pitfall, diving through its crazy orbit, but then the angle changed and Mike realized there was a series of shadows lined up in there, each one hiding the next. It was like a twisted string of dark beads, seen on end. The ship was headed right for the top of the string.

"What's *that*?" said Willingham. He sounded sober now, but thoroughly confused.

"Beats me," said Mike, telling the truth. MIDNITE hadn't mentioned this part.

The *Universe* homed in on the head of the string and dived through the first shadow. There was another one right below it, and another beyond that. The forward screen flickered so fast Mike began to hallucinate patterns. It was like pulse transmission on the speedway. The ship veered and swerved and zigzagged its way down through the string, connecting the dots as if in some insane computer compulsion. Mike began to wonder if something had gone wrong . . .

But then the twisting strand of shadows came to an end,

and just beyond it was the flashing cargo pod. "That's it!" he said, looking at Willingham.

Mike matched the orbit of the pod and eased the ship closer. When he was within fifty meters, MIDNITE's data cube keyed the ship's own automatic-retrieval program. Locks unlatched with metallic clunks and motors whined beneath them, as secret cargo-bay doors swung open on the belly of the ship.

The *Universe* maneuvered itself into position, merging the warp fields. A series of noisy grapplers clanked home, and the ship lurched toward the new center of mass.

"Heavy package," said Mike.

Willingham said nothing, and Mike couldn't see his face through the reflecting visor.

The belly doors whined shut. The computer verified that the pod was inside and locked down.

RETRIEVAL COMPLETE.

The ship reverted to local control. Mike took the stick and edged the *Universe* out of the pod's circular orbit, accelerating toward the surface of Clypsis. As the ship rose silently through the boiling radiance of the star's convective layer, Mike relaxed a notch, breathing more deeply. Maybe it was his imagination, but he was beginning to get *hot*.

"In case you're wondering," he said, "the race is over for us. I'm taking the ship directly to Pitfall—to the police hangar."

Willingham still wasn't talking.

Mike said, "You *do* know what's in that package, don't you?"

No answer.

The ship pushed out through the star, breaking suddenly into the glare of the photosphere, beyond which lay the inviting darkness of space.

"We made it!"

"Excellent," said Willingham. He had a gun pointed right at Mike's helmet.

Mike felt his stomach begin to squirm.

MIDNITE hadn't mentioned this part, either.

CHAPTER 20

Willingham said, "Just sit there and do nothing." He reached out and activated the radio circuits, filling Mike's helmet with static and harsh voices. Willingham shut them up. "This is *Universe*. I have experienced massive pump failure. Repeat, massive pump failure. Send the backup now. Home on my beacon."

The radio hissed and gurgled. "Copy, *Universe*. Backup on the way. Hang tight."

"Thank you."

The gun shifted about, but remained pointed at important targets on Mike's body. He wished he could see through the damned reflective visor, to know when Willingham was actually looking at him.

"Take the ship out beyond the spin-up circle and let her drift. Stay in the warp mode until I tell you."

Mike nodded, glanced at the screens, and brought the ship out away from the star. The warp engine whispered, and the *Universe* glided as serenely as a sleepwalker through the darkness. Mike was really starting to like the feel of it.

"That's far enough," said Willingham. "Shut her down."

Mike centered the stick, released the warp trigger, and took his aching hand away. He popped his faceplate for a breath of cooler air.

"Won't be long," said Willingham.

"Where'd that gun come from?"

Willingham didn't answer, and the lens of the gun didn't move.

"I feel like an idiot," said Mike.

"Be my guest."

"Are you going to kill me?"

"Be about time, don't you think?"

"What do you mean?"

Willingham laughed. "Kid, I must have followed you through every air duct and back alley in Pitfall. I thought I'd nailed you once with a bio-pak—but I was wrong. You damned near wore me out, and let me tell you: If I could fly this tub, I'd blow your brains out right now."

Mike flushed, hearing the words. His eyes darted about the cockpit, and he noted—quite irrelevantly—that the input light was flickering on the ship's engine computer. Several datascreens blinked, turned to garbage, and reset, then an irritating buzz rattled through his helmet.

"Stop twitching," said Willingham.

"Sorry, I didn't know I was—"

Mike became as light as thistledown and tried to float away. He realized his harness had come loose.

Willingham waved the gun. "Sit still, I said."

"I'm trying."

"Just do it."

Mike gripped his chair. "And all that time I thought Dover Bell was after me."

"He was, for a while. But after he ran into me in the tattoo parlor—and saw what I'd done to the folks there—he wanted no part of our little game. He even refused to kill you."

"He did?"

"Hard to believe, ain't it?" said Willingham. "Anyway, after that he was no use to Gajira—alive, that is. On ice, however... by the way, that was me in a green wig, trotting after you. We figured folks would remember the hair, not the man."

"Why'd you kill the people in the tattoo parlor?"

"They'd looked at your tapes, Mike. Strictly against orders. Who knew what they had seen, or what they might try to do with the information? Besides, the woman screwed up and sent the damned tapes into the Brain Bank. Made Mr. Gajira awfully mad."

"Would you answer just one more question?"

"Try me."

"What do you people want with all this HIPE?"

"Hey, we got competition, you know? We're supposed to let a bunch of upstarts ruin everything we've built up over

the years? Hell, no! But one big shipment—even sold at a loss—will drive 'em off the market."

"But there *is* no competition. That's just something MIDNITE invented to smoke you guys out."

Willingham didn't reply for several seconds, and again Mike wished he could see his face. Finally he said, "Are you serious?"

Mike started to answer, when a surge of static burst from his earphones. Now there was a tiny voice yapping monotonously at the bottom of a well of noise. Mike cocked his head, trying to make it out. The voice sounded far away, but getting closer. Mike looked at the quivering viewscreens. Was somebody coming? Then he remembered: Willingham's backup was on its way.

"They're calling you," he said.

"Who is?" said Willingham. "I don't hear anything."

"You're kidding me."

Mike strained to listen. The voice grew stronger, the static breaking up. Mike muttered, "Wait a minute. It's coming . . . it's coming . . ." Suddenly it was crystal clear, as if broadcast from inches away. The voice said, *My God, Michael Murray, what a squealhead you are.*

"Excuse me?"

Please take this man's gun so we can all go home.

"Take what?"

"Who the hell are you talking to?" asked Willingham.

His gun, his gun! Take his gun*! Here, let me make it easy for you.*

Willingham yelled in surprise as his harness yanked tight in emergency-crash mode. Mike stared for a moment, then reached out with both hands and snatched the gun from the astonished man.

Thank you.

Mike held Willingham back while he fumbled around with the gun, finally getting a good grip on it with his left hand. It felt weird there. Willingham tried to release his harness—as if there was anyplace to go. "Now *you* sit still," said Mike, leaning in close with the gun. Willingham settled down. "That's better."

None too graceful—but you got the job done.

"Who are you?"

You don't recognize my voice? Wait a minute, let me listen to it... The voice rambled incoherently for a moment, trying out various vowels and words. It shifted in frequency and timbre until—

"Speedball!"

That is correct.

"Where are you?"

I'm in the engine computer.

"But where'd you come from? MIDNITE told me you'd been erased."

Well, you know how I've been complaining that someone was messing with my tapes? MIDNITE decided to hide a copy of my pattern inside Clypsis—but he never told me. And when he was done, he erased the procedure from his own memory—in case the bad guys got to him.

"But how did he—"

I don't know, some sort of magnetic vortices in the plasma, set in motion as Pitfall dipped inside the star. Didn't you see that string of shadows? Those were cool spots protected by... well, you'll have to ask him to explain it someday. In the meantime, we seem to have a ship coming in.

It was a small deep-space runabout of radical design, coming right at them.

Mike, I think we better get the hell out of here.

"You don't have to ask me twice."

Mike reached for the stick . . . and the warp field collapsed.

Willingham must have thought it was awfully funny, because he just couldn't stop laughing.

"Speedball!"

They're trying to take control, Mike. This ship is full of access points.

"Can't you keep them out?"

I'm trying, but it's like plugging the holes in a sieve with toothpicks.

Willingham kept on laughing. Mike reached across and tapped the gun's output lens to his visor. "Would it be possible for you to shut up?"

It was.

When Mike looked up, he discovered the runabout had stationed itself in front of them, maybe fifty meters out.

She's got warp-screens, said Speedball. *Look*

The display shifted polarization, and Mike could see the shimmering zone of warped space that surrounded the ship. "Can they board us?"

I don't see why not.

"Son of a bitch!"

Mike raised the control panel and pried MIDNITE's data cube out of the hidden computer. He dropped the lid, grabbed the stick, and lit the main engines.

The *Universe* blasted right up over the warp ship's nose, headed for the nearest commercial web portal. Must have caught them by surprise, because the runabout just sat there. Exhaust products hit the warp field's surface, lighting up space with purple radiation.

Mike didn't have time to watch the screen. He put his attention on the main navigation board and plotted his run for the web portal.

Here he comes!

The runabout had spun around in confusion for a moment, but was now turned right and warping directly at them, its energy field gone milky and blurred.

"Come on, come on!" said Mike, jamming the engines into the red. Alarms bleeped and the techscreens flashed with vital messages:

MAX Q—TOR/FLX
FUEL PLENUM LOW PRESSURE
MAG LEAK CRYONICS 2/3/6
FLUCTUATIONS IN COMP POWER
ALARM 45/60—COMP/LOCK
LOW FUEL—D/T #2
HIGH TEMP—CRYONICS BAY
COOLING PUMPS OVERSPEED
ALARM 54/80—COMP/LOCK
ALARM 54/81—COMP/LOCK
LOW FUEL—D/T #4
RADIATION HAZARD—ASTRONICS BAY

* * *

''Caution,'' said the ship. ''Caution.''

''Screw it!'' said Mike, squeezing the throttle to the stops. A golden halo of light floated in space, and he aimed the ship right at it. The nebulous ring widened, then seemed to disappear. Mike entered the web with everything he had—and his pursuer was right on his butt.

''Get my warp drive back!'' Mike yelled. ''Or we're dead!''

I'm working on it.

The *Universe* jerked in sudden detonation. ''What was that?'' asked Mike.

How the hell should I know?

''Find out, will ya?''

Yes, master.

Mike ignored the sarcasm. He threaded the ship through the transition tube, then emerged onto the commercial web, headed for Beevee, the first planet out from Clypsis.

The proximity alarm blared.

Look out!

Mike was already jerking the stick. ''Ow! Damn it! I see the stupid thing!''

A nice fat freighter loomed up, filling the forward-looking viewscreen. Mike careened off the guy's turbulent wake, and throttled back to keep from losing control.

The proximity alarm reset and was immediately triggered again.

''My God,'' said Mike, as he dived beneath the private space yacht. He looked over at the long-range display. The commercial lane was choked with traffic, everybody trying to get home or make his deliveries before the Racing League cleared the web for the third leg of the Tricentennial Classic. ''Looks like we're a little early.''

He checked behind him. The other ship was right there, ducking the same private yacht. Mike wondered if his pal Defoe was in the pilot's seat.

''I can't outrace him,'' he said. ''Not if he has the warp drive and I don't.'' As he watched, the yacht shuddered and bucked in the residual wake of his pursuer's warp. ''Eventu-

ally . . ." said Mike, ducking the ship around another wide, slow freighter, ". . . he's going to nail us . . ."

Working on it. Speedball sounded preoccupied.

Mike tried to concentrate. His hand was really twitching like crazy now, and he was having trouble holding the gun on Willingham and flying at the same time. He was just beginning to think it might be a good idea to conk the guy again with the wrench when Willingham lashed out, reaching beneath the ship's control panel. Mike swatted at him, and Willingham grabbed Mike's bad hand, clamping down on it until Mike thought he'd pass out. Vaguely he could see Willingham fumbling again under the panel. "Stop it . . ." said Mike, but the words sounded weak and irrelevant. He raised the gun in slow motion, pressing it with great concentration to Willingham's upper arm. "Stop . . ." he said, but the man ignored him. Speedball jerked the harness tight, just as Mike pulled the trigger—tearing a long bloody strip through ten layers of suit material.

Willingham yelled and twisted away, clutching his arm. Mike slumped, his eyes going out of focus. It felt as if his right hand had been bolted to the furnace grate.

On the viewscreen, ships rose up like ghosts in Mike's path. He nudged the stick with the gun, first one way, then the other. The *Universe* moved sluggishly to avoid collision, then settled down in the groove once again.

Mike managed finally to pop the quick-release on the man's harness. "Put your arms through the inside of the belt." Willingham did one, but couldn't move the other. Mike put the output lens of the gun to Willingham's neck. "If you so much as wince, I'll open you up." The man didn't move, and Mike took his limp arm and shoved it under the harness. Blood dribbled out and floated away in pulsing globules. Mike set the zone clamps on the pressure suit, and the flow of blood diminished.

Working with his dead hand it took a long time to get the buckle snapped. He pulled the harness tight, then leaned back, sweating. "Should've done that in the beginning . . ."

He wedged the gun behind a strap and took the stick with his left hand. The panel in front of him blurred, then came back into focus. Something was happening . . .

He turned his head, blinking furiously, and looked at the sloping blank face of Willingham's helmet. "Hell'd you do to me?" The man said nothing, and Mike poked around under the console. He found the metal clips where Willingham must have kept the gun. "Nice." Then he felt a spring-loaded switch. Some sort of trigger?

"Speedball . . ."

I know. I'm checking.

"Oh, man, I feel . . . weird." He smiled. No, not weird, not at all weird. He felt strong, agile, invincible. The pain in his hand was fading. "Something's happening, man . . . something great . . ."

A single gesture of his fingers, and the *Universe* glided over the top of a long space-tanker. Mike rolled the ship out and pulsed his mains to wrinkle the fabric of space in the path of the ship behind. Perfect. Who needs turbo?

Mike . . .

"What?"

Speedball sounded upset about something, but Mike didn't particularly care.

How are you feeling?

Mike grinned. "Like a dragon on the wing."

Speedball kept quiet.

Mike casually flew a spiral pattern around the next freighter. Behind him the pursuing ship bounced off the warp ridges, but kept on coming. "So easy . . ."

They shot you up, Mike. They had your new suit rigged with a fatal dose, but I blocked the circuit. I shut it down before all of it could—

"What are you babbling about?" said Mike. Couldn't the tin idiot see everything was under control?

It's HIPE. They shot you full of HIPE.

"That's ridiculous!" said Mike, but instantly he knew Speedball was right, that he was in desperate trouble. He knew it was true, but he felt so pumped up with power and competence that all he could think was, This is the way I was meant to fly!

Mike let the *Universe* zoom right up to the exhaust nozzles of a big container ship before nudging the stick. Willingham yelped as the freighter filled the screen before

dropping away to the side. The *Universe* creaked and hummed with stress, and several inconsequential alarms tweeped.

Mike laughed.

He could feel his body balanced on the knife edge of perfect performance. He knew he could make this ship do anything he wanted. His mind was deluged by kinesthetic input, delighting in the calculation of speed and angle and power-phase vector. He knew every twitch, could feel the slightest acceleration. He was the quintessential pilot, a turbo version of himself.

Then, in the midst of this celebration, the stick went dead. The ship wallowed in the chop of the agitated web. Mike smiled, said, "Hey, Speedball. Don't fool around."

It's not me!

The ship began to roll and tumble. Attitude jets came on at random, then tightened into a pattern. The *Universe* peeled off to the right, headed for the shimmering wall. Mike whipped the stick back and forth, growing impatient. "Come on, now. Give me back my control!"

I'm working on it! That damned ship is cutting across our circuits.

"You better do something," said Mike. "Or it's gonna get messy."

Lights danced across his panel, and the scream of the turbines dropped in pitch, hesitated, and began to rise.

Try it now!

Mike jerked the stick, and the ship twitched, began to turn. Other jets lit off, trying to correct, and the ship squirmed under the hands of two pilots, each issuing conflicting orders.

"No good!"

I'll try rerouting the control pulses. And if that—

"Don't *talk* about it! *Do it!*"

The ship vibrated until the screens turned to hash, then—very slowly—the *Universe* turned away from the wall.

Stand on it!

Mike snapped the stick to the side, released it momentarily, then pressed it forward. The ship shuddered and responded, alarms screaming. THRUSTER MALFUNCTION—INPUT OVERLOAD.

Another space freighter appeared in their path, and Mike

shoved the *Universe* across its bow, scraping paint. He immediately jumped back across the freighter's path. The *Universe* hesitated, balanced on opposing thrusters. Mike jerked back on the stick, arcing the giant racer over the freighter's hot dorsal radiators, then around behind, flipping over as he came, and charging up along the belly of the craft, their radar targets merging on the screen.

A perfectly impossible maneuver, performed with perfection.

Mike grinned.

And he hated himself.

HIPE was flying the ship now, not Mike's own native talent. He never would have tried the drug, but now that he was dosed with it, he could see the attraction. To fly this well . . . one might even ignore the reality of what was to come—the downward spiral of diminishing talent and accelerating dependency.

But right now . . . *right now . . .*

The stick loosened in his grip, and suddenly the *Universe* was back in his exclusive control. "You did it!"

I breached their secure commlink. I got MIDNITE on the line, running decryption routines.

"Just get my warp drive back."

Working on it.

" 'Cause I'm running out of—"

Mike's big engines sputtered and died. "You see what I mean?"

Stand by.

"What do you mean, stand by?"

Uh, maybe you ought to look for a place to hide.

It was too late.

The warp ship climbed right up on Mike's tail. He managed to light his main engines for one last pulse—anything to discourage them—but the hot exhaust just spread across their warp field, dissipating in a shower of lavender sparks. Mike's engines cut off abruptly, his tanks dead empty.

The *Universe* clanged and shuddered, and Mike was thrown forward against his harness.

Willingham said, "Looks like they're getting close."

Close? *Close?* The runabout's nose was wedged into one of Mike's exhaust nozzles.

The *Universe* veered off toward the wall. Mike fired his thrusters until the fuel ran out, which didn't take long. The *Universe* continued to swerve, pushed by the brute force of the pursuer's warp engine.

"Come on, Speedball! Gimme something!"

Working on it.

Willingham laughed.

"Shut up!" yelled Mike. "What are you laughing at? They're killing you, too, you know."

"Screw it," said Willingham. "I got tapes in a safe place."

"So what?" Mike knew now it wasn't enough. *He* wasn't tapes; he was *right here*, wrapped in his own very personal body. He was *alive*, and he wanted to stay that way.

We're screwed, said Speedball. *They didn't just disable your warp engine, they blew the damned thing right off the ship.*

"Oh, no . . ."

Mike's heart was fluttering, missing beats, and a wave of dizziness swept through him, turning his stomach inside out. The HIPE was wearing off.

The viewscreen pulsed, filled by the glittering wall. Mike wondered what was it going to feel like, the coming disintegration. Would he burn up in an instant, like a lizard-bat caught in the flare of an engine's exhaust? Or slowly, subjectively time-shifted—an endless orbit through the interior of a star . . .

It was an image that made him smile.

Quite unexpectedly.

Twyla and Twyla on the datanet:

TWYLA (LIVE): Show me what's happening!

NET: *Image of the two ships approaching the wall.*

TWYLA (NET): His warp drive is gone. I'm getting a signal . . . MIDNITE has broken the encryption code . . . he's trying to relay . . .

TWYLA (LIVE): It's too late!

TWYLA (NET): There's always a chance.

NET: *Image of the ships—they're at the wall.*
TWYLA (LIVE): There isn't time!

The robot astronomy probe turned to lock on a marvelous source of x-ray emission, which was located at the outer surface of the commercial web that ran from Pitfall portal to Beevee. The glare of Clypsis was in the background, but fortunately the anomalous x-ray target was so particularly powerful the probe had no trouble maintaining a steady lock-up. Excellent data were taken.

A Racing League cameraship was standing off near Beevee in preparation for the Tricentennial Classic, which was to be passing through the region in an hour or so. Quite by accident a technician performing routine camera tests captured the exit of the two ships on tape—the brightest disintegration flare ever recorded. The next day he quit his job and went into business for himself, exhibiting the grisly tape. The Racing League subsequently sued to recover—and won—though bootleg copies continue to circulate.

The forward screen lit up in brilliant light, then went dead. The ship groaned and squealed, and the cockpit filled with a haze of smoke. Vibrations roared through the ship, and Mike gripped the sides of his seat. All he could think was, This is it, this is it!

Then the *Universe* shrieked; the haze vanished, and everything loose blew about in a swirling hurricane. Mike's faceplate snapped shut and locked; his suit tightened and ballooned in the sudden vacuum.

"We're breached!" he yelled into the radio. The ship had gone dead silent. Everywhere he looked, purple fire glowed through the walls, burning them away in a blaze of light. Mike stopped breathing and listened to the radio hiss in his helmet. "Speedball! Where are you!"

The *Universe* lit up from behind, as though a spotlight had been trained on it. Mike popped his harness and turned around to face the impossible. He was looking at the *outside* of the commercial lane, seeing the web right through the revealed ribs of his burning ship. A gleaming hunk of

hardware tumbled around back there: the nose of the run-about, sheared off and dragged along by the cargo pod's expanded warp field. The rest of the ship was lost in a dazzling glow of scintillating blue light.

At about the same time Speedball—with the aid of the encryption code supplied by MIDNITE—was infiltrating the warpship and shutting down its drive, Pitfall cops were busy rounding up Rinehart Weel and the rest of the Syndicate.

MIDNITE grabbed Weel on the way out of the pit. "Where's Gajira?"

Weel laughed. "Nobody sees Mr. Gajira."

"Today," said MIDNITE, "we're about to make history."

"Good luck," said Weel. "Tadashi Gajira has been dead for ten years—and nobody ever found his tapes."

"That's the way I like 'em," said MIDNITE, plugging himself into the Syndicate's computer.

Everyone who lived on the datanet had his own way of remembering where things were. MIDNITE's personal view of the net was a full-sized model of the speedway capital. He zoomed down the corridors and across the rings of an empty Pitfall, examining every crevice imaginable.

Gajira's scent was everywhere, hidden in computers and directories and smart appliances throughout the labyrinthine complex.

MIDNITE scoured the datanet, sending out search-and-replace macros that disabled the machines Gajira occupied, nibbling his data, bit by bit. In the end a decryption routine pounced on Gajira's secret metaphor.

"It appears," said MIDNITE, "there is a monster loose in downtown Tokyo."

Gajira stomped his way southeast down Harumi-dori. He kicked through the overpass, careened off balance into the Hankyu Department Store, and slapped aside the corner police box in panic. He bounded past the Sony Building, then turned to lean on the Fuji Bank, looking back. A flying disk rose hissing out of the moat at the Imperial Palace Plaza. It was coming this way, MIDNITE black.

Gajira snorted and roared, then tramped down the street to the Ginza. The black disk whined and spun and followed. Gajira turned left, running up Chuo-dori. He ducked behind Matsuya Department Store and watched the disk nose about in front of the USO. Gajira backed up slowly, and fell screaming into a missing data block.

The disk darted forward as Gajira scrambled up the crumbling side of the hole. His datanet was disintegrating.

Gajira batted feebly at the disk, then stumbled diagonally away, crashing across buildings toward Showa-dori. He was almost to the Ginza Tokyo Hotel, where he maintained an escape line, when the black disk swooped down on him, firing off voltage spikes.

Gajira howled as his data bubbled and flickered out. The disk buzzed closer, slicing off whole banks of memory. Gajira raged blindly, falling back. He was confused, tormented, and he thrashed about recklessly.

Terminals and datascreens lit up all over Pitfall as Gajira cried out, painting his enraged sorrow in wide slashes of color. His screen logo fluttered and rolled, full of holes, eyes flashing in practiced defiance. But now data was leaking out so fast he no longer remembered who he was or what he had striven for or why he fought the death that pressed down upon him with such heartless strength.

It wasn't fair.

The screens flickered and went blank.

Mike's radios had all burned up, so he couldn't call for help, but it didn't matter. The disintegration glow had been seen all over the system, and even now half a dozen ships were converging on them.

Mike's idea—to use the cargo pod's warp engine—had come to him as he pictured its extended orbit inside Clypsis. Unfortunately, the cargo pod wasn't rated for high power, and its warp drive burned out nine and a half seconds after Speedball managed to get it going. Still, the short-lived and diminished warp field had covered almost everything but the ship's skin, which burned down to a skeleton of reinforcing members. The fusion engines were untouched, though most

of the attitude thrusters had been clipped. The forward astronics bay was chopped off and melted shut.

All in all, said Speedball, *not too bad a deal.*

Back in Gajira's pit MIDNITE had one more surprise for Mike. "Keep the ship."

"The *Universe*?"

"Think of it as salvage," said MIDNITE. "Besides, it was impounded during the commission of a crime. You cooperated with me, so it's your reward."

Mike stared at the blackened ribs of the giant ship. "But it must still be worth—"

"Take it," said Jass. "Start your own team. You've got your master's certificate—thanks to Gajira."

"If it's any good."

"Don't worry about it," said Speedball, at home in his shiny new PV. "You've got friends in high places."

"And if you need money," said Raybo. "Well . . ." He had shaved and cleaned up and restored himself to recognizable shape. And no, he couldn't remember how he had gotten out of Gajira's pit. He said, "My estate is not fully depleted."

Speedball laughed. "I tried my best."

"Go on, Mike," said Tanya. "Larry can afford it. Sponsors are climbing all over him, looking for endorsements."

Mike smiled at her, then saw the way Twyla was watching him. "Gee, I don't know . . ."

His own ship, his own team . . . really? Was it really possible?

Mike looked at MIDNITE.

He was going to just give Mike the ship? *Give* him the ship? How many rules were getting bent out of shape this time?

Before I know it, thought Mike, my good friends will have me in jail.

"You're making me sick," said Jass.

Mike looked out at the folks assembled in the hangar. Only Scarface was missing, and Lek—poor HIPE-ridden Lek. Even now, without half trying, Mike could feel the distant, tickling call for HIPE in the base of his brain. Speedball told him it would die out, slowly, but Mike would always have to be cautious. One more dose and he'd be hooked.

"Your own team," said Twyla. "It's what you want."

"Yeah, but . . ."

"Don't screw around," said Jass. "God, Mike, sometimes you can be so dense."

"All right," said Mike. "I'll do it. But we'll combine teams. I want you to be the master pilot. I'll be your associate."

Jass frowned, and Mike added, "Look, I owe you an apology for the way I've been treating you the last week or so. Now, *you* know I'm sorry, and *I* know I'm sorry, but that doesn't mean I don't have to *say* it. I am sorry. I said some incredibly stupid things."

"I feel like a bum taking your apology."

"Do it anyway," said Mike. "And be the master pilot on our team. I still have a lot to learn. I mean, jeez, I'm only seventeen. Don't abandon me!" He meant the last part as a joke, but by the time he heard himself say it, he wasn't so sure.

Jass nodded, grinning. "I won't abandon you."

Mike turned to Twyla, wondering if he was always going to feel like an idiot with her in the same room. She was looking at him now, and he rather wished she wouldn't. Was Lek *really* gone?

Mike took his biggest chance. "We might have room for one more."

"An apprentice?" she asked, smirking.

"A pilot," he said.

She looked away, trying to hide her smile. "I'll think about it."

Mike fell asleep during Willingham's murder trial. He dreamed he was on a dinner date with Twyla Rogres, who was wearing a green wig and acting like a born-again squealhead. The waiter delivered their meal under a stainless steel cover, and when he lifted the lid, there was Scarface—alive and grinning, all those sharp little teeth lined up and gleaming. He winked sideways and said, "I'll be back!"

Mike woke abruptly to a commotion in the courtroom. The bailiff was hauling a familiar-looking lizard-bat away, and someone behind Mike said, "Little bugger was on your neck. Did you feel it?"

Mike yelled at the Klaat'k. "Scarface!"

The little animal squirmed in the bailiff's arms, looking back. No, it wasn't Scarface—but he smiled at Mike and nodded vigorously before the doors slid shut.

Mike slumped in his seat, grinning.

I'll be back, Scarface had said.

Thought Mike, Okay, pal . . . I'll be waiting.

Not surprisingly, Fyodor Willingham refused to cooperate during his trial, declining especially to disclose the whereabouts of hidden brain tapes—an annoying obstinacy that substantially enfeebled the order for his execution. In the end, MIDNITE was forced to authorize the use of certain semi-invasive brain probe methods. Unfortunately, the man's personality disintegrated into random squiggles on the screen, before flat-lining altogether.

An analysis of his burnt-out remains revealed that Willingham had been a parasite, living in the unregistered body of a brain-blanked man. In fact, according to Brain Bank scientists, Willingham represented a corporeal version of the ubiquitous Mr. Gajira.

MIDNITE now pondered the question: was Willingham the last of Gajira?

EPILOGUE

From an interview with Margie Phillips, conducted by Zara Treva on *Good Morning, Pitfall*:

TREVA: I guess not many little girls get to go on such wonderful adventures.

PHILLIPS: Don't be patronizing, Zara.

TREVA: Well, no . . . I didn't mean—

PHILLIPS: And it's going to be a long time before anyone else gets to go.

TREVA: Why is that, Margie?

PHILLIPS: Simple: only the *Spider* knew how to find the Old Web—and it's pretty messed up.

TREVA: But surely Speedball Raybo was monitoring the—

PHILLIPS: He probably was. But that particular copy of Speedball didn't make it, remember?

TREVA: Oh, yes . . . but why do you think the Old Web opened in the first place?

PHILLIPS: You have to look at the heat cycles of Clypsis, Zara. When the star was hot, we had a way in—but now that it's cooling off . . .

TREVA: But this is fascinating, Margie. Who do you think built the Old Web?

PHILLIPS: How should I know?

TREVA: I mean, do you think we'll ever meet them?

PHILLIPS: What a stupid question. Maybe they left already. For all we know, this galaxy was just an outpost.

TREVA: You mean, the Old Web might stretch all the way to some other galaxy?

PHILLIPS: It's pointless to speculate, Zara. Perhaps by the time Clypsis heats up again, we'll be ready to find it. I'll be twenty-eight years old by then. And you'll be—

TREVA: Just think: if they find the Old Web, we might be able to explore other galaxies.

PHILLIPS: Don't be silly, Zara. If we find the Old Web again, we'll *race* in it.

TECHNICAL DATA

Everyday life in and around Pitfall is led amid dangers terrifying to pre-spacefaring man. Some hazards, such as sudden fluctuations of varying gravity fields, are no more than inconveniences. But others, such as abrupt changes in the specialized atmospheres maintained for the different sentient races, are potentially fatal.

While there are protections against most of the perils one might encounter, consideration must be given to the needs of everyday life. The racing pits, for example, must be able to contain a breathable atmosphere for the mechanics, but must also give ready access to the vacuum of the race track.

Within Pitfall it is not uncommon for those beings who can afford pressure suits to wear them daily, thereby cutting down the risks should they need to pass through a zone of hostile atmosphere or take the transit cannon through vacuum.

Of course, the most dangerous part of the Clypsis system is the warpweb. Going "over the high side" is the most spectacular accident in all of sports, often leaving nothing more than a handful of debris.

HAYASHI

BAD MOMMA

HAYASHI

HC'S
1201
S
TRI-CENT
BAR'EM
SUSH
鉄
HAYASHI

2073
HAYASHI

HAYASHI

HAYASHI

HAYASHI

UNIVERSE
HAYASHI

We acknowledge the sacred land on which Cormorant Books operates. It has been a site of human activity for 15,000 years. This land is the territory of the Huron-Wendat and Petun First Nations, the Seneca, and most recently, the Mississaugas of the Credit River. The territory was the subject of the Dish With One Spoon Wampum Belt Covenant, an agreement between the Iroquois Confederacy and Confederacy of the Ojibway and allied nations to peaceably share and steward the resources around the Great Lakes. Today, the meeting place of Toronto is still home to many Indigenous people from across Turtle Island. We are grateful to have the opportunity to work in the community, on this territory.

We are also mindful of broken covenants and the need to strive to make right with all our relations.